SWEETHEART: PART TWO

EDITION 0

AN OMEGAVERSE BULLY DUET
BOOK 2

MARIE MACKAY

Note this is an ARC edition of Sweetheart, which means it will be going through one more round of edits before full release.

To those who cling to their dreams even in the darkest of storms

CONTENT

HOLD UP! Is there anything I should be aware of as a reader?

Yes! Let me get you a list so you know what you're getting into!

Threats of SA on screen. Reference to SA off screen. DV: Reference to and witnessed in flashbacks in non explicit detail.

Knife violence, gun violence. Torture (of bad guys).

Reference to a dog that passed before the events of the book. Death off screen, but love and grief explored within novel.

Anything else?

Primal play, collared alphas, group scenes, heats, cockwarming, CNC, mostly undiscussed, safeties present but still absolutely not representative of real life. (Don't do this at home).

~~No~~ chia pets were harmed in the making of this book.

PROLOGUE

4 months ago

VEX

I woke alone.

I woke—which was something, I supposed. I woke with a fragment of peace: the briefest huddle of seconds as my addled mind turned on and there was nothing wrong: Aisha was here. My mother was here.

And then I blinked my eyes open and reality crashed in.

I woke, today, at the beginning of what I knew was my ending, for I truly, finally had nothing left.

I was in a cramped room with an IV in an aching arm. The bag hooked to my windowsill above me was empty. The last of the fluids had drained, but there was something wrong with my arm.

I sat up, staring at it, trying to conjure the street smart instructions on what to do with... whatever had happened. My flesh was swollen and aching where the fluids had entered, looking like a sad blob of jelly.

My mind was sluggish, and I didn't care as much as I should.

Not now that I was alone.

Finally, I dragged up the lesson that one of the omega harm reduction clinics had given me. I thought perhaps the IV had gone interstitial... maybe? That word floated around meaninglessly for a moment. I didn't know what it meant, I just knew it was bad.

"For doubles, go warm," one of the sweet nurses there had told me. *"Double red or double blue—that means warm. But if it's both red and blue, go cold. And do it quick."*

I stared at my arm. Pale for blue, inflamed for red. It was pale.

I reached out and touched the swollen flesh. Cool for blue, warm for red. It was cool.

Double blue.

Double's meant warmth.

Good, because I didn't have any ice.

I staggered out to the bathroom, grabbing a towel and running the water until it was steaming hot. Then I wrapped it around my arm and left it there, waiting for the swelling to go down, finally forced to face my thoughts.

Still reeling from the drugs that had just blitzed my system, I was too shocked to cry.

Aisha was gone, and I'd all but crawled home and somehow jammed an IV into my arm with trembling fingers before vanishing from the world.

One more heat, I'd survived, but this time I'd survived it alone.

ONE

LOVE

Vex had been taken.

It was a truth that unravelled my sanity with every inch it seeped into my mind. Ebony had the phone now, expression dark as he played the video again.

"Just... turn it off." Drake's voice was strained. "We should text them, t-tell them we'll give them anything."

"Can't." Ebony's gaze was still fixed on the video, and I could see the fire in his gaze. I'd seen it before. That fire, once lit, would never be sated.

Not without vengeance.

Not without pain, or blood, or penance.

"Why not?" Rook demanded, trying to snatch the phone from Ebony's grip. Ebony took a step away, eyes burning.

"She was... she was really scared, mate," Rook said. "If it's about money, we just give it to them and get her back. It's simple."

"Nothing about this is simple," Ebony replied, but he was

distant, still scanning the phone screen intently, only half paying attention to us.

"Ebony, Rook's right—" I began, but I cut off as his blazing silver eyes snapped to mine. I realised he was closer to fully cracking than I'd ever seen him.

"You don't get a say!" he snarled. "You *let* this happen."

I grit my teeth. "We focus on Vex." I had to keep us together right now. "We're getting her back—and we're going to do it together. I'm with Rook, if this is about money—"

"If it *isn't* about money and we say we'll give them anything, we're on the back foot."

Drake made a strangled sound. "Who fucking cares if we're on the back foot, it's Vex—"

"There's nothing to stop them doubling down the moment they think we're desperate," Ebony cut him off.

"It doesn't make sense," Rook snapped. "Why take her and send the video if they don't want anything?"

"Could this be what they wanted? To... show us this and take her away?" I asked, my voice hoarse. "To hurt us?"

"No..." Drake's voice shook. "No, because then how... how do we get her back?"

There was a heavy silence as Drake looked desperately between us. His panic came through in his blackcurrant scent as it did in the bond, his grip on our connection slipping. It was all consuming.

He was terrified.

Rook was ashen. I could see in Ebony's eyes that he agreed with me—that there might be nothing they wanted beyond what they'd already taken. Our pack had enemies, too many to count. And too many had the kind of resources needed to pull something like this off and never get caught.

"If you hadn't stopped me, we wouldn't be here." Ebony's words were low and deadly as he squared me up.

"She..." I shook my head. "I didn't know."

"She's our *mate*. You treat me like I'm the broken one, but then you're the one who—?"

"Because of you!" I hit my boiling point, all the terror and guilt suddenly too much. *"You, Ebony!"* My aura was out, and I had his shirt in my fist as I shoved him back a pace toward the wall. "You were the only reason I let her go."

His lips were curled in a snarl, but he didn't retaliate.

But he was right. He wasn't the one who'd screwed up tonight.

I'd made the biggest mistake of my life. There should never have been a moment in which I didn't trust her.

My mate.

Our mate.

I'd failed her.

Still, I couldn't distinguish my pain from the hatred I had for the man before me. His expression was bitter as he stared at me silently. I *wouldn't* have made that mistake if it wasn't for him. I wouldn't have been afraid of loving her.

Still, he said nothing, and it fuelled my rage. "Don't pretend," I spat, "that you haven't spent your whole *life* making sure I couldn't have anything beyond this pack—beyond you!" I slammed him against the wall. "You got what you wanted, you piece of shit, *and it's cost you, and me, and her!*"

"No!" Drake was there, his aura out as he ripped me back, fury in his eyes. "We are *not* doing this right now! She's... she's alone. We can't fight until she's safe!"

Chest heaving, I took a step back, dropping my fist and trying to find order in my scattered mind.

"We..." The world was spinning. "We're getting her back."

"What do we do?" Drake asked. Again, I found my grounding as I looked at him. *He* was coming apart. I had to keep it together.

"We need help," Ebony said quietly. I glanced back at him. He was too still, even with his aura in the air.

"The cops won't get involved, you know that, right?" Rook asked.

Vex was a gold pack, and nothing in that video broke laws. The only claim we had on her was as a scent match. The Institute wouldn't help. It was up to us to make an offer to the pack who'd claimed her.

I took a breath, taking another step back and glancing around at them. They were all watching me. Ebony was the only one who didn't look afraid. He was coiled as if to pounce, his gaze fixed on me, a demand in it.

And I knew what that demand was.

I opened my mouth, then shut it, pulse skyrocketing. But Vex's fear still leached into my mind like liquid claws, seizing me, paralysing me.

She needed us.

"I don't care what we have to do," I said at last. "We get her back."

That was it.

All he needed.

His aura finally died in the air as he took a step toward the door.

"Just…" I held a hand up as he began to turn, still trying to rein in my scattered thoughts. "Everyone knows she's our Sweetheart."

My warning was clear: nothing could be traced back to us.

He nodded, and I felt him through the bond, a moment of soaring freedom. A vicious smile twisted his lips as I confirmed exactly what I knew he was hoping for.

Because never, in all my life, had I dropped my leash on my brother entirely.

EBONY

Hour One

I don't know how many times I'd watched the video as I waited in the office downstairs. At first, my stomach had dropped at the sight of Vex's fear. Now, it crystallised my fury, yet still was no less uncomfortable.

Was that why I watched it over and over—to numb myself to her fear?

It wasn't working.

It wasn't fucking working.

The tightness of my chest went nowhere.

She was still afraid right fucking now, and it was a violation of every one of my instincts that I couldn't save her.

I'd set the ball in motion for every resource I had available. Now, I just had to wait. I watched the video again, trying to unweave everything it had to offer me. The alpha's voice was distorted, making it impossible to identify. That wouldn't be enough to save him, not when I found out who he was.

Again, the video ended on that blurred frozen frame of Vex's tear streaked face.

Fury was ice cold fuel, seeping in every inch of my veins, smothering everything but the one truth with its claws deep: someone had taken my mate.

They were taunting her, and taunting *me*—

I almost jumped as the gate's buzzer rang through the office.

I got to my feet and made for it instantly. I'd told Rob we were expecting visitors so he didn't feel the need to come and poke his nose in. Everything we did tonight would be kept as quiet as possible. I buzzed the visitor in with barely a glance to the video feed of the front gates.

The woman who met me at the door was all too professional looking for the hour. It was the middle of the night, but she was still dressed in a white pantsuit. She had dark hair and a cool expression.

"Leighton Winston," she introduced herself, holding a hand out to me. I could feel her aura, ever present in the air along with her scent, vanilla cream.

A female alpha?

Of course my father had sent a fucking female alpha. Soren was a Hail Mary, but potentially the greatest resource I had. Of course, he'd do anything not to show his own face.

I ignored her hand.

"You better be good."

Her smile was cold as she looked me up and down, barely blinking at how I towered over her. "You have a missing gold pack. The cops won't bat an eye. Time isn't in your favour and as far as I can see, you don't have many options—"

"I have more resources than my dear old dad," I replied. "So if he wastes a second of my time—"

"If you *did* have options"—Leighton cut me off, voice icy—"I would still be the best. Now, I'm newly packed-up, and I have a post-heat omega at home desperate to carry on house hunting. So, trust me when I say it's in my best interests to get this mess cleaned up as fast as possible. Do you have an office, or am I expected to work in the foyer?" she asked. "Soren *did* warn me you were a neanderthal."

I knew there was a snarl on my face, but I took a step back.

She was right about one thing. We were short on time, and she had arrived within the hour despite how late it was.

I had no room to be picky. My mate was gone—had been *taken* from me. My fury returned at the thought of it. At the thought of that video.

Shoving it down for later, I set Leighton up in the office, but before I called the rest of the pack down, I took a seat.

"A couple of ground rules before we get started."

Leighton, who was just opening her laptop, lifted an eyebrow.

"There are certain types of information I need dealt with... discreetly. You don't take them to anyone but me, not even my pack lead. Is that clear?"

As if on cue, the burner phone I'd activated only half an hour before, buzzed in my pocket, and I tugged it out instantly glancing down at the text.

Unknown: What's the job?

Leighton reclined in her chair, fixing me with a calculating look, but this part was non-negotiable. For the first time in my life, Love had dropped his leash on me entirely, but I wasn't a fool enough to believe he could stomach every detail.

Finally, she shrugged. "Doesn't make a difference to me."

I nodded, then returned my attention to the text, already formulating my response.

No one, neither the piece of shit pack that dark bonded her, nor the law, would get in my way.

I wasn't just going to bring Vex home—that wasn't enough for my mate. I would hunt down every last person in this world that had ever caused her pain, and I would turn them to fucking ash.

TWO

VEX

Zeus's scent of stale cigarettes was sickening, choking my lungs with each breath.

I watched the slow drips of blood splash onto the leather seat of the limo.

My mates were gone.

The Crimson Fury pack didn't want me, and I didn't have the space to grieve. The next chapter, the worst I'd ever faced, was ahead.

It was my fault. I'd dared to dream, briefly, fiercely, with more determination than I ever had, and now the void I was dragged back into was darker for it.

"For a moment, I thought you had them. They were so protective at the Diamond Tides," Zeus said into the silence.

I didn't react. My tears were drying on my face.

This dread was similar to the first time, in the days right after I'd been bitten. But this time, I knew more.

I knew that Zeus Rogan was content with his disdain, but there were things that unseated even his disgust at the colour of my eyes. There were things that, despite his best efforts, made him want me. So I locked everything down so he wouldn't catch the faintest glimmer of my fear, or see another moment of my pain. I tried to pick through everything I knew about the Lightning pack. They weren't mentioned on many of the celebrity channels I followed. They'd had a decent moment of fame, some good movies and shows, and then they'd fallen from the public eye.

"Is this about Drake?" I asked.

It was the only reason I knew the first thing about their pack: Drake Jaccard had once been set to join them. I don't know what happened, or why he changed his mind.

Zeus's lips curved up at the edges, but he didn't spare me a glance, still reading something on his phone. "Oh, Vex. It's about so much more than that."

I clutched myself in the awful silence, the blood slowly drying on my trembling fingers.

Piece by piece, I let everything go.

My mates.

My hope.

The world was coming apart at the seams, and I didn't have anything to hold onto anymore.

Not Drake.

Not Aisha.

Not my mom.

Releasing them, it was like carving out pieces of my flesh, but I had to, now.

My fate, just like it had always been, was sealed.

DRAKE

Hour Two

. . .

"You're going to help get her back?" I asked, taking a seat in the office beside the female alpha. Her name was Leighton, Ebony had said.

It didn't matter that it was the middle of the night, none of us could sleep, not knowing she was out there, trapped and terrified.

I'd never felt so helpless in my life, and I was grateful for any help. The cops wouldn't help us get her back—which was sick.

Leighton nodded, glancing around at the rest of my pack.

"I'm going to do my best," she told me. "Ebony sent me the video on the way over here with a brief rundown of the situation, but we're going to come at this from all angles. Starting with Vex, I need everything you know about her."

"She's uh..." I swallowed, still finding it hard to focus. I pulled my phone out, hands shaking. "This is her..." I tried to pick a photo, but there were too many.

Ebony took the phone from me as I floundered. For a moment, his eyes scanned the gallery, brows drawn and head cocked as if he was seeing something he couldn't quite understand. Then the expression vanished, and he tapped a picture of me and Vex getting ice cream just down the road.

"I need everything, I don't care if it's truth or lies," Leighton was saying as Ebony began texting her photo after photo.

I nodded, glancing around at the others, hoping they would take the lead. I couldn't think straight.

What was *everything*? I knew a lot about her, but would any of it be helpful? Surely Love and Rook would have more useful information.

Only, every eye in the room was on me.

"We have... her Sweetheart application," I said. "Right?"

"I'll take that," Leighton said, "But I want it from you, too. We don't know how much of the application was forged. Vex Eden doesn't come up much through search engines, and her social media profiles are mostly private or hidden. I've got someone working on hacking—"

"I... I added her as a friend," I said. "But she doesn't have much on them at all. It's not just the private stuff."

Leighton nodded. "Then it's all the more important I hear from you."

"Okay..." I didn't know why the others weren't saying anything. One of us had to start talking. "Well she's nineteen. She uh... has—*had*—a friend named Aisha, but I think she passed, I don't know how. Her mother died when she was sixteen. She likes music, I um... I have her playlists..." I glanced to my phone which was still in Ebony's hand. "She loves Heart's new album—*Gilded*, plays it on repeat..." I trailed off.

Stupid.

That was stupid. None of it would be helpful.

"You're doing fine," Leighton said quietly, gaze fixed on me. "Keep going." She was a female alpha, so her aura wasn't like ours. Instead, it was always out. Right now, it helped to focus on it; I could feel her calm like it was mine.

"I don't uh... I don't know what was real. She never mentioned her dad, so I think maybe he was out of the picture. Did she... did she say anything about that to you guys?" I glanced around at the others.

They still hadn't spoken. Love was paler than I'd ever seen him, and Rook looked ill.

I don't know why they were leaving this to me. She'd spent loads of time with Rook. And I wasn't good at this. He'd know more.

How did I know so little?

Just her favourite fucking music?

She was my mate, and I didn't even know her mom's name. Love and her would have talked about real shit—I was sure of it.

"She never mentioned her dad," Love said quietly. "But I didn't talk to her that much." He glanced to Rook.

Rook shook his head. "I'm... I don't know. Drake knows the most," he said, looking to Leighton. "Vex and him..." He swallowed, eyes shifting in my direction but still not meeting mine. "She really liked him."

I opened my mouth to argue, but he got to his feet, jaw clenched. "I'm..." He wrinkled his nose. "I'm useless here. She hated me."

"She what?" Love asked, brows drawn.

"Sit down," Leighton said cooly. "You can mope later. I'm not done."

"I'm not going to be any help," Rook snapped.

"You can go when I say you can go," Leighton replied.

Rook's scowl deepened, but when no one challenged her, he sank back down into his seat.

Leighton continued shooting me questions about anything and everything: jobs Vex might have had in the past, her favourite places to visit, her schooling and registration status. I couldn't stop shaking, even when I tried to focus on the answers.

I'd taken my phone back from Ebony, anxiously scrolling through her photos, glancing down at them occasionally as if they might help. I kept regurgitating stupid shit, like how she really loved the otters at the aquarium and had once thought about being an animal trainer.

The silence of the others was like a constant scratching at the back of my mind.

I didn't understand.

She *didn't* hate Rook. She'd have told me if that was the case. And Love hadn't talked to her?

That made no sense.

I felt like I was in a parallel world, wondering why my brothers were lying in a moment like this, when there were bigger things to worry about than keeping secrets. She was alone right now, so afraid—

"You said she liked Heart?" Rook asked, cutting into my spiralling thoughts.

"Yeah…" I said. "Why?"

"Heart was at that charity signing event we did a few months back, right?" Rook asked, straightening in his seat, brows furrowed.

"Uh… I think so," I said, unsure why he was asking.

I knew a little about Heart—people had a habit of pairing our pack with him because of Love's name. He was a singer who'd skyrocketed to fame on social media alone. His latest album, *Gilded*, broke records for the first independent singer and gold pack to hit number one.

We hadn't talked to him at the press event, though. We'd opted for a beta-only signing so we wouldn't need heavy scent blocking drugs. We'd just returned from our last shoot in California. On set we had to take them a lot and our hormones—unstable as they already were—needed to balance. As an unbonded omega, Heart's signing was set up far from ours.

"Wait…" Rook was scrolling on his phone, suddenly focused.

"What?" Love asked, peering over his shoulder.

"There was a forum post a while back, it blew up. An omega claiming she was our scent match, but I think she said it happened at a signing."

It sounded familiar. Jas might have mentioned something about it in passing, but stories like that weren't uncommon—and we never took them seriously.

"Here, got it…" He paused, reading down the page. He ran his fingers anxiously through his messy hair. "It… fuck. It could be her." He turned his phone to the rest of us.

"This could have been tracked…" Ebony said.

Leighton's eyes were scanning her laptop screen, having

already pulled it up. "This post is four months old..." Leighton frowned. "She... posted online that she was your scent match *and* she was gold pack?"

My blood chilled. "What does it mean?" I asked.

Leighton turned to me, expression softening. "A post like this would have caught the wrong type of attention. If it was her, and I'll go on the assumption it was until we know otherwise, there is a chance she was taken for it."

"Taken... like... She was dark bonded because..." I swallowed, bile rising up my throat.

I knew the truth already. It had stared back at me from that letter, and I'd heard it in the video. But somehow, my brain hadn't fully realised it, not until I made myself say it now. My voice cracked. "She's in danger because she's our mate?"

A long silence followed as my brothers heard it, too. And I knew I'd fully lost control of shutting the bond down.

"Why haven't they asked for a ransom?" Rook finally demanded.

"If it was about money, we wouldn't be here," Leighton said. "That letter she left suggests it was personal. Do you have enemies?"

There was a tense silence, and I wasn't the only one whose gaze slid to Ebony.

"You could say that," he said quietly.

"Enough to narrow it down?"

"In this industry?" he asked. "People hold grudges. There's a lot of money to be lost if we step on toes."

Only, I knew there were people who hated our pack for more than just aggressive business decisions. Neither Rook nor Ebony were good at making friends, and when you were working closely with people for a long time... Shit happened.

We were blacklisted by a lot of people—not just in the industry. I know Rook, Love, and Ebony were cutthroat back when they were a prospective elite pack at the academy.

By the looks on my brother's faces, they felt the same. Love grimaced. "There's... a lot. Goes back to our academy days."

The academies that trained alphas for elite packs were savage, and there were only so many spots to enter the industry as a fully endorsed pack. For every spot claimed, a dozen others lost. A dozen packs of highly driven alphas with years of schooling to lose. That was a lot of alphas who resented the Crimson Fury pack before it even stepped a foot through the doors of fame.

The list was endless. Before I'd met them, there were alphas who had it out for Ebony and Love, trying to convince Rook to join them the night before the Crimson Fury pack was formed. They'd failed to qualify, and Rook had publicly dragged them for attempting to poach him. There were all of Ebony's targets over the years, Rickson Dagger pack, Ice and Fire—and I wasn't free of targets, I knew the Lightning pack hated me and Ebony. Then there were the problems brought on by fame itself. A few years ago, there was a scent matched omega who'd rejected a princess bond as a publicity stunt to get our attention. Those alphas started a hate group that the police had to shut down.

"This is one of the reasons why we didn't plan on having an omega," Love said quietly.

"I want the list," Leighton said. "But I'm guessing, no, not enough to narrow it down?"

Ebony scowled. "It *is*... likely that this is about more than money."

"That still doesn't tell us why they haven't asked," Rook cut in.

"The video you received wasn't just a taunt," Leighton said. "They hid their face and masked their voice—they're hiding, from you or from the law. And they went to the trouble of planting her in your home as a Sweetheart with the intention of getting you to fall for her just so they could rip her away. Yet, all they left was a note and a video without a request."

"*All?*" I asked, voice hoarse.

"They have your fated mate in a dark bond. If they wanted to hurt you, it could have been far worse. I doubt this was their ultimate goal."

"You mean, they changed their plans because we found out she's gold pack?" Love asked.

"They aborted the moment they found out you cancelled her contract. Perhaps they didn't believe you cared enough to trade for what they actually want, and it seems personal since they settled for a taunt."

"So..." Love's expression was stiff. "We have to convince them we want her back enough to give them what they want?"

"And... do you?" Leighton asked.

My eyes snapped to her, hackles rising, but Leighton didn't flinch at the hatred levelled on her from everyone in the room. "You need to get yourselves ready. If I'm right, what they want won't be an easy ask."

"We're ready to give them anything," Love said quietly. "That's not a question."

Leighton nodded, glancing at the rest of us, but none of us argued.

"So you think they tracked her from the post?" Ebony asked her.

"It's possible."

"Can you do that too?" he asked.

"Already have someone working on it."

Rook was glancing between them. "Why does it matter if we can track it?"

"It would tell us where she used to live, where she was taken from," Ebony said. He looked at Leighton. "If you get a location, I want it," Ebony said. "I'm not trusting anyone else with that."

Leighton smiled coolly, but nodded, glancing back to Rook. "We're coming at this from all angles, but if we can find when or how she was taken, we might be able to figure out who has her."

The world wasn't right, the room blurring in my vision as the story unravelled in my mind. I tried to stifle the imaginings of Vex making that post, so unsure, then her life crashing down around her because of it.

The phone gallery stared back at me. Vex, with a peaceful look on her face in the local forest walk. This had already happened to her. The dark bond was already on her neck. It had been since the moment she'd met us.

All those moments I'd seen a glimmer of sadness or fear in her eyes, and I had no idea she was carrying a burden like this. I could have been more.

I could have *done* more.

Ebony was saying something, but I couldn't process it.

"...Kinds of enemies we have aren't ones to stalk forums and turn up at the doorstep of an omega without getting noticed."

"It's much more likely she was taken first," Leighton replied. "Then sold as a gold pack with an established scent match."

Sold?

The word was like a lead weight, and I was sinking further from the brittle sanity far above.

No.

No one would do something like that to her.

But I'd grown up in the Gritch District. I'd heard warnings of just such things.

"That's a... a real thing?" Rook asked. He'd lost control of his hold on the bond. Love and Ebony were still locked down, so it was just me and him in the bond right now. I could feel his sickness, his guilt, as gut wrenching as mine was.

Leighton replied, but I couldn't take my eyes from my phone. "Dark bonding lowers an omega's chance at a scent match, though it doesn't remove it completely. Some packs prefer to buy gold packs with previously established scent matches to remove the element of surprise…"

I scrolled through my pictures again, finding one I'd taken of her sleeping beside me. My knuckles brushed her cheeks and there was a ghost of a smile on her face as she hugged my arm against her. I'd been stuck there, unable to leave until she woke, and it had been impossible not to snap a shot.

She was so gentle, so sweet in that photo. Nothing of the torment and terror that had been in her eyes in the video I'd just watched.

My throat was closing up.

Leighton was still speaking.

"…It's rare to find omegas with scent matches who have either been rejected or remain undiscovered—as is Vex's case. This makes them worth a lot. Add in a celebrity scent match, find the right buyer, and suddenly you have a valuable omega on—"

She cut off as I got to my feet.

"I just… I need some time. I think…" I couldn't sit in here any longer. "I've uh… I've told you everything I know. If you need anything else…"

"Drake—"

"It's okay." Leighton cut Ebony off.

"I can call you if I need anything," she said to me. "Let me know if you think of anything else that could be of use."

I nodded.

"Actually," Leighton glanced around at the others. "I have more than enough for now. I'll get to work. You should all try and get some sleep."

THREE

Hour Four

LOVE

Sleep was never going to happen. Not for me, not for my brothers.

The living room was as still as the bond. It was dark but for the pool lights outside that filtered in through the grand windows. I was cycling through everything that had just been said, fixated on Leighton's words.

Taken and sold.

That was what had happened to her, because of us.

I couldn't even feel Drake anymore. Ebony was out here, which never happened. His laptop was on his lap, and he was staring at it intently. Drake was at his side, knees to chest, shooting occasional anxious glances to the laptop screen. Rook was staring blankly at the aura boxing reruns that were playing on the TV.

"I… need to know what you meant," Drake said quietly.

He'd been working up to it for a while, I could tell by the way he'd been shifting in his seat, glancing at me and Rook with a hurt expression.

For a long time I said nothing.

Could we afford more fractures right now? Would we survive it?

"We're tired," I said. "Let's get her back, rest, and then—"

"She's alone," Drake cut me off. "She's alone, and... and anything could be happening to her right now, and she was taken because she said... she said we didn't want her."

I stared at him, the hollow pit in my chest tumbling open further and further.

My own failure.

I opened my mouth, then shut it.

"She had that bite on her neck the whole time," Drake spat. "And still, she could smile. She's the strongest person I've ever met. She doesn't deserve this. And I don't understand. She knew how much I cared about her, and she was with you all the other nights, I don't—"

"I didn't make her welcome," I said, heart tight in my chest.

I had to tell him now before this got worse. Even Ebony broke his attention on the computer, eyes calculating as he watched me.

"What?" Rook's voice was weak. "I don't understand, she was with you—"

"I told her not to come. I told her to focus on the rest of the pack. She didn't listen."

Of course, the reasoning for that was clear now. She'd been commanded to convince each of us. She'd been desperately running from a dark bond.

And I'd pushed her away—her own mate.

I'd made her feel unwanted.

Each memory from those nights was a sharp knife in my brain, challenging me in every quiet moment.

"I left her by herself, waiting for me until the morning."

"What?" Drake was staring at me as if he didn't recognise me.

"There's your answer," Ebony said. "Three out of four of us made her feel unwanted."

"Ebony—" Rook began, suddenly strained.

"Three?" Drake interrupted, glancing between Rook and Ebony. I blinked. Rook had said in the meeting that Vex hated him, but I'd tucked it to the back of my mind for later, unable to process every issue at once. Now, looking at his discomfort, I realised there was much more to it.

Ebony looked a little sour as he glared at Rook.

"Rook was blackmailing her into being sweet to him," Ebony supplied.

Drake stood, expression now something dangerous, sickness twisting it. "Blackmailed her into... *what?*"

My blood chilled, but Rook was shaking his head. "Nothing like that. It's still *Vex*, for fuck's sake, she'd have had my head—"

"She was running from a dark bond." My voice was icy. "I doubt there was much she wouldn't have done."

"It wasn't like that. I just..." He winced, not able to meet our eyes. "I wanted to get back at her for that first night when she... Look, I was pissed. I thought she was here for the fame."

A cold pit of fury simmered in my chest.

I knew I wasn't one to talk, but I'd only done what I had to protect her from getting between me and Ebony. But Rook...? I thought she and him were close.

"She..." Rook was ashen, eyes darting between us. "I was a dick, alright. I didn't know—"

"Didn't know what?" Drake asked, voice frigid.

Rook got to his feet, eyes a little wild as he squared up to Drake. "I didn't know she was our mate."

"I didn't know either!" Drake snarled. "I didn't know, and I loved her anyway!" Those words cut me short.

Loved her?

We'd all known. But hearing him say it...?

He looked ready to leap at Rook. "While the rest of you were treating her like dirt!"

"Enough!" The command of pack lead was in my voice, and it drew him up, if only for a moment. I hated using it. I didn't feel, for a second, that I deserved it. But... "We *can't* fall apart, not now—"

"You're blaming me?" Drake demanded. "After—"

"No. You... you were the only one there for her, but we can't. If this pack dissolves, the scent match goes with it, and then there is nothing in the world that can break that dark bond."

Drake's chest was heaving. He was on the brink of madness, his aura shivering in the air.

"We're it," I said, hating the truth of it. "We're all she has."

There was a wild look on his face, and he stormed from the room. I was after him in a moment, feeling the instability through the bond.

"Drake..." I caught up to him on the stairs.

I wouldn't give him excuses. He deserved better than that. The problem was, I didn't know what to say. There *was* nothing to say. "We failed her, but we're going to get her back."

He spun on me, eyes alight with fury. "Do you know what could be happening to her *right now*?" he demanded.

My stomach turned with vile sickness at those words. It was shit I was trying not to say—not to think—even when it was a boulder lodged right in the centre of my mind, unmoving, unavoidable.

"She's with a pack, Love. A pack that dark bonded her"—He shoved me a pace. I could see the madness that I felt through the bond from him, more unhinged than I'd ever seen. "You think if we get her back, you can just say sorry and it will all just go away?"

No.

I didn't, not for one second, believe that would be enough.

I'd failed Vex. So wrapped up in my own issues, I had missed every sign, every hint—and they'd been there. I'd *known* something was wrong. "I don't know how to fix this, but I will—"

"If—*when* we get her back, we offer her the princess bond," Drake said.

"Of course." That wasn't even a question in my mind. We owed her that.

It was the only bond that could save her from the dark bond, and it wasn't guaranteed, the pack she was with would have to give it up to us.

"I'm going to do everything in my power to break that dark bond," I told him.

He looked manic, though, running fingers through his hair. "It's... wrong. That we get a bond with her—"

"We're her best option."

"She's there because of us!" Drake shouted. "She's trapped with them because of us, *and we don't deserve her!*"

"I know."

Fuck me, I knew that.

"What about what they're going to ask of us?" Drake demanded.

"I'll pay it. I don't care what it is, I *will* pay it, and she will be fucking safe."

He stared at me, breath slowing just slightly, but I could still feel his instability through our connection.

"Drake, listen to me. We're going to save her—and not just the princess bond, I'm going to give her the world with or without us involved. I won't let a single member of this pack near her unless she asks, not me, not Rook, not Ebony. And she's going to get everything she needs to heal—"

"It's not enough, she shouldn't have to heal. Not for us—"

"I know!" I didn't mean to raise my voice, but it wasn't anger constricting my throat right now, making it hard to breathe. "I..." My throat was thick all of a sudden. "I fell for her, too. I was a coward... I was scared if Ebony knew..." I couldn't finish. "I wanted her to fix him, I didn't protect her from him—" I cut off, a wild laugh slipping from my mouth at the irony.

It had been Ebony in the end, who had fought for her. While I'd shattered her contract and allowed her to be stolen from our very home, *Ebony* had fought for her. "I w-was wrong."

I'd destroyed the contract.

I'd triggered the events that had caused her pack to rip her from us.

This was my fault—not Ebony's, not Rook's.

Mine.

Drake's eyes were darting between mine.

My voice cracked. "I will spend the rest of my life paying penance, if that's what it takes. But first, I need her safe."

VEX

Zeus's fist was around my arm as he led me up to the same room where I'd been locked for months.

He looked... off balance. I'd just met his pack—men I'd seen only hours before at the Gala.

"On your knees," Achlys had commanded, a cruel smile on his face.

He was sprawled out on a daybed, a gaming controller hanging loosely in his grip. His dress shirt was undone, and he still wore the dress pants from the Gala. His scent was non-existent, a lingering effect of the scent blocker they took for the night's events. "That's your place, right, little gold pack?" he asked as I sank to my knees, wracked with dread as I stared up at him. It was the first time I'd received a command from anyone but Zeus.

Triton had dropped onto the couch beside him, peering down at me. "If it isn't the little Crimson Fury slut we get to keep." His laugh was as slurred as his words as he sipped from his wine bottle. "Since she couldn't even seduce her own mates." He reached out and upended the bottle over my head. I let out a breath of shock, unable to move as the wine spilled through my hair, down my cheeks and eyes and neck, seeping into my gown. "Just as useless as the pack you're fated to, aren't you?" His eyes lingered on the wine that was trailing down into the neckline of my dress. It was a fight to fix my expression.

"You don't seem happy?" Achlys had leaned forward, sandy-blond curls swinging before vicious brown eyes. He grabbed my chin, forcing me to look at him. "Do you know how many people would kill to be on their knees before a pack like us?"

That was when Zeus had torn me away.

At my side, he was too tense, his grip on my arm too tight. Neither Achlys nor Triton had seemed happy as he'd dragged me from them.

I didn't have time to process the sinking feeling as I saw my room again. The same cream walls and dark carpet with the four-poster bed in the centre.

"I want you acting like our omega," he growled. "Get cleaned up." His eyes lingered on the drying wine and blood along my arm. The slender cut I'd made on my forearm was closing up already.

I was halfway to the bathroom before the truth of what he'd just said crashed in. I took as long as I could, blow drying and straightening my hair to perfection, dragging out the minutes as I tried to come up with a way out of this.

When I finally stepped from the bathroom, robe wrapped tightly around me, I had the faint makings of a plan.

Zeus was seated on the side of my bed, phone in hand as he scrolled, his shirt half undone, sleeves rolled up. It was strange, seeing his face after all the time he'd spent behind the mask.

For a moment, my gaze was fixed on his phone.

Had they replied?

I grit my teeth to fight my tears. If they had, surely he would tell me. If they had, it would mean they wanted me back—and that's what he wanted, too.

No news meant they didn't.

They were gone, and it was just me.

His dark eyes were cold as he looked up to me, eyes sweeping over my body. He was furious, I could see it in the tick of his jaw, as if he were trying to search for something I'd done wrong.

"I want to negotiate." I'm proud of how steady my voice came out. My world was in pieces, but I didn't have time to linger on that right now.

There was a faint curve to his lips as he lowered the phone. "And what, exactly, do you think you have to negotiate *with*?"

"You…" I swallowed. "You like it when I leave the bond open." I knew how much he liked feeling my terror, and the state of my end of the bond wasn't something he could command me on.

"You're offering to leave the bond open, in exchange for…?"

I'd thought this through, a dozen times in the bathroom and still my words were weak. "I'll clean and cook, and be… whatever you want out of your omega. But I don't want…" My voice failed me at last at the absurdity of what I was trying to say. "I don't want…"

"You don't want us to touch you?" he supplied, eyebrows raised. "We already have people who can cook and clean."

"You have people who want to fuck you."

His eyes flashed with a glimmer of humour. "You know what we *don't* have around right now?" I stared at him, not liking the malice in his tone. "Someone who *doesn't* want us to fuck them but has to put up with it anyway. It's a harder spot to fill, you know? And my pack has certain... preferences that are hard to cater to."

When he got to his feet, I almost stumbled a step back, the height difference enough to stop my heart. He moved more quickly than I could anticipate, fist closing in my hair. Then I was being dragged to the bed, where he threw me down. With a gasp of panic, I flung myself away from him, but before I could get across the bed, his weight crushed me against the blankets. A sob of terror caught in my chest as his fists closed around my wrists, pinning them against in place.

"W-wait!" I begged, throwing my weight against him, but he was so huge I could barely even draw a breath beneath him.

"There it is." His voice was hot in my ear. "See, that wasn't so hard, and the bond is wide open."

Then, he was gone.

I scrambled to the other end of the bed, the world spinning, tears blurring my vision before I turned, each breath getting caught halfway up my throat. I was shaking.

He had a nasty grin on his face. "What do you have to negotiate with again?"

The bond was still open. It was like fighting with a broken shutter in a storm, trying to get it closed.

"Then why... what's keeping them...?" I couldn't finish.

"You think you're *that* fuckable?" He laughed.

"You said... you told me—" I cut off, trying to get my thoughts together. "Why are you in here then?"

"You want to know the truth?" he asked. I realised, a little late, that I didn't think I did. "You've been gone too long, and while my pack wants their turn, *I* have certain... instincts that are hard to ignore."

"Like... what?" I asked.

"Come here."

He settled into bed as I was forced to cross toward him. My blood chilled as he dragged me into his arms. I could feel his delight at that as he swept the hair from around my shoulders.

What was he doing?

I jumped, a low whine slipping from my chest as I felt his teeth graze the back of my neck. I struggled, but his growl stilled me, something primal and vicious in it. I remained frozen as he sunk his teeth in, renewing the bite. Then he held me for an age, and I felt the satisfaction radiating from him.

At the bite. At my terror.

"I could though, couldn't I, little omega?" he whispered at last. "I could break you right now and all of that spirit would be gone, but where would be the fun in that?"

FOUR

ROOK

The others were all doing shit, and I was useless. We'd offered them money and received crickets.

Nothing but silence all day.

I was shaken, and the house was a swamp of tension that I couldn't handle. Space was what I needed, just a moment out of this nightmare so I could get my head straight. I did the thing I always did when I was in a hole: I went to the *Celebrity Round Table*.

They weren't an official TV show. It was basically a frat house channel that posted videos dedicated to celebrity watch. They'd become big enough to attract guests.

I needed a distraction more than anything.

"Harrison!" Venice Parker greeted me as he opened the door. He wore a robe that hung open to reveal a tanned six pack. By the looks of it, they were getting ready to film.

"Caught you in time?" I asked.

"You want in?" Venice asked, his smile full of delight.

"Sure fucking do."

"Rook!" Kimberly's delighted squeal sounded, and the pretty raven haired beta was hurrying toward us. I kept my eyes on hers, uncomfortable with her obscene cleavage that I'd once very much appreciated.

"Hey," I said, fixing a smile on my face with a nod. "Was bored. Wondered if you had room."

"Always!" She was ushering me in.

I'd expected as much. Popular, they might be, but they were nowhere near the level of fame my pack had. They were always enthused when I turned up. They were an alpha beta pack, known both for their talk show and the much more adult films that they released. I'd been invited to join that sort of production a few times, though I'd always declined.

They *loved* the Crimson Fury pack, and visiting always made me feel better.

I slumped down onto their ridiculous, glittery red couch beneath the studio lights as they finished setting up. Janine put a bit of makeup under my eyes telling me I looked like death, and Rory shoved a beer into my fist that I took numbly.

This *would* help.

The cameras turned on, and we were live. It wasn't acting, wasn't even near the same thing, but it was the closest I could get.

There were drinks and laughter and drama, and it didn't take me long to realise that even with the cameras rolling, it still wasn't working. All I could think of was her.

The pain she was in, believing we didn't want her.

I hadn't known.

I hadn't known she was my mate.

Never would have dreamed of—

"There was a leak from The Sweetheart Agency that there's no more contract between you and Vex Eden." Kimberly's words snapped me back to reality. "You have no idea how relieved I was to hear that," she was saying. "And I just want you to know, Rook, that we're all outraged for you."

"What?"

Vex?

Why was she talking about Vex?

I couldn't move for a moment, staring at Kimberly with a blank expression.

The video flashed in my mind... *Vex, a terrified mess of blood and tears...*

Every one of my hairs stood on end. Panic began to set in, my face a rigid mask and it was all I could do to keep it up, years of acting kicking in like a defence mechanism.

My omega was somewhere in this city, alone.

I could do nothing about it.

But what was I doing here, among these foreign scents?

"...A violation, what she did," Janine added. "The Sweethearts give hope to all your beta fans out there. To hear an omega infiltrated that—and a gold pack? *And* tried to seduce you, hoping scent and hormones would be enough? I'm mad—and I have a bunch of boyfriends." She giggled. "But seriously, you should see the outpouring of support online. We're angry for you. No one's seen her since the Gala. Smart move, if you ask me. There are mobs out for blood."

I stared at her, unable to process the thoughts misfiring across my mind.

No.

She didn't understand.

It... It wasn't like that.

"But how do you feel about it, Rook?" Venice asked. "Having someone try to take advantage of you like that?"

I opened my mouth to tell them Vex wasn't like that, then

halted. We were live... I couldn't—shouldn't—say anything right now. There wasn't enough information.

"I think what gets me is the fact she pretended to be a beta," Kimberly put in. "It's *such* an uphill battle for us in this industry, we don't need omegas taking that from us, too. Elite packs like yours give us something special. Omegas always win with packs, so having a few out there that want betas... it's always given me so much hope."

I blinked, still reeling.

This... this *was* part of the brand. Most of the fame was fuelled by the beta population, and our pack had stationed itself perfectly to receive that affection.

"Come on, let's hear it from you, Rook," Venice nudged me. "For all of the Cinderellas out there—all the Sweetheart hopefuls who have your poster on their wall. There's still a chance, right?"

It was a mistake coming here. I should have known there'd be questions—questions I couldn't answer. I'd just wanted to get away from it all. My throat was tight as I got to my feet.

I didn't process what they were saying around me. My name was called, but then the lights were gone. I'd made it to the front door.

I took deep lungfuls of air, staggering toward the car where my driver was still waiting for me.

"Take me home," I rasped, as I stumbled into the Lexus doors.

We didn't make it. I had to tell him to pull over halfway there so I could throw up on the sidewalk.

I was shaking by the time I climbed back in, rubbing my face as if it might free me of the flashes of her terrified eyes, pleading through the phone screen.

What was happening to her right now?

We just... we just had to get her back.

What the fuck did that pack want? Why wouldn't they tell us?

I just needed her back and safe.

There was a bang on the screen between me and the driver. I looked up to see his eyes on me in the rearview, wide and unsure.

My aura...

Fuck.

My aura was out.

I shoved it down with difficulty.

When I finally got home, I'd barely stepped into the foyer when I heard the bang of an office door. Drake stormed toward me, eyes lit with fury.

"What the fuck—?" I cut off as he seized me, slamming me against the door.

"You're a fucking pig!"

"What?"

But he was unhinged, aura out. *"Rook fucking Harrison agrees that Vex Eden is an enemy of the fans.* Now Janine Wiser is holding votes across her socials for which fan looks best next to our pack, *while your mate is fucking gone!"*

"I didn't... I didn't say anything." I blinked, looking from him to Love. "I didn't say anything."

"Exactly!" Drake shoved me again, violet eyes furious. "You didn't defend her while she was being slandered by—"

"What was I supposed to do?" I demanded. "I mean... I *left,* but was I supposed to throw away years of work, when we don't know what's going to—"

I cut off as Drake's fist split the side of my face.

"We're getting her back, you fucking idiot. And then what will you say?"

"Why *were* you out on an interview?" Love asked.

"Fuck... I don't know. I was stressed, alright—?"

"You know who's stressed?" Drake spat. "Your fucking mate. And while we try to convince that pack we want her, *you're* on an interview making it seem like—"

"I didn't say anything!" I repeated, panic seizing me. "I left."

"Why didn't you say anything, when they were slagging off your mate?"

"I..." Fuck. I looked to Love. He was silent, but his scent, vanilla winter, had the same edge of rage as Drake's. "I want her back. I just... I can't deal with it like you guys can."

"Deal with it?" Drake asked, affronted. "That's all you're thinking about? Yourself? When—"

"I know!" I spat. "I know, and I can't stop thinking about it, alright? Thinking about what if they don't reply, what if we can't get her back—"

"We all are," Drake hissed. "The rest of us aren't going out and—"

"She loved you!" I shouted, seizing him by the shirt. "If she never sees us again, she loved you!" The word was choked. "She... she hated me. I made... made her life miserable."

Their disgusted expressions were too much. I was shaking again, and once more I felt my aura flicker in the air, out of control as the true demon of the night finally reared its head. "That c-can't be the only thing she ever sees of me."

"It won't be." Ebony was the one who spoke into the silence. "We're going to get her back. We've got an address for her old place."

I blinked, trying to process that. It wasn't everything, but it was a start. "Why are we still here?"

"It's late," Ebony replied. "You lot try and get some sleep, we'll leave the moment I get a reply from the building owner.

"And you—" Love jabbed me in the chest. "Aren't leaving this house alone until she's back."

"What about the Dragon Hunter's announcement?" Ebony asked, glancing briefly between us. "It's tomorrow. That's not shit the contract is flexible on."

"I don't give a shit about the Dragon Hunter's contract!" Love spat, turning to him.

I tensed, unsure what to think of that. I got it—I really fucking did. We needed to get her back. But what he was talking about—sabotaging the greatest career opportunity we'd ever landed?

We didn't have to lose both.

And it wasn't just about the opportunity.

I needed it. The gruelling hours on set, nothing to think about but the job. Here, all I had was endless hours and a time spent with a frat pack that had left me feeling more hollow.

On set was the only time I was ever good at anything. And they were there, always at my side. My heart quaked at the thought, but where would we be, if something went south with Vex? If Germany wasn't coming up to distract us?

Packs had fallen apart over less.

Nothing was fitting quite right in my head.

All I knew, was that I couldn't lose her and lose them.

I couldn't do it.

I couldn't lose her—it wasn't even conceivable, but if they weren't on the other end of it...

I shook my head, trying to dislodge the spiralling thoughts.

The others weren't thinking straight. We were all fucked up in our own ways, and this job was the only thing that kept us straight sometimes.

"It'll get him out of your hair," Ebony said smoothly, ripping me from my spiral. "It's a scheduled event. If we don't turn up people are going to start asking questions. We don't want any press on this. When we get her back, I don't want their attention, it's not fair to her." I could see the cold calculation in Ebony's eyes. "We'll go to Vex's old place first thing tomorrow morning, see what we can find, then I'll take him to the interview and make sure he shuts his mouth on *anything* regarding her. You stay with Drake, make sure Leighton has everything she needs."

I wrinkled my nose at those words, but held my tongue.

I'd never had Love look at me with such coldness. "Not one

single fucking line of slander, Rook, or I'll blow up the Dragon Hunters contract myself."

FIVE

Hour 36

ROOK

"Where the fuck are we?" I asked as Drake scanned street signs before looking back down at the map on his phone. The four of us were making our way down unfamiliar, grimy streets. Not a single person who'd passed us by hadn't looked shifty to me—though my judgement might be off, it had been over two days since I'd slept.

"Nowhere good," Drake murmured, more tense than usual as he eyed the surrounding streets. I glanced at him, knowing he'd grown up in the Gritch District himself, but even he looked uncomfortable. "We're five blocks further than the last street my mom would let us go near."

We'd parked a few streets from our destination, since one road had been blocked off with yellow crime tape. Ebony had driven, since he'd caught a nap earlier, which was better than the rest of us could say, and we'd taken Drake's van, as we didn't want to draw attention to ourselves. We were supposedly heading to Vex's old pad—the place she'd been taken from all those months ago.

I felt that familiar world-numbing anxiety at the thought of her current circumstances, amplified by my fatigue.

Right now, we were all dressed as inconspicuously as possible. Ebony had his long hair in a ponytail, tucked into the back of his jacket, and both he and Love were wearing caps. I had my hood up and a pair of sunglasses on, similar to Drake. We might not last too long before getting spotted, but it was enough for a quick trip.

I didn't know what we would find, but it had to be something.

This morning, one text had come through to Vex's phone, words that still made me sick to think about: *'Not very convincing'*.

It was a single reply among the dozens of messages we'd sent by now. That we would make an offer. That we just needed to know what they wanted in exchange for her safety. Even, on Leighton's advice, asking that Vex be kept safe during negotiations.

We were begging. Begging a pack with all the power in the world over us. And that was the only response we'd received.

It was my fault.

They must have seen the broadcast from the Round Table. I couldn't swallow past the rock in my throat, and I shoved my fists into my jacket pockets. Shame, guilt and fatigue were my constant companions.

I forced my focus back to the alleys around us, a little flare of rage in my chest.

Why were we wasting time?

This literally couldn't be right. We were in the Gritch District —I hadn't even been here before. Mates were supposed to be compatible—there was no way Vex had set foot in a place like this, let alone lived here.

We left the main street behind, as Drake led us down an alley with towering walls that dimmed the sunlight overhead. Bricks were cracked and withered, with layers of graffiti across them, both fresh and faded. A foul stench wafted from a sewage vent with a dented top. I was tense, my aura on the edge of bursting free, and it felt like every shadow was watching, returning my anxious scrutiny with twice the intensity.

It was the kind of place that flinched with every movement, not nearly as barren of life as I'd first assessed. Movement down a smaller alley caught my attention, and looking closer, I spotted a makeshift tent between two dumpsters.

Love looked more off balance than I'd ever seen him. Ebony was expressionless, which was how he got when he was presented with something he wasn't sure about. Pure intake. He was stripping every inch of this place down with that ice-cold gaze like the psychopath he was, as if he might be able to exact revenge on the street corner itself for existing near Vex. Knowing Ebony was in the bond with me didn't usually bring comfort, but right now we needed him. She needed him, as much as it killed me to admit it.

I was fucking useless in this.

As we stepped deeper through grimy walls, I became even more on edge. My breath caught as what I'd thought was a pile of old rags shifted, then peered up at me with golden eyes as I passed. I found myself staring into the gaunt, wrinkled face of a homeless woman as she puffed on a pipe, huddled against the wall.

"There's been a mistake," I said again, hurrying over to Drake, who was still glancing from his phone's map to adjacent numbers. He wouldn't find the right one—I was sure of it. Vex hadn't lived here—she wasn't like any of these people. "Get Leighton to check again," I demanded.

None of the others answered, but I noticed Love's jaw was set.

How could they believe this was where Vex had lived?

We were getting curious looks from anyone we passed, and I tugged my hoodie further down, shooting a glance at Love and Ebony.

"Fuck!" I jumped out of my skin, my aura bursting out as a rat skittered from beneath a soggy cardboard box.

"Get a grip," Ebony snarled.

I wrinkled my nose, straightening myself and shoving my aura down. "We have the wrong place."

"Would you shut the fuck—?" Ebony snapped, something vicious in his voice, but he cut off as he almost ran into Drake, who'd finally come to a stop.

He was staring up at one of the tall buildings before us. Up a few worn concrete steps was a red door with peeling paint.

LOVE

We entered the lobby of the run down apartment building. Inside were a few ratty seats and a dusty coffee table.

Ebony was on his phone already, his eyes darting around the place. The phone rang a few times, and then I heard a muffled answer on the other end.

"We're here," Ebony said. There was a faint reply, and Ebony hung up.

I looked to him.

"Owner. She lives on the property. It's our best shot at getting information."

A few minutes passed with no sign of the owner. An alpha passed us in the foyer, dark eyes scanning us up and down as he slipped out the front door.

Rook was tense. "Did she live here *alone*?" he hissed. "With alphas like that, about?"

"I do give them their own floor," an unfamiliar voice said, and I glanced over to see a wizened old lady leaning against the frame of one of the side doors. "They are a little more destructive, I tend to find, especially around these parts. Have to charge them a bit more for repairs."

"Are you the owner?" I asked, crossing toward her and holding out a hand.

"Sure am." She took mine, shaking it with considerable strength given her small frame. Her grey hair was tied up in a bun, and she held a cane firmly in one hand. "I'm Tammy. Now, what are you here about?"

"Vex Eden," Drake said. "Do you know her?"

The woman's bushy brows rose, and she took us in again with new interest. "Now what's it to you?"

"She's..." Drake trailed off, glancing back at me. "She's our mate."

"Is she now?" The old woman put her hands on her hips, glaring at us. "Thought you lot looked a bit too clean for this area. Where are you from?"

"Citrine—" Rook began, but I shot him a look.

Too late. "Citrine Hills?" She cackled. "I hear you fart diamond dust up there. And here I was, thinking the universe had lost its sense of humour."

Rook looked a little put off, but the woman fixed her hazel eyes back on me.

"Is she alive?" she asked.

"She is, but she's in trouble. She was taken from here a few months ago. We wanted to ask around, in case anyone saw anything."

"I can do you one better," the woman said. Then she hobbled over to the little desk and fumbled in a few cupboards. "I never did this for the money, you know? There's just too much danger in these parts. So, when she never came back..." Tammy shook her head. "Well, I hoped..." She sighed, then tugged something from a box and handed it to me.

A key.

"She's number eleven, on the second floor, here." She bustled around the counter and ushered us up a flight of stairs.

"You... kept her room?" I asked, surprised.

"Couldn't forever, but sometimes... Well, you never know. And if they do come back, they're worse off than ever. A place to stay can be the leg up they need to get back on their feet."

Worse off than ever?

What kind of trouble did this woman expect Vex to get involved with?

"She was always sweet," Tammy said over the horrendous creak of the stairs as she led us to the second floor. "Hurrying in and out of here all day with Aisha. She was full of adventure, that one. Always meant for better than this."

There was no elevator, just sticky carpets and a musk in the air, that I would be willing to bet never went away.

As the door to the next floor opened, I was met by a jumble of noise. Thin walls did little to smother ongoing music from a number of rooms. There was a loud thud from upstairs, then the sound of someone smashing on a door with a yell. As we filed onto the landing, an aura split the air. It was from upstairs, I'd guess, just reaching down onto this floor, but it was huge and unstable.

"Now... let me see," Tammy said. "Vex's was just down there to the right." She pointed. "Suite eleven. Hope you find what you're looking for, and she..." Tammy seemed uncomfortable for a moment. "I tidied up a little, but it looked like there was a fight in there when I went in."

I knew the blood had drained from my face, but the old lady was already on the first step down.

"Tammy." I caught her before she vanished. She looked up at me curiously. "How much was Vex paying? We'll cover the missing months." I'd double it for what she'd done for us.

She considered me for a long moment, eyes calculating, then she shrugged. "I won't say no if you've got the money." She tugged out a pencil and a scrap of paper from her pocket and held it against the wall. I could see the faint tremor in her hand as she wrote, then she folded it and handed it back to me. She gave me a quick smile and then began down the stairs. I glanced down at the paper for a second, then frowned, deciding I'd be more than doubling it if that's all she'd been asking, and I'd do it for every month Vex had ever lived here.

I hurried after the others as they began making their way down the hall.

A door to our right creaked open, and tinny metal music leaked out. A slender male omega with shaggy red hair stepped from the room, booted foot barely creaking against the floorboards before he caught sight of us. He froze, cigarette between his lips, lighter halfway from his hoodie pocket. Golden eyes darted across all of us, then he was back through the door before any of us could blink. It slammed, and I heard the click of locks and a chain.

I frowned.

Was he *afraid* of us?

But Drake was already pushing past me, checking the numbers until he found eleven.

This was it.

Vex's place.

Her room was much too small for the amount of character it packed. It was smaller than I'd ever seen a living space, and my first instinct was to search for a door to a second room that didn't exist.

There was a long silence as we all stared in disbelief.

It was taking me a moment to process what I was looking at. There was a bed, a cramped desk, an old TV. An overflowing set of drawers was crammed beside a little vanity.

It was decorated floor to ceiling with... well, Vex.

"Fuck." Rook muttered. "How is this possible?" He was

striding across the tiny space, peering out the murky window as if it might give him some answers. "What about the bathroom?"

"Shared," Drake muttered, nodding to the door. "Community kitchen too, I'd guess."

"I don't... understand." Rook sounded floored. "She was supposed to be from... I don't know, like a rich family."

"Her whole application was forged," I muttered.

I felt sick as I stared around at the chaos of the space. There were posters everywhere, some of which reflected our pack back at us.

There were a lot of DVDs, a photo board, and a—

"Oh..." Drake trailed off, hurrying to the corner where he crouched down.

"What?" Ebony asked, still at the entryway, brows furrowed. So far, he'd been as stunned as me.

Drake stood up, a bowl in his hands.

"It's... I don't..."

I stared at it. It was a pink dog bowl, and it had a word hand painted across it in black.

'Aisha'.

"You said Aisha was..." I didn't finish, a stone dropping into my stomach. He'd said Aisha was her best friend.

Drake set the bowl down, eyes scanning the photos that were pinned up around the vanity's mirror. Then he tugged one down, eyes wide. In it, Vex was beaming, her arms wrapped around the neck of a St. Bernard that was almost the size of her.

"She really was... alone before us," Drake said quietly.

She had been.

Just an omega and her dog, living in a place like this...

Vex's tear-streaked face haunted my vision as I stared around numbly. Drake and Rook were arguing and Ebony was rummaging through drawers.

I couldn't move, grief suddenly overwhelming me.

This tiny pocket of space that was her—all of her—in every crack and colour.

My mate.

There was something harrowing about it.

Propped up against the mirror was a board covered in more photos and clippings. I picked it up, staring at the coloured collage as I sat down on her bed.

It was titled: *'Vex and Aisha's impossible dreams'.* She'd taken a marker and crossed out the 'im' impossible, and beside it was a clipped quote: *"Dare to dream."*

There was a photo of stone steps leading up to a temple, surrounded by trees on a sunny day. Vex had pinned the words: 'Meet the temple monkeys in Kathmandu.'

There was a beautiful photo of the Grand Canyon at dawn and pinned to that one were the words: *'Take momma's ashes and sing her lullaby at dawn.'* That one was crossed out, and marked complete. Beside it was a Polaroid selfie of Vex and Aisha at the Grand Canyon.

A photo of a recording studio was labelled with: *'Produce one song that sounds kind of half decent and someone might want to listen to'.* I couldn't help a small smile, though it fell away at the next one.

There was a picture of a classic perfume. *'Go on a date with a guy rich enough to buy me Lava and Ashes Perfume on a first date'.* She'd crossed that one out. I scowled. That was unnecessary, we could buy her enough of those for a lifetime.

There was more, though, a dream house, a dream nest—to which she'd stuck a dozen little clippings of things she might buy if she had the money.

I glanced around the room briefly, stomach clenching. It was nothing like the nest in her pictures. I could see echoes of it, weak attempts. Edison bulbs were traded for tacky, coloured christmas lights across her vanity, only half of which worked. Her photo wall was cracking, just an old cork board that looked halfway to its grave. Blankets were ratty and thin, the huge bed was, instead, cramped, even for a one person, and the mattress was caving in. She had four pillows, all worn and old.

It was the last dream on the board, though, that truly did me in. In the bottom right, was a clipping of us. Pinned to it was her scrawled handwriting that said: *'Meet the Crimson Fury Pack.'* There was an arrow toward it with another scrawled note. *'Thank them for speaking up about gold packs.'*

I set it down, staggering to my feet. The world spun, and I made for the hallway, looking both ways until I saw the cracked door. I headed for it and found a grimy bathroom. Crashing to my knees before the toilet just in time, I threw up violently.

I could have fixed this. We could have given her everything she dreamed of. Instead, I'd left her shivering on her knees, night after night, believing I didn't want her.

Now...Were we too late?

She was gone. Alone and terrified, and still somehow fighting. Battling hopelessness with a strength displayed in every inch of her room.

Someone was crouched next to me, hand on my shoulder.

Caramel and brandy.

"You alright?" Rook asked as I finally leaned back.

"We..." I wiped my mouth with my sleeve. "We were supposed to protect her."

Only an hour ago, I'd been so furious with him I hadn't even been able to look at him. When the text had come in, taunting us for not wanting her enough, I'd seen red.

But my own grief was overtaking that now, and I could see the agony in his expression. "I know."

SIX

VEX

It was a moment I claimed from years of dreams.

I stood in line for hours surrounded by energised fans. But quiet and broken wasn't how I imagined I would be when I finally met the Crimson Fury pack. I shouldn't be here, I knew that. Yet, what I clutched in my hands belonged to Aisha, it was pink and glittery, just as bright as she had been. She'd loved their pack as much as I had, literally leaping with excitement when their movies played in my cramped apartment. I smiled, grief washing over me, the pink glitter twinkling through tears.

She'd died for me.

I could get this signed for her.

I was jostled forward in the line, almost at the front, and finally the tiniest spark of anticipation lit. Today, I would meet the Crimson Fury pack for the both of us.

And that was the moment I caught the first sweet hint of caramel brandy.

. . .

Silence smothered the world. Movements and sounds were distant echoes.

That truth was sinking in slowly; despair was a fist around my throat.

I wouldn't survive this.

I didn't want to.

Water splashed against the bottom of the glass as it filled. It was the only thing in the world. A command hanging suspended in nothingness.

I waited for too long. The water spilled over the edges, wetting my shaking hand, cooling the command as it did.

I could wait like this for a few moments more.

Rainbow prisms danced in the water for just a moment, then the tears faded, as if even they were too afraid.

I jumped at the sound of movement. My eyes snapped to the broad mirror, reflecting the bathroom back at me. Mine was a face I didn't recognise, even with the golden eyes and silver hair and the peach streak I'd fought for.

All for nothing.

And he was here, too.

Zeus.

When had he come in?

I stared at him with sunken eyes, water still flowing over my hand. He folded his arms, leaning against the doorframe, tucking his phone into his pocket. I lingered on the movement, the sight of his phone stirring something so distant now.

It felt like it had been forever... Zeus still didn't speak.

They aren't coming. The whisper in my mind was reassuring now, a lifeboat to cling to.

"Are you going to give me a show?" Zeus asked, dragging my attention back to him.

Those words threatened the cool silence in my mind.

I withdrew the glass from the sink, but when I tried to pass, he shifted, blocking my way. I didn't know what to make of the look he was giving me, something caught between anticipation and annoyance. He'd been irritated since the moment Triton had swaggered into the room.

"He wants water," I muttered, ducking around him.

When I exited the bathroom, I hated the sight that met me just as much as I hated the sight of Zeus. Triton was seated on the side of my bed, topless, his chestnut waves framing his cruel smile. "See, you can't keep her all to yourself, Zeus."

I fixed my gaze on the floor as I reached him, having seen enough of the delight in his eyes as he watched me follow commands.

He didn't take the water from me straight away. "What do you think? Will she have a better gag reflex than Drake?"

The silence turned to a high pitched ringing.

Drake?

I looked up at him, the full truth settled into place. Drake's fear. The past that haunted him.

And *this* pack.

Reality crashed in, a cresting wave of crystal shattering against marble. And in that moment, it felt like I shattered with it.

DRAKE

I spun as I felt Ebony's aura split the air. He had frozen, staring down into Vex's bottom drawers that he'd been digging through.

"What?" I asked, crossing toward him. He stood, chest heaving, and I saw a large IV bag in each fist.

"Heat drugs," he sounded furious. "Black market."

"How can you tell?" I asked, peering at the bags.

"The Trograst—it speeds the heat to a day, but it's so dangerous it's banned. Why would she—?"

"If she's self administering," I cut in. "Means she's out cold.

Can't have an IV running on yourself for too long. Risk is too high."

"These drugs could kill her," Ebony snarled. "Is she too good for the free clinics? What the fuck was she thinking?"

I opened my mouth, then shut it, truly taking Ebony in. "She's not stupid," I said, putting a hand on his arm. "If she didn't go, there was a reason."

Ebony flinched back. "Like *what*? Our money funds those clinics. What are they there for if my mate is using this shit instead?"

His fist closed around the bag and it burst, flooding the room with a strong iron-like scent before he flung the sopping plastic at the wall.

Shit.

I'd *never* seen Ebony crack like this. But then in the drawer, beside where he'd found the drugs, I spotted a stack of papers. They were all PSA posters with Ebony's face. It was one of his campaigns about gold pack safety.

We only stayed a little longer, waiting on Love to sort arrangements to have her stuff brought home. Since we hadn't expected to find anything of hers, we didn't have the boxes to pack it all up.

"Did you find anything useful?" I asked, looking to Ebony. I wasn't sure what he'd been looking for.

He was tense, bag of drugs still clutched in his hand, but he didn't reply.

"Maybe we should ask around before we go," I said as Rook shut the door to Vex's room. I examined the space and my eyes fell on the door that had cracked open as we passed—the one with the red-haired omega within.

Love caught me by the shoulder as I made for it. "He looked nervous."

"He's an omega. If she trusted anyone, it was him."

I knocked on the door, then took a step back, waiting.

There was a long pause, and nothing happened. I tried again.

Finally, the door cracked open, its chain snapping taut, and one golden eye peered out at me intently. I noticed he leaned back slightly, hand resting on his hip. I had no doubt he had a weapon.

"What do you want?"

"Not here for trouble, I just wondered if you know Vex," I said, forcing myself to relax.

His gaze darted behind me, and I hoped the others weren't crowding the hall.

"Yeh... I knew her."

"We think she was taken from her room. Did you... see anything?" I asked.

There was a long pause. "Why do you care?"

"She's important to us."

Again, a pause. Then finally, the door shut. I heard the sliding metal, and then he opened it properly, glancing from me to the others.

"She wasn't lying, then?" he asked. "About matching? She told me it happened, but didn't say how."

"She knew you well?"

"I mean... kind of." He shrugged. "She always had good drugs."

"What?" Rook asked, surprised.

"Heat drugs and shit. I don't know who her dealer was, but they were clean as they come. She got extras and shared them with me. I appreciated that. Can't be too careful."

"I'm Drake," I said, holding my hand out.

"Yeh..." He trailed off, a frown on his face that told me he knew exactly who I was. He took my hand though.

"Gambit."

"We're trying to find her. Did you see anything?"

"I don't know. Maybe? There was some weird shit that whole week, but I was..." He winced. "I wasn't all... here." His eyes darted down the hall, and his voice dropped. "I had a bad heat cycle right before. Was out of it for ages."

"But you did see something?" I asked.

He shrugged, eyes snagging on something behind me. "Is she uh... going to need that if she has you lot?"

I turned to find him eyeing the pouch of heat meds that was still intact in Ebony's hand.

"They expired last month," Ebony said.

"Mine expired half a year ago." Gambit shrugged. "I could do with it."

"We're not giving you drugs like that—" Love cut off as I backed toward Ebony and grabbed it from him, then crossed back toward Gambit.

He took it from me gratefully.

Then I stood back, letting Ebony fire off a few questions. Gambit seemed willing to answer them well enough, but I still wasn't sure how any of this would help us find her.

"I don't get it," Rook said. "If you live across the hall from each other, why not just help each other through it? Then you could use the safer drugs."

Gambit snorted, looking between us like Rook had made a joke. "You don't tell *anyone* if you're in heat. Never. Doesn't matter how much you think you can trust them. You know how much money someone can make, ratting out a drugged up omega halfway in? Enough for better drugs for the next few years. Nah, Vex wasn't stupid."

My stomach twisted in discomfort. I'd grown up in the Gritch District, but this? This was layers and layers more desperate of a place than anything I'd experienced.

"Some alphas will pay a lot for that, you know? Cut off the drugs, and we wake up halfway through, not sure what's happening. Then, if we're lucky, they'll dump us back on the street when it's over and that's if the Hounds don't get you on the other side."

"Hounds?" Love asked.

"Traffickers," I said, glancing back at him. Even I knew that slang.

"Why are you gold pack?" Ebony asked. I winced at the blunt question, but I could feel he was still on edge through the bond.

Gambit set the bag down and folded his arms, finally comfortable enough to remove his hands from whatever he had tucked into his belt. His features held the boyish handsomeness of a lot of male omegas, but he looked rough around the edges. There was a jagged scar on his temple, and those bright eyes were hardened. "Because I never went for the injection."

"You chose it?" Rook asked, surprised.

Gambit eyed him wearily, then wrinkled his nose with a shrug. "It's not like it is topside. Even if my eyes weren't gold, doesn't keep me safe. Seers can only identify if a dark bond was forced. If we don't have golden eyes, it can still look legal even if we're forced into it. Torture, blackmail—you name it. There are packs who prefer that, but if they do ever get me, with these eyes, there's a chance I get out."

I shivered at that thought, knowing what he meant. Gold packs, just like rogues, weren't bound by the laws the Institute put in place. The ones that made us less prone to violence.

Gambit's meaning was clear as day. As difficult as it might be, it *was* possible he could free himself by killing the alphas that bit him. An omega with the injection could never kill an alpha that claimed them, just like I could never kill an omega I bit.

Gambit and Vex—even Ebony, as a rogue—weren't locked in by such rules.

An omega was in dire straights if those were the options left; if golden eyes were chosen as a warning. The question wasn't if Gambit would be a target; it was what kind. And that, I realised, might have been the decision Vex was faced with, too.

We had to get her back.

I returned my attention to Gambit. "What year were you born?"

"'06," he said, then winced as the age-old trick caught him. I did the math quickly.

Fuck.

Too young to be on his own in the world like this.

How old had Vex been when she perfumed? How long had she lived in a place like this? When omegas perfumed in their early teens, their heats were often delayed. If they did happen, they were mild and easily managed by over-the-counter pills. It was only when adulthood crept in that everything changed.

"Alright." I dug in my pocket, finding one of the many little notebooks I kept with me in case I had a strike of inspiration for a part I was practising for. I jotted my number down on a page, and tore it out, pressing it into Gambit's hand.

"Next time you're in... trouble," I said, avoiding the word heat. "You can call. I'll make sure you're safe."

He stared down at the number for a long time, jaw clenched.

"She really is your scent match?" he asked again, glancing back up at me like he wasn't sure he believed it. "Guess it makes sense," he added. "No other reason topsiders like you would give a fuck about one of us."

I could practically feel the shift of my pack behind me. The discomfort through the bond at those words.

"She *is* our scent match," I confirmed. It would, perhaps, help him trust us.

Still, he looked unsure, as if he was a moment away from handing me back the number.

"You know who we are," I said quietly. "We don't have any use for black market bribes. You're Vex's friend. If you call, we'll make sure you're safe."

"He's barely an adult," Rook hissed as we made our way down the stairs. "We're just leaving him there like that?"

"He has our number," I replied. "He can call if he needs anything."

"We can do more than that," Rook said. "He's too young. That room is tiny, and he's gold pack for fuck's sake, by himself, just like Vex was. He shouldn't be in a place like that."

I considered Rook curiously. "There's a million kids like Gambit in the Gritch District. He and Vex aren't anomalies. You can't just go in and rip them all out of their homes."

"That's not a home. That's a room. It has a fucking communal bathroom!"

"Let him call us," I said. "I think he will."

"What are you going to do if he does?" Ebony asked curiously as we stepped back out into the grimy street.

I shrugged. "Make sure he's safe."

There were dozens of ways to deal with heat if you had money. Private heat clinics always had spots.

"I don't get it," Rook was saying. "Gold pack is for life, why not just get the injection and never go back?"

I turned to him with a frown. "Never go back?" I asked. "You can only live where you can afford. Most people who grow up on that side of town don't think they're ever getting out."

That had been me.

That was why I'd worked so fucking hard—harder than Rook ever had to work. Not just for me, I'd wanted my whole family out.

We hadn't even made it to the car when my phone buzzed. I was relieved to see a text pop up on the screen.

Unknown number: Tell me when she's safe, yeh?

Me: I'll do that. Thanks for the info.

Me: Reach out if you need to.

I held my phone up to Rook. "He'll call."

"Send me his number," Ebony told me from the driver's seat ahead.

"Don't scare him off," I muttered, sending it over and adding Gambit's name to my contacts.

"Do you think we found anything that's going to help us get her back?" Rook asked, gaze fixed on Ebony. I felt a weary flutter of hope in my chest. Ebony was the one who seemed to have a dozen plans while the rest of us were at the mercy of Leighton's updates and the damn phone Vex had left behind. But he'd been cagey about them. Still, he'd been set on visiting where Vex had lived.

Ebony opened his mouth as if he were going to snap back at Rook, but then noticed my desperation. He sighed, clenching his jaw. "Nothing I'm doing is likely to get us results in the short term."

I swallowed. "So our best bet's still...?"

There was a hateful look on his face, but he nodded. "We still need them to ask for a trade."

"What he said about gold packs and dark bonds," Love said. "It's not like... it's not so simple, is it?"

It wasn't unheard of, gold packs killing their alphas, or rogues killing their bonded omegas, but it wasn't common.

"He's right that it's possible, but the dark bond makes it a thousand times more difficult," Ebony replied. "Vex would be fighting the dark bond as well as her own instincts as a bonded omega. It's not just *hard,* it's all but impossible. You have to be more than just desperate or afraid. The drive it takes isn't something that can be planned for."

"But... if she did?" Love asked.

Ebony's eyes darkened. "Then she'd be at the mercy of the rest of the pack before we could get to her."

VEX

Drake?

Hearing my mate's name on Triton's lips was the final confirmation of what I'd been afraid of since the moment I'd seen Zeus's face. Fury hit me like a strike of lightning. Instinct smothered everything, the world, the commands.

My Drake. The one who'd loved me, despite how broken he was. Despite his pain and monsters.

Monsters I was facing right now.

The glass of water in my hand shattered as I smashed it on the bedside table.

I lunged forward, snapping that last fragile thing I had left: the piece of me that was a bonded omega. The world was red, the shattered glass clutched in my fist. I was being ripped in two, the bite on my neck pure agony, my veins on fire.

I didn't care.

Screaming rang through the air. It was a desperate sound tearing from my own lungs. Strong arms grabbed me, tossing me easily to the ground, and the world went black for a moment, pain splitting my back.

I blinked, breathing ragged.

I was on the floor.

The glass was scattered around me. I was shaking beneath the agony of the dark bond, a thousand knives across my skin.

But all I could see was Drake, the fear in his eyes when he'd looked at the pack—and how he'd confronted them for me, anyway.

They'd... hurt him.

The world came into a blurry focus. Zeus was helping a furious Triton to his feet.

I sobbed in despair.

He was alive.

I'd just splintered into a thousand pieces, and he was still alive.

I'd smashed the glass against the bedside table and lunged for him. Then... then Zeus had kicked me into the wall... I thought.

"—*Little gold pack bitch!*" I could hear Triton's fury.

I hope he killed me.

He couldn't...

He wasn't a rogue, and I was his bonded omega...

"*Enough!*" Above me, Zeus was between me and Triton, blocking him. "Go get cleaned up you fucking idiot."

Blood trailed down Triton's chest, a nasty, gaping wound below his clavicle, but he listened to his pack lead with a snarl.

I hugged myself, lungs feeling like stone. It was over.

"*Find your voice, find your strength.*" My mother's words whispered, but it was far too late for dreams.

I had no strength left. Not for my voice, not for my hope.

Not for my dreams, that had always left me more empty than before.

"Come here." Zeus's command was jarring. I was picking myself up, my soul shaken, too fragile to fight it. It had just tried to shatter the cage that held me, tried to shatter myself.

I had no more strength left.

He took my wrists, turning my hands in his, examining them. There was a cut on one, though it wasn't deep. He looked amused. "You really are a wildcard, Vex. If we keep you, I'll enjoy punishing you for behaviour like that," he told me, reaching up and tracing the dampness on my cheeks.

But there was only one word of his that stuck.

I stared at him.

"If?" My voice was a rasp.

"You're mates have been harassing me," Zeus said. "But I need to know if they can put their money where their mouth is."

"W-what?"

Zeus tossed his phone onto the bed beside me.

I stared at it.

There were texts from my mates—from the phone I'd left. Demands like, *What do you want? Are you looking for a payout?,* or *We will negotiate for her return.*

Zeus lingered on one of the few replies he'd sent: *I've grown attached to her, you know? It's got to be good.* There were more from them below.

We're willing to negotiate if you don't hurt her or touch her. Tell us what you want. Name it. It's yours, but return her unharmed.

These texts had gone back... I scrolled... they were endless. They'd been asking for me since the moment I'd been taken.

They wanted me back?

Instead of relief, I felt a twisted, sick panic at that.

It had to be a trick. I'd already... I let go of that possibility, I'd had to. I didn't know how to hold onto it anymore.

Zeus's knuckle brushed my cheek, and I jumped. "It's Triton who was harmed, though, not you. Do you think I should up your price—just for damages?"

"Th-there's still a price?" My voice was hoarse, but that was all I could focus on.

They were trying to get me back—if it wasn't another cruel prank.

"There is, but I need to know those mates of yours are serious this time," he mused. "That they understand how close I am to keeping you."

But... What Triton had just said... What if the price was about Drake? I... I *couldn't* let Drake near this pack ever again.

Zeus's fist closed around my arm, and he shoved me onto the bed. "Let's find out, shall we?"

I was winded, the blow still making it hard to breathe. Then Zeus was on top of me, his weight pinning me down.

Panic blitzed by every other instinct, and I opened my mouth to scream, but then his phone was in my face once more.

He was recording.

Drake... *Drake was going to see this.* I couldn't let him see how scared I was.

I was disoriented as he shot the video, panic and fury mingling as he taunted me, choking me for my mates to see.

Finally, it was over. Zeus's weight had vanished, and I curled up, trying to process what he'd said in the video.

Was there a chance for me?

"I need to know *just* how committed they are, and I intend to make them sweat. But on the bright side." I jumped as he leaned close and pressed a kiss to my temple, his voice a low murmur, "maybe you didn't fuck up so badly after all."

Fresh tears blossomed in my eyes. I didn't know what to do with hope right now. It was too much.

But how?

How was it possible?

Was it Drake—fighting for me?

I wanted him so badly, and this time, the thought of him was impossible to push away. His blackcurrant wine scent, and the safety of his arms around me.

SEVEN

Hour 40

LOVE

Ebony and Rook were at the Dragon Hunters interview. I didn't envy them that job.

I'd finally managed to get a short nap, but it was haunted by nightmares of chasing Vex through a dark forest, never able to catch her.

The channel where the interview would be hosted was running on the TV in Vex's room. I didn't usually watch our interviews, but I couldn't risk Rook screwing up again.

The sun was already starting its descent as the afternoon stretched on. Vex's phone was on the edge of the bed, plugged in to charge indefinitely so we wouldn't miss anything.

I stared down into the boxes of Vex's things that I'd arranged to be brought from her apartment.

"This is her stuff," Drake rasped. "Her nest. We should let her pick where it goes."

I nodded numbly.

"We can…" My voice was too hollow. I cleared my throat. "We can put the rest of it up." I'd rush ordered a bunch of stuff under the pretence of giving Drake something to do, but to be honest, I needed it just as much.

Hopelessness was starting to dig its claws in.

It didn't help that I was staring down at her dream board. Numbly, I began hanging some lights that matched the pictures.

When.

When she was back.

I wasn't ready to face the possibility that we might never see her again.

The voices on the TV addressing the Dragon Hunter franchise grated at my mind though the interview hadn't begun yet.

I didn't give a fuck about the stupid franchise. She was still out there.

She was suffering right now.

When I heard the buzz of a phone I jumped, lights tumbling from my hands.

Adrenaline blitzed through my exhausted system, but Drake got there first, tapping the phone open, eyes scanning the screen.

"It's another video."

My stomach dropped. Drake paused, and I felt his terror through the bond.

"If you want me to tell you what's in—" I began.

"No," Drake hissed, then hit the play button.

Vex was the only thing I truly saw as she lay upon the sheets of a bed. She was staring up at the camera, golden eyes shocking in their brightness and fury. She was terrified, I could see that beneath everything.

Her face was pale, and her eyes were haunted.

"I can't understand why you want her back," the distorted male voice said. "She's a brat. That's why I avoid omegas—shallow cunts, the lot of them." He laughed. "You know the first thing she ever fought me on?" The alpha's fist closed around her neck.

The whole world stopped. I shifted forward, my breath catching, but he didn't press down.

She was so small, fighting beneath him.

Terrified.

My throat was closing up.

"Hair dye," the alpha's distorted voice was half a chuckle. "Then it was nail polish, and makeup, and fucking outfits." He snorted again, but I could see the pain in her expression.

"What have you got to say about that?" he asked. I saw him draw back just enough for her to catch her breath.

"I didn't..." She struggled, voice thick. "I didn't want you... taking anything else from me." Her lip quivered, but she didn't take her eyes from him. I saw a fierce hatred in them, one that lit the smallest spark of hope in my chest, even if I couldn't identify why. "I didn't want you telling me how I was supposed to look!" She was losing it, nails clawing at his arms as her voice became hateful. *Or how to be for them!"*

The alpha snorted. "She's going feral." He slammed her back harder into the bed before I could snap my gaze away from the phone.

Drake shifted forward, though, jaw clenched with fury as he watched.

"And that's all?" the alpha was asking. "The best you have to offer? A pretty face?"

"This is a taunt," Drake hissed. "He's playing with us. There's no—"

I held a finger up, eyes fixed on the screen.

"Luckily for you," the alpha went on. "It seems that might just be enough for them. Would you like to go back to your mates, Vex?"

She stopped fighting him, her chest heaving as she stared at the camera. That flash of desperation that crossed her face was enough to shatter my heart.

"But the question is," the alpha murmured. "How badly do they want you back?"

And with that, the video cut off.

There was a horrible silence, and then I downloaded the video and sent it to Leighton, Ebony and Rook.

"It's a challenge," I said. "They're... asking what we'll give up."

"We told them to name it," Drake said.

"I get the feeling they're about to."

EIGHT

VEX

The Dragon Hunter's interview played on Zeus's phone as he sat beside me on the bed.

He'd just sent them the video he'd recorded, but I still didn't know why. I almost shut my eyes as I saw Ebony and Rook on the screen for the first time in what felt like an eternity, my chest becoming tight. They were seated on interview chairs in front of a screen decorated with huge dragons flying across a landscape of mountains.

We watched only for a few moments before Zeus tapped out of the stream and went to his texts. I read the one already drafted.

"You get one chance to prove your devotion, and I'll send her back until her heat. Then, maybe we'll negotiate. But I want proof up front, tell Rook to announce on live TV that you're dropping the Dragon Hunters contract."

. . .

He pressed send, and my heart was in my throat.

Zeus was still too close, holding me against him. "What do you think he's going to do?"

They wouldn't... I knew their job was their whole lives. I was just... just a gold pack omega, who'd lied to them. They wouldn't give up something like that for me.

"Why?" I asked. "Why ask that?"

He returned to the interview, and I couldn't peel my gaze away from it, heart thundering in my chest.

"We have you, and some of them are still acting like playboys. I want to see them give up what they care about most."

As I watched, Ebony glanced down to his side where he sat, subtly tapping on his phone and reading it. His gaze slid to Rook.

"He knows," Zeus whispered. "Now, what do you think they're going to do?"

ROOK

Cancel the Dragon Hunter's contract?

We were right in the middle of the interview, and they'd finally replied with a demand, and a promise that they would send her back.

It should have been the greatest relief in the world after days of this torture, except that the instructions were for me—not any of the others.

Only... Let go of the Dragon Hunter's franchise?

Our big break.

But Love's decision had come instantly.

> Love: Rook, you're fucking doing it. No arguments.

Panic rose in my chest, making it hard to focus. I'd never had stage fright before in my life. I loved the spotlight, and the cameras, but as I looked up at the interviewer, I froze.

It was only last night that I'd been staring at another camera. Drake was right, that was a mistake, and what I'd done hadn't been missed. It was why the instructions were for me.

Would we have had her back already if I hadn't?

I opened my mouth, knowing I was supposed to do something. I was supposed to fix this.

But I was the one who'd broken it.

I was the one who had convinced her we would never want her.

I got to my feet in a daze, ripping my mic from my jacket, bile burning my throat. But I didn't make it one step outside the room before Ebony caught up to me, shoving me against the wall.

"I can't do this," I rasped. The world was spinning. I couldn't focus, but then I felt his hand palming my neck, other fist in my shirt.

"Rook!" He snapped. "Focus."

I blinked, meeting his raging silver eyes. A wild laugh bubbled up my throat at this foreign affection. Ebony fucking hated me. "You can't just treat me like I'm Drake and expect it to w-work."

I saw the flicker of a sneer on his face. "Oh, I'm not, Rook. It's this, or I'll put you through a fucking wall on live TV."

I swallowed, those words straightening my thoughts a little. "I just... I need a moment."

"I knew you were a piece of shit, Rook, but this is a new low—"

"I want her back," I rasped. It was the truth. Even faced with losing the greatest opportunity we'd ever been given... it was nothing in the face of getting her back. "I swear, that's not—"

"Then what is the *fucking* issue?"

"I don't..." Fuck. I wasn't built for this. I couldn't... In that moment, I didn't care that it was Ebony here instead of Love. I could feel myself cracking.

"Why is this happening?" I rasped. "I d-don't understand. Drake fell for her, y-you and Love wanted to protect her, I can't be the one to fix it—"

"You know what they're probably doing to her right now?" Ebony hissed, snapping me from my spiral.

My blood turned to ice, and I opened my mouth to stop him, but he was already speaking. "Right now, your mate is probably getting *fucked* by other alphas. You don't get to have a breakdown. You'll go back to that mic, you'll say the words: *'We are dropping out of the Dragon Hunters franchise'* , and then you'll get in the fucking car so we can leave. And if you don't, I swear I'll chain you to that Alpha's Hook in the garden and pry each of your fucking nails off one by one, and I think Drake and Love would be glad to watch."

My lips were parted slightly by the time he finished.

"Is that clear?" he snarled.

I nodded numbly.

Finally, his hand dropped from my neck, and he was shoving me back into the room.

Somehow, the cogs in my brain started moving again. The freefall into infinity had halted.

Ebony's words cycled in my head.

I picked up the little mic I'd dropped, not seeing the interviewer or the room full of watching eyes.

The words were ash on my tongue, coming out mechanically.

There might have been a shocked silence after I spoke. There might have been an uproar that followed.

I might have stepped away, or Ebony might have grabbed me and hauled me from the room. At some point, open air hit my lungs and then a car door slammed, making me jump.

The world crashed back in, and I realised my hands were trembling.

"What if it doesn't work?"

"It will."

"Do you think... do you think that's what's happening to her?" Again, nausea roiled in my stomach, but it was long empty by now. The things he'd said about what might be happening to Vex... I couldn't shake it from my mind.

"If it is, I'll make sure they regret it a thousand times more than she ever could."

There was a long silence that followed that.

"Thank..." I swallowed. "Thank you. For... for that."

Ebony's expression became twisted for a moment. "You don't deserve her, Rook. You're a speck of dirt stuck to a diamond."

"And... you... you think you deserve her?" I asked, a shaky laugh in my voice.

For a second, I didn't think Ebony even knew his answer. He spoke after a long pause. "At least I'll protect her."

When we got home, an agonising hour passed before another video came in.

It was simple and short, but brutal. With a fist in her hair, Vex was dragged to the door of a limo and shoved out onto tarmac. The video shifted briefly to its surroundings, and I saw a parking lot and shops, ones I recognised—

"It's... it's the strip mall down the road," I said, heart in my throat. "She's... she's just—"

I cut off, spinning as I felt an aura flare.

Drake was already out the door.

DRAKE

I ran faster than I ever had in my life.

My feet slammed against the pavement, not a care that my aura was out on this quiet, residential street. The world was a blur, the sun too bright.

I turned the corner, the street ahead a straight line to the shops.

Never, in my life, had I felt fear like this.

I'd be too late.

It was a trick.

She wouldn't be there.

And then ahead, around the side of the shops and beside the brickwork, I saw her figure curled on the tarmac, solitary and vulnerable.

"*VEX!*" The shout came from me without thought, as if sending sound ahead of me would stop this hallucination from slipping away.

She looked up, eyes wide.

It was her.

Twenty feet.

It wouldn't be real.

It was a nightmare. It was why I hadn't been able to sleep. Because I knew this is what I'd be met with if I did.

Her expression crumpled as she saw me, and she tried to get to her feet. She was weak, stumbling the moment she straightened, crashing back to her knees.

Fifteen feet.

I could carry her home.

She didn't have to be strong right now.

I had strength for her.

Ten feet—and this was the point where the dream would end in a nightmare.

This was the moment I would wake—reaching for a blank ceiling with nothing but the fading scent of raspberry treacle, and the image of haunted, golden eyes.

Five feet.

Please, not this time.

Please...

Then I collided with her, my jeans ripping on tarmac, my hand around the back of her head to catch her as I failed to stop my momentum, sending us both into the ground.

My own breath caught, each one thicker and thicker as hot tears broke free.

She was real.

She was in my arms, and she was real. Her scent of raspberry treacle was real, filling my lungs.

Her fists were at the back of my shirt, low heaving sobs coming from her chest as she clutched me to her tiny frame.

"I've got you," I told her.

I could do nothing but hold her close, unburned adrenaline shaking me to the bones. "I've g-got you, Vex." My voice was a thick stammer as I made a promise I'd hit the grave before breaking. "I'm n-never letting you go."

Never again.

I'd die fighting for pack lead if Love even hinted we might leave her behind.

Finally, she released me just enough that she could draw back. Her pale face was streaked with tears, makeup free, nose a warm pink.

But her eyes...

All of those pictures and videos paled beside the real thing.

They were golden and... breathtaking.

Real.

This was the woman I'd fallen for, and it was the first time I'd ever truly seen her.

Footsteps sounded behind me, my pack's scents filling the air, but I couldn't take my eyes away, afraid to even blink.

"Vex!" That was Love kneeling at our side.

Vex tensed, those perfect eyes drawn in fear all of a sudden.

"N-no!" Suddenly, she was trying to break free. "W-wait! Rook—"

What?

I turned to see Ebony and Rook. Ebony stood a few feet back, but he wasn't looking at Vex. Rook was behind him, half a step from... I blinked.

I'd not taken in anything other than her.

But Rook stood a foot from a long back limo that was still in the parking lot.

Every instinct switched to high alert, and I was drawing her closer. That's where she'd just come from.

Could the alphas still be in there?

I'd kill them.

Love got to his feet, something hateful on his face telling me he was thinking the same thing.

We all were. The bond between us, for the briefest second, was unified with a sickening hatred.

A need to act. To—

"Please don't!" Vex's desperate voice shattered all my instincts to pieces, sending a splintering divide between me and my brothers. She was trying to stand, still shaking. "Don't!" she begged again as I stood, helping her with me.

"But..." Rook looked lost, lips half parted as he stared at her, still a foot from the limo. "I don't..." Rook looked to me, to Love, and then to Ebony. I could feel his uncertainty through the bond. His panic, too.

I got it.

A lingering flash of my alpha instincts was still trying to claw out, wondering why Rook hadn't ripped that door open already.

I wasn't processing properly.

None of us were.

None of us except Ebony. "We check it," he said. So fucking sure.

"No!" Vex's gaze was darting between us all desperately. "You can't."

"Why would it still be here?" I asked Ebony, trying to detangle this chaos. "They wouldn't have stayed."

Right...

That wouldn't make sense.

And we couldn't, not if she'd told us not to.

"Rook, *check it*," Ebony growled.

"She said *no!*" My aura split the air. *"Love!"* I turned to him, afraid to let go of Vex. "Tell them no."

Love was frozen, eyes sliding from Vex to Ebony and Rook.

Then, after a tense silence, he spoke at last.

"No." Love's word was a solid command directed at Rook.

Relief washed through my system as Rook shifted one pace toward us.

"She's in a fucking dark bond," Ebony snarled, holding up a hand as if to bar Rook from changing his mind. "She could have been commanded to stop us."

"Why would—?" I began.

"This pack is *taunting* us." Ebony cut me off. "Doesn't seem far-fetched, that they're just out of reach—watching their command steal our chance of solving this?"

"Enough!" Love snapped. "We're taking her home."

Shit, I could see the waver in Rook's expression, could practically feel him shaking the command off. He could defy a pack lead's order. Do it too much and our bonds would grow weak, but by his expression, he'd risk it.

"Please Ebony—R-Rook." Vex's trembling voice sent cracks

down my heart, and I could hear the fresh tears in her words. "*Please* listen."

This wasn't right.

We'd got her back.

She wasn't supposed to be afraid of us.

There it was again from Rook through the bond, the faintest flicker of insecurity.

I don't know how we'd become this tense, as if by even touching that door something bad would happen, but I could feel it from Vex.

"I..." Rook was staring at her, an apology in his eyes as he took a final step back, hand outstretched.

Fuck.

They wouldn't.

"*Rook.*" Love took a step toward him, but Ebony shifted back, an attempt at blocking both of us.

"Check. It. *Now!*" Ebony snapped.

"N-no!" Vex dived from my arms, and I was right after her. Ebony and Love's aura hit the air next as he went for Rook.

I threw the first punch.

Vex tried to launch past us, but Ebony caught her arm. He took my second punch in the jaw, but his fist caught at my shirt even as he staggered, stopping me from getting by him.

"LOVE!" I bellowed.

He better—

But it was too late.

"NO!" Vex's sob split my heart in two, and I caught sight of Rook, who'd already ripped the door open.

ROOK

I thought I was done breaking. That I was in as many pieces as it was possible for a person to be in.

But that last plea from Vex shattered me again.

I could keep breaking until there was nothing but dust, I realised.

And it didn't matter.

For the first time in my life, I agreed with Ebony.

It was the right choice.

And Vex hated me, anyway. She'd hate me forever, so it might as well be me. Ebony, at least, had a chance.

So I wrenched the door open, my aura joining the others, a part of me expecting to be attacked.

But there was no one inside.

I stepped in, Love crashing in behind me, just a second too late. Now, instead, all his instincts were on high alert for a threat as we both stared around the inside of the limo that was almost entirely empty.

Outside, I could hear Vex's choked sobs. She wasn't begging anymore—it didn't even sound like she was fighting, as if just opening the door was enough.

The inside smelled too clinical—the first sign that something was wrong. There was no trace of raspberry treacle in here. Even if the alpha had been wearing dampeners, her scent *should* be here.

Naturally, my eyes fell to the only object within.

A little black book rested on one of the leather seats.

With my heart in my throat, I reached for it, a chill sliding down my spine, the sound of Vex's sobs behind me.

"Rook?" That was Ebony, peering in behind us.

I was already slipping down onto the seat, turning the first page.

My stomach dropped.

Again, the writing was that faded brown.

Dried blood.

Vex's blood.

Nice job, assholes.
Get her back for five seconds and you're already fucking this up.
Here's a secret about her time as your Sweetheart: Every time you broke her fragile little omega heart, she would crawl back to the bathroom and write about it just for me to see.
Now, you can see it, too.
The command is still active, and will only stop if you've all read this book back to front.
PS. Now you've seen it, you better keep it safe. It's the ticket to negotiations.
She'll tell me if you lie.

My hands began to shake as I stared at the page.

Ebony shoved past Love toward me, trying to snatch it from me, but a growl slipped from my chest.

For once, he listened.

I turned the first page. I didn't want to, and I *had* to all at the same time.

Then the next, and the next, ice seeping through my veins at the words before me.

NINE

VEX

Scalding hot water streamed over my body.

It wasn't enough to burn away the ghost of Zeus's touch on me. The way he'd always held me close... I didn't understand it. He found me vile, yet he'd barely left me alone. He'd been annoyed when Triton visited, and I'd felt vindication through the bond when he'd shoved him from the room, dripping with blood.

It wasn't something I'd focused on at the time, but now I was standing beneath the water, trying to blitz him and his pack from my mind, it was all I could think about.

That and the book.

Zeus's command was clawing at me. I needed to write in it for the pain Rook and Ebony had given me, but they still had it.

Would they all read it before I had it back in my hands?

A choked sob escaped my chest. They were going to see everything. Rook was going to read everything I'd ever written about him.

He... he already had.

There was a knock on the door.

"You doing okay, Vex?" Drake's voice floated in, shattering my despair, if only briefly. I stared at the door through the glass encasing the huge shower. He was waiting outside. He'd told me he would be whatever I needed, but I'd been too much of a coward to ask him to come in here.

I'd just needed five minutes alone, to cry without making him feel worse before I could face him. It had been a long five minutes, and I felt the same.

I still wanted him.

I turned off the shower and all but stumbled out of it, wrapping a towel around myself and fixing my expression the best I could as I opened the door.

He was right outside, and the steam from the shower flooded from the bathroom, lifting his blackcurrant wine scent into the air.

Beautiful. Comforting.

Everything.

His violet eyes were worried and flutters of raven hair framed his face. There were dark bags beneath his eyes, and his skin was papery pale as if he were sick. He looked like he needed a good sleep. I opened my mouth, unable to rip my gaze away, and then realised I had no idea what to say. I didn't even know what I wanted. The desperation must have been clear in my eyes because he frowned.

"Can I come in?"

I swallowed, then managed to nod.

He slipped into the room, taking me in with a frown.

"Have you slept?" he asked.

I shook my head. I'd barely got an hour at a time. Zeus barely left me alone, and I'd laid awake the whole time he was there, terrified.

"Then let's get you ready for bed," he said. He picked me up and set me down on the counter, then took a spare towel and began squeezing my dripping hair.

Once done, he fetched me a silken cream dressing gown, but I stopped him before he could help me into it. Instead, I tugged on his shirt gently, trying to find the courage to tell him what I needed.

I didn't need to say anything else before he was tugging his top over his head. "You're lucky Love forced me to freshen up last night or there'd be no way."

I found the first moments of a real smile on my face as I clutched it to my chest. He began helping me dress, which included a set of ridiculously fluffy socks that I swear hadn't been in here before.

I jumped as his aura split the air, and he stifled it in an instant. But he was absolutely still, eyes fixed on my stomach. I looked down quickly, only to see there were purple bruises from where Zeus had kicked me into the wall. It ached, but... well, everything ached. My wrist was sore from the way he'd pinned me to the bed, my body was stiff and exhausted from a lack of sleep.

"It's not as bad as it looks," I whispered.

Still, Drake didn't move, unable to drag his eyes away until I tugged his shirt down over the bruise.

"It... it was self defence. That's all."

Finally, those captivating violet eyes met mine.

"I... hurt one of them and they uh... they had to drag me off."

His brows pinched, but he nodded stiffly. "Okay." He swallowed. "Yeh, I mean, 'course you did. I... I don't think Rook's ever recovered from the spoon incident."

I smiled, though it felt empty in the strange silence that followed. "I... like the socks," I whispered. "Did you get them?"

"Love did," he said. "And the..." He waved at the counter behind me, looking a little confused. I glanced back to see over a dozen boxes of Lava and Ashes Perfume. That was my favourite—

not to mention stupid expensive, and more than I could go through in a lifetime.

"If you think that's weird, you should see the linen closet," Drake said. "I didn't know there were so many types of fabric you could make a sheet out of."

Those words were good, right? I felt the faintest glimmer of warmth, somewhere in my chest, but it was fuzzy and barely recognisable. I sank against the lean muscle of Drake's bare chest as he lifted me up and carried me out to my room.

It felt... different in here, but I hadn't looked long enough to identify why.

I couldn't stop staring at him as he set me down on the bed. He was stunning, even with tired eyes and messy hair.

He dimmed the lights, and then plugged his phone in. I didn't say anything, knowing my phone—the new one that Zeus had given me—was still in the bathroom. Its charge would last until I woke, and I could check it then. I didn't need it with me.

Drake grabbed a tub of moisturiser, knelt before me, and began to massage it into my legs.

I nudged the pot, reading it. The brand was famous for both being expensive and completely scentless. Drake caught me looking. "There was no way in hell I want anything getting in the way of my mate's perfect scent." He punctuated each of his last words with gentle kisses on my legs.

Again, I felt that murmur of happiness in my chest, the bubble of a stream echoing through a forest so dark and dense I couldn't tell where it was coming from. He was so sweet and gentle it was... it was too much. I felt my breath catch as tears returned in full force. He paused, looking up with a frown.

My lip quivered, and I shut my eyes.

I'd thought, for what had felt like eternity, that I would never see him again.

I'd let him go.

The soft touch of his palm brushed my cheek and the bed shifted as he sat beside me.

"I don't..." I choked. "I don't know how to be what you need."

There was a long pause and he tugged me into his arms. "What do you think I need?" he asked me gently.

"I... I don't know. Anything. I should be happy I'm back, but I just feel..." I couldn't finish.

Empty.

Worthless.

Like I'd failed him by letting him go.

"You don't need to be anything, Vex, and you don't have to see anyone until you're ready. You don't have to hear their apologies, nothing. If you don't want me here either, I can—"

A low desperate sound rose in my chest and he cut off. I reached for him, even with my eyes squeezed shut, gripping his wrist deathly tight.

"I want to stay with you," I breathed.

"I'm... I'm staying—I don't... I don't ever want you out of my sight again. I just need you to know whatever you ask for is yours."

I didn't really understand the offer. They'd given up everything to get me back. Their entire career had taken a hit for the gold pack omega who'd lied to them.

I shook as he drew me closer, wrapping his arms around me protectively and sinking down into the sheets, drawing blankets around us. "We failed you, Vex. I failed you."

I shook my head. "You didn't."

"I did, and I'm so sorry I didn't see it. I should have. I'm your mate, and I wasn't enough. I should have—"

"Please don't say that." My voice was thick. "You..." My chin quivered. "You were the only one who was enough."

He held me tighter. "Love wants to speak to you. They... all do, but I don't think the others..." His voice became tight, the blackcurrant wine in the air edged with a dark fury. "You just... you let me know when you're ready to see them, alright?"

I bit my lip, eyes darting to the door. "I could... I could see Love I think. Maybe after…"

"After sleep," Drake said.

I nodded.

Love was the only other one who had tried to stop them opening the door. My chest tightened at the thought of the limo. Of the book.

Were they reading it right now?

I'd have to add to it when I got it back; that command was a constant tug.

Swallowing back another round of tears, I held Drake closer. It was strange to be back with everything in the open. Knowing who Zeus was. Knowing now why he'd used scent dampening spray in the limo to hide his own scent.

Drake would recognise it.

Drake knew the whole pack. Triton and his cruelty and his foul scent of old beer. Cerus and Achlys... though I knew less of them…

I knew they'd hurt Drake, but I was forbidden from speaking a word of the pack who had bitten me, with layers of foul trigger commands warning me away from even considering fighting that order.

The shower wasn't enough. I still felt as if Zeus was everywhere.

"I want…" I swallowed, feeling my tears come back. "I want to forget it all. I just... I want him gone."

I regretted the moment I'd spoken. I shouldn't have mentioned a 'him' at all. I couldn't imagine what it must have been like for Drake when he'd learned the truth of my bond. But then... he'd seen the videos…

What did he think of them?

I hated how frightened I'd been. I knew Drake would never say it, but he must think I was so foolish. I'd chosen my eyes and now I couldn't handle the pack who'd bitten me—

"That, Dreamgirl, is something I can do." His sweet words were enough to stifle my fears, and his voice was so confident that I peered up at him. The smile on his face was genuine. He shifted, fingers winding through my hair, tugging my neck back gently as he brushed his cheek along my jaw.

Blackcurrant wine became all consuming. It took me a moment to realise what he'd done. When I did, an unexpected purr rose in my throat, and my fingers dug into his arm.

He'd scent marked me.

"You're safe Vex," he breathed. "You've only seen the smallest part of what we're going to do to keep it that way."

I swallowed, shrinking, unsure of how to process that. "I love you," I whispered, instead.

That truth was safe, even among all of this uncertainty.

I could see the sadness in his eyes, as if he knew I wasn't ready for the promise he'd just made. Instead, he pressed his lips to my forehead and whispered, "I love you too, Dreamgirl."

The sense of safety warred with dread as sleep swept me away at last, a single, lingering thought souring my peace: this comfort could only ever be make believe. There was no promise in the world that could convince me that this nightmare was over forever.

Drake was a part of their past, and I could never allow any trade to go through that might put him back in harm's way.

No matter what it meant for me.

TEN

LOVE

I had to haul Rook from the limo with Ebony.

He was gone. There was a void where he'd been in the bond. It was like he'd just... vanished. The experience even drew Ebony short, I could see it in his slight crease of a frown.

He wouldn't let the book go, and I had no idea what it was, but I could feel the creeping dread in my system as I stared at it clutched in Rook's shaking fist. Drake and Vex were gone. He'd carried her back to the house, his fury through the bond, as suffocating as Rook's absence.

I could, at least, trust Drake to take care of her.

When we get him into the living room, Rook slumps on a couch, setting the notebook down at last. Ebony grabbed it before me. He lingered on the first page, eyes narrowed as he scanned the text. Then he flicked through the rest of the book quickly— too quickly, jaw clenched and expression dark. He hesitated only on one page, I noticed. The way his frame tensed slightly was the only giveaway that something had bothered him. Then he handed the book to me.

"They're trying to get in our heads," he said. "And apparently"—he nodded to Rook—"it's working."

I opened the first page, scanning it, heart dropping like a stone as I read the words scrawled across the page. There was no way I could read the rest like Ebony had, each one would be a dagger in my chest. But even if I could I wouldn't, not unless she knew. She'd begged us not to open that door, and now...

"We fucked up." Rook's voice was hoarse as he looked at Ebony. "We chose wrong."

With difficulty, I ripped my mind from the horror of the page I'd just read. I had to deal with this.

"We didn't," Ebony said as if it were that simple. "The outcome doesn't change anything."

Rook gave him a sickened look. "We should have listened to her—"

"There was no choice." Ebony glared at Rook. "Our mate was dumped from a limo in a parking lot. When we got there, it was still there. There's only the *illusion* of choice so she'd hate us for it."

"She told us not to," Rook spat. "She told us not to, and we didn't listen to her."

"Because she's fucking dark bonded!"

Rook was back on his feet, anger finally forging past apathy. "Of course it doesn't bother you," he snarled. "You're a fucking void, Ebony. Why did I think that might change because of her?"

"Because," Ebony sneered, rounding on him. "You've still never cultivated two healthy brain cells to rub together in that petri dish you call a—"

"You won't see her. Not unless she asks for you," I said, cutting them off before auras got involved again. "We can't fight like this. It's what they want." I hated to admit anything Ebony said was right. "We all want the same thing."

"Do we all want the same thing?" Rook demanded, flicking a

hand in Ebony's direction. "Because he doesn't seem to give a fuck." He looked incensed for a moment. "How can you read that without blinking?"

"I want her safe," Ebony said. "And you two are more worried about her liking you."

"I want her happy!" I snapped. "What's the point in any of this if we destroy her ourselves?"

"You're too emotional," Ebony shot back. "Is she going to be happy if she ends up with that pack? We have her back, and we still have no idea what they want. We need to get ahead. If that means she cries over me reading that book, then Rook's right—I don't give a fuck!" He was in my face, lip curled, fist balled in my shirt and voice raised. "I can make my mate happy when she's not dark bonded to vermin."

Then he shoved past me toward his room, leaving me and Rook alone.

"Fuck." Rook hissed. Then he kicked the coffee table hard enough to send it toppling. "Fuck!"

With that, he was gone too, vanishing into his room. We were the only pack in the world who could save her, and we were falling apart, piece by piece.

Come the negotiation, would there be a pack to back her at all?

It had been hours since the fight. I was alone, sitting in the hallway outside her room. Vex's notebook was still clutched in my hand, but I didn't open it. I wouldn't do anything without speaking to her. The command was clear that I had to eventually, but she couldn't write in it if I had it.

She was with Drake. Safe.

As the hours ticked by, my mind began to spiral.

Drake was with her in there, asleep too, but I wouldn't sleep until I knew there were no more surprises waiting for us. I couldn't. It wasn't that I wasn't tired, but there was no way my mind would calm enough to allow it anyway.

Get her back for five seconds, and you're already fucking this up.

The words in the book were true. We'd screwed up, and the possibilities of her commands were endless. If we all went to sleep, and she left or got hurt... what kind of mates would that make us?

But... What if it wasn't enough that I had the book with me? What if they changed the command? What if there were more we didn't know about?

How would they change it, anyway?

Last time... I frowned. Last time, she'd been given a phone—one she had left with us. But aside from the videos we'd been sent after she was taken, everything else—the contacts, the texts, they were wiped clean. All but for a few photos she'd taken at the Gala. We'd determined either the phone was programmed that way, or Vex had been deleting all correspondence after it was complete.

Either way, they had kept ongoing communication with her before. Now we knew about them, they would surely be more careful, but they wouldn't risk not speaking to her at all, would they?

I frowned, shooting a text off to Ebony and then getting to my feet. Ever so slowly, I cracked the door to her room. I wouldn't see her, not until she was ready. But this... this was different. And she wouldn't have to know.

I peered in and spotted her asleep first, tucked into Drake's arms. I tried not to linger on them, and my eyes fell, instead, on a phone on the bedside. I recognised it as Drake's from the case.

Maybe she hadn't been given one?

I scanned the rest of the room. I'd been through it a dozen times while she was gone, setting things up and making sure it was perfect. My eyes were immediately drawn to the pile of clothing on the bathroom floor that hadn't been there before.

I crossed toward the bathroom silently. My heart was thundering in my chest, and I wondered if this was a good idea at all. I searched the discarded clothing until I found it—the same kind of phone as she'd been given before. Nothing in it mattered, Leighton hadn't been able to trace the numbers on the last one, but... was there a way to protect her, anyway?

When I slipped back out of the room, Ebony was already waiting for me, arms folded. He was alert, though there were dark shadows beneath his eyes. He'd been catching naps over the last few days, but nothing substantial. I doubted his lack of sleep had anything to do with anxiety, more likely it was the pure vicious fury and drive we'd been feeling through the bond from him. That was why I'd texted. As *pissed* as his decision earlier had made me, if there was anyone who could figure this out, it was him.

I shut the door, then turned to him, holding the phone up. "What happens if we take it from her?" I asked. "They won't be able to give her any more commands, right?"

Ebony frowned, running his tongue along his teeth, eyes darting between me and the phone as he worked through that. "Could be risky. I doubt they haven't thought about that. We don't know what commands it might trigger if she can't access it."

"What does that mean?" I asked.

He shrugged. "I read a case where an omega was forced to rip her own nails off for every day she wasn't able to access the computer she was being commanded to use for a job."

I winced, but I wasn't ready to let go of the idea. "What if... she didn't know it was gone?"

"What do you mean?" Ebony asked, head cocked, and I could see his brain already working a million miles an hour on the question.

"Can we copy it?" I asked, but Ebony was already snatching the phone from my hand, examining it.

"If... she doesn't know then nothing will trigger. This... this could be what we need."

"Okay..." That was good. That was something. "Do you think she might guess what we've done if no commands are coming through?"

Ebony glanced back up at me. "Why wouldn't they come through?"

I frowned. "Because... the whole point is to protect her from them?"

Ebony scowled like I was an idiot. "The point is to protect her. Period. And we can't do that because they're always one step ahead. If I keep her phone and relay the texts to the new one, neither will ever know. I can set up call forwarding, but I'll need to find out if there's a way to record the conversations somehow. That way they'll speak like there's no one else there. We won't get a better chance at information."

"Wait. If they send a fucked up command, you want to forward it to her?" I asked. "After what you did earlier—"

"You don't have to like it. *She* doesn't have to like it, but I intend to free her of that bond."

I stared from him, to the phone. I could order him to give it back. Ultimately, I was in charge of how we handled this. He could try and challenge me for lead again, but there was no guarantee there, and a challenge like the one he'd made—it wasn't good for a pack.

We both knew we had to keep this together for her.

But... I believed him.

Before I could open my mouth, though, he spoke, something tense in his expression. "You are... emotional about this—"

"She's—"

"Just, wait!" He cut me off. "You were right, earlier when you said... What's the point if we destroy her? She needs... she needs more from us." It looked hard for him to say. "We don't know how this is going to play out. We don't know what they're going to ask for or how careful they'll be—even in negotiations. I want every option on the table when it comes to freeing her, and that..." He scowled, looking uncomfortable for a moment. "That also means her."

"What?"

"She is the last line of defence," Ebony said quietly. "That's what they did to us, isn't it? Sent her in like a trojan horse? She lived in our home," he said. "Got close to us."

"And?" I asked, unsure where he was going with that.

"This didn't let her into their *home*, Love, they let her into their pack bond. That gives her power, whether or not she knows it—whether or not *they* know it."

I stared at him, mind working through what that could possibly mean. "Let me deal with this. You don't have to be a part of it." He lifted the phone. "I'll have the copy back before she's even awake. You need to convince her to fight for us."

He stepped away, tucking the phone in his pocket as he made his way back to his room.

I spoke before he could turn the corner. "You have to try, too," I said. "You're her mate just like we are."

He looked back at me for a brief second, and I felt him through the bond in answer, which was a white flag from Ebony even on a good day. What I felt from him surprised me. He wasn't reluctant, like I was expecting. He was... unsure.

Then he turned the corner and he was gone.

ELEVEN

DRAKE

I awoke to my worst nightmare.

My arms were empty.

Vex was gone.

Panic constricted my chest as I staggered from the bed. Through the curtains, I could see only the faintest traces of morning light outside.

"Vex?" I asked, staring around the dim room.

When I turned the lights on, I still couldn't see her anywhere. The bathroom door was open, and there was no one inside.

Had she left?

Maybe her commands had told her to leave right after she arrived, and this was all just a taunt. My mind flashed back to the last time.

I'd stumbled into her room, terrified of the fight between Love and Ebony downstairs. Only when I'd entered the room, she was gone.

It was a moment I'd never forget.

The worst moment of my life.

After one last sweep of the room and bathroom, I made for the door. I had to tell the others.

When I slammed the door of her room open, however, I almost tripped over something solid. I looked down to see Love seated on the floor, back against the wall, staring up at me.

What was he doing?

"She's gone," I said, not even trying to keep my terror from my voice.

He was on his feet in a moment, brows furrowed. "What?"

"I j-just woke up, and she wasn't there," I said. "What if... what if she—?"

"No. She didn't leave," Love said. "I was here the whole time."

Looking at him closer, I realised he looked more exhausted than ever.

Had he still not slept?

Perhaps he'd been afraid of the same thing as I was right now —of a repeat of that moment. Of finding her room empty and our mate gone.

It was the first reprieve I'd felt from my terror. If he'd been here the whole time, maybe I'd missed something. Love was already through Vex's door, though, and I followed.

He scanned the room just as I had, peering behind the couches. He rubbed his face, blinking viciously as if it might shake him awake. No, he definitely hadn't slept. His braid was loose and coming apart, and his face was downright gaunt.

"She didn't leave." He was so sure, and I believed him.

Then he frowned, eyes catching on something. I followed his gaze, trying to figure out what he'd seen. He was staring at the three huge moving boxes of her stuff.

He crossed toward them in a moment, examining the tops, which were halfway open. Then he froze, something pained in his expression.

He clenched his jaw, gaze finding mine, confirming what I was wondering.

I stepped toward them, peering into the box that was full of her clothes. Sure enough I caught a glimpse of silver-brown hair with a wisp of peach, and from what I could see, she was curled up tight. My heart broke.

Love was stepping away, expression pained. "I think you should..." He swallowed, clapping me on the shoulder. "She's not... uh... she's not ready to see me, yet."

I stopped him. "She is," I said. "She told me."

"I don't think it's right that I—"

"You're pack lead, Love. That's your mate. She needs you."

LOVE

Vex looked so small and fragile, curled up in the box of her old clothing, clutching it against herself, along with a large, pink dog's collar.

"Vex," I whispered gently, in case she was sleeping. I heard the door click shut as Drake left me with her.

I was met with one brilliant, golden eye blinking open and peering out at me. She looked so afraid. For a long moment, we just stared at each other, and I realised I had no idea what to do, so I reached out and took her hand.

Her grip was like a vice in mine. She was trembling. For a moment, it was almost impossible to keep it together. But she needed me to keep it together.

"I'm sorry," she whispered thickly. "I didn't mean to worry you."

I shook my head. "You don't owe me an apology."

Quite the opposite.

How many times had I gone over this conversation in my head

while I sat outside her room. I couldn't apologise either, not yet. Not like this.

She deserved better than this.

"Do you want to stay in there?" I asked.

"I..." She trailed off. "I don't know. I got in and now I don't know how to get out."

"Do you want..." I began, but she shifted so both her golden eyes met mine, and for a moment, it was hard to remember what I was saying. "Do you want *me* to stay?"

She nodded.

There was another long silence. "You... went... to my place?" she asked, at last.

"Your landlord kept everything," I said. "I thought... maybe you'd want it here. I thought—when you were ready, I could help you make this like... home." I didn't dare say the word nest.

I didn't deserve to, after what we'd done. We'd hurt her again. We just got her back, and we'd hurt her again.

I hated them.

I fucking hated Ebony and Rook right now.

The raspberry treacle in the air seemed to wilt, and I noticed she squeezed the collar tighter.

"When Drake said Aisha was your best friend," I said. "I didn't know..."

"She was the best friend I ever had." Her voice was hoarse. "She was... my protection. The only reason I felt safe."

Another long silence passed, and I could see her chin shaking as she warred with tears.

Vex was a new person to me now. There was so much about her I'd assumed. All of it was wrong. Before this, she'd had almost no one. The room had been evidence of that.

An omega and her dog.

No friends. No family.

"I um..." She paused, then the next words came tumbling out.

"I matched you when I snuck into one of your beta-only sign-ings." Her whole frame tensed as if she were afraid of what I would say.

I squeezed her hand tight in mine. "I know."

Her golden eyes found me again, confused.

"We saw the post you made," I told her.

Her chin quivered, and she glanced down at the collar she was clutching. "Everyone who replied told me I was selfish and horrible for going to your event."

"No—"

"They were... I mean... they *were* right."

"I don't think you're selfish, Vex," I told her.

There was another long silence, and I didn't say anything else, feeling as if she were building courage for something.

"Are you... okay?" she asked.

"Don't worry about me. I'm just..." I swallowed. "You're back. That's all that matters. It's all I care about."

"I... I wanted to thank you."

"For what?" I asked.

"You tried... you tried to listen to me. About the limo..."

"I wasn't enough to stop them."

She squeezed her eyes shut tight for a moment. "Did you read the book?" she asked.

I could feel it like a weight on my soul, tucked into my pocket as it was. "I will, if you want me to. I would... I would like to rid you of that command."

She shrugged, so clearly unsure. "I..." Her voice shook. "I would, too. But it's a lot, when I wrote it, I was..."

"I'll read it," I said. My heart twisted at what she might have written in those pages, of the pain they held. Pain I'd given her. But I didn't want what I said right now to be tainted by that book. She deserved these words from me because I owed them to her, not because she asked, or because I witnessed the pain she'd never wanted me to see. I wouldn't let her suffer more because of my cowardice. Not for one second.

"I think... I think I'm ready to get out," she whispered.

"Okay."

"But... uh..." She looked nervous. "I might... need help."

"I can do that," I said, wondering how long she'd been in there.

I reached in with my free hand, but she gripped me tight for a moment, gaze nervous. "I, um... I might cry. It's not you."

She was right.

By the time I'd helped her up and scooped her out of the massive packing box—along with a bundle of clothes and the collar—there were silent tears tracking down her cheeks.

Holding her in my arms was an indescribable feeling, even if she was trembling—which was all wrong. Too long, she'd been with that pack, and I was afraid of the wounds she now carried— ones she had because of me. How much had happened in that time?

I had become a different person in that time.

But she was safe.

She was here.

I wasn't stupid, though, even as I tried to find ways to deny it. I was looking at a woman who had sought safety in a box because my pack wasn't enough.

She was broken because I had failed her. I shoved back the burning in my eyes. I couldn't crumble, not until I had given her the world.

Right now, she was raspberry treacle, the scent of earth and fur that lingered so faintly on Aisha's collar, and blackcurrant wine. There was an edge of a claim in the latter scent. Drake had marked her. That settled my instincts. She was wearing my pack's claim. It was small, but *something*.

I owed Drake another thanks, as well as another apology.

Where would we be without him?

Where would she be—with no safety in this place but for the fading traces of a friend long gone.

She deserved better.

I set her on her feet, helping her steady herself as she wiped her eyes with the sleeve of Drake's shirt.

I would give her better, starting right now.

VEX

To my utter shock, Love sank to his knees before me, a tremor in his grip as he took my wrists.

I stared down at him. His dark braid, which hung over his shoulder, was messy and loose. His eyes were lightless from fatigue, yet they were full of an intensity that stilled me. His scent, vanilla winter, was edged with sorrow, and I didn't know if I was comforted by it or not.

I shrunk in on myself, unsure.

What was he doing?

"Vex." His voice was rough as he spoke words that stilled the world. "I would like to offer you the princess bond."

My mouth popped open as I felt something intangible settling between us; the faintest bond that lit with his offer.

"I..." I tried to find my voice. "Can you... can you do that?" I asked, completely unsure. A princess bond had more steps to completion than any other bond. There was an offer made by the pack, acceptance of the omega, a bite upon the neck, and finally, unification. Love was starting the first of the steps.

He could never rescind it.

"I did my research," he said. "I can make the offer. But they stand in as your proxy for acceptance. We can't do anything else until negotiations, but I can't take this back. I just need..." He swallowed. "I need you to know that you're going to be safe," he

105

whispered. "There is nothing in this world I won't give them, do you understand?"

More tears burned my eyes, and suddenly, I couldn't look at him, gaze fixed on the glass chandelier above.

"You don't have to do anything," he told me. "Never again will it be your job to make us like you. It's our job to discover if we will ever be worthy of you."

My fingers clasped tighter on the collar as I got my tears under control.

I thought....

For so long, I thought I'd lost everything.

All that time I'd been alone, left to decide what mattered.

And now...

I felt hollow.

Broken.

There had been a fleeting moment when Drake had been running toward me. When he'd swept me up in his arms. And Love was there, and for just one heart stopping second, I thought maybe the last week could vanish, that maybe there was something to save.

I don't know if it was seeing Rook and Ebony beside that limo, or if it would have happened anyway, but it felt like everything had come crashing back in.

I felt like I was in a dream again.

"I'm sorry, Vex." Love's voice was unsteady. "I'm sorry for everything. I fucked up the night of the Gala. All of it was my fault."

I swallowed, my throat suddenly dry.

There were moments about that night I still didn't understand. I'd thought they'd discovered I was gold pack and cancelled the contract. That they didn't want me. But then they'd asked for my return.

"I didn't know you were an omega. I thought... when we were

at the Gala... I thought you were trying to trick me..." He shut his eyes. "The things I said to you, I never should have—I *should* have had more faith in you."

"You didn't..." I swallowed. "You didn't have any reason to have more faith in me."

I'd thought about it a thousand times. What had happened that night, it scored scars across my heart that I didn't know would ever heal.

But *that* part, at least, I knew was the truth. I needed to be able to separate where to place this pain. There was too much, and I couldn't afford to make a mistake.

"I should have known, watching you and Drake, that you were the real thing. I should have known because I always hold people at arm's reach, and I still fell for you. But I was a coward. I cancelled the contract in the limo on the way home. I thought you were..." His voice caught. "I was scared of how much I cared, I couldn't see past my own shit long enough to see the truth, and you were the one who paid for that."

My chest tightened as I stared at him, the tiniest blossom of hope lighting in my chest at those words.

On the ride home?

But that was before the article.

"It w-wasn't—" I had to stop, getting my quivering chin under control. I looked up again at the lights above. "It wasn't because I'm gold pack?" My voice was a harsh, thick whisper.

I'd played it out a thousand times in my mind: My mates learning I was gold pack, then they'd been disgusted, which had turned into a claim: they didn't want what I was, but maybe they'd rather make that claim than see another pack take their scent match.

An alpha's pride.

But I was trapped, and it would be an offer I had to take.

Love was staring at me, eyes wide with shock. "Vex. No."

"B-but... you're an elite pack. You can't..." The grip I had on the collar was painful now as I tried to shove the tremble from my voice, a thousand taunts from Zeus crowding my mind. "You can't have me around now that everyone knows the truth."

Finally, the tears broke free again, spilling from my eyes in a flood.

He reached up, as if he wanted to cup my cheek, but hesitated. I clutched his hand in an instant, and then without really knowing if it was me or him, I was sinking down into his arms and he was holding me close.

"Fuck. Vex, not a single alpha in this pack cares what colour your eyes are."

I shook, holding him for a long time, not sure if it was because I wanted his embrace or because I needed to hide the tears.

Finally, I leaned back, and Love cupped my cheek, sweeping the remnants of my tears away.

"W-what about Rook?" I asked. I'd been most afraid about him, and during the interview... he had looked upset, even when saying the words Zeus had demanded he say.

"He hasn't mentioned it. If he ever does, I'll break his jaw."

My smile was weak.

But somehow, he just looked more upset, expression crumpling again. "I'm so sorry. I fucked up so badly." Suddenly, he couldn't meet my eyes. "When we got home and we saw the article about you, I still didn't know you were a scent match until Ebony... Ebony wanted to claim you. I told him we couldn't because I couldn't... couldn't let someone like you get caught in the crosshairs of this pack. And knowing you were our scent match, it terrified me even more. He... challenged me to claim pack lead for you. We were fighting when Drake realised you were gone."

I stared at him.

Ebony had fought to keep me?

I wasn't sure what to do with that information.

"If I'd known you were dark bonded, I'd never have hesitated," he looked so desperate, as if he needed me to understand. "It was never because I didn't want you, it's because I wanted you safe."

I nodded, throat still thick. "Well..." I said weakly. "Now you're kind of... stuck with me."

His smile was soft, eyes finally filled with something other than worry.

"I... *always* wanted an omega," he said quietly.

My chest loosened at those words, and for a moment, I couldn't take my eyes from him.

"Always," he said, again, brow creasing. "But a scent match? That was a dream so far out of reach that I couldn't even conceive of it. Not with Ebony. We're not *stuck* with you, Vex. We want you here—all of us want you here."

Slowly, I nodded, letting those words sink in. Those were words I'd once been so desperate to hear.

I wanted to feel... *something* now.

But the day was choked with terror and relief, and a million fears crowded my mind. So instead, I curled back against him, sinking into his touch and willing that to be enough for now.

"I have a lot to make up for," he murmured, wrapping his arms around me. One hand gently resting on the back of my head. "But I'm going to prove to you I'm worth your love," he whispered. "Let me find a way to earn your forgiveness."

There was a long silence, and my breathing eased as I inhaled vanilla winter.

His apology settled slowly across my mind like a light blanket, smothering cracks and open wounds that would one day still need healing.

I thought this might be enough, just for today.

"You're here with us now," Love said. "The negotiations,

they'll just be one day and then it'll all be over. You'll never see that pack again."

Again I nodded, the words like a salve on a burn, something to rest in, even if they felt like the fairytale ending I wouldn't get.

Nothing about the pack I was bonded to was simple. Love was saying what he had to believe, but he was wrong. It wasn't just one day. It was a crossroads: A moment in which just maybe, there was a real future for me—or a moment in which my life finally slipped off that cliff entirely. That question still hung over my head, a constant scratching in my chest, demanding to know if I would be worth enough, no matter what Love said to me now.

"But after, Vex. We'll manage your heat however you want us to, whether that's with us, or not."

I leaned back, looking up at him, lips quirking up with humour I was so desperate to feel. "I don't know if Drake has the stamina on his own."

Love's smile was a reward in itself. "I'll do you a favour, and never tell him you said that."

I curled up against him again, still clutching Aisha's collar, happy to linger in this tiny moment of peace.

Love wanted me. He hadn't known I was gold pack when he'd cancelled the contract, and there truly was an offer of a princess bond between us. He was telling the truth, enough to commit him and his whole pack.

His hand brushed my hair affectionately. "They said the nego- tiations will happen when you go into heat, I thought... if you want drugs—"

"No drugs," I whispered. There were drugs that delayed it, and drugs that suppressed heat. I'd taken the stronger of the two, the ones to push it off. The more I messed with either kind, the worse it would get.

It wasn't a command from Zeus—he'd said nothing either way. "Every time I put it off, it'll get worse. I've already put it off once.

When it hits I'll only be able to suppress it for a day or two." Enough time for the negotiations—which was exactly what Zeus wanted. Me, right on the precipice of my heat—the greatest bargaining chip on the planet.

It was too dangerous to risk delaying it. If—and it was a big if —the negotiations would go in my favour, how long would they last? I wasn't ready to think about my heat hitting before they were over.

"My heats... they're erratic," I said, knowing I needed to tell him this now, with Aisha's collar in my hands, or I'd chicken out. "I've drugged up too many times. Sometimes I know for ages ahead of time, sometimes they come quickly and violently. My last one... I was out when it hit. Didn't take ten minutes for it to burn through every scent blocker I had. I was... I was three streets from home. And then..." I closed my eyes. "I was stopped by these alphas." My stomach dropped, panic spearing my veins at the memory. But I forged on, knowing I needed to say this to him. I owed Love this explanation for the choice that had changed all of our lives.

"Aisha... she's the reason I got h-home." My voice shook. "I could barely see straight or walk... and I... I... left her."

"You had to," he said, and I could see the fear in his eyes, even just hearing it. "She wanted you safe." His grip on me tightened.

Blood still roared in my ears at the memory. Waking alone and grieving...

My voice was choked. "I used to watch movies all evening, and she... she loved yours so much." I found another faint smile at the memory. "She'd always bark when Rook would come on—I had to skip his scenes if it was too late, or I'd have people knocking at my door... but then..." The fragile smile on my face vanished in a second. "I woke up from my heat, and she w-was g-gone. And y-your signing was that week. I'd never thought of actually going, but I wanted..." I clutched the collar closer to my chest.

"You were going to get us to sign her collar?" Love asked.

I nodded. "It *w-was* selfish—"

"Hey, hey that's not true. And the scent match, the chances were so low." He tugged me close. "She was there for you in the most vulnerable moment of your life." He paused, something caught in his voice. "If you'll let me, Vex, I'll sign that on the day we're enough to live up to Aisha's legacy."

TWELVE

DRAKE

The next morning, I woke in a cold moment of dread. It didn't vanish until I'd opened my eyes to find she was here. Vex was still in my arms, present and trusting me to keep her safe.

I released a breath, propping myself up at her side, keeping my arm around her. I couldn't take my eyes away. She was so beautiful, and looked more peaceful now than she did when she was awake.

Both Love and I had read the little black book last night. We'd had to, to break the commands she was bound to, even if it was something she'd never wanted us to see. I'd digested every line, as I imagined Vex tucked away somewhere, drawing blood, alone and in pain. Now, I couldn't shake them.

Dear Drake: You don't want me.

Dear Drake: Please don't leave me. I can't do this without you.

I knew what the last one was about. It was from the morning I'd woken and almost hurt her. It was why I'd pleaded with Love yesterday to sleep on the bed instead of the couch the moment she said she was okay with it. I didn't know when my own nightmares would surface again, when I might wake in the night, not myself. But if Love was here, he could keep her safe.

Now the notebook was in the office downstairs, untouched. Vex was free of the command, and we were chained to the truths she'd never wanted us to see.

I held her closer, despair getting the better of me, wishing I could be more for her. I felt the faintest rumblings of a purr in her chest as I did, as if she was trying to soothe my pain.

Love stirred at my side, rubbing his eyes and glancing over at us instantly, as if he had woken with that same dread I had. His eyes snagged on her, and I saw a softness in that look. It was new from him, not something I'd ever see him offer anyone before. But there was sadness in his eyes, too. He'd locked the bond down the moment he'd read that book yesterday, and I hadn't felt him since. When I'd asked him about it, he'd just shaken his head and refused to answer. There was more in there for him than there had been for me. More for all of the others—and all of it had been worse.

I tried to bury that familiar stab of anger at him as I thought of it. But I trusted her, and she felt safe around Love.

"She hasn't forgiven me," he whispered, as if reading my mind. He sat up carefully, so as not to disturb her, and rubbed his face. "And I don't want her to, not until she's ready. She needs real healing, not something forced on her because she's looking for safety—which, for her, is almost impossible." He cleared his throat. "It's why we owe you a debt I don't think any of us can ever repay."

I frowned.

"You offer her the safety no one else has. She can do the rest as she needs. So... Thank you for that, Drake."

I nodded, feeling the ongoing vibrations of her purr against my chest.

"She's… different," Love said. "Even from before when she would spend time with you. She's… running out of strength."

He was right. It was harrowing, the lines in that book, and the change I'd seen in her since she had returned. There was an emptiness in her eyes that hadn't been there before. It meant we'd failed. Her nightmares had found her, and there had been no one there to protect her. Something happened in a person, in moments like that. Left alone to face the darkness, she'd reached for the only thing remaining for protection. That empty void that stole hope and love and passion, in exchange for a cold armour, promising protection for just one more day.

One more hour.

One more minute.

I tried hard not to think about what might have happened in those days in which she was taken. She'd said nothing about them aside from the one comment when I'd seen the bruises on her skin, and I couldn't be sure if that was the dark bond or her choice.

The way she'd been able to hold herself before, with a smile for me, even when I knew now she must have been terrified, was gone. Her fake smiles were rigid, and the real ones, rare. She could tell me it was because she was tired, but I knew the truth.

She hadn't touched her makeup, and the boxes from her home remained unpacked. She made me give her another of my t-shirts, and anxiously held onto the hem throughout the day.

She'd left the room once with me and Love yesterday, joining us in the downstairs kitchen while we cooked a full roast just for something to do. She'd sat on a barstool, chopping vegetables, content at least. Then Ebony had crossed the foyer to the office where Leighton occasionally dropped in, and Vex had gone tense. I don't know if it was Ebony, or just the introduction of anything outside of the bubble that was me and Love, but she'd looked afraid.

"No," I told Love, holding her closer beneath the warmth of the sheets. "Strength isn't something you can take from someone."

I believed in her strength, I'd seen it hold up against monsters I couldn't even imagine. In the videos, I'd seen it in the face of the alpha who had left that bite on her neck. I'd seen it over and over and over. She was a woman who would fight until there was nothing left. That was her beauty. That was what she had to offer.

It wasn't Vex's strength that was failing right now.

"Do you know what it's like to give and give until there's nothing left?" I asked. "Only for someone to turn their back and walk away?"

I did.

I knew what it was like to break myself for people who walked away the second they thought there wasn't anything more to take.

I'd given what had felt like an eternity, and finally, Ebony had pried me from what had slowly turned into the worst nightmare of my life. But I'd had the strength to survive, because I'd known what I was fighting for. I'd been where Vex was; in the aftermath. In that moment of silent shock, when it was safe everywhere but your own mind. For me, unlike Vex, it had been over for good, and still I'd struggled.

My brother, Rickard, had visited once. It had been the familiarity I'd needed—I'd missed—and I'd been about to open my mouth and tell him everything.

"You left the Lightning pack for one that's barely even formed?" he demanded.

I drew up, frozen. He'd just arrived, and I'd fallen into his arms, shaking. He was my big brother, and he'd supported me through everything. When I'd seen him, it was the first time since Ebony had dragged me from that house, that I'd been able to cry.

"I..." I drew up, looking into his eyes.

"What the fuck is going on?" he asked. He seemed angry. That was... it was okay. He didn't understand, not yet. When he did, he would be relieved. I'd never seen any of them after I'd joined the Lightning pack. I'd been too scared, not trusting the face I would have to put on if I did. Not trusting the lies I would have to tell. But now, I was free, and I still had a chance to make something of myself with the Crimson Fury pack.

"It's fine. They're an approved elite pack," I said. "They're just new."

"That doesn't guarantee success like—"

"I'll get her into another facility if I have to," I said, quickly. "Ebony's working on it now. She won't even notice." I knew that's what he was worried about. We all were.

My mother had a rare bone disease that left her needing medication and around the clock care. That kind of treatment wasn't something my family could have dreamed of before I joined the Lightning pack.

"What about the money?" he asked.

"I don't... I don't know. We haven't talked about money yet. But it'll be fine, there's no way I'll let mom—"

"It's not just mom, it's about the rest of us?"

"I... I don't know yet."

"You left them without knowing?" he asked.

"I h-had to. I told you, it—"

"It's a fucking job, Drake. You do the job, you get paid. No one said it would be easy."

"Just... listen to me. It wasn't just the—"

"Years, we all put in to make sure you kept that academy scholarship. I got nothing, no help, no time, no nothing. And then you go and drop the Lightning pack without even telling us? This isn't just about you, Drake. It's fucking selfish."

.   .   .

That had been the last time I'd seen him.

They'd come back. I knew they had. But I'd been a coward and I'd asked Ebony to deal with it. My mother had kept her place in the facility—I would never punish her—but I'd never seen them again.

And now that very pack who had once saved me... my brothers who I'd trusted... Well, we were the ones who'd done it to her. *We'd* failed *her*, when she was fighting so hard.

"It's *not* her strength," I whispered. Love didn't get to strip that from her. "It's her hope." The thing *we'd* broken. "We have to fight as hard as she has, to give as much as she has, or how can she keep trying?"

THIRTEEN

ROOK

"I don't have anything *to say to you."* That's what Drake said when I caught him grabbing food in the downstairs kitchen last night. I'd been hiding out there, unsure what to do with myself. Beside it was a small living area and TV where Rob usually spent time, and I didn't want to risk Vex seeing me if she wasn't ready. At least, that had been the plan, but as the hours went on, I was getting more and more unsure.

"Please just—" I began.

"I read the book." Drake spun on me, shoving me in the chest. "You made her feel like nothing."

"I didn't... I mean... I know. But it wasn't just me. What about Love and Ebony? We need to figure out how to—"

"Love is sorry—"

"I'm sorry!"

"You don't know how *to be sorry!" Drake snarled. "And you know what, out of all of us, you were the only one she compared to the pack who bonded her?"*

Panic rose in my chest as he spoke the words I was scared of hearing. The ones I hadn't been able to shake since I'd read them. But he didn't get it. "I am *sorry! The moment she lets me—"*

"I hope she doesn't!"

"How can you be okay with the others, but—?"

"I trust her *judgement on Love." Drake shoved me again. "I'm not okay with Ebony, but I don't get it with you—you had no excuse Rook!"*

"Drake!" I tried to tail him as he plated leftovers from the meal they'd made earlier, but he spun back on me. I'd never seen him like this. He was Drake. The quiet one, the kind one. Having him level his disgust on me like this, it was unsettling.

"And what about me?" he demanded. "Even if you couldn't get your head out of your ass long enough to see her as more than a beta. You knew how I felt!"

"I know. I just... Tell me what Love did to get her to—"

"Love thought he was protecting her!" Drake slammed his fist onto the counter, aura splitting the air. "He was wrong, and he told her that, but what were you doing?"

"I didn't know—"

"If you say that one more fucking time, like it makes it okay—like if she wasn't, if she was just any old beta who I'd fallen for—then it would have been fine?"

"I want to make it right—"

"Then you can stay down here and make sure she never sees your fucking face, you piece of shit!"

I forced the memory from my mind as I tugged on my shoes in the foyer.

"Where are you going?" Ebony poked his head out of one of the offices. It was the second morning since we'd got Vex back, and still, she hadn't asked to speak to me. The only consolation I had, was that she also hadn't asked to speak to Ebony—as far as I knew.

"Out," I snapped.

"Where?" Ebony demanded.

"It's my fucking—" I shook my head. "Doesn't matter, I'll be back later. It's not an interview or... or anything... *public*."

"Family meeting?" Ebony asked, eyes trailing the suit I'd put on. It was the only one I owned, and my pack was well aware I only wore it for one reason.

I shot him a glare. "Am I *allowed* to leave for that?"

"I can't imagine why you'd *want* to."

I ignored that, slamming the door to the garage behind me and crossing toward my BMW.

He didn't get it and never would. Ebony hadn't lost a wink of sleep when he'd dropped his mother from his life—though she'd made it easy. She lived on the other side of the country now, with no intention of bothering him. She'd turned up to Love's door one day with train tickets for the two of them to start a new life.

The meaning had been painfully clear: Penelope Hightower considered herself a mother of only one son—and that son had made it clear he wouldn't leave Ebony behind.

But *their* mother was a different breed of stress. I couldn't so easily rid myself of the pack that had raised me. They were an elite pack of mega famous musicians, and well-known enough that keeping a relationship—even for appearances—was beneficial. My stomach turned at the idea of being disowned by them like Ebony had been. Sometimes I wished I could care as little as he did.

As I made the drive, I found myself stuck, again, on the words Vex had written. Each time I thought of them, a different line stuck, sinking claws in and not letting me go.

Dear Rook: You were supposed to be better.

I wasn't used to feeling this way. Drake may not believe me, but I wanted to fix it. I wanted to do better for her, if she'd just let me tell her that.

All the others were doing something. Drake and Love were with her—Love had offered her the princess bond for fuck's sake. Ebony was busy with Leighton, but all I had were those phrases, all from her, all telling me how much I'd hurt her.

My mate.

And I didn't know how to fucking fix it.

I arrived at the get together already high strung. The meeting was at a restaurant so high end it didn't even have a menu. The Stallion was a favourite spot for the Harrison Pack.

I was led to a table with a cream table cloth, golden ornaments and cutlery, and three people seated at it: two of my pack dads and my mother with a few plates of Hors D'oeuvres.

Fuck.

There was no one else, and no seating available for any of the eight siblings to join. I dropped into the seat, a scowl on my face.

This was a goddamned ambush.

Felix was the pack lead, and Benjamin was my biological father, so it made sense it was the two of them. Plus, I knew Lucas and Philip were out of the country for a concert this week.

My mother, the world renowned singer, Goldie Harrison, was wearing one of her signature cream dresses that perfectly contrasted her rich, dark skin and bright eyes—both of which I'd inherited. Her scent of cinnamon buttercream never failed to comfort me, even when she was getting on my nerves.

"It's been a while, Rook," she said. "You look terrible."

I grimaced. "Thanks, mom."

"Well," she prodded. "Tell us, what's going on?"

"Why did you drop the Dragon Hunter's franchise?" Benjamin asked. Right. He didn't even stop to say hello before he pounced.

I swallowed, jaw clenched. Of course, this was what they wanted to know. The last week was a blur of fatigue and desperation, but I should have known this part would catch up to me. "I don't want to talk about it."

"It's a fool's move—"

"I said I don't—"

"After all this time, going against our advice," Benjamin said. "And you *finally* found something to make us proud, all to just... throw it away?"

I grit my teeth, not wanting it to show on my face how much that hurt. I was Benjamin's only biological child in the pack so his expectations of me had always been higher. Of course, I failed those expectations at every turn, no matter how hard I tried.

"Why am I not surprised?" Felix muttered. "You were always listening to your grandmother when you should have been spending your time—"

"Don't bring gran into this," I snapped.

"You're the oldest, Rook. We always pushed hard." My mother paused, glancing at Felix. "We recognise now that the whole... acting thing was our own failing."

"What?" I asked, glancing between them. It was a surprise to hear any of them take responsibility for anything.

"We pushed too hard, and you pushed back—I mean, of course you did, you have a spine on you, just like your father."

I blinked, trying to keep up with the conversation.

They were still *stuck on this?*

It didn't matter how many times I told them I'd chosen acting because I loved it—not because I was trying to get on their nerves —they wouldn't believe me.

"We've been trying to give you space," Benjamin said with a nod as he served my mother some of her favourite Mango Fritto Misto. He was rewarded by a sweet sideways smile from her. I lingered on that for a moment. I should figure out what Vex liked. That would help.

123

I wondered what she'd want if I brought her here? Had she ever been to a place like this before?

Would she even like it? It was pretentious as fuck, and I hated it, but then... I'd seen where she'd lived. Might this be a *good* kind of different...?

Fuck me. I didn't know where to start. The dreamboard was in her room, and there was no way for me to go in there without disturbing her. I'd tried to remember what was on it, but I hadn't been paying nearly as much attention to it when we were there. I'd been in shock.

"But this is going too far, now," Felix went on. "What was it? Some game by one of the Hightower brothers again—? I said they'd be your ruin, son." I saw him rub the back of his right hand absently as he spoke. I felt a rare spark of gratitude toward Ebony —the only moment of gratitude he ever had and ever would earn from me.

"They are not good enough for you, Rook," Benjamin said. "And now they're going to sabotage this, too?"

"You have a strong aura, I've been saying for years, you should be pack lead," my mother said. "They wanted your name to climb their way to fame, you should be the one—"

I grit my teeth. "I *don't* want pack lead." I knew those words would land on deaf ears as they had every time I'd said them before.

"When are you going to grow up?" Felix asked. "No *true* alpha doesn't want to be pack lead, it's in your blood—stop running from it. We didn't raise a layabout."

For the hundredth time, I wondered how pleased my parents would be if Ebony had been theirs, instead of me. Born into my family, he would have excelled. Instead, I was a disappointment to a pack who would have preferred a cold psychopath, while he was stuck with a mother who thought he was a monster.

"Can we drop this? The contract's gone—and it wasn't Love or Ebony's fault."

Still, I could feel that ancient pit of hopelessness stretching open beneath me as I looked around at them. Was it possible that the Dragon Hunters *would* have been enough?

Maybe with it, I'd get smiles from them instead of this never ending disappointment and frustration. It's why I stayed away from my family as much as I could. It was one thing to endure it, it was another to see them shower my siblings with praise for following the paths that had been laid out before them. It didn't matter that I was doing better in my career than any of them ever had, even before Dragon Hunters.

I hadn't chosen acting to disappoint them. I'd wanted to show them I could live up to their legacy—but doing something I loved as much as Felix and Benjamin loved piano, or as much as my mother loved her singing.

"What about this gold pack drama?" My mother asked, startling me out of my thoughts. "You should be getting ahead of things like that."

"Why do you even know about that?" I asked—like I didn't know the answer, they watched my career like hawks.

My parents had tried everything to get Love and Ebony out of my life, bribery, blackmail, threats. And when none of it had worked, they'd turned up themselves, ready to escort me out—which had been a big mistake.

Before that day, I don't think Felix Harrison had ever truly *lost* in his life, but there was one thing he valued even more than the idea of his children living up to his pack's legacy. And of course, finding weaknesses was Ebony's specialty.

So they walked away, and I got my pack.

But I believed they hid annoyance at my successes and took great pleasure in my failures, even while fronting disappointment.

"You cannot be associated with things like that, Rook," my mother said evenly. "It's worse than tacky career choices."

"What... what is?" I asked, trying to backtrack through the conversation around my spiralling thoughts.

"It's bad enough that Ebony's a rogue." Benjamin's lips were drawn as he said that, as if it disgusted him. "You can't afford PR like that."

"Like...?" I stared at them stupidly for a second before I understood. "Like Vex?"

All of their eyebrows shot up, and I regretted saying her name.

"Oh no, dear, you weren't actually involved with her, were you? I mean I know she was a Sweetheart, but you told me it was Ebony's—" She cut off, eyes darting to Felix. There was a definite unspoken rule between them that Ebony never be named, and if he had to be, he was 'that rogue Hightower brother'.

"She's... important."

Felix's eyebrow shot up. "Sort yourself out, son. The first omega who wanders on into your life, and you're—"

"No. That's not... it's not like that." They could needle me all they fucking wanted, but I wouldn't hear them talk about her. It was... impossible. They could never know. I knew, just from this. What would they say if they knew we'd already offered her the princess bond. Right then, I was so glad for Love's commitment to her, he had always been stronger than me. Better than me.

You were supposed to be better...

That's what she'd written.

And I couldn't be, not if I did here what I'd done in that stupid round table interview. Not if I let them slander her and did nothing.

"Wait for a mate, Rook," Benjamin said, eyes kind, though I knew he was just nervous about the thunderous expression on Felix's face. "I know you don't want one yet because of your jobs, but later. That's the better way to go about it anyway, if you ask me—especially with the state of your career."

"What does that mean?"

"Come now, you don't believe it's *random* do you?" my mother asked. "You scent match someone deserving of your station. Look at me and your fathers." She glanced between them proudly. "Truly ideal."

"We worked hard and proved ourselves," Felix was saying. "We got an omega worthy of that. If you ask me, you aren't... there yet. Still too immature, especially giving up career opportunities like this. You don't want to be like your cousins now, do you? The Morrison pack were always slacking, never took anything seriously, and who did they match with?"

"Josie comes from a rich family—" I began.

"From engineers and ... and doctors—in the public sector?" Felix scoffed. "Hardly elite, hardly *special*. Anyone could do those jobs. You do not come from mediocrity, Rook. Not Benjamin, nor your mother—they're special, with music sought out across the planet."

"Don't waste that, son," Benjamin said. "And your mother's right. Get the contract back, work hard, and when you do find a match, they'll be worthy—"

I was on my feet in a moment, sickness twisting my stomach.

Worthy?

I'd hurt her.

I was the one who wasn't worthy of her.

"If I..." I had to steady my breathing, and I couldn't meet any of their eyes, pulse roaring in my ears. "If I ever court an omega, she will *never* meet any of you."

"Rook!" My mother's voice was harsh as she got to her feet.

But I was shoving the chair back and walking away before she could finish.

Benjamin caught up to me as I reached the doors. "How dare you walk away from your mother like that—"

"Don't *touch* me!" My aura flared in the street, and Benjamin took his hand from mine, brow furrowed.

"Rook, you will go back in there right now and apologise—"

"I don't owe any of you an apology," I snarled, stepping back from him.

Only her.

She was the only one I owed an apology to. I understood the truth now. I understood how wrong my parents were. I had hurt her; I was the one who'd failed. Who wasn't good enough. It was simple, devastating, and yet… it was better this way.

It was me who wasn't worthy of her. I had never been, and I didn't think I would ever be.

FOURTEEN

VEX

> Rook: I want to apologise, Vex. I'm downstairs.
> I'll wait as long as it takes.

I'd stared at that text for a while. The others had told me that he wouldn't see me until I asked. I'd been too much of a coward so far. And now... *he* was the one asking. Drake was pissed when he saw it, since they were supposed to be waiting for me, but I was a little relieved to be honest. So I told him and Love that I wanted to do it.

I was wearing one of my favourite sweatshirts, having found the courage to pull it from one of the boxes. On the cuff were the words my mother had embroidered all those years ago.

"Find your voice, and find your strength."

I clutched that cuff in my fist nervously as I peered around the downstairs kitchen. It was where Rob usually cooked, though I knew he was staying elsewhere for a few weeks. To give me space and privacy, I guessed. So they were cooking for themselves. And Drake had told me Rook had been spending time in the small living area behind the bar so that I didn't accidentally run into him.

Rook got to his feet the moment he saw me step into the small space, eyes wide.

"Vex." His voice was rough. There was caramel brandy lingering in the space, and it set me on edge. It was a scent I had fallen for once, that I was programmed to fall for—only now, its sweetness made me nervous. He was wearing a suit, which I'd never seen before, and he looked different. His eyes were haunted, and his face was drawn, dark hair a mess.

Had he been suffering while I was gone, like Drake and Love had?

It was probably the toll this was taking on his whole pack, a little voice whispered. *Not about you.*

Did I want it to be about me?

Of all of them, I was most frightened of what Rook had to say. He'd so easily rejected me. I was the reason he had dropped the Dragon Hunters contract...

"Will you talk to me?" he asked.

I took a few steps into the space beyond the kitchen, looking around at the TV and armchairs, lip caught in my teeth.

It was just beginning to feel safe, but... I knew he'd seen the book—had seen how much he'd hurt me—and it wasn't just the dark bond. I'd cared enough, been desperate enough, that he'd hurt me, even when I was nothing to him.

"You're angry," he said, taking a step towards me. "And you have every right to be—"

"I'm not," I whispered. "I'm not angry."

He paused, paling a shade. There was a strange silence, before I finally found my voice again. "I don't... want you to pretend to want me just because..." I trailed off.

Just because what?

The others wanted me back?

There was a princess bond between us now.

He frowned. "I'm not pretending."

"You hated me." Those memories had been larger than life for too long. "I can't see how that's changed just because you found out I was…" I couldn't finish, not wanting to say the word mate.

When I was with Zeus, I'd gone over each night with Rook in my head. He'd always felt different, as if getting his love had been in reach. But each time he'd pushed me away. I'd desperately wondered how I'd do it differently if I could do it again. I had challenged him over and over, but if I could have just… been what he'd wanted, then maybe… maybe things would have been different, and the contract would have never been destroyed.

I hugged myself.

How do we come back from that?

I didn't have an answer. I wanted one, but I didn't have it.

He closed the last few steps between us and reached up, perhaps to touch my cheek, but seemed to think better of it. It might have been my expression, or the way I shrank back, staring down at my fist, which was still balled around that inscription. "I don't hate you." Rook's voice was weak, but I was too scared to look up at him. "That's not… I never hated you, Vex."

Finally, I dared glance up. His jaw was clenched, and he looked so unsure.

"You never wanted me." It was so hard to keep my voice steady.

I wasn't enough for him. Of all of them, I knew he cared about his image the most. My gold pack status would never fit in next to that.

Rook shut his eyes, taking a deep breath. "You said, in the book, that I… uh…" He looked sick for a moment. "That I reminded you of them…"

My heart pounded at those words. At the reminder that he had read them. They weren't just words, they had each been like a carving across my heart. Truths given while I was curled up alone, with tears tracking my face, my hand shaking as I was forced to write them down. No matter how I hated what they said, or hated how pathetic they were.

"I've been really stupid," I said. "I get why you wouldn't want to see me."

"Drake and Love, they—" I began, but Rook cut me off.

"*They* want to salvage their relationship with you."

I flinched, knowing my shock was plastered across my face. Terror hit my system, as real as if I were in a room with Zeus.

"No, no. That's not..." Rook began, his expression breaking, and I could see his panic for a moment. "That's not what I meant. I don't... I don't deserve a relationship with you. I know that now."

I stared at him, a horrible weight settling in my stomach as I heard those words.

What?

Was that supposed to make me feel better?

Or was this his way of distancing himself, so he could salvage his image?

"But I will protect you." He was still talking, and it was hard to keep up. "I don't care what it takes."

Protect me? But he hadn't... he hadn't protected me. And now he was trying to find a way to keep me at arm's length?

"I don't want that."

He frowned, eyes darting between mine, but I didn't get it.

How did *he* not understand?

He'd just said he didn't hate me, but he didn't want to try, either? I clasped my fingers together, unsure of what to do. "I don't..." My voice shook. "I don't want protection from someone who's given up."

"Given up?" he asked, so perfectly confused. "You want...?" He trailed off. "You think we can...?"

Panic rose in my throat at the hopelessness in his eyes. "I d-don't know." I sounded desperate, as I cracked around the edges.

Why was he making me *figure this out?*

He stood, looking down at me with those pretty chestnut eyes that had failed me over and over.

I needed him to stop looking so lost.

It was like bars of a cage, closing in from the final side.

I'd thought maybe... I *could* talk to him, but I was wrong. I couldn't do this—not if he was going to give up.

Like a rising flood choking me, I was consumed with the terror of what he was threatening right now—stealing away a dream he'd already stolen a thousand times. At my own fury that he would do what he'd done, and then give up.

"Vex..." He swallowed. "I don't want you to think I'm like them. I'll do anything to change that. Just tell me what to do to fix this."

Tell *him*?

Why did he think I knew what to do? I was lost. I felt like I was swimming through tar in the pitch black, the only touchstones, Drake and Love. More than I deserved.

He reached for me, so desperate.

"Don't..." I pulled away. My lip was trembling. Pathetic. Weak. In front of a man who'd done nothing but hurt me. I hugged myself tighter, fighting it, shoulders bunching as I scrambled for a way out of this.

"I will do anything for another chance," he begged. "Just tell me, and I'll do it."

He wanted me to find him another chance, when I was drowning?

I'd been with Zeus, not him.

I was the one with that darkness lurking on the other end of the bond, a promise of hell I'd never escape if I failed.

Knowing I didn't deserve more.

Everything—I'd given him *everything* down to my own tears and heartbreak, and it hadn't been enough.

I broke in that moment, a wild, furious scream tearing from my lips, then I was slamming my fists into his chest. *"Try!"* The last of my sanity was ash in the wind. "I want you to *fucking* try!" My voice broke, tears flooding my face, all the rage scrambling to keep a hold and save me from the void beneath.

He was my mate.

The one person who was supposed to have saved me.

"I wanted more," I choked out. "You gave me cruelty I never wanted, and now you have guilt *I don't have any use for!"*

He was staring at me, shock in his eyes as I clutched his shirt. I hated how fucking pathetic and open I was right now.

I hated that I had to say it.

I hated that his expression was still blank.

"I want better than that," I choked. *"I want you—"* I shoved him again with all my might. *"—to have been better the first time!* I want you to be more now! I want you to prove all my fears were wrong, instead of giving me more. I want to be worth enough to you, that you'd risk being wrong, and you'd try even if you find out *you can never fix it!"*

Or find out he could never fix me...

The need to scream those words sucked me dry: mind, body and soul. The world spun, and I didn't realise I was falling until he caught me. I could hear his unsteady breaths.

I tried to tear free—I had to leave. I didn't want to look at him. I didn't want to risk seeing that confusion in his eyes.

Uncomprehending guilt.

Caramel brandy still lingered in the air, and I was sobbing with my entire body as I tried to tear from his grip. *"Let me go!"*

"Vex! Please, I'm sorry." His voice shook, and he was drawing me into his arms, trying to get me to look up at him. "I'm so sorry. Just... please. I just need a chance to make it right—"

"Let me go!" Finally, I tore away hard enough to break his grip, only then I found myself staggering back too violently, losing my footing. I crashed to the ground, a whine slipping out as the bruised area of my stomach flared with pain.

I jumped violently as an aura split the air, and I was on my back in an instant, eyes wide. Rook looked worried, but when he stepped toward me I scrambled back.

It wasn't rational. It was pure, terrified instinct. I'd been here before... It was hard... It was just hard for me *not* to react.

He lifted his hands up. "Are... are you okay?" he asked. But I couldn't reply. "I'm... I'm trying to..." He swallowed, stepping back again. "I c-can't get rid of it. I'm trying." He looked wild, running fingers through his hair. "I can't... fuck. I'm not going to hurt you." He sounded so desperate, but I could barely hear the words, blood roaring in my ears.

"P-please just... just let me go," I whispered.

I didn't want to cry again, not because of this. All of this was wrong, the aura was wrong, my fear was wrong.

"Please!"

He took another step back, and there it was again, the thing I didn't want to see: how lost he looked. I turned, staggering to my feet and making for the glass doors that led to the gardens.

Love and Drake thought I was talking to Rook. They wouldn't come looking for a while.

I needed air.

I needed to breathe.

FIFTEEN

EBONY

If Vex thought, for one moment, I hadn't installed cameras around this entire property to alert me when *anyone* left, she was sorely wrong.

My phone had buzzed the moment she'd run into the gardens this evening. "What are you doing?" I demanded, striding toward her as she huddled before a dead firepit.

She jumped, spinning where she sat, and got to her feet quickly as I reached her. I paused for a moment, noticing the tears streaking down her face. "I-I wasn't going to stay long," she stammered.

"You can't be outside without one of us around." My initial anger was waning at the distraught look on her face. Had something happened? Or was this just part of the healing process we knew we'd face when we got her back?

"Why?" she asked.

I cocked my head, trying to figure out if she seriously meant that. "Our job is to keep you safe."

"I'm in the garden...?"

"I don't trust anything is safe without one of us here," I snapped. Plus, the pool was less than ten feet away.

What if she fell in? I'd worked far too hard to see my omega die like that. I'd have to fence it off, or teach her to swim, but I doubted she'd be open to that right now.

She wiped her eyes angrily, then folded her arms and squared me up with a bratty look. "That's too bad because I don't want your company."

I narrowed my eyes, stifling the affrontement that surfaced as she said that right to my face.

Fine.

But she was mistaken if she thought I gave a shit about her feelings on this. I took her by the wrist, hauling her back toward the house.

"Let go of me!" she hissed, throwing her weight against my grip. When I didn't flinch, she leaped at me instead, sinking her nails into my arm. I just turned on her and tossed her over my shoulder instead.

"Fuck *you*!" she screamed, gripping my shirt, trying to kick and scratch at me however she could. "Let me down! I don't want to go back to my room yet!"

"I'm not taking you to your room," I told her mildly as we reached the doors. "Rook's still up, you can hang out with him."

"N-NO!"

Her struggles re-doubled, and when I let go of her with one hand to open the door, she almost managed to launch from my grip.

Fuck.

I just managed to catch her in time as she tumbled from my shoulder.

"You were the one taken!" I dragged her upright and pinned her against the door. "Why are you *insisting* on being difficult?"

"Difficult?" she demanded. "I just want to sit in the fucking garden."

"You're my omega!" I spat, grip closing on her shoulders. "You won't be taken on my watch ever again."

She opened her mouth, but the fury died on her expression as her eyes darted between mine. Her whole body language changed, chest suddenly heaving, and her jaw clenched.

I frowned, letting her go, not sure what I was looking at. I could read anger, but I didn't know what this was. Then her face crumpled, and—to my surprise—she burst into tears.

Uh... okay.

I wasn't sure what to make of that.

I also wasn't ready for the million thoughts cluttering my head, each a demand or idea of how I could fix it—and all likely entirely wrong.

But Vex had returned to us, off all her scent blocking drugs, and there was an unaccepted princess bond between us now. Every goddamned instinct was screaming in my head, more vicious than a drug in my bloodstream.

"I've got you, Vex. I'll always keep you safe."

Shit.

Don't think about that right now.

Those words—the ones I'd offered, and she'd written in blood —wouldn't get out of my fucking brain.

The discomfort, that knot of threads I couldn't untangle in what was usually a perfectly oiled system, it was back. The same feeling, the one I hadn't been able to place, since the moment I'd read the book Rook had pulled out of the limo.

Her pain, because of me. And one line that I couldn't shake.

It was like Drake, but a million times worse: she was mine. It was my job to protect her; I couldn't be the one to hurt her.

That day I had lied with ease, just as I always had. And yet, never had a lie so painfully caught up with me as this one had, because I had to convince her that those same words were now my truth. And now she was crying, and I had no fucking idea why.

How was *anyone* supposed to plan for a mate?

Here she was standing before me: an entire free thinking, emotionally sensitive person around which my whole universe now orbited, and I didn't... I didn't know why she was crying.

My job was to *not* make her cry, and I'd done it without intending to. I'd driven her to tears before, but those times it had been on purpose. Here I was flying blind.

I was successful in life because I picked the battles I fought. I chose my goals to match my strengths and then I trashed the competition without blinking. But this... this was different.

This was a battle I couldn't bow out of, and yet it required my greatest weakness. Manipulation—that I excelled in: changing minds, making people do things I wanted them to. Easy.

But changing their feelings?

Only, Love was right, I couldn't sit this one out, watching from the background. I needed to be a part of her healing, too. Before I knew what I was doing I had her in my arms and I was sitting us down on a nearby daybed. I tucked a lock of hair behind her ear.

What would I be doing if it was Drake?

He was quieter than this, I had to read a lot more into smaller tells. Vex was still trembling, tears flooding her face.

"Love said..." Vex hiccupped. "He said you... fought for me."

I considered that, though I still couldn't piece together why it had caused her to cry. "Not hard enough."

"I thought... when you found out, and you didn't say anything... I thought it was because..."

"Because I didn't want you?" I asked.

She nodded.

Ah.

I grabbed hold of that. She needed reassurance. I'd already

considered this and come up with a game plan. I hadn't intended to offer it so *soon*—though I hadn't thought she'd want to see me for a while longer. But it was the best option, and the most valuable thing I had to offer.

I shifted my thumb, stroking her cheek ever so gently, waiting. Finally, she peered up at me, something curious in her gaze at my touch.

Good.

This was the beginning of the reassurance. But by the time we were done there would be no moment in her life that she'd felt more safe. "I'm sorry. For everything. You deserve so much better than what we put you through."

"What?" she asked, eyes glittering with insecurities.

But I knew *this* was what she needed.

I'd rehearsed it in my head. I'd done my research on all the kinds of apologies it was possible to give. So, making sure my voice was steady, I went on. She'd heard my expression of regret, next, I needed to accept responsibility.

"I was... selfish. I treated you in ways I never should have, and that's on me. There's no excuse for it."

Now, offer restitution.

"There is nothing I won't do to make this right. Nothing I won't do to free you of that bond. I will be whatever you need of me. I can't... I can't allow you to be unsafe..." I glanced around at the garden. "But I will give you space, if that's what you ask for."

Repent.

"You can't trust this, and I can't change what happened—but I promise I will never hurt you again. I want you to feel safe with my pack. I want you to know that you matter to me, and... not many people in this world matter to me."

Ask for forgiveness—but don't force it on them.

"If you'll let me, I want to earn your forgiveness."

She stared at me, confusion clear on her expression.

But I'd seen this before. It's how the process worked. The moment I tried to change—to give someone like Love or Drake what they needed, there was this same confusion. Then they understood what I was offering, and they conceded.

It was the foundation of all the important relationships I had in my life.

So, I waited for her to understand.

"Are you...?" She swallowed, staring at me with that perfect little crease on her forehead. "Are you... *lying* to me?"

I shifted, taking her in, a little surprised. Vex was emotional, but she wasn't stupid.

"This *is* the truth: I want you to be safe and I want you to be happy."

She frowned, trying to untangle that. "I don't want a mask from my mate, Ebony. I want *you*."

I felt an unexpected weight in my chest. None of the others had questioned this part, knowing the solution I offered was better than the alternative. Better than the impossible. "I don't think you understand what you're asking for."

"Tell me, then." she said.

I straightened where I sat, gaze darting out to the gardens for a moment, calculating. "Let me tell you what you could have, if you let me give you this, instead."

She chewed on her lip for a moment, but nodded.

So I did. I painted her the picture I'd already been planning since the moment I realised she was my mate.

"You could tell me what you like, what you're afraid of, your favourite food, comfort movies, all the things that make you upset or angry. The way your perfect date would go, the pet peeves you have about men. What you'd love someone to do for you when you're upset. Anything, Vex. Anything in the whole world, and I could be that for you."

I'd done it with Drake to a lesser extent. He was like a puzzle, and I had to keep track of the outcomes of different behaviours, but it had worked. I knew how to make him feel better.

I *wanted* to do that for her.

She didn't trust us, and trust is what we needed to earn from her. I *could* treat her like a queen.

"Would you... enjoy that?" she asked.

I frowned.

Enjoy it?

Enjoyment wasn't the point. Every time I protected her or put a smile on her face, it was a win. She was my mate, that was hard wired into me, and I could ride that victory. It was a game I'd never had in my life before, one that gave me hits of satisfaction I'd never felt so easily.

I wanted to be someone she could trust, and I wanted her to let me close, so I could have her around. Love had made it clear that I wouldn't be allowed near her without her consent, so I couldn't force my presence on her.

Even if I did, there truly was something tangible to how much I liked the idea of making her want me. Of exploring everything about her that made her smile or laugh or fall for me more. Of exploring the lust that had me in a chokehold every time I looked at her. I wanted to know how to make her beg for me, how to make her scream my name and make her so high on ecstasy that her body gave out and she had no choice but to let me hold her.

Explaining that, however, would ruin it for her, and then neither of us would win. "I would... *enjoy* being someone who made you happy," I said at last.

The word enjoy was wrong on my tongue, the lie uncomfortable in a way that lies weren't usually. But to tell her I *needed* to be someone that made her happy? I thought she might just run.

"But it wouldn't be the real you?" she asked.

I opened my mouth, then shut it, oddly stumped by that question. She didn't want me without the mask—she might think she did, but she didn't.

"You're my mate," she whispered. "The universe put us together."

"And I can be what you need."

Her jaw ticked, expression tightening. "Not like that."

"You don't want what you think you want—"

I cut off at her visceral reaction. Her eyes blazed with fury, and her hand clamped around my neck as she squared up with me—even caught in my arms like she was. "Don't you *dare* tell me what I want."

My blood heated, and I had to shift so she wouldn't feel how rock hard I got at the fire in her eyes.

She *was* my mate.

I don't know how I hadn't seen it.

But... I had. The whole time, I'd known she was special, but without a name to it, without understanding, I'd shoved her away, afraid of attachment without claim.

Even now, I didn't have that claim. Not the way I needed it.

"I want you as you are."

I stared at her, mind going a million miles a minute as I thought out what that might truly look like.

Freedom?

Or... or something else.

Would I lose her?

She didn't seem to think so, but she wasn't like me.

"I will accept nothing from you if it isn't real," she hissed. Her hand was still clamped around my neck, and I lost myself in that moment.

I shifted so I was on top of her, delicate neck in my palm as my thumb pressed against her jaw so she couldn't look away from me. Her breath caught, hair scattered around her on the cushion, eyes wide as she held mine. She wasn't afraid. Instead, a daring curiosity danced in her eyes, and it was—for a fleeting moment—the first time I'd seen the fear gone.

I'd done that.

My time with her had pulled her from the void entirely.

It was the moment of confidence I needed to forge on, to take this dare of hers and make it into something real.

She was going to understand, though, what it meant. "You're an omega, Vex. Do you really want someone who can't offer you the care and attention you crave?"

She frowned, furious for a moment. "I'll have Drake, and Love, and..." She trailed off, not ready to bring Rook into this, yet. She looked determined, though. "I want something real."

For a single breath, my mind ran away with that idea. I imagined a world where I didn't have to hide, and she would stay at my side all the same.

Yet... not even Love could tolerate all of me. He saw glimpses behind the veil, enough to turn his stomach and make him never want to look again.

"You're afraid I won't want you?" she asked.

I let out a breath, humour in it.

Of course she wouldn't.

"I don't know why you would ever ask for that, with what I've just offered you."

"I've spent too long hiding what I am to want that life for someone I'm supposed to love."

Love?

And there was the problem.

But it was as if she could see the conflict in my eyes. "There's a way to make it work," she whispered. "Or we wouldn't be mates."

I wasn't usually so irrational to wish words to be truth when I knew they weren't, but I caved in that moment. We were so close, her breath tickling my cheek, her silvery hair scattered about her freckled face, bare of makeup and utterly captivating. Eyes of liquid gold dared me to never blink, to never look away for even a moment, lest she turn to smoke.

So fucking beautiful—even more so, in what she was trying to offer me.

"I still... I still haven't forgiven you," she whispered. I realised I'd shifted closer, much too transfixed. I understood what her words meant, despite the lust burning in her eyes. She wouldn't let me close.

Not yet.

"If you don't want my apology, Vex, I'll earn your trust back my way."

"How?"

"Say you want me how I am, and I'm yours. I will burn the world to the ground if anyone dares try to take you from me again." Her word trumped Love's. Her word was everything. "They can get on their knees and give you the apology you need, they can be sweet and put you back together piece by piece. But I will be your hound. I will bury the bones of anyone who has ever hurt you."

She stared at me, completely taken off guard. Her lips were parted, her breathing heavy.

"If that's... who you are..." She swallowed. "I want *you.*"

I didn't let her go, a rare moment of worry hit my system.

What if she was wrong?

What if she saw what I was, and wanted to run. But then... I wasn't going to lose her. Love would bite her no matter what, the dark bond on her neck meant she would ask for that, no matter what I was.

If she became frightened of me, we could return to pretence. I could treat her like a princess until she forgot the monster beneath.

"Alright," I said, realising too long had passed between us.

She frowned, shifting beneath me, clearly unsure. I released her, getting up. She got to her feet too, looking a bit shaky, but I caught her before she could leave.

"You said you wanted this, Vex, so let me start with this. Tell me who took you from your home."

"What?" Her eyes were wide, darting between mine.

"I said—" I took her chin, forcing her to look up at me, my words absolutely sure. "—Who took you from your home?"

SIXTEEN

LOVE

Something changed in Vex the next morning.

I woke to find her and Drake huddled at the windowsill, staring at something I couldn't make out.

"I don't think it's a potato, I think it's a—" Drake cut off as he noticed me hurrying over.

"What's going on?" I asked.

"Vex has gifts," Drake said.

"Gifts?" I asked. She turned to me, and I almost drew up with surprise at the look in her eyes. She was glowing. I stifled a moment of irrational jealousy.

"Gifts from Drake?" I asked.

It had to be.

No way would any of the rest of us get a reaction like that—

"Ebony," Drake said, shooting me a look that told me he was just as confused as I was. Vex had already turned back around, examining the line of peculiar things.

I followed her gaze, taking in the four objects lined up on her windowsill.

A crystal swan.

A print of a single eye, and behind it were black and white swirls like an optical illusion.

A pitch-black choker with a lock dangling from it.

But the last was the oddest of all. It was... I leaned closer. It was familiar. It resembled a potato, but it was a brown sack, stuffed full and tied off at the bottom. On it, a terrified, frown was scribbled on with a sharpie and it had two small buttons for eyes.

"I don't get it," Drake said.

"It's a chia pet." I knew that with certainty. "We made them when we were kids—stuff little sacks full of soil and chia seeds, then water them every day. They grow chia grass for hair. Our nanny made Ebony make one, and he drew a face on it just like that." I nodded toward the one on the sill.

"So... I have to water it?" Vex asked.

"Once a day or something like that."

Vex nodded, scrambling to her feet and making for the bathroom. I was left to exchange a very confused look with Drake.

"She's... different," I said.

"Yeh. I mean... she said she fought with Rook, but she didn't mention Ebony..." He looked back to the lineup of objects. Then he reached over and picked up the glossy print with the black swirls and a singular eye.

"This looks like the 'Evening Stars' logo, right?" he asked. That was the interview Ebony and Vex had attended the other week.

"Yeh, I think—" I cut off as the scent of raspberry treacle in the room changed, something anxious in it. I looked up instantly to see Vex had drawn up in front of us, a glass of water clutched in her hand. She was staring at the print Drake was holding, her face paler than usual.

"Are you okay?" I asked. She glanced up at me, then fixed her expression and nodded, though her scent became no more settled. Her eyes darted back to the print.

"Are you sure?" Drake asked, obviously concerned. Her fingers were gripping the cup so hard they were white.

"I'm... fine." She glanced between us guiltily, and then back at the print, clearly unable to keep her eyes from it.

Oh.

Oh.

"Uh... mate," I reached over, tugging it from his grip. Her scent spiked an edge of panic, but then I placed it back down on the sill where it had been before. Then, just like that, she was back to normal. Well... she was *this*, which wasn't normal, but it was... it was good.

She settled back down before the sill, placing the cup carefully next to the chia pet. "How much do you think I should water it?" she asked, peering back at me.

I pulled my phone out to look it up.

Drake still seemed confused, until he caught her reaching out and adjusting the Evening Stars print once, twice, and then a third time, each time throwing a guilty glance Drake's way.

His eyebrows had vanished into his messy hair as I read out how much she was supposed to water the chia pet.

"Is she... nesting?" he mouthed at me.

I opened my mouth, then shut it, giving him a non-committal nod. But it was hard not to think so as I watched her drizzling just the tiniest bit of water onto the chia pet, brows drawn with a focused expression only inches from the horrifying thing.

Drake looked back at me, absolute bewilderment on his face. *"Ebony?"* he mouthed again.

I shrugged, just as baffled as he was. I'd asked my brother to try with her, and it seems he had. Oddest of all, it seemed to have worked, and I would be lying if I said that didn't make me a little jealous.

When Vex looked back to us, her eyes were a bit brighter than they had been yesterday. "Do you think uh... maybe we could unpack a box, today?"

VEX

I was tired of being broken and fragile and exhausted.

I wanted to be strong enough that I could take something back. Despite the bond on my neck. Despite the commands and the alphas lurking in the back of my mind.

Truly, I had no idea which part it was: screaming at Rook, demanding Ebony *refrain* from turning himself into the world's most flawless mate, or perhaps it was finally knowing where I stood with them all. But this morning I'd woken up in Drake's arms feeling... better. Not perfect, but a little less fragile.

And then I'd seen Ebony's gifts, and the room had changed.

Right now, it was like they were the centre of the space. Everywhere I moved, they tugged my attention back to them. The point of safety, of... something right.

There was one other thing that felt a part of this room, tucked deep in the back of the linen closet. But it was a reminder of my desperation, and I felt a little guilty considering it. So, with Love and Drake, I began unpacking one of the boxes they had brought, and suddenly the room had more anchors in it, balancing it out. Each one made it feel more right. I placed Aisha's collar, which I'd previously returned to the box out of nerves, on the table beside my bed.

Love and Drake were both being so patient with me. They'd promised me that, and yet it was more reassuring to see it. Love was nervous in a way I never thought I'd see, but I noticed he brightened more each time I found a place for one of my things.

Still, I couldn't look at my makeup. It was in my bathroom where I'd left it, along with my straightener and curler, and in the afternoon, Drake caught me shoving it all back in the drawers. It was more of an issue now that the rest of the nest—room—was starting to feel more safe.

He stepped up behind me, wrapping his arms around my waist and catching my wrists gently. "What are you doing, Dreamgirl?"

"I just... I don't want it anymore," I whispered, meeting his eyes in the mirror.

"That's okay," he murmured. "Just... tell me why?"

The answer was out of my mouth before I'd even thought it through. "It's stupid and I don't need it." I shut my eyes right as I said it, hating that answer.

"I don't think it's stupid," he said.

Foolish, insecure panic caught up to me: a fear I never would have felt before all of this. "Do you not like..." My breath caught, the words turning thick as molasses in a split second. "You won't like me if I don't—?"

"You'd be my dream girl no matter what you wear or do with your hair," he said.

My heart calmed, if only for a moment.

"But I don't think it's stupid if you do love it," he finished.

Carefully, I set the eyeliner down, then turned so I was facing him. Violet galaxies held mine, sure and sad, piercing me right to my soul.

My mate, who never missed my pain. Not for a second. Not even buried in the depths of a video meant to do so much more than challenge something as inconsequential as my passions.

"And that's all?" Zeus's voice was like daggers in my mind. *He was pinning me by the neck, forcing the camera in my face so they could all see how weak and stupid I was. "That's all? The best you have to offer? A pretty face?"*

"I love that you love it," Drake whispered, drowning out Zeus's taunt. "I love that you sing to yourself when you do your hair.

153

That you enjoy putting on makeup so much sometimes you wipe it all off and start over just because you want to go again. I love your hair and style because it's a reflection of you. And I love..." He trailed off and when he spoke again, his voice was thick. "I love that you fought for it. You don't have to fight again, but I just want you to know I don't think it's stupid."

I reached up before even thinking about it, hands cupping his cheeks as I drew myself up to my tiptoes, face just inches from his.

I knew they were worried about the dark bond—about commands that might be hiding around every corner, and I couldn't say anything about it, even to tell him there was nothing to be afraid of right now.

He leaned closer, cautious, and I dragged him down to me and pressed my lips to his.

A purr rose in his chest. He lifted me and set me on the counter so my legs could tangle around him and drag us closer.

It was, for a few brief seconds, enough to stop the world, to challenge each doubt and monster lurking around every corner. After, when I stepped from the bathroom, I left the counter how it was, messy and scattered with makeup.

Next was my clothes. While Drake went to grab us a late lunch, Love helped me dig out all of my favourite sweatshirts. They were all oversized, worn with age, and each had an inscription on the cuff. They were the most precious things I owned, aside from Aisha's collar. My mother was gone now, and she'd never be able to inscribe the lyrics of a song ever again. I'd always been so careful about wearing them, not wanting to ruin them.

Right now, I'd lined up my favourite three and I was looking between them.

The inscriptions read: *I'll stay with you until the first break of* day', 'Find your voice and find your strength'—the one I'd worn yesterday. And the third, the one with the inscription that meant the most, even if I never wore it or never spoke it.

Choosing the former, I tugged it on (over Drake's shirt), not caring that it was warm out today. Love helped me hang the others up on a rack all of their own, keeping them separate and easy for me to identify by inscription.

"So, did you speak with Ebony?" Love asked.

I glanced at him, a little unsure. "Yes. Last night."

"And was it... okay?"

I nodded. "He tried to apologise."

"Tried to?"

"Yeh."

I didn't really know what to think of the conversation I'd had with Ebony. It felt right, but even he'd been concerned at my choice, which was unsettling. No one had ever asked that of him before, I knew it, but I had to have faith in this match.

And then... what he'd asked me...

Perhaps it should have been the most unnerving moment of the night, but instead warmth coiled in my stomach at the thought of it.

I will burn the world to the ground if anyone ever dares try to take you from me again... I will bury the bones of anyone who has ever hurt you...

Would he?

Could he, even?

The gifts were a promise, though I had yet to figure them all out. And I chose to believe in that promise.

Something about Ebony seemed detached from the world, as if he were capable of things that normal people weren't. I believed him, even though it was madness. Even though I didn't know the first of what I'd just given him when I told him the truth.

But if I could believe in him for the past, then maybe, just maybe, I could hold onto hope for a future, too.

"I told him I didn't want him to pretend anything for me," I said, watching Love carefully. "I want him as he is."

He set down a pile of clothing and turned to me, ocean blue eyes fixing me with all of his attention in that unsettling manner. He took a long moment to reply before he finally spoke. "*That* is a daring thing to ask of Ebony."

I shrunk a little, anxiously gripping the inscription of the cuff I wore. Just like they had with Rook last night, feeling those bumps of the embroidery beneath my fingers settled my nerves.

"I know," I said.

"Do you know what those gifts mean?" he asked.

"I'm figuring it out." I felt a smile tug at my lips. "Do... do you love him?" I asked. If there was anyone in the world who could help me understand Ebony, it was Love.

He considered that for a long moment. "Yes."

"Do you think he loves you?"

"I don't know. But does love have to be reciprocated to be real?"

"Is that why you chose the name?" I asked.

He smiled. "I was fourteen. I chose the name to piss off Ebony."

We were silent for a while as I unfolded a few more of the sweatshirts, examining each carefully.

"What is it that you value?" Love asked at last. "When you learn that someone loves you?"

I considered that for a long time before answering. "There's just... something safe in knowing they'll be there no matter what. Even if you fuck up or make mistakes."

He nodded, running his tongue along his teeth. "I believe Ebony is as capable as offering that as any of us are. It's just the criteria, the reasoning, *that's* what makes some people uncomfortable."

"Like what?" I asked.

"He values me. I will always be the one who has known him all his life, who took an interest and can challenge him. That's never going to change, no matter what I do."

"But... that's still not love?"

He shrugged. "If a mother loves her baby because it's hers, we call that love. Because the child is now entangled in who she is and what she has done, because she values becoming a protector and nurturer." Love took a breath, not meeting my eyes for a moment. He was different when he spoke about Ebony, more open. I couldn't take my eyes from him as he brushed away a loose flutter of hair that had escaped his braid. "How is what I am to Ebony any different? Or even him to me? He is... concrete. No one can replace what I am to him, and no one would ever be able to replace what he is to me. Love is just entanglement and identity. Identify that and it's safer. If you don't, you leave it to the mercy of titles that can fail in the face of misplaced expectations. I've seen first hand how little a mother's love, the kind of love that trumps all, can be worth."

"So... yes?" I asked, though I wasn't quite sure what question he was answering anymore.

He shrugged, but nodded. "I think, if we were capable of perfect love, then maybe my take would be different, but we aren't. There is no guarantee of absolute love, not even in blood. My... *entanglement* with Ebony is worth more than what some people have. It's up to you to decide if that's enough for you."

I think I already had, yet hearing this from Love was comforting. "But uh... you don't trust him, do you?"

"No... I don't."

"I want to," I said quietly.

"And in that, Vex, you will be in uncharted territory." He

smiled, unperturbed, and perhaps I saw a glimmer of curiosity in his eyes. "We could get one framed," he suggested, lifting one of the sweatshirts. "If you wanted."

"Maybe... just not yet?" Doing that felt like making a commitment to this room. I didn't think I was ready for that yet.

Not when it could still be taken away...

I swallowed back that thought.

Love didn't look upset at all, already back to straightening the sweatshirts in the rack.

That night, when I settled into bed, crawling back into Drake's arms, and this time twining my fingers into Love's, I had time, briefly, to wonder upon what Love had said about Ebony, and to wonder upon the gifts he'd left. A smile touched my lips before sleep found me with ease.

And for the first time, my dreams were silent.

SEVENTEEN

Day four. Chia pet's 1st day of life. Hair length: 0cm.

EBONY

I knocked on the apartment door, trying to measure my expression, the early makings of a thrill humming in my veins.

When it opened, I was met with the face of a woman I'd now carved into my memory for a second time. She was the first person to have harmed my pack and walked away. Only, I was back this time, and it wasn't for Love.

It was official as of this morning: I was courting Vex. The promises had been set, and this time, unlike the words written into that book in blood, I wouldn't break these.

I smiled warmly, and Alana Swan's eyes went wide, her bright red lips popping open. I was dressed well, with a few buttons of my shirt undone. My hair was up as usual with a few wisps framing my face. I was everything that made the image of Ebony Starless absolutely devastating.

"Alana?" I asked, and the smile on my face was easy. She was the woman who'd found my mate, collapsed and vulnerable at the

Diamond Tides, and made the choice to ruin her life. Now, she was here before me, and I would return the favour in kind.

"Yes..." She was breathless, knuckles white on the glass of wine she clutched. "E-Ebony."

I held a hand out to her, and she took it. "You spent some time courting my brother," I said, thumb sliding along the back of her hand gently.

"I...I did." Her smile was nervous, darting between the movement and my gaze.

"And then..." I paused for a moment, letting her linger in her nerves as she tried to figure out what could possibly bring me to her doorstep. "You saved my pack from one of the greatest embarrassments of our career."

Slowly, I lifted her hand, bowing just slightly, and pressed my lips to her knuckles. It turned my stomach, giving her even that, but I took comfort in reminding myself that it was a kiss of fate.

By the way she pressed her palm to the wall and her face drained of colour, I thought she might have almost fainted. In the next moment her cheeks flushed deep pink. That was cute when it happened to Vex, but Alana was nothing but vile.

"I... did? I mean. Of course, but... but how can I help you?" she asked.

"I wondered if you'd allow me to give you a gift of thanks."

Alana's eyes lit up. "I mean... I didn't do it for a gift, but who am I to say no? Would you... would you like to come in?"

"Are you sure I'm not intruding?"

"No no, not at all." Her high-pitched laugh was grating. "Come in. Can I offer you a glass?"

"I wouldn't say no," I replied. "You have a partner, right?" I asked as I stepped into a pristine living area. "You went with him to the Diamond Tides?"

I knew of course, because Evan Sorowitch was unwittingly a part of this now, too.

Alana, who'd made her way to the kitchen island and unhooked a wine glass, paused ever so briefly, not looking back at me.

"We... aren't serious." She found a broad smile as I slipped into one of the bar stools and glanced around.

Not serious?

"Ah." I offered her a smile as she passed me the glass.

Yet, this expensive apartment was *his*.

Of course, I understood. It would be rather inconvenient, I knew, for her to be in a committed relationship, when a man with a hundred times her partner's wealth turned up at her door with a gift.

Alana wasn't independently wealthy. She found her lifestyle by jumping from rich man to rich man—most of whom were in the movie industry, as that seemed to be where she was most comfortable.

She'd become more proficient over the years. At least in her time with Love there had been an attempt at a true relationship before money and fame were brought in. He'd wanted to keep it a secret, after all. But now she went for men who were happy to be public about having her on their arm.

As we drank, I engaged in a dull conversation about the industry, my pack, and Love, though I stifled that topic quickly so I didn't ruin my own plans. And I counted every time she placed those manicured fingers on my arm in affection.

"So... a gift?" she asked as she finally finished her glass. I could tell she'd been itching to bring it up, but she was practised in hiding that desperation of hers. Come across too intense, and she would never have been able to snag the richest celebrities that would allow her into their spaces.

"Will you join me?" I asked, nodding toward the door. "I'll show you."

She didn't argue, and I took great pleasure in watching her

shut the door to her apartment, pulling out her keys and locking it, knowing that it was the last time she'd step foot in such luxury.

I led her down the stairs and out onto the street. It took only a few minutes for us to reach the little side ally in which I'd parked the rickety old van.

"The gift," I said, stepping up and sliding open the rusting side door.

She frowned, looking into the interior that had been gutted of all but the front two seats. Instead, there was a ratty slim bed and a boxed off area for a toilet.

"Go on, get in and I'll show you."

She looked so perfectly confused, but like the idiot she was, she climbed in, heels wobbling on the uneven flooring. Shame, really. She'd be stuck with those heels for a while.

I stepped up behind her and slid the door shut. She spun, a frown on her face as she looked at me, ducking down against the low roof.

"Solid van," I said, climbing up into the front passenger seat. "Half converted to one of those travel vans that hippie girls love. The bed looks a bit uncomfortable—but it's yours and that's what matters. Couldn't get you one with one of those nice composting toilets, but it does have a bucket. Very economical."

"What are you talking about?" she asked, staring at me from the back. I shrugged, pulling a set of keys from my pocket and putting them in the ignition.

"A place for you to stay," I said, as if it were obvious. "But this was only half the gift."

As if on cue, police sirens rang out down the street.

She glanced between me and the street outside where the sirens were growing louder. "What do you mean?"

"That apartment we were just in is about to be raided for drugs. Successfully, I might add, since Evan is rather entrenched in less savoury means of making money. He likes his expensive cars, and pretty birds on his arm. There's only a few ways to make that happen when you're a c rate actor."

Alana's face blanched.

"On the bright side, you aren't in there, which means you do, in fact, have a chance to flee."

"To... what?"

"To flee."

She was staring at me with a blank look.

"There's a storm coming to New Oxford," I told her. "And you, Alana Swan, are right in the middle of it," I told her. "All those *alternative* means in which your partner makes his money are about to see the light of day. Only, he's not alone, is he? Our profession is *infested* with these vermin, making their money on tainted drugs, keeping the best for themselves—and that... that doesn't even begin to scratch the surface."

"It's not..." She shook her head. "I have nothing to do with it."

"Ten days, you have, before the lid is blown open and Alana Swan is planted right in the epicentre. You've dated a dozen others who'll be outed by the end of the week. It will be all but impossible to believe that you had nothing to do with it."

"W-why are you doing this?" she stammered.

"You came for Vex Eden because you are a pathetic jealous bitch," I said.

"N-No!" Her jaw clenched. "I helped you. I'm n-not responsible for a gold pack's status. If she didn't want it, she should have chosen differently. Her issues are hers to figure out."

"My *mate's* issues are mine to figure out."

Alana froze, her eyes going wide. Her mouth opened, then she shut it. "I... had no idea she was..." She trailed off, clearly finally realising the reality of the situation she was facing. "I didn't know."

"I can only imagine you didn't," I said.

And it changed nothing.

I knew the movie industry back to front. Since I was a teenager, I'd been tracking every inch of it in order to get ahead—it was how I'd secured Drake for our pack.

Sex and drugs, that's what these idiots preferred to dabble in. Conquer the industry without falling prey to it, and it was easy to reach the top.

The direct connection between the highest and the lowest creatures in New Oxford was not news to me: the rich funded crime that punished the poor—though the depravity... Since digging deeper over the last week, I'd discovered the *depravity* was bottomless.

What *was* new, however, was how it had become personal. That it was my mate who had suffered.

There *would* be retribution. And Alana? She'd managed to slide her way right into the middle of it all.

There was only one truth I didn't yet know.

"My question for you, Alana: do you know the sources your partner uses to make the money that keeps you so comfortable?"

Her face was still all too pale. "I don't know what you're talking about."

"Good," I said. "Because I'm giving you a chance to get out. I even went to the trouble of getting you a new identity."

I tugged open the glove box and withdrew what was within. In each hand I held a passport, one blue, one green. A US passport with her new identity, or a Mexican passport with her new identity.

Self preservation would tell me the rest.

If she truly didn't know, then she was guiltless—in that, anyway—and she would see no reason why she needed to take such drastic measures and flee the country. The information I gave to my contact next week would reflect that.

If she *did* know, then self preservation would tell her that her best bet was to cross the border to Mexico as soon as she could. Equally, the information I gave would reflect that.

I watched her strained calculation as her gaze darted between both passports. For a moment, she reached for the blue, her fingers shaking as she did. Then her eyes darted up to me anxiously, and she snatched the green from my fingers so fast she might have thought I would take it away.

I straightened, a vicious smile curving my lips.

Vex had been right about me on the day of Dean Trance's interview. I didn't give the first fuck about gold pack rights. Yet, I hadn't lied to her, either. I didn't hate them, and I certainly didn't give a shit about the colour of my mate's eyes.

But Alana Swan was a different kind of monster, it had been reflected in her actions at the Gala. She'd been willing to target Vex while she couldn't fight back, and then blast her across the internet.

The flavour of Alana's sins didn't matter to me. I was here because she'd come for my mate. Her sins served only to light my way to the kind of punishment I offered. The kind of punishment that brought Vex the justice she deserved, without overstepping what she would want if she was here.

And now I knew the full truth: she was a woman just as willing to jeopardise the safety of a gold pack omega as she was willing to step upon their corpses to reach a diamond ring.

And Alana had shown me herself.

She reached out to me, lip trembling pathetically, but I caught her wrist.

"Careful," I murmured as I let my mask fall away completely. "I promise to snap every finger that touches what is hers."

Her eyes went wide with terror and she drew away sharply, but my fingers bit down on her wrist, not letting go.

"I've already counted six times tonight. So that's... six fingers?"

Her face went deathly pale. "W-wait... I didn't know," she stammered. "I-it's not fair if I didn't know."

"And when you knelt at the side of an omega who couldn't fight back and chose to destroy her, was that fair?" I asked mildly.

"Please Ebony," she begged, ugly tears flowing down her cheeks. "I d-didn't know."

"How about, since I'm feeling nice, I'll make it six less days I'll give you to run? Though I'd be fast. Crossing that border will be infinitely more difficult once you're on a watch list."

Her mouth worked like a fish out of water as I released her wrist.

"Don't do this," she begged. "Just let me get there. I'll l-leave, I swear."

"Four days, that leaves you with. You're going to have to drive quick. At least you don't have to worry about finding a place to stay."

I grinned, opening the door of the van and stepping out. I was lying to her of course. I wouldn't be setting off the New Oxford fireworks for Vex until I was ready—and that wouldn't happen until I'd found the location of one particular alpha. He was mine, not the police's, and *fleeing* wouldn't be an option for him. But Alana didn't need to know that.

"W-wait, Ebony, just—"

"Better get going, Alana, or I'll make it seven less days."

I slammed the passenger side door right on her horror struck face.

Snapping bones was its own satisfaction, but imagining the desperate terror of this foul woman lasting days as she fled across the entire country? Imagining her face when she realised I'd taken everything, right down to her phone, which was now in my pocket.

Now *that* was priceless.

I supposed I *could* mention to her that I'd drained her bank account into gold pack charity funds, cancelled her credit cards, and that this shitshow of a van had a broken fuel gauge and less than ten miles of gas in its tank.

But I wouldn't.

Her issues were hers to figure out.

EIGHTEEN

Chia pet's 2nd day of life. Hair length: 0cm.
  Time until execution: 7 days

VEX

"You're in a *very* good mood today," Love noted as I snuggled next to him in bed, scrolling through a movie list on the TV.

I glanced up at him, trying to measure my expression. "Am I?"

"If I didn't know any better, I'd say it happened the moment you found a certain gift smashed to pieces on your windowsill this morning."

I shifted, looking back at the TV screen and continued scrolling, fighting a blush that was creeping up my cheeks.

He was right on both accounts. I'd woken to find a certain crystal swan with its head snapped off on my windowsill. It flipped a switch within me, something primal and etched into the constructs that made me an omega. Ebony was fighting for me. And maybe this giddiness made me a horrible person, since I had no idea what the shattered swan truly meant.

What Alana had done wasn't something I'd lingered on, not

with everything else. It was like a dagger digging into layers of scar tissue, pain I'd felt before, cruelty I'd been taught to accept as normal—as my own fault for a choice I'd made. And next to Zeus... it had faded.

But the broken swan was Ebony's way of telling me *he* wouldn't accept it—that maybe there was a world where I didn't have to, either.

He was doing exactly what he'd promised he would do—at least, he claimed he was. I'd told Love I wanted to trust Ebony.

I'd been warring with urges to break out into spontaneous song—or purring—all day. And I'd been losing those battles.

Now, we were waiting on food and Drake. There'd been a disaster in the kitchen, and he'd shooed us both upstairs so I didn't witness the food casualties.

They'd asked if there was anywhere I'd like to go out today, but I wanted to stay like this a little longer, spending the day with them in my room.

I liked this.

Me and Love and Drake. It wasn't the whole pack, like I might have dreamed of once upon a time, but it was something. And it was sweet and it was feeling safer by the day—by the hour, even.

"You put makeup on." Love said. It was an observation rather than a question.

"I... did."

"I like it."

I fought a smile, snuggling closer, trying to get him to lift his arm up and put it around me. I wanted cuddles from him. I'd had *loads* of blackcurrant wine cuddles, and I wanted some vanilla winter ones. I ached for some chestnut and twilight grass too, if I was being honest, but I wasn't ready to face that.

"You're getting very... physical today," Love noted.

I froze, eyes wide, unsure what to make of that. "I'm... sorry."

"Don't be," he said. "I just want to be sure I'm reading it right," he said. "Am I... reading it right?"

"I could... I could do cuddles?" I said, a little nervous.

He cocked his head. "If you're comfortable enough for cuddles, then that changes things."

"Does it?"

"Of course," he said, getting to his feet.

"Uh. *What* are you doing?" I squeaked as he began tugging his shirt off. My cheeks burned far too hot at the sight of his pale skin and rippling muscle. He just ignored me, stepping to the foot of my bed and—

"Oh my god!" I grabbed the pillow beside me and jammed it over my face. "You can't do that!" When I peered over it, he was still on his knees, palms in his lap, eyes down.

"No no no..." I flung the pillow at him, but he didn't budge. He didn't even look up. I scrambled over and dropped to his side. "You *literally* can't do that."

"Why ever not?" he asked, eyes fixed downward.

I grabbed him by the arm, then let go because he was all... bare and... and sexy. *"You have to get up!"*

"If you give me a command that involves getting up."

Shit. It was way too hot in here. "What am I supposed to ask for?"

"Anything you want."

"What if Drake comes back?"

"What if he does?" Love asked evenly, eyes still fixed on his hands.

"Please get up!"

"Oh, I don't think so." I could *swear* there was a smirk on his lips. "If memory serves, you didn't give me a choice."

"Why did you take your shirt off?" I stammered. "Are you... are you trying to *seduce* me?"

He didn't need to answer, of course—seduction had been the entire goal for me, after all.

Oh fuck.

I grabbed his shirt, and—instead of huffing it, which is what my raging hormones were demanding right now—I shoved it into his lap. "I command you to put your top back on."

"I..." He was unsure as he looked up at me, head cocked. "I don't know if I'll allow—if you can do that."

"You never tried—wait, *why* didn't you ever try that? You could have just told *me* to... to put on a Snuggie and sleep on the couch."

What *would* I have done, then?

"I couldn't engage with it!" he hissed, though it might have been the first time I'd ever seen him blush. "I just... I thought you'd stop coming."

"Okay. Well, I'm going to try that—"

"I'm not wearing a Snuggie," he said. "We don't even *have* a Snuggie."

"An oversight."

His eyes narrowed, then he reached into his jean pocket—to order in a truckload of snuggies for me if the last few days were anything to go off of—but caught himself and returned his hands to his lap.

"Dammit Love!" I groaned. "I can't handle this."

"If it would make you feel better, you can leave me here all night."

"No. No no no. You don't understand. There is no way in hell I can handle you all... chiseled god topless kneeling at my bedside all fucking night."

There was literally no way. But Love had to cough roughly to cover his—

"*Why* are you laughing?" I demanded.

"I'm not." He cleared his throat.

"Tell me. Now. *That's* a command."

He looked up at me, keeping his face as straight as he seemed capable. "The experience was mutual."

"No—*you* didn't feel like *this*. You didn't even know I was an omega."

He raised an eyebrow. "I didn't need to know you were an omega to know you're the most beautiful woman I've ever seen—coming into my room wearing barely a thing."

My retort stalled at that, blood turning boiling hot as he went on.

"Do you know how uncomfortable it was to have an erection *that long* in one night? At least when *you're* aroused, you aren't depriving surrounding tissue of blood."

I stifled a giggle. "Oh, well I'm sorry the experience was *so* taxing for you."

There was a beat, and the humour died from his eyes. The silence hung between us for a long moment, and when he spoke, his eyes dropped back to his hands. "You should..." He swallowed, jaw ticking. "You should leave me here for a couple of nights at *least*."

"I'm not going to do that," I said. "Ebony can be my vengeance hound." That was how he'd put it. My eyes drifted to the windowsill where the broken swan remained before I looked back to Love. "Frees me up for other things."

"Things like what, Princess?" he asked.

Fuck.

I gripped my sleeves in distress as that nickname did things to me. *"I don't know."*

But this was impossible. *How was I supposed to cope?*

I couldn't take my eyes off of him: pale skin, rippling muscle, and he was intimidatingly huge, he and Ebony had to be over six five. His raven braid hung over his shoulder, free wisps curling around his high cheekbones.

And he'd apologised to me.

And every day he was devoted to packing that with as much meaning as he could.

And he'd offered me a princess bond.

And now he was kneeling at my bedside, all *'your wish is my command'*, sinful and devastating.

And Drake was going to walk in any moment, and then I'd have to explain it all.

NINETEEN

VEX

Drake walked in to find me happily hugging a mound of pillows as Love gave me a back massage. A rom com played on the huge screen on the far wall, and I'd switched to a tank top and shorts to make the massage easier (but Love still insisted on being topless).

"The lasagna?" Love asked.

Drake dropped down onto the bed beside us with a sigh. "It's *possible* I'm spoiled and out of practice. I blame you. Ordered in instead."

Drake glanced a few times between us and the rom com, and I noticed him shifting a little closer as if curious.

"You've never asked me to give you massages," he said. I could swear his voice was wounded.

"I was coerced," I replied. Though, I couldn't say this wasn't nice. It was very nice, and Love's scent had shifted into something pleased, which was undeniably charming.

"Coerced?" Love asked with a chuckle. "You are the one in control here, Princess. You could command me to stop, and I'd go back to kneeling at your bedside, waiting to be whatever you wanted."

"Love!" I glanced at Drake in horror as heat rushed places it had no right to. He was frozen, staring between the both of us.

"Lead of the Crimson Fury pack," he went on. "And you could use me however you wanted."

A whine slipped from my chest, and *fuck me*, I knew my scent had just hit the room like an aphrodisiac. My eyes darted again to the side, locking with Drake, who was still fixated on me instead of the movie. There was a part to his lips, and something feral burned in his eyes.

That didn't help.

That didn't help one bit.

Love shifted forward, voice just a breath in my ear. "Is this too much for you?"

"I…" I swallowed. Fuck. Slick had pooled between my legs. I couldn't look at Drake right now, though I could feel his gaze scorching me. The air was thick with blackcurrant wine and vanilla winter, each edged with want, and my hormones were responding in kind.

"Are you *trying* to turn me on?" I whispered.

He leaned very close to my ear, speaking just for me. "Maybe I'm putting on a show for Drake." His touch slid to my hips, fingers curling around to my inner thigh as he pulled me back against him.

"I did *not* command you to do that," I whined.

"Actually." His breath was hot on my neck. "When I asked what *kind* of massage you wanted, your words were, and I quote: *'I don't know, anywhere it's supposed to be good'*."

I actually shuddered as he lifted one hand and curled it around my neck, drawing me firmly against him. "Imagine what that could mean," he said. "What I could do to you?"

"Not that I'm complaining, but uh how did we get here?" Drake asked, dumbstruck.

"It was her idea."

"It was not," I whined. "He's *filthy*."

"And you," Drake's fingers tangled in mine, and all of a sudden I couldn't look away from him. "Don't seem particularly upset."

It was hard to be upset when Love's scent was like a blanket of need for *me*. He wanted *me*, and knowing that—feeling the truth behind the words he'd offered me the other day—it was like riding a high.

"Do you want him?" Love asked, thumb grazing my jaw.

A sound of desperation rose up my throat. "Yes," I whispered. I did.

I wanted them both, but Drake... even seeing the burning desire in his eyes right now, it was making me desperate.

"Do you... want to?" I knew he wanted to move slow, he'd told me that.

But Drake was shifting, and then his lips pressed to mine.

"I want you, Dreamgirl," he said, as he drew back. "There's never a moment I don't."

"Okay..." I was breathless as Love released me, but he drew my chin up to face him, eyes serious. "You'll say if there was any reason you didn't want to keep going?"

I stared at him, parsing through that before settling on the cold and obvious truth. He was scared that there might be trigger commands from Zeus.

I shook my head, making doubly sure the bond was shut down tight. "You don't need to worry," I whispered. "I promise."

Not tonight.

Not for Love or for Drake.

I could see his uncertainty, though. I didn't know how much a promise was worth, not when it came to a dark bond.

But what could I say so he understood?

That I want this? I'd already said that.

So instead, I met his eyes, fingers cupping his cheeks. "I'm not afraid," I said. "But I thought maybe... I want you to hold me, so he can touch me, but I can't touch him. If... if that's best?" I glanced at Drake, I wanted to give him that option. It was our first time, but truly his first time with intimacy like this. Before, when I'd given him control, it had made him feel safe. He had a half smile on his face as he tucked my hair behind my ear.

"Are you sure you'd be okay with—?" Drake began.

"It would be... really hot..." My cheeks blazed again at the thought of being trapped between them. Of Drake taking me while Love held me.

"Your wish is my command," Love said, repositioning me between his legs, so I was facing Drake, who was staring at me with a burning expression.

Love's knuckle brushed my cheek, a gentle caress that trailed so slowly down to my neck. My veins lit with fire at how his fingers paused at my chest, nearing my nipple. He hovered there for a long moment, tracing the area and making me wriggle in his grip. He clamped down on my hip, holding me tighter with a chuckle.

I was reminded of the first night I met him, when I'd teased him with a kiss.

There had been fire between us. Something real.

Then he reached down and tugged my shirt up and over my head so I was seated between his legs in nothing but my shorts and panties. He secured my arms behind my back with only one of his, so I was held on display for Drake.

"Do you need to be fucked, Princess?" Love growled. His free hand slid down my torso, brushing my nipple, and then slipping lower.

"Yes." My voice was nothing more than a desperate whine. I was heady with need, lust blitzing through every instinct.

All but one: With every scrap of power I had left to me, I held shut the bond I had with Zeus.

He wouldn't have this. None of them would.

"Are you sure?" Drake asked. "You want it like this?"

"You don't?" The question was an embarrassingly desperate plea. I gasped as Love's finger found my clit, every nerve set alight again.

"God yes, Vex. I just want you to be sure—"

"Drake!" I begged.

Then he was there, right before me with blazing violet eyes, and I moaned as I felt his hands running up my body right as Love slipped a finger into me.

I was shivering with relief as he pulled my shorts and panties down before tugging his clothes off. Then, palming his rigid cock with one hand, he dropped his other hand between my thighs and, along with Love, slid two fingers into my centre, gaze pinned on me as I moaned again, arching against him.

Slick pooled between their fingers pumping slowly into me with two different rhythms. I bucked against Love's grip, far too desperate, a feral sound loosing from my chest.

"Fuck her," Love commanded.

"You're terrible at not being in charge," I breathed. Love chuckled, and I felt his kiss on my temple.

Then Drake shifted and I let out a breath of relief as he repositioned me easily, lifting my hips enough so my legs could straddle his. His girth pressed against my entrance. Then he bowed over me, pressing his lips to mine. I couldn't move an inch between Drake's hold on my hips, and Love, who still had my arms behind my back. I arched, letting out low needy sounds as Love began circling my clit, and Drake nudged my entrance again. My slick made the movement easy, and still, I let out a whine of shock at how big he felt.

He lingered there, stretching me out, and then slid in with a groan, filling me completely, his tip brushing that spot that was making me see stars, before pulling out and pressing back in, tongue driving deep into my mouth as he did.

"You're taking him so well, beautiful," Love murmured.

The sounds I was making as Drake rocked into me were nothing short of completely wild. I couldn't take my eyes from him. The way his expression creased with pleasure with every thrust, neck muscles tense, low sounds of pleasure rising in his chest.

The air was a tangle of their intoxicating scents.

My mates.

"Let her go," Drake breathed at last.

I blinked up at him, eyes wide. Love was releasing me, though, and then Drake shifted, moving me with him. Then he was pressed over me, one hand taking mine and holding it against his chest.

"I want *all* of you, Vex."

"You're sure?" I whispered.

"I am," he breathed. I saw his eyes flick to Love for half a moment. "We're safe, Dreamgirl." His fingers bit down on my hips and I groaned as he held me still, drawing out and driving back into my core. I arched against him, eyelids fluttering, groaning as I felt the base of his knot press against me.

"I want you to be my first," I whispered.

He paused for a moment, surprised.

"You've never...?" Again, I shifted up against his knot, just enough to feel the stretch, then shook my head. I'd *dreamed* of knots—what omega didn't? But I'd never fucked an alpha before. I'd been too nervous, worried about attachments or claims I couldn't control.

"You don't think I'd take your first without giving you one of mine?" I asked.

His smile was dazzling.

I wanted all of *him.*

Then he shifted us so I was on top, hands pressed to his chest to keep myself steady. I cupped his face, sinking back over him and loving how his teeth caught his lip with the pleasure of that.

We were both panting, right at the edge of a climax. I returned to the pace we were at before, each time letting his knot press against me, not even trying to control the sounds I was making as it did.

And I knew when it was the right moment. Drake tensed, grip on my waist becoming vice-like.

I reached out for Love, too, needing him. He was there, fingers winding gently through my hair, helping me stay steady as I trembled, one hand on Drake's chest, the other twined in Love's.

One more stroke, and Drake groaned, straining to hold back.

"Take him, Princess." Love's voice was low in my ear, his fingers slipped to the back of my neck, hand almost large enough to circle it entirely. "I want to see the moment you take his knot."

Again, I stretched over him, wanting this to last forever right at the edge of ecstasy as I got lost in violet galaxies. "I love you," I whispered.

I heard the sound of Drake's growl as I pressed down over the base of his knot, a noise of shock slipping from my chest as our bodies locked.

"Fuck." Drake groaned, gripping me mercilessly as he rocked into me. "I love you too, Dreamgirl." I felt the heat of his seed filling me as I moaned, the orgasm sending me into oblivion.

TWENTY

LOVE

Vex was everything.

We were in a nest of raspberry treacle so sweet it put to shame every dessert I'd ever tasted. And right now, I couldn't look away from her pretty golden eyes, glittering in the dim light of the room as she stared at me.

Drake was beneath her, still locking her in place, a low rumbling purr in his chest that I could see was soothing her as much as it was keeping her turned on.

She wore nothing, bare skin glowing beneath the warm light of the Edison bulbs I'd hung above us.

"Love?" she whispered.

There was something needy in her voice.

She was my undoing, I already knew that. But hearing her whine my name with desperate eyes fixed on me, as her body still trembled from the orgasm Drake had given her...

Fuck.

They were connected right now, she was locked against him, trapped by his knot.

It was impossible not to think about that as I straightened, reaching out and cupping her flushed cheek. She nuzzled into my touch, golden eyes not leaving mine for one moment. Then her teeth grazed my thumb before she took it between her lips.

I groaned, moving closer. I was careful, though, positioning myself at her side, while not imposing on Drake's space. This was more than I'd expected from him already—not that I'd planned any of tonight—aside kneeling for her. But if I had, I wouldn't have assumed Drake would be willing to take this step with me here.

With Vex, he was different. I could feel it from him through the bond, nerves scattering in the face of her passion—and not just her passion for him. It had happened before that even, when she was opening up to me; he was deciding to trust where she decided to trust.

He spared my movement only the slightest glance. I felt the shift in him only because I was searching. It was fleeting like a missed heartbeat: just the faintest flutter of anxiety. But then he relaxed palms resting on her hips as his eyes traced her body reverently. "You want him too, Dreamgirl?"

I tilted her chin up so she was still staring at me, lips pressed around my thumb.

"Are you sure you want to test me right now Princess, while you're trapped?" I asked, free hand closing around her hips and drawing her back just a fraction. I felt the resistance, and she let out a little moan, eyelids fluttering, and her body shifted back instinctively as she locked herself back over his knot.

Drake groaned, too, and I could only imagine how it would feel if her perfect body was squeezing *me* like that.

Clearly, her vulnerability was only turning her on more.

The nip I got from her was impatient, and I felt her wriggle against him.

I was rock hard at the thought of it, but I didn't think... not yet. I wasn't ready to take this step, even if she was. There was still too much I hadn't made up for.

And it wasn't just her.

Drake never spoke about his trauma, but there were some things in a bond that were hard to miss. I was quite sure a large part of why we'd been safe to him was because we were easily distinguishable from his past. Sharing Vex, however, complicated that.

I didn't want even the faintest shadow of anything uncomfortable tonight. It could be good in one moment, and ruined the next.

Still, I would let none of that stand in the way of their pleasure, not when she was trembling between us, begging for more. I could watch her come apart a thousand times and never be bored.

"Tonight, Princess, you belong to him." I dragged her back a fraction, loving her little moan as she struggled from my grip, body clenching over his knot again. Drake tensed beneath her.

I ran my touch around her hips and down her stomach to her clit. "But that doesn't mean I can't find all the ways I can get that pretty little body of yours to squeeze him."

She let out a moan as I played with her, and now I was looking for it, I could see the moment she tightened over him again. "Good girl," I breathed, then I drew my touch away, pleased at her needy little breaths. Instead, I cupped her neck, enjoying the breathy sound she made as I squeezed just tight enough that she would feel it.

"Fuuuck," Drake hissed, jaw clenched as her grip jumped to my arm. "God, that's hot, Vex."

She was breathing heavily now, and I wanted to see her climax again.

My free hand dropped to her nipple and I twisted just hard enough to get another whine and full body response. Drake's breathing was as heavy as hers was.

"You shouldn't dare me to play while you're so vulnerable," I breathed in her ear. "Can we get him to fill you again?" I flicked her nipple and squeezed her neck once more.

She moaned and I was rewarded by a new, desperate sound from her. I knew she had a beautiful voice, but no one could have prepared me for the way those sounds came out in the bedroom, sweet as a birdsong. And fuck me if it didn't make me reconsider every thought I'd had about taking it slow.

What I did next wasn't planned. Actually, it was a moment of pure madness.

I leaned close, sweeping her hair around her neck then froze, mind momentarily wiped blank.

It was the first time I'd ever seen it properly: the bite that leeched darkness across her skin like ink.

There was one moment of ice-cold fury. One moment in which all of my instincts flared, seeing another alpha's bite on her. It was, right before my eyes, the thing that stood in my way, that gave all the power I should have to another pack.

A humiliating weakness.

Failure.

I shoved away every doubt, fear, and inadequacy, instead, doing the thing that appalled every instinct and sent a shiver down my spine.

I pressed my teeth over that very bite.

My burden, not hers.

Never hers.

My bite wouldn't do anything, it couldn't—I could no more form a bond with her than she could accept one, but when she came apart this time, it was different. Drake had reacted quickly, as if he'd known what I was going to do. Pushing himself upright, he cupped her cheek in his palm, directing her eyes to him as she trembled in my grip. The sound she made was half pleasure, half shock as she melted between us.

I felt a thousand things in that moment: my own shame and doubt, my need to fix this—to protect her. I felt Drake's love for her like it was my own, a breath of air after drowning, something pure, true and guiltless.

And I felt her too, I felt her want for me: a desperate need amidst darkness, but that part was a piece my mind conjured, perhaps in a cry for validation at what I'd just done.

After, she lay against Drake's chest, breathing heavily, eyes squeezed shut.

I think...

I think I'd fucked up.

There was something wrong.

When he finally released her, she grabbed her shirt and hurried to the bathroom.

Shit.

Shit.

I tugged on my braid anxiously, internally kicking myself. Drake was staring at the bathroom door, a frown on his face.

Too long passed.

"That was..." I swallowed, rubbing my face. *"Shit."*

It had been instinct, raw and real, and yet... I don't know how she felt.

I hadn't meant to upset her. In the moment it felt like a gift, but in hindsight, it was sort of fucked up. And it wasn't like she could read my mind. It was supposed to be a sacrifice of my pride, but perhaps... Had she thought I was shaming her?

When the bathroom door finally creaked open. She didn't appear in the frame straight away.

When she did, she hurried across the room to stand in front of me. She wore one of her cute oversized tops with the lyrics embroidered on the sleeves (which she clutched desperately as she stared at me), and her eyes were undeniably red-rimmed.

Fuck.

"I... I'm s—" I cut off as her hand snapped to my mouth, and there was a flash of that fire in her eyes even as her lip trembled. Then she clambered into my arms, her back against my chest, and she drew my embrace around her like a blanket. Her face was buried in the crook of my arm, so not even Drake could see her expression.

Then, I felt the heat of what I knew had to be tears against my skin. I didn't have time for doubt, though, because at the same time her purr rumbled to life, and it was enough to obliterate every one of my fears.

TWENTY-ONE

ROOK

> Me: does your gold pack friend have any advice for me? I need to know how not to fuck this up.

In desperation, I'd sent Prey the text. She'd been at the Gala with that gold pack—the one who'd read me the riot act over bedding fabrics.

> Prey: I'm not going to lie, her experiences aren't exactly conventional.

> Me: I'll take anything.

> Prey: Alright. I'll forward you her responses, idk how useful they'll be.

Next, I'd received what might have been the strangest lists of dos and don'ts I'd ever read.

1. Never ever ever ever tell her she can't have waffles.

2. Ever.

3. Hide your suits if you do. But don't.

4. If you put a gun to your own head, make her hold it and tell her she can pull the trigger, she'll trust you forever.

5. Escort her in all elevators.

6. Make sure she knows her eyes are pretty.

7. Give her a princess bond. She'll really like it.

8. Don't try to torture her, but if you must, then make sure to crack like a big baby and hold her all protectively in the shower afterwards. She'll love it if you cry too, but some of my alphas aren't very good at that.

9. Giving her a big red button to blow up buildings owned by baddies is also good (if there's no one inside), but don't lie to her about if there's someone inside.

10. Do not unknowingly take her virginity with hate sex. It might sound hot, but my alpha's never recovered so I don't recommend. Though he's really into the praise and worshippy stuff now so I don't know if he broke in a bad way (???). Maybe do it.

I read it four times, but I don't know if it helped. Maybe I really did have a lot to learn about omegas.

. . .

> Me: Well, that's fucked up.

> Me: Was the gun loaded?

There was a pause.

Prey: she says yes.

> Me: Damn.

So, I'd spent the rest of the day back at the drawing board. That evening, however, I'd felt something through the bond I couldn't escape.

Naturally, I'd grabbed a bottle of whiskey and got piss drunk.

I found Leighton working late in the office downstairs, a notebook at her side, and laptop open. "Do you need something?" she asked without sparing me a look.

"They're banging her." I slumped down on an office chair two down from her, setting the whiskey bottle down before me. "They're banging her, and she still fucking *hates* me."

Leighton didn't pause her work. "Get out."

Uh... who the fuck did she think she was?

"This is *my* house. I can... I can go wherever I want," I told her, trying to keep my voice steady.

Her response was to open her phone and type something out.

"Do you have an omega?" I asked.

She sighed, eyes finally flickering up to me for just a second, before returning to her work.

"Of course you do," I snorted. No way Ebony would let her step foot in this house if she was unbonded. "What do you do when you fuck things up with him?"

"Her."

"Oh..." I rested my head on the back of the chair with a sigh. "What do you do when you mess up? When you... fuck shit up... with her, you know?"

She raised an eyebrow at me with a cold smile. "I wouldn't know."

"Ah. You do look..." I waved at her clean dress suit with a vague gesture. "So... *perfect*."

She spared me one blank look, then returned to her laptop.

I sighed, larger this time. "Apparently, she didn't like the pity party I threw for myself."

"Right," she said, mildly, continuing to type. "Because there's nothing in the world that screams alpha more than a pity party."

I grinned bitterly, raising the bottle to her before taking another sip.

"So you went and threw yourself another one." Her words were so quiet I almost missed them.

I straightened, a sneer on my face at the challenge. "What would you know?" I asked. "You don't have a clue what we've been through."

"I know what she's been through," Leighton finally fixed me with a derisive glare. "Tell me, what did *you* go through?"

"My scent match was bitten by another pack."

"Poor you. Especially when that little black book of hers made it clear you cared about her so *deeply* before you knew she was your mate."

That drew me up. "You read it?"

"How do you expect anyone to help without all of the information?" she asked.

"Why *did* Ebony's dad pick *you*?" I asked.

"Ebony believed Vex had too many arrogant men interfering in her life already."

"Really?" I straightened, shock breaking through the whiskey haze.

That was... thoughtful of Ebony. Unexpected.

"No," Leighton sighed, rolling her eyes. "I'm here because I'm the best, you drunken idiot—and you're wasting my *very* valuable time, which I should be spending on *your* omega."

I wrinkled my nose hatefully, but a low chuckle from the door drew up any response. I directed my scowl at Ebony instead, catching the irritating scent of twilight fucking grass. "The fuck are you doing here?"

"She texted," he said, looking down at his phone, reading from it. *"I don't work in environments with pests."* He grinned. "Figures." He grabbed me by the arm and dragged me to my feet.

We were almost at my room when I tried to rip away from him, turning to the hallway. "I think... I should go and find her and tell her—"

"No." Ebony was in my face in a second. "You're not ruining her night with your drunken idiocy."

I wrinkled my nose, but I could barely see straight by this point, and he was probably right.

"Are you going to... tuck me in?" I asked with a hiccup as he shoved me onto the bed.

"What are these?" he asked, ignoring me as he sifted through the books still open on my duvet.

"Books on omegas... I got them today... I thought I could... I don't know... maybe do something fucking right. Then I realised that's stupid, and I'd screw it all up anyway, so, you know..." I lifted the whisky bottle. I wasn't going to admit to him I was drunk because I knew they were banging her.

Sickness turned my stomach as I thought of the parts in those books I'd read about the way omegas felt about their scent matched alphas.

A feeling of attachment like no other...

Sensitive to rejection...

Benefit from re-enforcement via action and words...

I took another long swig. Ebony picked one up, and a growl was up my throat before I could stop it. "They're mine!" I lunged for him, heart suddenly in my throat.

I needed them.

I needed... *anything* that might mean I could give something to her that wouldn't blow up in her face.

Not going to happen...

Ebony's lip curled as he stared down at me, but then his eyes fell on my nightstand and he tossed the book back on my bed, crossing toward it.

"You stole from her dream board?" he snarled, picking up the photograph I'd left there.

"No!" I was on my feet in a second, hand closing around his wrist. "I was going to give it back!"

We were both frozen for a moment, staring down at the selfie of Vex hugging Aisha in a park.

"Please don't tell her," I rasped. "I'll give it back, I swear."

He didn't move, and I still couldn't take my eyes from the picture.

"Do you think... is it real?" I asked.

"The dog?" Ebony asked.

"No—*her.*"

"What do you mean?"

"She's always smiling in those pictures. But I just... I don't know if it's real."

"What makes you say that?"

"Because... she had nothing. You saw her place. She... she had nothing."

Ebony was looking at me like I was mad, and it took me a second to realise I was asking the wrong person.

But... I didn't need him. In a way, she'd answered it herself. She'd answered it in blood, in words that couldn't have been a lie.

Dear Rook: For one second, I thought I was safe. You ruined it. Sometimes, you remind me of him. I didn't come for your money or your fame. I came for you. I hate you for not seeing that. I hate you. I want to.

But I'm not even strong enough for that.

I didn't understand.

Would it have been wrong for her to come for what I had, when she had so little? Would I have done that, if our roles were switched?

Ebony dropped the picture back on my nightstand. "Give it back tomorrow." He stepped away, clearly about to leave.

"She said... she said in those notes... she said she didn't hate me," I said. He paused, turning back to me. "I can't... I can't get it out of my head... That's how sweet she is, you know?" I hiccupped again, more violently. "And she is so good... So sweet and caring and *didn't* hate me so much that... that she wrote it down."

"I know, I read them—"

"No. You don't. *Every* word was a choice... And she bled to..."

Oh *fuck*.

Tears were burning my eyes. In front of Ebony. Not that I

could stop fucking talking anyway. "She... she bled to say she didn't hate me."

"I don't think that means what you think it means."

"It means she's too good for me."

Ebony snorted. "I stand corrected."

"You know the difference between what she wrote about me, and what she wrote about all of you?" I asked. "I didn't get it at first, why she didn't want my apology, when she let Love in. And then I realised... well... she'd told me—it just took a little time to piece it together. And now... now I can't stop thinking about it."

Ebony paused, genuinely curious. "What?"

"She was wrong about what she was afraid of with you, with Love—even the like... six fucking syllables she wrote for Drake. But for me?"

He stared at me, brows furrowed.

"She was right..." I felt the crushing truth of that. My face must have gone a sickly shade because, with a disgusted look on his face, Ebony dumped one of my garbage bins and tossed it at me. I stared into its black depths, next words echoing. "She *is* enough for Love, you *do* want to protect her, and Drake does want her. But me? I don't think... I don't think she knows that I'm..."

Fuck. Me.

My voice shook. "I don't think she knows if I'm different from the fucking pricks who bit her."

I didn't know if I was different.

Ebony was staring at me.

"I want you to prove my fears wrong, not give me more," I said.

"What?" he asked.

"That's... that's what she said to me, when she was throwing my apology back in my face—rightfully, obv-obviously. It's why she can... she can look at you. It's why she can't look at me."

"Are you done?" Ebony asked, folding his arms.

"I think so?"

He turned to leave again. Probably good. I was never going to live this down.

"You know... It was like... I could feel her tonight."

Ebony paused, glancing back at me.

"That was one hell of an orgasm from Drake. It was like... like I could feel her with them in the bond."

Ebony didn't say anything, but he stared at me with eyes narrowed. Finally, he made to leave again.

"You're... doing things to make shit better for her," I asked. "Right?"

He didn't look back.

"Let me... let me help."

"Not a chance in hell, Harrison."

"Just... give me something to fucking do."

"Go find your own shit to do," he said before slamming the door.

EBONY

Trying to burn Rook's pathetic sobbing face from my brain, I returned to the office where Leighton was working.

My contact, the one helping me orchestrate the fireworks I had planned for next week, had put me in touch with the man that could make it happen.

> Unknown: We want the same thing. I can give you what you need, locations, names, places.

> Me: If we want the same thing and you have that, why do you need me?

> Unknown: I need what you have.

Me: What's that?

Unknown: I know the Gritch, you know the topsiders.

Me: But you still want the favour.

Unknown: you get nothing without it.

"What is it?" Leighton asked She looked about to pack up her stuff.

Most of her work she could do remotely, but it helped to reconvene occasionally. Soren was right, she was good.

"It's a job."

"What kind of job?"

"I've got to set up a..." I peered down at my phone. "A two-hour security blackout in the East Centennial Institute building," I said. "And a guy to get in and out with something small."

I had no idea why that's what he needed, and frankly, I didn't care. I'd get it organised, and never think on it again. Then he'd give me what I needed for Vex.

She considered me. "You're aware of the kind of resources that will take? Even your leverage on Soren—"

"I have the blackout covered." That was the sort of thing money could buy if you knew where to look. People on the ground, that wasn't where I excelled, and where my dear father did—Leighton was a testament to that. "All I need is someone who can get in and out of an Institute building during the blackout without drawing attention."

Leighton tilted her head, considering. "That, I can get you no problem at all."

Good.

Another thing sorted.

Shutting the phone off, I headed back to my room. I was on edge, and it wasn't hard to identify why. It was *great* that Drake and Love were having sex with my—*our*—omega. I winced.

Really, *really* fucking great.

But it was just damned distracting.

Strangely, though, I agreed with Rook. I had thought—for just the faintest moment—I could feel her. Impossible. Except, unlike Rook's wishful thinking, I hadn't the imagination to conjure up what a force like Vex might be like in this bond. Yet, I could still feel her like light burned behind my eyelids upon a blink.

The phone on my desk buzzed.

A text from Vex's phone, the one I'd copied.

I read it and reread it a dozen times, grappling with my side of the bond so that neither Love nor Drake would feel my fury.

> Pack Lead: If you ever let something like that happen again, I swear I'll find a way to kill you myself you filthy rat.

A *death* threat? From her own pack lead? There was no way it was real—even if he could kill her, it would be suicide for his pack bond.

No.

I didn't think this was a true threat at all. It was an alpha's aggression. He was angry—*furious*—at something that had just happened.

I stared at the text for far too long.

There were a few things about it that stuck out as odd.

The first, and most obvious: the language made it clear he wasn't a rogue, or there wouldn't be a question as to whether he could kill her.

Second, the phrase 'something like that' didn't fit if he was referring to her being intimate with us. *Sex*, they had to have anticipated between scent matches. They would either accept it, or they would have given her commands surrounding it. This text was referring to something unexpected.

What could Vex, Love or Drake have done to get a response like that?

Finally, the last thing that stuck out was the death threat itself. The part that turned my world red with every re-read.

'I'll find a way to kill you myself'.

Those words held a darker truth: Vex's execution had already been discussed.

After an age of staring at it in silence, I took a breath, then screenshotted the text and sent it to Leighton. She was creating a bullet proof legal defence for my actions protecting Vex. A death threat on my mate was just another thing added to the arsenal of things to justify what I might be forced to do if it came to it. It was becoming more clear by the day, how necessary that might be.

I was about to forward the message to Vex's duplicate phone, when I hesitated.

In my mind's eye, I saw the flash of colour and life and freedom that I'd thought, for a moment, had *been* her in this bond with me.

Slowly, I tucked the phone back in my pocket.

I would forward it—I *had* to.

But it could wait until the morning.

VEX

When I woke up in the morning, my pack bond with the Lightning pack was still... off. Like an open live wire that occasionally sparked.

Last night, after Love had pressed his teeth to my bite, I stood, trembling in the bathroom, fingers gripping the counter, warring with fury. It had been white hot, frightening, and absolutely not mine: Zeus's furor was such that it was as if he was physically present beside me.

It had been unconscious, but when Love's teeth had found my neck, I had reached out to him. Like a bird taking flight as if there were no bars in the way, I had tried to say yes to his offer.

To his bond.

To his pack.

And the following collision had rattled my cage with a ferocity I was still feeling the tremors of.

The dark bond between me and the pack that sought to chain me had opened. It had been the only moment in my life in which I didn't regret them being with me: as I tumbled over that cliff, with Love's teeth at my neck.

Now, I woke to his purr at my back, and a sense of safety I had never felt before. No bond he offered could last, but this moment would.

I was scared of the fury waiting for me. But now I was sure. *I* had chosen in defiance in a world that sought to rip choice from me. And this time it hadn't been a choice of fear or desperation.

The bite on my neck still held power, but it was no longer my only truth.

Love wasn't just my mate or my alpha.

Love was *my* pack lead.

TWENTY-TWO

Chia pet's 3rd day of life. Hair length: 0cm
  Days until execution: 6 days

ROOK

I pulled up before a rather dull-looking apartment building—if a little less broken down than the one Vex had lived in.

We weren't all that far away from Vex's old residence, but those few blocks did wonders for changing the kind of characters I was seeing on the street. From here, I could see a few kids shooting hoops, and groups of teens clustered around a mom-and-pop pizza joint.

I wouldn't let that fool me, though. I was sure I would find nothing good in the home I was about to visit.

I'd woken this morning with a splitting headache, and discovered that in a drunken stupor, I'd taken Ebony's suggestion to heart. I was going to find my own way to help Vex.

So, I'd texted Gambit (after previously stealing his number from Drake) a rather dramatic message trying to convince him to accept any help at all. I stood by one thing: he *was* Vex's friend, and we hadn't done enough. It was the only thing I could offer her right now without making things worse.

To my utter shock, he'd replied.

I peered up at the apartment building from the windscreen of Drake's van, double checking it was right. Then I scrolled through my conversation again.

> Gambit: What kind of help are you offering?

> Me: Name it.

> Gambit: Like... we talking money?

> Me: What do you need?

> Gambit: There's just this one debt I can't cover. If I get it managed then I'm set.

> Me: What is it and how much?

> Gambit: 10k, but I've saved 1.5 already.

I'd stared at that for a long time. 10k was nothing. If that's all it took to set him on the right path then I could do that today. Gambit was in need, and I had more than I knew what to do with.

> Me: I can cover it all, just tell me how.

After that, he'd asked me to write a cheque to a *'Kit Miller'* and given me an address to mail it to.

I'd come in person, though. He hadn't told me what it was for, but I couldn't imagine it was anything good. I wasn't stupid enough not to realise 10K was a big deal in places like this. I wanted to give it to them directly and make it clear that whoever it was, that they were to leave him alone after.

My hood was up and I had a cloth mask covering my face from the nose down. The only thing they'd know about me was that I was an alpha. I had the height and build to be intimidating, but just in case, I'd tucked a gun into my satchel as I ducked out of the van.

I headed up the steps to find the buzzer system was broken, though the front doors were unlocked, and I got to the second floor without any difficulty.

I located number 214, then paused for a moment, taking a breath as peeling paint and worn wallpaper stared back at me. I'd be in and out. I just wanted them to see me so they knew Gambit had people in his corner.

I lifted my hand and knocked loudly.

My heart raced and I realised this might be a really stupid plan.

But what else did I have left?

Ebony had told me to find something to do, so I had. I was done hurting Vex. If I could make *this* right, well... that was something.

It was a start.

The door opened, and I tensed, senses on high alert. But instead of thugs like I was expecting, I was looking down at a small beta woman holding a wooden spoon in a faded apron. In her hair were specks of grey, but the auburn beneath matched Gambit's perfectly. Instantly, I caught the smell of something delicious and savoury in the air.

The woman frowned as she saw me, then took a small step back.

I released the death grip I had on the satchel, realising how threatening I might look, tense as I was.

"How can I help you?" she asked, worry lines creasing her forehead. She had green eyes that were as kind as they were tired.

"I..." I wasn't sure what to say. A motherly looking woman in a dusty apron wasn't what I had expected at all.

A child who looked to be no more than ten poked her head

around the woman. She, too, had bright green eyes, auburn hair and a scattering of freckles just like Gambit.

Was this... his *family*?

The woman caught the kid with her arm just as she tried to step toward me, a curious look in her eyes.

"Go help Kit serve up," she said sternly, though she didn't take her gaze from me as the child darted away.

"Kit..." I said, and the woman's eyebrows rose. "I'm here for a Kit Miller?"

The woman folded her arms. "And what do you want with her?"

Her?

"I... I have something from... from Gambit."

Her eyes went wide. "You... you know my Gambit?" The spoon almost slipped from her grip.

"I... yes," I said, not sure what to make of that.

"Do you know where he is?" she asked. "Here, here come in!" Before I knew it, she had me by the arm and was hauling me into the little apartment. I was met by a small coat area, which was scattered with jackets, coats, and shoes of all sizes.

"You don't know where he is?" I asked. Gambit's place *must* be within walking distance of here.

She glanced at me, something wounded in her eyes, but she didn't reply as she ushered me past the messy coat room and into the main house.

"Here, don't worry about the shoes. Come in, come in. Gambit's friends are always—"

"Gambit?" someone asked.

I was assaulted by chaos as I stepped into the tiny home. It was a boxy room with kitchen, living room, and dining room in one, and it was bustling with life. There was a steaming pot on the stove, which looked to be the source of the homey smell of chilli. Bags, clothing, stacks of paper—a lot of *things* were crammed everywhere. The old wooden dining table could barely fit the seats around it, and there were quite a few more people than should fit in a space as small as this.

"We're just about to serve up," the woman told me. "You'll join us," she added. I opened my mouth to argue, but she was already pointing her spoon at each of the room's occupants—all of whom looked like replicas of Gambit at different ages—and all female. "This is Kit, Petal, Justine, May, and..." She frowned, eyes narrowing as she glanced around the room. Then she shouted, voice sharp enough to make me jump. "*Layla!* It's supper, *how* many times have I asked? Oh—" She turned to me with a smile. "And I'm Terra."

Kit, I noted, was the oldest aside Terra, and looked to be in her early twenties. She was clutching a stack of bowls, but was frozen as she stared at me.

"Did you say Gambit?" she asked again.

"Yes," Terra said. "This is Gambit's friend, uh..." She looked at me expectantly.

"You don't know his name?" Kit hissed.

"I was about to ask," Terra said, affronted.

"You can't just invite strange alphas in without—"

"Gambit's friend!" Terra snapped. Then looked at me with the same fierce expression and raised eyebrows.

"I'm... Rook," I said before I could catch myself. I hadn't considered a fake name, just as I hadn't anticipated being swept into a family home and offered dinner. "But I shouldn't stay," I said as Terra began setting the cramped table for another.

"Nonsense." She waved a hand. "My son's friend coming over and not staying for supper? I won't have it said of me."

I swallowed, looking back around. Kit was still watching me, as were a few of the others with wide eyes, though the youngest, Petal, who barely reached my thigh, had returned to her colouring book.

"Gambit's friend?" Kit finally managed to ask. "Or...?" She trailed off.

"Or what?" Terra asked, glancing back between us.

Justine, the kid who'd appeared at the front door, was edging up to me, her eyes still wide. "He's an alpha, Momma," she said. She reached out and poked my leg.

"Justine—!"

"You're an alpha, right?" she asked, her voice a loud whisper.

I nodded with a smile, though she wouldn't see it through the mask.

"You smell like candy," Justine said, stepping right up to me confidently.

"Thank you."

"I know he's a..." Terra trailed off, then she blinked, gaze snapping back to me. "Wait. You're not...?"

"Oh..." I realised what she was saying. "No. No, Gambit's not pack. He uh... he knows my omega." I almost winced as I said that, knowing how little I deserved to call Vex mine.

"Ah..." Terra said. "Well. Good. I mean, of course. He'd not bond to a pack without..." She patted down her apron anxiously, looking around the room as if searching for something, a glaze in her eyes.

It was at that moment a gangly teen—Layla, so I assumed—slouched into the room, eyes fixed on an old gaming console in her hands. She drew up a few steps in, however, and looked up, staring at me in confusion. "Uh... What's going on?"

"We're serving dinner," Terra said pointedly. "And we have a guest, so put the game away and don't be rude."

Next thing I knew, Terra was at my side again, hustling me to the table and almost manhandling me into a seat. "No allergies, dear?" she asked.

"No, but I really—"

"Good, good. You'll like it. Gambit's favourite. Afterwards, you can give us what he sent."

"Gambit sent something?" Petal asked, looking up from her colouring book.

"Yes, yes. But let's eat."

Around me, the room came to life as bowls were passed to Kit, and demands were made for serving amounts.

"I can uh... help—" I began.

"Don't be silly," Terra said as she set a bowl of chilli and cornbread before me. "Drink?" she asked, though she was already pouring me a glass of water and setting it down.

"Thank you," I said awkwardly.

Justine clambered into the chair on my one side, which caused a fight between her and May, who looked to be perhaps seven or eight, and wanted to sit next to 'Gambit's candy friend'. (They settled on surrounding me from both sides).

Kit was the last to sit, and I couldn't help noticing that she had a limp as she brought her bowl to the table to join us.

"Rook," May hissed, tugging on my arm and drawing my attention back to her. "How are you going to eat with a mask on?"

Ah. Shit.

In this sort of proximity they would likely recognise me instantly. I tugged my mask down quickly, sticking my spoon into my chilli and hoping not to draw much attention to myself. I had never been uncomfortable with fame until this moment, yet somehow it felt... wrong right now. As if it didn't have a place here. My fame had nothing to do with Gambit, or why I'd come, yet it still had the power to change everything about this moment.

And I realised I didn't want it changed.

I was met with a few double takes and a long silence.

By the end of it, everyone was staring.

Finally, it was broken by May, who let out a squeak of derision. "You *big fat liar!*" She jabbed her spoon into my tummy.

I raised my eyebrows, entirely unsure of what to make of that.

"Your name isn't Rook," she told me. "I know for a fact it's Danny Davis."

I bit back a smile, finding it easier to keep my gaze on her than the rest of the stares in the room.

"You... have me there," I said. Danny Davis was a racer I'd played in one of our earlier movies.

"Gambit's friend is a *race car driver?*" Petal, the youngest, asked, eyes wide.

"No, he's a film actor, you idiots," Justine countered.

"He's not!" May snapped. "And I'm not an idiot." She turned back to me. "Do you drive cars or do you... *film actor?*" she spat the last two words out like they were dirty.

"I, in fact, do both," I told her, fighting my grin.

She folded her arms and gave Justine a smug *I-told-you-so* look.

"Danny?" Petal asked me through a mouthful of cornbread, her eyes wide. "Did Gambit get *me* anything?"

"I'm afraid not. Just Kit," I said, and my chest tightened at the heartbroken look in her eyes. "This time, anyway. It's uh... Kit first since she's the oldest."

Even if Gambit wouldn't help me, I'd get gifts for the rest of them.

"Oh. Okay." She nodded to herself like that made sense. "Can you tell him I miss him?"

Terra's smile was tight as she pressed a kiss to Petal's head. "You can tell him we all do."

For the rest of the meal, no one mentioned my job once which I was grateful for. Terra tried, a number of times, to prod me for Gambit's address, but I kept it to myself. I'd ask him after, but if he hadn't given it to them, it must be for a reason.

Not a reason I could fathom.

There was life in this home that I'd never felt before, and

strangely, it didn't matter that it was small with rickety chairs and peeling wallpaper. The closest I'd ever come to existing in a place like this was in my movies.

My childhood dinners—if graced by anyone more than my mother—were cold and quiet and hosted across wide marble dining tables set by paid staff.

Even my relationships with my siblings were overshadowed by competition set on us by the expectations of elite pack parents. Ones who were far too busy to be present every day. Everything was framed by achievements and success.

You want for nothing, Rook. Do you know how many people in this world can say the same?

I'd doubted a thousand things in my life when it came to my own worth or success, but never before had I doubted the truth of those words, the pillar that held up everything I was taught. The cornerstone, the launch pad, the thing that gave me no excuses to be a failure, because *I'd wanted for nothing.*

You can be grateful by having something to show for it.

Where others had excuses, I had none, for there had been no need left unmet.

I'd had everything.

An absolute truth.

The very foundation of what I was.

A splintering crack, begun by Vex, followed by that book she'd filled, and finalised by this moment, fissured through the truth that I no longer could be sure was absolute at all.

I swallowed, shoving that away. I would... I would examine it later. Right now, I was desperate to fix things with Vex. I was a wreck. No conclusion I came to could be trusted.

I was quieter than usual, content to watch the dinner play out before me, not wanting to disturb it with what I had to offer.

Petal finished first and slipped from the table to grab her

colouring book. Then she clambered onto my lap and set it out to show me her scribbles.

"You're getting so good!" Justine told her. "I love the flower page."

"It is lovely, Petal," Terra said. "Keep it up."

I glanced at her and the warm smile she had for her daughter that looked so genuine.

"Do you like it?" Petal looked up at me with big green eyes.

"I..." I stared at the scribbles of colour.

It was terrible.

I've heard enough mediocrity, son. Don't waste my time until you can play well enough to be worthy of being remembered.

"It's..."

"Of course he does, honey. It's lovely."

But Petal was still staring up at me.

"I love it," I said, the words stiff.

"Do you think Gambit would like it?" she asked.

"I'm..." There was something stuck in my throat and I had to clear it. "I'm sure he would," I said.

"Okay..." She paused, and then she ripped the page out. "Here. It's for you, because you came and he didn't." I opened my mouth to refuse, but she looked almost angry at me, as if it was my fault Gambit wasn't here. Then she was furiously scribbling *'Dany Dayviss'* across the top and shoving it into my hand.

I thanked her, truly realising how odd it was, that I was here with his family, and I barely knew a thing about him.

After, when the table was cleared, Terra sent the others away to give us some space. It was only me, her, and Kit, who watched me wearily, as if she wasn't sure what to expect.

I fumbled in my satchel, making sure they didn't see the gun I'd brought—and thank god it wasn't loaded. When I straightened, envelope in hand, Terra placed her hand on my arm.

"Is he alright?" Terra asked me. "Is he safe? You'd tell me that, wouldn't you?" Her worry lines were back now the younger children weren't here.

"He... is." Well, not what I would quantify as safe, but he seemed to be managing.

I set the letter down and pushed it toward Kit. She opened it and looked inside. Her olive skin went ashen and her eyes went wide.

"I can't take this," she whispered, pushing it back toward me.

"It's from him, not me," I said, as Terra peered at it, and her face went white as a sheet.

"I won't cash it—"

"Kit..." Terra whispered. "You should..." Her eyes darted toward me. "You should think about it."

"I don't want the money," Kit said again. "I want him back. You can tell him that."

"Kit baby," Terra whispered. "You're in pain every day."

Kit's lip trembled. "I don't care. I w-won't take it."

"Don't take it," I said. "And I'll have to come back with a bag of cash."

"She *will* take it."

"Mom—"

"No. You'll take it and you'll get the surgery, honey. You're on your feet every day at that damned restaurant."—Terra turned to me sternly—"It's her leg that was hurt. But she *refused* to stop working after the injury, even when we can get by without—"

"We can't."

"Well, it's a non issue. You'll get the surgery, and your leg will be better—" Terra's voice shook a little "—And you can work yourself to the bone then, alright?"

Kit's jaw was clenched as she glared between us, and I thought the glittering tears in her eyes might be from fury, but she didn't argue when Terra pushed the check toward her.

"Just... you tell him to come *home*." Her voice broke with that last word.

I swallowed. "I'll do that."

Alone and back in Drake's minivan, I felt strangely... *something*.

Off.

Wrong in a way I couldn't put my finger on. I pulled my phone out to text Gambit, trying to ignore it.

> Me: Kit's mad at you. She says she'd rather have you back.

> Me: Why the fuck don't you want to see them?

> Gambit: You went to the house????

> Me: I dropped it off. Your mom fed me dinner.

> Gambit: For fucks sake.

> Gambit: Did you tell them where I was?

> Me: No. But I think you should.

My breathing was heavy as I typed it out, and I couldn't stop staring at my phone until his reply came in.

> Gambit: I can't.

I was already furiously tapping out my response when he replied again.

> Gambit: It's too dangerous.

I paused, staring at that, unsure of what it meant.

> Gambit: Kit needs that leg surgery because of me. We were out together when someone attacked me because of what I am.

I froze, staring at that reply, heart sinking in my chest. Omega or gold pack? Or perhaps both in a place like this.

> Gambit: We've never had anything but betas in the family. We weren't prepared for what happened.

I stared for another age, but he sent nothing else. I tucked my phone in my pocket and started the car. When I got home, and had thought about it, I typed out another reply.

> Me: I said I could help you get sorted. That didn't help you at all. Why did you ask me for this?

I'd looked at the text for too long, but then deleted it without sending it. I stormed up to my room, mind spiralling like it never had before.

Somehow, I didn't know what to do with myself. I felt like ants were crawling beneath my skin, making it impossible to sit still.

I pulled out the picture Petal had given me and placed it on the bed beside the picture of Vex and the open omega studies books. I stared down at them.

Something was wrong with me. I was shaking.

I crossed to my nightstand, a tremor in my hands as I picked up the trophy Vex had smashed. There was nothing left of it but the base and inscription on the plate.

'Enora Harrison, Radiant Aura Award, 1993'

My grandmother's. It was her fault I was here at all. That all of this had happened. I set the trophy down next to the two pictures, and finally my heart settled, if only a little.

Acting is not what it used to be. You were raised better, and if your grandmother keeps filling your head with shit about following your dreams, then you won't be seeing her any longer.

This was it. *These* things before me, they were what was wrong.

My gran had ruined me, Vex hated me—even when I had *everything* and she had *nothing*, and Gambit was a fucking prick for setting me up like that.

I grabbed Petal's picture. Vex had already broken the trophy—done the job for me. Finally, I could put my finger on what I was feeling.

I was... I was so angry. I was angry, and these—these stupid fucking things.

They were what was wrong.

My tremor got worse as I looked down at the picture. I'd lied to Petal. Had told her it was good. Only, I couldn't tear it. I couldn't move.

Furious, I found myself screaming at the stupid picture that I'd lied about. *"How does that help, if she wants to get better?"* Still, my hands shook as I tried to rip it. *"It fucking won't!"*

Anger blitzed through my system, trapped, unable to go anywhere, and I still couldn't move. My eyes fell on the picture of Vex, smiling. She shouldn't *be* smiling.

It was a lie.

It had to be a lie.

She had *nothing*.

It felt like my chest was caving in.

Why did it feel like my chest was caving in?

Only, I'd moved without realising, dropping the picture on the bed, and instead reaching my trophy cabinet. I had my own Diamond Tide's award in my hands, and finally, fucking *finally* it felt like I could move.

None of this was my problem.

None of it.

It wasn't my fault I'd scent matched to Vex or that I wasn't good enough for her. I hadn't signed up for that dinner—for seeing their fake fucking happiness in their house that was falling apart.

I hadn't signed up for any of it. Not their sad looks or lying about a five-year-old's shitty colouring.

"Now Petal is going to be mediocre for the rest of her *fucking life!*"—I flung the stupid trophy at the wall and watched as it exploded into a million pieces. *"And it's my fucking fault!"*

"Sweet mother above," a cool voice drawled from my doorway. "What the *fuck* is going on?"

I spun to see Ebony leaning against my door frame, eyebrows raised.

"I don't want to *fucking* deal with you right now!"

"Well too bad, because frankly there's nothing more interesting in my life right now than finding spoiled little Harrison screaming at his trophies before he *executes* them." He kicked the door shut behind him.

"I'm not fucking about Ebony. *Get. Out!*" I was on the brink of crossing toward him right now and putting him through the wall.

"Rook, you're a mess in the bond. Talk."

"Talk?" I asked with a breathless laugh. "To you?" Like *Ebony* fucking cared.

"It's either that or I knock you out before Love and Drake feel the need to poke their heads in. I won't have it getting back to Vex. She's still recovering from the last tantrum you threw."

I stared at him, a snarl on my lips. "I just... I don't *fucking* get it!"

"Get what?"

"I convinced Gambit to let me help him."

"Did you?" Ebony asked, looking genuinely curious. "And?"

"That's the fucking problem. I'd offered him anything in the world to help, and he sent me to give his sister money for surgery."

Next thing I knew I was seizing the next closest trophy I could find.

"And that... makes you angry enough to break your trophies?" he asked, as if I was genuinely posing him with an interesting puzzle.

"It's fucking *stupid!*" With a flare of my aura, I flung the trophy at the wall and watched it shatter.

"Is it?"

"He's a fucking idiot. I gave him a chance to get out and he blew it!" I threw another trophy and watched as it shattered. "What if I never offer again? What then? And instead of getting himself out, he sent me to have dinner with his sweet goddamned sisters who were missing him because he was too much of a *coward* to visit them!"

With another growl of rage, I sent another trophy from the shelf flying.

It wasn't enough.

None of this was enough.

I spun on Ebony, who was still watching me with perfect calm. *"Well?"*

Ebony shrugged, watching me intently. "Sounds like he's a good kid."

"A good...?" I let out a laugh, running my fingers through my hair wildly. "Don't you pretend to be normal *now*!"

"Sure, *I* think it's stupid. He was thinking about his family before himself, that's what the world would call selfless. Caring. *Noble.*" His eyes flashed with derision at that last word. "You've never done well with people who are good, Harrison. Even *Drake* makes you uncomfortable sometimes."

I stared at him. *"What?"*

Ebony actually laughed, folding his arms and giving me a

condescending look. "You are the only person who chose, with eyes wide open and no loyalty or obligation, to enter a bond with me. If I were to guess? I make you feel better about yourself. But *what* has ever given you the impression you *like* good people? We don't *see* good people."

"Vex is good."

"Based on your drunken blubbering last night, that's going *swimmingly* isn't it?" Ebony sauntered further into my room without a care and leaned against my bedpost. "Oh, but it's worse than that. Vex isn't just good. She needs *you* to be good for *her.*"

"I just..." I winced, hating that he was the only person that I could talk to right now. "I don't..." I broke into a wild laugh. "I don't understand. We have everything."

"What?" He considered me for a moment. "The pack?"

"We're rich and famous, and we have *everything.*"

He raised his eyebrows, as if wondering where this was going.

"So why...?" I trailed off, trying to figure out what I was trying to say.

"Why what?"

"Why doesn't it *feel* like it? The money, the house, the fame— it's what everyone wants. *We have what everyone wants.*"

"Yup."

"Then why isn't it enough?"

"Speak for yourself. I'm fine."

"Because you're fucking broken!" I snarled. I was striding toward him in a moment, so lost in anger I couldn't even remember why.

Ebony didn't flinch as I squared him up, a rather noncommittal look on his face. "Because this is what I knew I wanted," he said, still fixed on me with interest. "Is this what you always wanted, Harrison? Or is it what you were *told* to want?"

That drew me up, deconstructing the last thing I had that

could easily fuel my rage. I was supposed to be sure I hated Ebony. *That* was supposed to be easy.

"It's what everyone wants," I snapped, knowing how unhinged I sounded right now. *"We have what everyone wants."*

"And?"

Fuck.

Finally, I closed my fingers around the knife that had been lodged in my throat since the moment I'd made her cry the other day. *"And none of it means anything if she hates me!"*

The silence was smothering and completely terrifying. Finally, Ebony broke it. "So... How do you fix it?"

"I don't fucking know!" I didn't know how to stop hurting her. I couldn't even conceive of the pain I'd put her through. "She's... she's real, and I'm this... this empty shell with nothing to offer anyone! Every time I try to fix it, I make it worse. It doesn't matter what I do."

"That's because you're a loser."

"Could you—"

"No. You are. You always have been. You've fallen face first into everything good in your life."

"No! I worked hard—"

"Everyone works hard." Ebony snorted. "Not everyone has the leg up you had—and if you can't see that, you'll never be enough for her."

"Right. Great. That's why you're here? To tell me that I can't ever be good enough—"

"You have everything you need to be good enough, Rook. You hit every criteria for transformation, but none of that matters if you won't accept it."

"I want to!" I couldn't fight this *feeling*, it just *kept. Coming. Back.* "You think I *want* to be the kind of person who would hurt her? Who reminds her of *them* because I'm too fucking blind to

deal with my own shit? I just... Every time I try, I hurt her more! I don't know how!"

"And that makes you... angry?"

"I'm not angry!"

"You aren't?"

"No!" I shouted. "I'm... I'm..." I didn't say it. I couldn't, not to Ebony, not even now. But he knew. Of course he knew, and he was looking at me in a way that I didn't like one bit. "I'm not Drake!" I shoved my fist into his chest, though still, he didn't react. "And you don't get to puzzle me out like one of your little... psycho's pets."

"What are you scared of?" he pushed.

I...

Fuck.

"I don't know." I swallowed. "Of *this*. Of... figuring this all out —all of this shit I should have figured out before." My voice cracked. "What if I'm... I'm too late to change? What if it doesn't matter, and I try to be better and I can't?"

Ebony shrugged. "That's where I max out, mate. No—" He cut off, gaze pausing at my phone on the bed. Then he frowned, picking it up.

"What?" I asked.

His expression went dark.

"What is it?" I asked again.

"It's your sister."

"Which one?" Not that it mattered, barely any of them texted any more.

"It's Rayne... Rook, what the *fuck* did you do?" he asked.

"What do you mean?" I demanded, trying to read it. "I didn't do anything."

But Ebony was reading the text out. *"What did you say to mom? The parents are convinced you're about to ruin everything for some gold pack con bitch. They're digging up dirt on her for the press. Last I saw them like this they convinced Aunt June to kick Elric from the will. You need to call them. I can't talk them down."*

My blood turned to ice.

"No..."

"What the fuck did you say about Vex?" Ebony asked, now angry for the first time.

"Nothing... I..." *Fuck.* I shouldn't... I should never have said anything when they brought her up. *"I was defending her."* That's what Drake had been mad about—*I'd* been mad at myself for not defending her at the round table.

"Not to your parents, you *idiot!* They're crazy, Rook. Did you see the smear campaign they did on that beta your brother shacked up with? You think Vex needs that right now? Do they know she's here? They're going to—"

"No. No. They don't. We can get ahead of it. I can—"

"You can *what?"*

"I don't know. I just... Fuck. Just *help me!* Why come in here and offer to help if all you were going to be was useless?" I seized him, rage and terror burning away everything else. That's all he was—fucking useless.

Not me.

He was a void of a human.

I hated him.

I hated that I was bonded to him.

I hated that, even after all of this, he hadn't thrown a single *goddamned punch—*

"Oh..." Ebony cocked his head, something startled in his expression as he dropped my phone back on the bed. "Oh... *dude."*

"What?"

"You..." He breathed a laugh. "A fucking prat as always."

"What?"

"This..." he laughed. "This is going to be rough. You're *way* too late."

"Late for what?" I was fighting the urge to throw him through the wall if he was cryptic for one second more.

"For drugs—and there's no way in the seventh circle of hell I'm letting you *near* her like this."

"What the fuck are you talking about?"

"Playboy Harrison is about to have the worst few days of his miserable life," Ebony taunted, true delight in his eyes. "You're going into a full-blown rut."

TWENTY-THREE

EBONY

"What am I going to do?" Rook had me by the shirt, eyes wide. It wasn't that I didn't think he was capable of a meltdown like this, but his aura and scent had shifted in the last minute: indisputably a rut.

I grinned. "I don't know Harrison. Better figure something out quick. What do you *usually* do to keep away ruts?" My voice was almost singsong with delight.

His face went ashen.

We both knew the answer.

I rutted often—too much alpha in me, that was just the way it had always been. Love and Drake did sometimes, but Rook? God was he blindsided right now—enough of a playboy to have never fully rutted.

"I can't..." he whispered, coming to the conclusion I'd reached half a minute before. "She's... she's not... I can't hurt her again."

"You're not *fucking* her," I said, alarmed.

Maybe *not* the same conclusion.

"I meant I'm not fucking anyone else!"

Oh.

Okay, yes. Same conclusion.

"I didn't... *fuck!* I was stressed. I didn't realise."

It was really hard to fight my grin.

"Help me!" he growled, letting go of my shirt to shove me.

"Help you through your rut?" I chuckled. "Mate, even if I swung that way—"

"Fuck you!" he snarled. *"What* am I going to do?"

"You've got three options, the way I see it. A clinic can put you in a big metal box and give you as many drugs as they can to keep you under—worst goddamned experience of your life, I hear, but you'll survive. Or you *could* cleave from the pack and go bang a bunch of chicks," I said, hopefully. "Spare us the rest of your miserable existence."

It wasn't *really* an option. There were only four of us in the bond; if one of us cleaved there was a decent chance our pack's scent would shift enough to destroy the match with Vex, and I wasn't giving her up.

He grabbed me by the shirt again, eyes wild. "I'm not betraying her!"

"Or we could go to the pits."

"The... what?"

"You could fight it out," I said with a shrug. "But there isn't a safe arena in this city that can keep it on the downlow."

He stared at me, mouth working for a moment.

"Take me." He was wringing his hands, breathing shallow. "She's... she's good, okay. And she'll probably try to help, or feel bad if she doesn't. I don't... I don't deserve that."

"I'm not going to be your rut-nanny."

It was a lie. I'd be a rut-nanny to watch Rook have the shit beaten out of him in the pits any day.

But I wanted him to beg.

"Fuck! Please! I... I need you to. She can't... she can't see me like this. Y-you're the only one who can do this for me."

"Why?" I asked, a little surprised.

"I'm not... I don't... like who I am, Ebony. I want..." He ran his fingers through his hair, trying to come up with a way to say it.

Damn. He looked like he was about to cry again.

"You want me to make this miserable?"

"That's what you do, right? Break people?"

I grinned. "I don't know if you deserve the privilege, Harrison."

His expression turned into a snarl. *"You're the one who said she needs me!"*

I sighed, like it was a hard choice. "Fine. I'll clear my schedule and make this the worst rut of your damned life."

"Wait... Wait..." His eyes darted down to his phone. "First, we need to do something."

"What?"

"It's... it's for her. And my parents. And anyone who watched that fucking interview where I didn't defend her. I need to fix this. All of it."

I raised my eyebrows, grin widening as he told me what he wanted.

"You're going to need to be out for that," I said. "Can't half ass it. She deserves better."

"Yeh, I know. I want everyone to know she's the only thing in the world I care about."

"If you put one dent in my Lambo, I'll carve you into pieces and toss them over a bridge," I snapped as we sped down the streets of New Oxford to our first stop.

They didn't build these cars to be alpha proof, which was a sin. If any company came out with a car for alphas, I'd be first in line.

"How many times?" Rook asked.

"How many times what?" I glanced at him sideways as he clutched himself in the passenger seat of my car.

"How many times...?" He groaned, a low growl slipping from his chest as if he couldn't hold it back, but when he spoke, he was stifling a grin. "Have you cut people up and dropped them over bridges, you fucking psycho?"

I grinned. "Drunk or sober?"

He loosed a rather unsettling laugh, then another growl. *"FUCK!"* His back slammed against the seat, one knee coming up. *"I feel like I'm on fire."*

"Watch the fucking dash!" I snapped.

ROOK

When we pulled up before a glowing street sign, the plans were laid, and I was at the edge of cracking completely. Ebony reached over to the glove box and took out a gun.

"Oh... Wait. What the fuck—?" I cut off as he flipped the weapon in his hand and cracked the side. It came apart in an instant, revealing itself to be a gun only in appearance. Within was a compartment containing a number of vials of drugs.

"Uh... I don't want anything in my body that you'd rather people think is a gun."

"I can get a licence for a gun," he muttered, checking the labels until he found what he was looking for.

Was that supposed to make me feel better?

I caught a glimpse of one of the vials.

"Is that Agritox?" I snarled, eyes wide. "You can't have that." It was poison to alphas. Literal fucking poison. "It's controlled, isn't it?" I asked. "They track it?"

I'd heard it compared to nuclear waste in how invested the government was in keeping an eye on it. I looked around like special ops were going to pounce from the shadows any moment.

"Chill," he said as he drew up clear fluid from a vial into a needle he'd got from God-knows-where.

"You aren't injecting me with anything until you tell me what it is."

"Novastra. You're going to have to be really out cold for what you want."

"Oh... okay." It was a heavy sedative—definitely not an over-the-counter med. "It'll work even if I'm in a rut?"

"For an hour or two, maybe?" he said with a shrug. "We'll have time if we get a few people on it. And—better, it'll be so much worse when you wake up. You can put on a real show."

I nodded, still hesitant.

"Fuck!" I swore as Ebony jammed the needle into my arm without warning.

"Countdown," he said. Silver storm eyes were more delighted than I'd ever seen them as he watched me. "Thirty seconds."

The world began swimming. "I want... I want it ruined."

"What?"

"My reputation."

If I entered the pits tonight, the whole city would pay attention. I didn't want Vex in the spotlight, but that ship had sailed. I needed to change the narrative.

"By the time you're in that cage, Rook, the world will see you as a whole new man."

TWENTY-FOUR

LOVE

> Jas: Look. Ebony told me to make sure none of it got back to you tonight, but this is going a little far.

> Jas: Channel 39.

As I turned the TV on, I was met with complete insanity. It was the *'Firedome Alpha's Arena'* casting station. It was the one Rook put on sometimes and hosted a range of different fights, including aura boxing, but that wasn't the focus of the channel as we turned it on.

It was rut fighting.

"Fourteen rounds in the cage!" A very enthusiastic commentator was saying. *"That's the previous record for a single rut cycle, and Rook Harrison is on twelve! He's looking to take the crown for his princess!"*

"His... what?" Vex's voice was faint, and her face was pale. But I didn't answer, completely stalled with shock as the camera finally panned back to the cage.

Rook was definitely in a rut. He looked wild.

He wore nothing but a pair of dark camo cargo pants. His black hair was stuck to his forehead, his rich brown skin glistened with sweat, and he was staggering to his feet over the bodies of two collapsed alphas. Blood trickled from his lip, but he wiped it clean, chestnut eyes on fire as he stared around at the stadium of people that were making a deafening roar.

As he straightened, face twisted in a snarl, bruised fists clenched, we saw that across his chest was tattooed three, huge black letters.

'VEX'.

Above the 'V' in her name was a simple black crown: the symbol of a princess bond.

"Oh. My. God..." Drake whispered.

Vex got to her feet, eyes orbs of shock, leftover pizza forgotten in her hand as she stared at the screen.

"There weren't many people betting on him taking the crown, but it looks like Rook Harrison is more than just a pretty boy celebrity."

"That's... my name," Vex whispered, dumbstruck.

Yes. Yes it was. I couldn't take my eyes from it as the camera panned around him.

"But it's going to... it's going to ruin his image. Everyone knows I'm gold pack—and he's supposed to... he's not supposed to commit t-to me."

Well. Rook was committing.

Hard.

Irreversibly.

In the most insane, idiotic, Rook way that I could have ever fucking imagined.

Vex stepped toward the TV, almost absently. "Everyone... Everyone is going to see it..." But I thought her eyes might be shining.

"Yup." That was true. Jas was updating me. Social media, blogs, new stations and radios, it wasn't *going* to be everywhere. It already *was* everywhere.

"Stay tuned, ladies and gentlemen," the commentator was saying. *"Rook Harrison is going into his thirteenth round—the fourth with double opponents, and he doesn't look close to stopping. Two more wins and he sets a record, beating the legendary fourteen round title champion, Arsenal Gray."*

"While they send in the next alpha," the other said. *"We've got someone on the line who can shed a bit of light on this mystery tattoo—now, our phone lines are flooded and I've been told to tell you to keep it civil, everyone, we're not hosting anyone looking to spread hate."* There was a pause, and then the sound of a phone connecting. *"Kate, is it?"*

"Yes! I'm... I'm a huge fan of the Crimson Fury Pack."

"Tell us—what do you know about the tattoo—?" But Kate was so excited that she barely let him finish.

"She's an omega! A *gold pack* omega!"

"She?"

"For those of us who keep up, we know Vex has been with them for a while! We thought she was a Sweetheart, but then it came out she was a gold pack. But she's their scent match—she has to be!"

"Hold on, hold on—if she's their match and she's with them, why do you think Rook is in the cages?"

"He's making a statement—it's for her and it's for us! You see that symbol above her name? That's a princess bond. They've offered her a princess bond!" Kate was so excited she was breathless, but the commentator didn't get a chance for a word in. *"The media have been horrible to her, but I bet you anything the press were just making it up that she was lying to them. I think they knew, and were using the Sweetheart stuff to keep the relationship on the downlow. But she doesn't deserve any hate. She was on an Evening Star's*

interview with Ebony the other week, and she was so real, and cool, and funny.

"And for the fans out there who are mad, you need to get a life. The Crimson Fury pack are beta-friendly, but everyone forgets they've been pro gold pack from the start! No wonder they got a scent match like her! We get less chances to be seen than anyone, and now Rook's making a statement for her. No one can challenge this! I think we should just be happy for them!"

"Thanks for the info, Kate! If you're a new viewer tuning in for our unexpected celebrity watch, we're giving a crash course in Rut Cages. Can you give us the low down once again, Preston?"

Well...

Holy. Shit.

Vex had gone from pale, to bright pink in the cheeks as the commentator continued.

"...The alphas in there go until the cycle ends—they fight until they're out from a hit or collapse. That's a cycle, folks, then they rest until they wake, and then they go again. Sometimes they can go through three or four cycles before the rut is over. And yes, they can bow out between cycles, but transitioning to drugs is a painful process—and most prefer the fights over sedatives in a tin can."

The other commentator jumped in. *"And in answer to calls of people worried: a rutting alpha is about as tough as you can get. This isn't boxing, there's no ref in the cage. We're here to watch nature at work. Alpha's lose interest the moment their opponent is out, we've never seen it go further.*

"It's Stadium policy, we never pull them in the middle of a cycle —not unless we have to. They fight until they're done. They're here to get their rut out of their system, and we won't risk letting a dangerous alpha back on the street. Rook Harrison knew that when he entered. He's going to fight until he's finished—and by the looks of it, he's got a lot more fight left in him."

"It's easy to see why. If you're looking for it, every time another

alpha touches that tattoo on his chest he goes wild. Our seers are telling us his aura is off the charts. This gold pack is clearly why he's fighting tonight—I sure hope she's tuned in."

"Are you... okay, Vex?" Drake asked her, stepping to her side.

"I... yes. It's just... it's not what I expected. Did you know he was in a rut?"

She glanced at me, but I shook my head. She bit her lip, looking torn between excitement and nerves. Then a word tore our attention back to the TV.

"...Casualties are rare. Alphas have used aggression to get ruts out of their system since the beginning of time. They're built for this. Remember that Rook isn't just a pretty boy actor, he's an alpha first."

"Casualties?" Vex asked, face pale.

"You heard him, it's not going to happen."

"But..." She gripped the sleeves of her shirt. "He's my mate. I should be there!" She was already crossing toward her closet.

"Vex." I hurried after her. "I don't know if it's a good idea—"

She spun on me, eyes wide. "He can't get hurt because of me."

"It's not because of you—if he gets hurt, it's because he's a melodramatic prat."

She wasn't listening, instead grabbing a jacket and hurrying toward the door.

"I'm not taking you," I told her.

"Drake!" She turned to Drake. He looked between us anxiously. "I... I think Love's right. I don't think you should go. Places like that aren't exactly safe—"

"Then I'll go by myself." The door slammed behind her before I could reach her.

She literally couldn't, *right?* Drake gave me a look before we were after her.

"You don't have a bank card, or a car, or a bus pass—" I began.

"I'm going." She said, already halfway down the stairs.

"Vex, I don't know if going there and seeing him like this is a good idea."

"He's my mate and he's in a rut! I should *be* there." She looked distressed as she rushed down the driveway.

"He's been a prick, and I don't want you going because he's set this up so you feel you have to. Neither does Drake."

"Then I'll go by myself," she insisted.

"How are you going to get there?" I asked as she unlocked the side gate and headed out into the street. "It's too far to walk."

She didn't have a current bank account—and as a gold pack in a dark bond, the government considered that her pack's responsibility so there was fuck all we could do about it right now. She didn't even have any cash as far as I knew.

She spun on me, eyes blazing. "I got by just fine without alphas before," she snapped. "He needs *me*." That might have been sweet, especially with the determination in her eyes as she said it, but in the next moment, she shoved her hand out into the road with her thumb up.

Right in front of me.

Like it was just a *normal* thing to do.

She was an *omega*. A *gold pack*, for fuck's sake.

I grabbed her hand and shoved it down. "You are not *hitchhiking* across New Oxford at 9 o' clock at night."

"Try and stop me," she snarled, trying to rip her hand free. "See. What. *Happens!*"

"It's dangerous!"

"In this neighbourhood?" she asked, finally getting free of my grip and sticking her hand out again. "Don't you have like… security patrols to get rid of fans and paparazzi and shit here? I'll be fine."

"Vex—"

"Besides, what's anyone going to do? Kidnap me and dark bond me?" A mad giggle rose up her throat as she took a step away from me, thumb still out. "My stupid fucking pack'll be so mad, they'll have to come hunt me down." She looked a little unhinged with desperation. "You know, they never told me I wasn't allowed to get kidnapped."

"Okay—okay!" *Fuck.*

And fuck Rook for this stupid act.

I glanced back to Drake, but he was already hurrying back to the garage. "Fine. But for the record, I think this is a shit idea."

TWENTY-FIVE

ROOK

Everything around me was a blur of colour and sound and light that all jumbled together, not making sense.

All I knew was the fire burning through my veins, the feel of the auras around me—each a threat and a challenge. One I couldn't lose.

I didn't lose. Not ever.

It was who I was.

And I wasn't done. I hadn't finished. I needed to go again, needed to throw the next punch, to take the next burning hit. My body ached, from bruises and wounds; from hormones that scored my system.

I was alone.

I knew that to my bones.

I couldn't feel my pack any longer, I thought maybe I'd been the one to shut them out.

Right...

That sounded right.

I'd been upset earlier, and I didn't want them knowing. I didn't want them taking time away from her again because of me.

Another hit, and pain exploded in my back as I was slammed up against dark metal bars. This alpha... he was tough, eyes burning with rage as he grabbed me.

But his rage, his fuel, it was nothing to my shame.

I grabbed him, shoving my aura further than I ever had before. With all my might I flipped us, catching his head on the bars and he collapsed in an instant.

Each time one fell, it was a validation—he didn't lose because I was born with more, because I was richer, or because I had something he didn't. This pain, the agony of shame I carried, it wasn't make believe. It was real.

She needed that.

So I clung to it.

I sank into it, the isolation, the shame.

She didn't want me because I wasn't good enough.

And what I had here, it was made of more than dust and ash —than the trophies, now in pieces on my bedroom floor. It was a pain that maybe, if I let it, could turn me into something new.

So every win was proof: the playing field was even, unlike everything else in my life. When I got up, and another alpha fell, it was tangible. Evidence of something I could have spent my whole life searching for before now, and never found.

And just like her, *this* was real.

EBONY

Struggle.

That was, I realised, what I needed.

I couldn't respect a person if I didn't see their strength. And it was hard to gauge the strength of someone if you never saw them struggle. And never had I seen spoiled-brat-Harrison struggle a day in his life.

He had over-bearing parents that fucked his mind and expectations of himself up from a young age, and too much money to understand the value of anything. But as far as struggles went, it just wasn't all that much.

Tonight, though, I witnessed something different. Which was actually rather uncomfortable, because I was discovering a certain amount of respect for his dedication.

For the dozenth time, Rook was spitting blood, broken and panting through what might be a cracked rib.

This arena wasn't like underground fight pits. It was regulated, with a dozen cages active at all times, some with rutting alphas, some with professional fighters. Since Rook had already been half in a rut when we'd arrived, I'd co-signed all his waivers as his pack mate. And now this arena was full, and, I'd been told, the line went three blocks down.

He'd got the media's attention, just like he'd planned, and that tattoo would be known across all of New Oxford by morning. A claim. A statement, one even his parents would have a hard time unseating.

Again, Rook got up. Shaking and trembling. And again. And again. Another fight. Another win.

His actor training, the small stints he'd done learning various martial arts, they were nothing compared to the other cage fighters. It didn't matter though; he was outlasting them.

He just *wouldn't stay down.*

More than that, he never actually lost himself beyond recognition, worthless, witty quips coming from his mouth to an alpha that was about to put him in the fucking ground.

It might have been pretty fucking hilarious, only, he didn't stop. It wasn't what I'd expected: for him to win fight after fight, until he'd taken the title. Until he was in more fights than any other alpha had been in a single cycle.

I didn't notice my phone blowing up until I caught the oh so overbearing stench of vanilla fucking winter.

Fuck.

Love grabbed me by the shirt, shoving me back into the bars of the viewing cage we were in. "What the *fuck* have you done?"

"His choice." I sneered. "I'm just the chauffeur."

"Get him out!"

"Can't. He needs to be the one who—" I cut off as the scent shifted.

Blackcurrant wine and... *fuck.*

Fuck.

"What did you bring her for?" I glared between Love and her. My beautiful omega with worried golden eyes, anxious raspberry treacle filling the air in moments.

"He's my mate!" She looked hurt.

I shoved Love out of my way and crossed toward her. "This is what he wanted. Let him finish. The rut has to be half out of his system by now."

"Why didn't he tell me he was rutting?" she demanded.

"It was last minute. We didn't have many options."

"You *could* have told me."

"He..." I scowled. "He didn't want you to try and fix it. He didn't think he deserved that."

"But it's my job—"

"Vex," Drake said, frowning. "That's not true. You know that's not true."

Vex jumped as Rook was slammed against the cage wall at our backs, a low groan sounding in the air. He was on the brink of collapse as the alpha gripped him.

Good.

Maybe this would be when he finally—I winced as his aura

flared out of control and he headbutted the alpha with all of his might.

The man crumpled, ending his seventeenth fight.

"Rook!" Love was at the edge of the viewing area. *"Enough! That's an order."* There were two layers of metal bars between us and him. The cage's bars and the one's containing our viewing area. Above, the crowd roared, the first rows ten feet above us in a circular stadium that looked down on the cage. Rook, barely recognisable from the bruises and swelling on his face, turned to us weakly, taking in Love.

"I... I can't."

"You can," Drake hissed. "Get the fuck out!"

Rook shook his head. "You don't... you don't get it. She wants you, Drake. She told me to figure it out myself. That's what..." He wiped away another smear of blood, fingers curling around the bar of the cage, dragging himself up. "That's what I'm doing. So *fuck off!"*

"No, this isn't what I meant!" Vex's voice shook. "Get out!"

Rook stared at her for a long second, eyes glazed over with something uncomprehending.

"Ebony..." he said, eyes finding mine, and I could barely hear him over the crowd. "I... I don't think I can stop."

"You won the title, Harrison. You've done better than any other alpha that's been in that cage. You can give it up now."

Some alphas collapsed between fights, ending the cycle there, exhaustion catching up to them as hormones burned out.

"I c-can't, Ebony. I haven't... I haven't hurt enough."

"Rook, please!" Vex begged.

Rook stared at her as if he didn't know what he was seeing. "It's not enough, Baby Girl."

"It is, okay!" she shouted, trying to reach for him desperately through the bars. "It's enough."

Rook blinked, hand reaching out to hers for just the briefest moment, and then he pulled back. "I don't think you're even real," he said. "You wouldn't... you shouldn't have come here for me."

"N-no!" Vex called. *"ROOK!"* But he ignored her.

He wiped away the blood trickling down from his nose with a grin and turned away from us. The roar of the crowd rose again, even more deafening, as the next two alphas entered the ring. Rook had to hold onto the bars for a second to keep himself steady, then his aura flared.

"ROOK!" Vex screamed again, reaching for him.

I felt the faintest flicker of him through the bond, it was gone in the next instinct, and his scent of burning chestnuts turned feral again.

"Get him out!" She turned on us, eyes wild with terror. "It's too much!"

"I can't, Vex. That's not how it works."

"He's mine!" she snarled, grabbing me by the shirt. "He's mine and I'm telling you *it's too much!"*

There was a deadliness in her eyes. I couldn't explain the power she had in that moment. She was beautiful, wild, and I could swear her golden eyes were almost their own source of light in the dim viewing area. Then, she was gone, back at the bars, screaming his name as Rook crashed to the ground once more.

"No one's gone this long before," Drake hissed. "We don't know he won't get hurt. That's how alphas die in these things. Take too many hits while the adrenaline's high."

"Drake!" I snapped. She didn't need more panic. "Enough. You shouldn't have brought her!" I turned on Love. "Why would you come? He's going to be fucking fine." He *would* be. The death rate was lower than ruts dealt with out of cages.

Though Drake... fuck. He *was* right. No one had gone this long before.

"You think I can control her—?" Love began.

"I think she deserves better than this—"

"This is not better!" Drake spat.

"I didn't know he was going to lose his fucking mind. He was too late for proper drugs. Would you rather he ended up burning through sedation in one of those clinics? *Un-fucking-natural*, that's what—"

"*VEX!*" Drake's shout cut me off, his aura splitting the air. "*NO!*" I looked over to see him diving toward the edge of the viewing ring.

Where was—?

My blood chilled as I spotted her, a rare moment of absolute fear spiking my system and not just Drake's and Love's through the bond. My own terror flooded through me as my aura flared.

Vex had climbed the viewing ring's bars, fast—much too fast.

At the top, the bars were wider—still not enough that one of us would have fit though, but Vex was tiny. Drake moved quicker than I'd ever seen him, climbing the cage after her. But she was through, leaping from one set to the next right as Drake reached out for her.

"*NO!*" Drake's bellow was lost in the roar of the crowd. He was too late. Vex didn't look back. Her eyes burned with determination, fixed on her mate.

She slipped through the last bar and I thought my heart might have stopped as my mate tumbled down into an arena with three rutting alphas.

Rook was down, I realised. He was shaking, aura flickering in the air.

Vex threw herself between him and the two alphas, shielding his body with hers as she turned on them, and in that moment, her scent hit the arena like a bomb, golden eyes blazing with a wildness I'd never witnessed before, and it was as if the whole world came to a stop.

TWENTY-SIX

ROOK

I was in the dream I'd lived a thousand times in the last hour.

She was there, screaming my name.

Her fists closed around the metal bars separating us, only... she looked too upset. She'd been calmer in the previous visions. I didn't want her to be upset.

With the ringing in my ears, it took me a long time to understand.

Get out?

She was asking me to stop?

What kind of vision was that? I could keep on. I had more to give. More to prove.

You might die... a little voice whispered.

No... *no no no*. That wasn't the plan. I mean... I deserved it, sure. But... but she didn't. If I died, the loss... with just the four of us... it was possible I could shatter the scent profile, destroy the match.

But... Well, I wasn't pack lead.

I wasn't an anchor like Drake.

I'd never had a presence like Ebony.

If I died... that would be the smallest piece of the pack to fall away. Maybe they would be fine without me.

And I couldn't stop hurting her, no matter how hard I tried. She would be better without me. Again, I staggered to my feet and wiped the fluids from my face.

Blood or tears, I wasn't sure.

It didn't matter.

I'd go until I couldn't anymore. I'd break until there was nothing left.

If I survived, maybe there would be something on the other end, something real. Something that was enough for her.

My aura was cracked, frayed and vicious. It was broken... I'd pushed it too far. It was waning.

But I wasn't done.

The next hit came, sending me into the metal bars. A new, bone deep pain flared across my whole body.

My aura was waning. Too soon. Every hit was like a monster chasing me, ready to catch up. It was then that I realised I might have gone too far. If I let go of my aura now, what would be left?

Only when I reached for it, I felt it shudder.

As it wavered, I choked, something hot and thick coming up my throat, an iron tang on my tongue.

Desperately, I grappled with aura, needing to hold on, but it was slipping away. Danger sounded in my head. I couldn't let it go. *I couldn't*—

And then, I seized it—clinging to it with a strength I didn't own. And everything in the world vanished except the hallucination that wasn't a hallucination.

The raspberry treacle was real.

She was real.

And she was above me. Everywhere.

She was... she was here.

No.

That couldn't be possible.

It... it couldn't be.

The alpha auras in here were unhinged, doused in rage, though something about them had shifted, sensing the other energy in here: her.

I heard a low guttural growl above me, resonating into my very soul.

She was a presence, the likes of which I'd never experienced before. Raspberry treacle, but not sweet or nervous—or afraid like she was in my worst moments.

The scent of my mate was edged with fury and danger.

She was everything in that moment: the smell of fresh morning dew on green leaves, of roots diving deep into soft, cool soil, deep and grounding, of the prickles of a raspberry bush. And there was a fiery hot edge to the sweetness that formed her scent, something vicious in it now.

Protective.

So absolute, so all consuming, that it almost froze me completely, down to each breath in my lungs.

It *should* have.

Except...

She couldn't get hurt for me. I couldn't...

I grabbed her and—with all my waning strength—turned us both so I could shield her with my body.

The movement set off a reaction in the cage.

The suspended moment of stillness shattered, and I could sense one alpha move, about to strike again—the energy in this cage as familiar as the beat of my heart.

Below me, she was breathless. Golden eyes, brighter than I'd believed possible, were desperate.

"N-no!" she moaned. Tears flooded her face, as she grappled with my cheeks, speaking—no, *begging*...

I reached out to her, knowing I needed her closer. I needed to —but before I could seize her and drag her close, pain split my side and I was jolted into the cage, crashing violently into the heavy metal bars.

One pulse of my heart beat.

Two.

Three.

The world was reforming. Not quite right. Something was... something was missing.

She was gone.

My breath came ragged.

The fresh raspberry bushes, the fury, the sweetness, the morning dew and cool soil, her golden eyes.

Gone.

I was left, fingers halfway curled through her hair, the desperate motion I'd been making to drag her tighter against my chest.

Too late.

Vex was limp in my arms, eyes peaceful and closed, glistening crimson blossoming rapidly through the roots of her hair.

DRAKE

She shouldn't have been faster than both me and Ebony, auras out, my heart almost gave out as I saw the scene before me.

I'd never seen Love like this, Ebony was dragging him from an alpha trying to unlock the cage. Instead, he threw himself bodily against the bars, a low snarl loosing from his chest.

And then—far too late—the door was opened. Love was through before any of us, but I was on his heels.

The two alphas were there. One was towering over Rook and Vex. Love wrenched him back and slammed him against the wall of the cage. Security swarmed in, dragging him off, barring the other alpha as I crashed to my knees before Rook and Vex.

She was... *oh my God.*

She was—

Another snarl erupted from Rook's chest as I reached for her, panic making it hard to think straight, and then he was drawing back, still curled over her to keep her protected as his free hand closed around my throat.

"Rook!" I gasped. But he wasn't there.

My brother wasn't there.

His eyes were wild as he held her limp frame against him, trembling, mad with terror.

"ROOK!" I tried again, knowing I needed to reach her.

Blood matted her hair.

She wasn't moving.

She wasn't—

"Ebony!" Rook choked, eyes finally shifting as Ebony crashed to our side. "She's gone!" Rook's voice was choked. His whole body was shivering with exhaustion. "I... Why was she here?" Rook asked, voice cracking. "I don't... I don't understand. I was trying to..." His expression broke, desperate eyes finding mine. "Everything I do... it... it hurts her. I thought this... I just wanted to do something right. She wasn't supposed to g-get hurt."

"It's not your fault." It wasn't.

It was mine. All of ours. Hers. *What had she been thinking— climbing into the cage?*

"Why... why was she here?"

The medics were trying to get close, but Rook's grip tightened on her if anyone who wasn't pack got near.

"Rook, look at me," Ebony said firmly. "We need to get her help." Someone had passed him a monitor, and he was slipping it onto Vex's finger.

"I c-can't... I can't hurt her again. I've already hurt her so much, Ebony. I just wanted to do something that would protect her. From m-my parents. From me. To make her see maybe I'm not... I'm not like her monsters. That she doesn't h-have to be afraid..."

All of us were glancing down to read the monitor. Something in my chest loosened as I saw the numbers pop up on the screen, showing pulse and sats. "Rook," Ebony said, voice eerily calm. "She's going to be okay. It's a head wound. They bleed a lot, but you have to let her go."

Rook just stared at him, uncomprehending, grip still a vice.

"I always disappointed my parents... you know." His eyes found Love. "And then with you, with the pack, it was different. Until she came, and then you... you saw the truth. And y-you're all..."

"Hey, it's fine, mate. You're going to be fine—"

"I know you all think I'm worthless," he whispered, tears flooding his cheeks. "And now my family is going to try and break her l-like they b-broke me. And I j-just wanted to... to do something good for her... Just... once."

"This wasn't on you," Love said firmly.

"Rook," I whispered. "You have to let her go. Please. No one can help her like this."

The lighting in here was odd. I glanced up, just for a second, to see why. Black curtains had tumbled down the cage walls.

Privacy curtains... But... no.

They did that when...

A low growl slipped from my chest.

No.

She wasn't dead.

She wasn't.

The monitor was showing life. Her pulse was right there. Another thing was being passed to Ebony, who was closest to Rook.

"Thirty seconds," a voice said, quiet enough for Rook not to hear. "Give it to him, and he'll be out in thirty. Then we can treat them."

"I'm going to give you this, okay?" Ebony was saying. "It's for her. If I give you this injection, she'll be okay, alright?"

Rook stared at him, then finally nodded.

He jumped as Ebony jammed the needle into his arm and injected it in an instant. Rook's breathing became ragged.

"You're both going to be okay," I said.

Thirty seconds.

I counted.

Still, nothing.

Still, Rook remained clutching her.

Another thirty. Then another.

Then Ebony gave him another shot.

For seven and a half minutes, Rook fought the drugs, trembling and terrified, before he finally sagged, eyes rolling back in his head. We were there to catch him and pull her from his arms.

TWENTY-SEVEN

LOVE

"Now to the question New Oxford is blowing up over: Who is Vex Eden?"

"The gold pack who dropped into a cage with three rutting alphas to claim celebrity actor, Rook Harrison, when he was—and get this—in his eighteenth round of cage fighting."

"To put that in perspective, the previous record's owner nearly died in the cage at fourteen rounds and never competed again."

"If you ask me, after today, I'd be surprised if we see Harrison in the cage again."

We were in the hospital, and the tinny sounds of the news reporters from Ebony's phone were grating at my sanity.

Vex and Rook were stable—thank fuck—because *I* certainly wasn't.

They were in adjoining rooms, as I'd refused, despite medical advice, to put them in the same bed. She wouldn't have her waking up, disoriented, in Rook's arms on an Arkologist's recommendation just because he'd been a *fucking* idiot. Not until I knew more had changed between them than just instincts and hormones.

I didn't care how many worried looks Drake shot me. If I had to pay the price with Vex, I would.

Vex was currently stable with either me or Drake in the room, but the nurse had told us (at the least) not to close the door to Rook's room. Oddly enough, his vitals hadn't stabilised with anyone present but *Ebony*. So, my brother was angrily standing in the doorway between Vex and Rook's rooms, phone playing a news station on full blast, and he was watching it intently. Drake had even edged over to see.

"*She's got to be their mate, though, what else would possess an omega—any omega—to do that?*"

"*Before the calls come in, let's dispel some myths, folks, before this gets out of hand.*"

"*Myths like what?*" Another voice asked.

"*She didn't mess up like some people are saying. Quite the contrary. Look at how bright her eyes are—rare to get a moment like that caught on camera. That, ladies and gentlemen, is a feral gold pack omega, protecting the alpha she's claimed. She looks ready to kill for him. Mayson and Piers—the other two in the arena with them—were in ruts, running on nothing but instinct, and she wasn't soothing them. I'll be as clear as I can, say what you want about them, but gold pack auras—scents, whatever you like to call it when it comes to omegas—they're strong.*"

"*So you're saying... she wasn't trying to calm them down?*"

"*Not in the least. That was a challenge.*"

"*Doesn't seem smart.*"

"*Have you ever been around a feral omega? Not to mention a gold pack one? I'm curious to know what would have gone down if Harrison hadn't shielded her like he did.*"

"*What do you think would have happened?*"

"Well, there was a moment—look, if you pause it. There was a moment where they both stop. If you ask me, they might have backed off entirely."

"You really think so? She's still just an omega."

"Ask any alpha in that arena what they felt the moment she turned on them like that. It was a challenge most domestic alphas aren't used to. Take Mayson, he's no rogue—he's a bank manager for Christ's sake, staring down the barrel of thousands of years of evolution."

"So... it was Harrison that fucked up?"

"I mean, I'm not saying I blame him, but it may well have ended better for both of them if he'd let her do what she climbed into that cage to—"

"Shut it off," I snapped.

I couldn't take it.

Drake glanced up at me from the phone, eyes hurt. "We should know. I mean... it's kind of... I don't know—"

"She almost died," I ground out.

"Protecting him," Ebony said quietly, gaze falling on Vex again, an intense look in his eyes. "Protecting *our* pack."

There was a long silence. "Fine." I swallowed. "Just turn it down."

I was still coming down from the absolute terror of what had just happened. Never, in all my life, had I felt anything like I had the moment I saw Vex crouching over Rook's body, looking out at two rutting alphas who were primed to murder her.

It wasn't just her. There had been a moment, when we'd got to the hospital, that the doctors had been worried about him. He'd fought too many rounds... any longer...

I clenched my fists. I should have done more before this—should have noticed that he was getting this close to a rut. I was *supposed* to be his best friend, and I hadn't noticed. I'd been so angry. And now it was Ebony who'd been there, and she stopped him, not me. She'd *claimed* him.

They'd said that was good.

That should be good. It *was* good, I was just...

You weren't watching her... My nails dug into my palms. *She got hurt while you were fighting with Ebony.*

I felt like I was living a replay.

Fuck.

But what had *she* been thinking? No one could have predicted that.

And it was televised.

I looked up, blood running cold. Would the pack who held her bond punish her for this?

"Have they texted?" I asked Ebony when Drake dipped out to find a vending machine.

He glanced up, frowning until he realised what I meant. Ebony tugged the second phone from his pocket, glancing at it, then shook his head. "Nothing. But it's late. They might not find out until the morning."

"They might have felt it through the bond."

"Less gets through than you think. She's strong. She keeps them out."

There was a knock at the door, and I looked up, half prepped to see Rook's parent pack—Ebony had warned me they were on the prowl—but instead I was met with a rather unexpected sight.

I crossed toward the door and pulled it open, heart in my throat. "Prey?"

And she'd brought... friends. Well, one familiar gold pack omega—the one with chestnut hair who we'd found with Vex at the Gala. At her side was an alpha—presumably hers. He was tall and slim, and saddled with a stack of boxes that smelled of sweet baking. The snow white of his shaggy hair and one red eye marked him as a seer—an alpha who could read auras. But he certainly didn't look like he worked here—he wore a hoodie and had a scar up his left cheek.

"Hi..." Prey said, dragging my attention back to her. Her smile was a little anxious. "We heard about the situation. Thought we could stop by."

"I..." Visitors for Vex? "Yes."

Ebony went rigid as I let them in, furious gaze fixed on Prey and the second alpha.

"What are you doing?" he asked.

But the omega was already shaking Drake's hand, then mine, and Ebony's—who nodded stiffly, eyes still on Prey—as she introduced herself as Havoc, and her alpha as Kai.

"This is good," One of the nurses was saying, trailing them in, eyes on Vex. "Her heart rate is better. Does she know your scents? We usually find that reaction happens when an omega finds a person's scent comforting."

I felt Ebony bristle through the bond, and his eyes snapped to Prey like a lightning bolt.

"How is she?" Prey asked, eyes meeting mine. "Rook texted with an update."

"He did?"

"Wanted any tips we could give on how he could get her to trust him."

"For the record," Havoc declared. "My suggestions were much more reasonable than climbing into cages with rutting alphas—but it was pretty cool. I'm glad they're alright though."

"Love—"

I crossed toward Ebony, stopping him before he began. "If they settle her, they stay."

"You're okay with an unbonded alpha soothing your omega while—"

"They were there for her when no one else was," I said under my breath. "They're good for her, and you're going to be fucking grateful."

"There for her?" Ebony demanded.

"Yes."

I'd been able to piece together what they'd done in hindsight. From the fire in Prey's eyes when she'd found me at the Gala, to all the truths that had come outside.

"She wasn't just there for her, Ebony. Prey found *your* omega *in* heat, and she protected her and brought her back to you—to all of us. Of course Vex finds her comforting. Get a grip."

Ebony's jaw was still firmly clenched, but he did pause, eyes calculating as he glanced back over at Prey, who had taken a seat at Drake's side.

I came out of the bathroom next, however, to hear the monitors in Rook's room beeping.

"What the fuck is—? *Ebony!*" I snapped. He'd shoved Drake out of the way and was unceremoniously clambering into Vex's bed. I pinched my brow with a sigh as he drew her against him and twilight grass filled the room as he scent marked her before I ripped him off and shoved him back into Rook's doorway.

Havoc had laid out her gifts, which included three boxes of various waffles from Betabutter's Waffle Truck, and then clambered onto the foot of Vex's bed before pulling out some string.

"What's her favourite colour?" she asked.

"Peach and sage," Drake said instantly, shuffling his chair closer and watching. "What are you doing?"

"Friendship bracelet." She lifted her arm to reveal three. "You get one, and then all your friends get charms to put on it. I had to get three. The first one is mostly my dad. Then my pack got me so many I needed another one. So then I got a third for friends only or they'd take up all the space."

There was an awkward silence in the room, and then Havoc's eyes brightened with realisation. "You don't need that many friends. I only have Prey, so she just got me eight charms." Another beat passed. "But I mean... if I got another friend, I could trade some out." Havoc glanced to Prey for a second, nervously. "That would be okay, right?"

Prey nodded with a smile, and it was hard to ignore how she looked at Havoc with a warmth she'd once had for me.

I slumped down into the chair beside her and watched as Havoc and Kai were taking it in turns throwing chocolate raisins into each other's mouths—to Drake's entertainment.

"She's a scent match?" Prey asked me quietly.

I nodded, jaw clenched.

"I'm sorry we were too late," Prey said. "When we found her, I didn't know someone had already been in."

"I know." I swallowed, still hating to think of that night. We were talking quietly enough that the others couldn't hear, especially with the news still blasting, and I wanted to clear Vex's name. "She wasn't lying to us because she wanted to."

"I wasn't making any judgements—"

"She wasn't trying to trick us. She didn't have a choice." I swallowed. "She was dark bonded—*is* dark bonded. Still."

I really don't know what had made me say it, but Prey was just... she'd always been steadfast.

It wasn't exactly a secret, though we didn't want the press finding out, but I trusted Prey. She was one of the few people in the world I trusted absolutely.

Prey's only reaction was to go still, intense eyes fixed on me with that steadiness I remembered so well. She was always calm. I felt it in her aura, jasmine and myrrh, like a blanket upon the room.

Prey reached out slowly, her hand taking mine and giving it a squeeze before letting me go. "I'm so sorry, Love."

"Thank you for... you know. For being there for her when I wasn't." I'd left her that day when she was going into heat. If I hadn't... what would have happened?

How much less might she have suffered?

"I... I almost lost her," I whispered. "Too busy worrying about... About Ebony, and the pack and what it would mean."

"You want to know what I think?" Prey asked.

I sighed, rubbing my face and bracing myself. "Yes." She had never been one for sugar coating anything.

"I think you need to give yourself a little more credit when it comes to Ebony."

"What do you mean?"

"You're his cornerstone, Love. You need to have faith in what that means."

"He's the reason you—"

"You don't need to remind me of what happened," she said, and I saw the briefest shadow of sadness in her eyes, but it was gone in a moment. "You know he didn't just blow up my chance with your pack—he blew up my chance at the Rangers show, too?"

"I know. He—"

"Do you think he hated me enough to go the extra mile?" she asked.

I considered that, unable to help glancing at my brother who was shooting dark glances our way.

No.

That part hadn't sat right with me. Prey had been so upset about what had happened between us, she'd been ready to throw in the towel on movies entirely. Instead, she'd looked at a TV show with a dozen more seasons to go. A fresh start—almost a new career.

Except Ebony had stolen that from her, too.

The only explanation I had was that he'd done it to punish me. To drive the point home that I wasn't allowed anyone but him.

"It wasn't well known, but I was about to swap managers to get that role," Prey went on. "I was dropping mine for Lucas Rivers."

I paused, eyes narrowed.

"And then less than a year later all that shit comes out about him." She wrinkled her nose. "Convenient timing, too, when you jumped right in with his replacement on the City of Dusk spinoff movie a week later. Contract fell right into your laps."

I stared at her.

No. That hadn't been convenient at all. I knew Ebony had triggered that landslide himself. I hadn't argued for the filth he was unseating.

Except *if* he'd known beforehand...? I leaned back, considering that.

Was she suggesting he'd *protected* her? It felt too wishful when it came to Ebony. "He didn't hate you, Prey, but he didn't like you."

"No, he didn't." She smiled, elbowing me and returning her gaze to Havoc and Kai. "But *you* did."

They stayed for a little longer, providing a welcome distraction— even if it did include one tense incident, in which Havoc almost choked on a raisin. (Kai had been half way to heimlich's and Drake had his finger on the call bell before she'd spat it up like a cat).

Afterwards, Havoc finished making Vex *three* friendship bracelets with different combinations of colours (just in case), and placed one gently on her wrist. With my approval (and to Ebony's utter horror), she scent-marked it *and* got Prey to as well.

Then she added two silver charms: a waffle for her, and a falcon for Prey—for her famous movie, *Hunting Falcons.*

"Nice seeing you, Love, Drake." Prey nodded to us as they gathered their stuff to leave at last. "Ebony." She served him a particularly warm smile that, for Prey, was loaded.

TWENTY-EIGHT

VEX

I woke to clinical lights and a dull, aching pain in my abdomen and a splitting headache.

Warm arms surrounded me. I blinked sleep away, trying to ground myself.

Blackcurrant wine and vanilla winter were in here. Twilight grass and... Something was wrong.

Where was he?

I caught it, the scent of caramel brandy was there, but faint.

Too faint.

That low wounded groan... it was from me.

"Vex!" That was Drake at my side in a hospital bed, arms around me.

"Where...?" I croaked, my throat dry and sore. "Where...?"

"Just in the next room. He's okay. He's resting."

The next room?

"I..." Fuck. "What happened?"

"He was being an idiot, staying in there that long," Love growled.

Images rushed back. Rook, weak and bloody on the floor... His aura was unstable, blood and sweat glistened on his cheeks...

He could have died.

He *almost* died.

More than anything though, it was what I'd seen in his eyes as he'd looked at me through those bars.

He was alone.

"I..." I need him.

My voice wasn't working.

My chin quivered pathetically, and then I was scrambling from the bed. I got barely a step before I buckled, a whine of agony rising in my chest. Love caught me, but I struggled from him. Finally, I found my voice. *"I need to see him!"*

The world was spinning, but I didn't care, a deeper instinct driving me on.

I didn't stop fighting Love's grip until I felt the unstable aura split the room.

ROOK

I awoke with my world still crumbling down around me. A sense of dread collapsing in on all sides.

I'd fought the blackness sweeping me away, the sound of her pain echoing in my mind, haunting me through pain and restless sleep.

It was that same sound that woke me, dragging me awake through agony and drugs.

Vex.

Vex!

The world spun, pain splitting my head. Everything was too bright... Everything was spinning...

Where was she?

I could hear her cries...

She was the first thing that came into focus, expression broken with distress. Someone was holding her—fighting her. Crimson seeped into my blinkered vision, and I reacted before thought, a low growl in my chest as I ripped them from her.

Someone tried to grab me, but I flung them back, ignoring the searing in my whole weary body.

She was right here.

She was hurt.

Because of me?

I wouldn't let her hurt anymore.

"Vex!" I crashed to my knees, fumbling for her.

God... *she was alive.*

Her eyes were open. She was all but on her feet, though I was steadying her, hands on her hips.

"Rook?" She was desperate, but the pain cleared from her expression as she took me in. "You're... You're okay?" Glittering tears beaded in her eyes.

Fuck.

I helped her sit on the edge of the bed, even when every instinct was screaming at me to drag her into my arms right now. To hold her close and never let go. I fought those urges, remaining kneeling before her, instead.

The image of her below me, eyes closed, blood blossoming through her hair, it was like a stake in my heart that I couldn't rip out. One that made demands, set my hair on end, left adrenaline streaking through my system and my aura almost impossible to stifle.

But I couldn't act on it.

I'd chosen to climb into that cage, I'd chosen it so I could fix this with her. But I hadn't wanted her to turn up, to worry for me, or get hurt again.

So I crushed those instincts with every ounce of my will,

needing to give her better. I ignored them, even when she was reaching for me with golden eyes full of desperation. "Rook...?"

I caught her wrist, my own panic stronger than even my most violent instinct. I wouldn't react like I had before—trying to fix this for me but with no consideration of her.

She was only broken because I'd fucked up.

"Vex." My voice was rough. "I need to tell you... I'm sorry." I cleared my throat, ignoring the twisting of my heart as her lip trembled, eyes darting down to where I held her.

She froze at my voice, blinking, and the glimmer of a beading tear vanished with the motion.

Each moment in the cage had been cold and dark. I'd known my mate was in the world somewhere and didn't want me.

That was true agony.

"The whole time you were here, I made you feel..." Like... that. Worse. And for so much longer. "I'll spend the rest of my life fixing this." Again, it took all my might not to drag her close. "I'm so, *so* sorry for everything, and I want to start making it up to you—when you're ready. I didn't mean for you to be there. I'm just... I'm sorry, and I—"

"What do you think you're doing?" A sharp voice asked.

I looked over to see a woman in a white coat leaning against the doorway, arms folded. She was a female alpha, and had taken enough scent dampeners that I couldn't catch her scent. Even her aura was faint in the air.

What did she think she was doing, interrupting this? "Who the fuck are you?"

"Henreka Davis, Arkologist on your case."

"We're kind of having a moment—"

"We're seeing a spike in heart rate—"

"I'm fine!" I snapped.

"It's *her* heart rate," she said, eyes shifting to Vex.

I turned. "What?"

"Never in my life have I seen such a foolish display. She claimed you on live TV, Mr. Harrison. Why are you treating her so coldly?"

Claimed... *me*? My mind didn't have time to consider that for her last words. I wasn't being *cold*. "I'm *apologising*."

"You're fighting your instincts. She's reading it as rejection."

"It's okay!" Vex's voice was breathy.

"I... What?" I looked back to Vex. She was still tense, eyes darting between us. "Y-you are?"

"I..." She shook her head. "No. No, of course not. It's nice... what you're saying. I didn't want to—"

"I'm not rejecting you."

"I know... I know you're not." But her voice went up a few octaves, a slight tremble in it.

"But—"

"Mr. Harrison!"

The moment I shifted to glance back at the Arkologist, Vex whined desperately, kicking her legs, her bottom lip quivering.

Okay.

Shit.

I gave into *everything*, staggering to my feet and dragging her against my chest.

She was different now, and I couldn't put my finger on why. The whole world had shifted once more.

I was hers.

No matter what happened, I was hers. And that knowledge, it didn't come with shame this time. Instead, I was determined to be someone worth that.

I sunk onto the bed, drawing her head back gently so I could brush my jaw along hers.

A scent mark.

I'd never done that before. Not to anyone.

Her purr was instant, and I felt arms wind around my neck as she clutched me against her.

My heart was warm.

Vex had claimed *me*?

My own purr rumbled to life, matching hers as I held her tight.

That was a gift I would never let go.

TWENTY-NINE

LOVE

My face was still sore from where Rook had clocked me.

Fucking bastard.

I hadn't been *hurting* her.

The nurse had given me a look that said, *'you have no one to blame but yourself.'*

Vex, in full omega mode, spent the rest of the hospital stay curled up in Rook's arms—with the exception of when I dragged him to the shower, (the reek of blood and sweat was getting a little much, and she deserved better than that). During that time, she dangled her legs over the edge of the bed, staring anxiously at the door until he returned.

Being in her arms was making Rook purr like a motorbike which was, admittedly, a little sweet. Plus, I could swear there was a glint of smugness in her expression as she worked around his death grip of a hug to adjust pillows around them both.

It settled my heart.

She was... happy.

That was what mattered.

"Can we go home?" she asked, the moment the Arkologist came back in to check on the two of them.

"He's got a bit of a rut left in his system. He'll need watching, but he's good to leave. His wounds are healing quickly—that's normal, especially in a rut, and yours weren't too severe," she finished.

"Okay, but..." I glanced between them. "You said the rut is *almost* over. He's not going to have to..." I trailed off.

"Is he going to have to stick his dick into anything before it's over?" Ebony supplied the question for me.

Dr. Davis chuckled. "She's doing a fine job of balancing him already."

"She is?" Rook asked, confused. "But I mean... we haven't..."

Dr. Davis rolled her eyes. "It's always the elite packs who miss that memo. To be crude, your omega doesn't *have* to have sex with you to balance you through a rut—though, she's welcome if that's what you'd both prefer. Omegas well in tune with their instincts can settle an alpha without much more than skin on skin contact. We haven't needed to give Mr. Harrison anything for his rut since he arrived."

Vex puffed up at that, drawing Rook closer still.

"So... we can go home?" Drake asked.

"I'm going to prescribe them both another pain killer for lingering injuries. As long as you don't separate them, let her take him to the nest, they'll be fine."

"Oh..." Rook looked weary. "No, no, I can't go into her—" He cut off as Vex spun on him, eyes blazing. "I'm uh..." He shrank perceptibly. "I'm yours, Baby Girl... We can do what you want."

Getting them home was a relief.

Rook's family had been blocked from visiting the ward no less than three times. I didn't put it past his family to eventually find a way around the security.

Sure enough, once we were home, his family were at the gates within the hour.

Ebony caught up as I went to meet them.

"What are you doing?"

"I want to deal with them," he said.

"You do?" I asked, surprised.

"He needs someone to fight for this."

"You think I won't?" I asked, affronted.

He side-eyed me. "You're still lukewarm."

I stopped walking for a moment, catching his arm. "Is it good enough for you? He pulls that stunt and she just forgives him?"

"It's who she is. What gives you the right to devalue that?"

"It's not her I'm worried about. It's him…" I rubbed my face, torn. But how was I supposed to just forget everything that had happened?

"He's doing the best he knows how to do and has been for a while now."

"His best is—"

"Shit. Yeah, I think we're all clear on that, but you can't keep people around despite their flaws like a saint, and then take issue with them when it's convenient to you."

"What's that supposed to mean?" I asked.

"It means he was trying, and you weren't there to help, but you're happy to turn up and do the criticising."

"I'm focused on her," I said. "She deserved that."

"I'm not saying that was the wrong choice."

"Then what are you saying?"

"This pack has the same flaws as it always has. You allowed that then—were willing to turn a blind eye then—so you don't get to take it out on Rook now."

I stared at him, jaw ticking. Was it possible that this was about more than just Rook?

I'd never seen Ebony defend Rook a day in his life—and he wasn't just defending Rook. I could see it in his eyes: he would die on this hill.

Actually... that wasn't entirely true. There had been one day of his life that Ebony had defended Rook, though I'd thought it was simply about securing Rook's spot in our pack so he wouldn't have to deal with Prey.

Except my understanding of Ebony was, perhaps, more incomplete than I'd previously imagined. Or was Vex changing us —changing him?

He was right though. And he'd been there when Rook went into a rut. I even believed that he'd done what he thought was best for them both—as insane as that was. And, fallout aside, maybe it was.

"Okay." I nodded to the group at the gates. "Your call."

It had, after all, been the Harrison pack to whom Ebony had made his defence of Rook the last time.

I didn't like Rook's parents one bit. I knew he kept his distance when he could, but his relationship with them was complicated.

They were musicians, renowned in their circles, and they hadn't liked Rook packing up with me and Ebony. The last time I'd seen them had been the day that they'd come for their *final intervention*' as they'd called it—which had proven prophetic, even if not in the way they'd hoped.

At the age of seventeen, Rook still needed their signature to approve his place in our prospective elite pack. Instead of giving it, all four of his fathers had turned up at the door to bring him home.

. . .

"Sign the papers." Seventeen-year-old Ebony sounded bored as chaos erupted around him.

Casually, as if his fist wasn't closed around the onyx blade that was jammed into Felix's hand, he picked up a pen.

"One twist, and I don't know if your tendons will ever recover enough to play." He peered up at the other three alphas around the table, all with their auras out.

"Anyone touches me, I might just... slip." He leaned back where he sat, and pressed the pen into Felix's free hand.

Felix could have come for him after that, there were certainly enough witnesses, but just like everything else Ebony did in life, it was calculated. *"He'd never want it getting out to anyone that he'd been bested by a seventeen-year-old nobody."*

That's what he'd said, and he'd been right.

At the gates to our home—which I had no intention of opening—we were met by Goldie, Rook's mother, Benjamin, his biological dad, and Felix: pompous pack lead.

Felix Harrison didn't shy from much in the world from what I'd seen, but his face blanched a little as Ebony stepped forward to take the lead on the conversation. I couldn't quite fight the smile at the edge of my lips.

"Rook is recovering."

Felix stiffened, but Goldie was full steam ahead. "How long before he'll see us?"

"Before he's well enough to tolerate irritants?" Ebony asked, gaze sliding to her. "Never. You aren't welcome here. Don't come back."

"You can't stop us seeing our son," Benjamin snapped.

Ebony's gaze flickered to him, but he said nothing else, waiting.

Again, Goldie wasn't having it. "What's this nonsense about the gold pack—?"

"Careful." Ebony's voice dropped, each word sure. *"Any slander of our mate will be treated as slander of the whole pack."*

Felix went stiff, glancing between us as if trying to find the trick.

"She *isn't* Rook's mate." Goldie Harrison just sounded so damn sure it made my stomach turn.

"We've offered her the princess bond," Ebony said coolly. They knew already, they had to, they'd seen that tattoo, but Goldie didn't look ready to believe it. "And she's... considering."

I appreciated that from him.

Vex didn't need anyone prying into the dark bond. Not with the amount of media attention she already had.

"Considering?" Felix spluttered. *"Considering?"*

"You aren't welcome near my pack," I said. "Leave, or security will have remove you."

I could easily dial it in. This street was full of famous residents, and the patrol would have them removed in an instant.

Goldie stepped right up to the bars of the gates, her voice shaking with fury. "You've... destroyed him."

"You destroyed him, Mrs. Harrison." Ebony said coldly. *"Vex* is doing her best to pick up the pieces."

"I don't believe it," Goldie's voice was a truly irritating pitch for a woman so renowned for her vocals. "I thought the two of you were bad enough—then the Jaccard kid, and now this?"

I winced.

Wrong move.

At the mention of Drake, Ebony went from glacial to sub-zero.

"Without you leeches," Goldie was snarling. "My Rook would never have matched with an omega like—"

"Like *what*?" Ebony asked, clear and cutting. "An omega who would throw herself between rutting alphas to protect him?"

There was a sneer on his face as he took a step back. "You're right. Rook's moving up in the world. His omega bloodline doesn't host quite such *calibre*."

With that, he turned to leave.

Goldie's eyes bulged, and she was half mad with rage. Benjamin had to catch her from leaping at the gates. I turned, following Ebony as Felix's curses chased us down the drive.

There was still a shadow in Ebony's eyes as we made our way through the front door. "You aren't allowed to do more. Not to Rook's family."

"Vex's success will be enough," he said quietly.

I was left pondering one thing as we returned to Vex's nest. "What do you think about what she did in that cage?" I asked as we walked up the stairs.

He glanced at me, then shrugged. "Reckless and stupid."

Yet, I could see it there again, that flash in his eyes. Now she was safe and well, it was clear that he was absolutely smitten by what she'd done.

He was right on a good number of things today, the least of which being how harsh I was on Rook.

I might have to reckon with another harsh truth.

I'd thought it was fear that led me to isolate our pack from omegas and scent matches, but it may well have been pride. Who was I to decide Ebony couldn't handle a mate—that he would hurt her?

He was proving me wrong every day, and our pack was changing because of it.

THIRTY

LOVE

When we returned to Vex's nest, it was to find Rook and Vex still cuddled on the couch. Drake had put on Aura Boxing—a questionable choice since I wondered if it *would* even be Rook's favourite anymore.

The two were bundled in blankets and pillows, and Rook had her clutched in his arms like he might never let her go.

Drake was at their side, a lingering smile on his face as he glanced at them.

"Still high?" I asked, dropping down beside him. The pain meds Dr. Davis had given them weren't light.

"As kites," Drake replied.

Rook was slumped back, squeezing her tight in his arms, voice a low whisper. "I don't know what to do, Vex. You deserve to be happy, and you deserve mates who care about you. But I don't have the right to be on the same fucking hemisphere as you, and I don't know what to do about that."

I felt a little pang of guilt as his pain came down the bond.

Maybe... Maybe Ebony had been right. Maybe this pain had been here the whole time, and I'd been ignoring it.

"Well, it sounds like booking a flight would be a good start," Vex replied, a cheeky sparkle in her dazed eyes.

He looked around dramatically, then grabbed his phone from the cushion beside him. She giggled, but shoved it down, forcing him to meet her eyes again. "Don't... don't actually leave me."

"Okay. I won't. Not ever."

Listening to them muttering to each other like teens with too much gossip was quite sweet. Drake had to keep burying his face in his jacket so they wouldn't hear him snickering.

"I'm the luckiest man in the world now that you'll let me hold you," Rook was whispering much too loudly. "You're so perfect. You're funny, and *so* kind, and your eyes they're... they're pretty. Not just pretty, Vex. Like when I saw your real eyes for the first time—I didn't even know it was possible for anyone to be that beautiful."

Vex's cheeks were glowing pink as she pushed herself up, swaying slightly, golden eyes struggling to focus on him. "You're really pretty too," she whispered.

"More than Ebony?" he asked.

She swallowed, lips parting as she considered that. "I'm not allowed to say that."

Rook nodded, with a frown. "Okay. I get it."

"I *really* like the tattoo." She ran her fingers over it gently, as if she couldn't believe what she was looking at.

"I'll get more. Anywhere you want them."

"Will you?" Her eyes shone.

"Anything for you, Baby Girl. My perfect, sweet, kind, sexy omega." He brushed her cheek, and she leaned against his palm, purr rumbling to life. "I'd even..." He trailed off, his own cheeks going pink as if he was mustering the courage for something big.

When he spoke, it was in a slurred rush. "I'd even get one on my face if that meant you'd sit on it."

Drake shoved his fist to his mouth, choking back his laughs at my side, and even Ebony's face was split with a grin. Vex's laugh was goddamn heart stopping.

After Rook's scent mark, Vex kept doing it back to him as if forgetting he was *thoroughly* marked already. I noticed she'd done it *three* more times since the pretty eyes comment. The nest smelled as if a bakery shop had exploded in the middle of it.

They settled into quiet cuddles for a while before Rook spoke again. "Vex..." His voice was low and worried.

"Yes?"

"I'm a little... concerned about... well, about the others." He dropped his voice even more, though not nearly enough so that we couldn't hear him. I side-eyed Drake and Ebony, who were watching with interest.

"What do you mean?" she asked.

"Well..." He glanced at us and his eyes narrowed before he looked back to her. "I'd like to know what they did to apologise. I want to make sure it was good enough."

I straightened, irritation flaring. "You've got to be fucking joking—"

Drake grabbed my arm, but Rook wasn't backing down. He was glaring at me.

"It's a valid concern," he said. "I just... Look, this was really hard. I had to do a lot of stuff to know how to get this right—"

"Rook." Vex tugged his face back to her.

"No, I'm serious. I had to go to a family dinner with all of these kids, and then there were the trophies and the cage—"

"Our apologies were *fine*," I snapped.

"All I'm saying is that how do I know you guys know how to apologise properly?"

"You just missed the boat, Harrison," Ebony snorted. "Most people learned a while ago."

"Bullshit. I think I would have noticed."

"Stage three of social development: initiative vs guilt," Ebony supplied.

"What does that mean?"

"It means Drake and Love went through the uncomfortable process of learning to form a genuine apology approximately between the ages of three to five."

Rook, even high as he was, didn't seem to see the joke. His eyes went cold, expression turning sour.

"I want him out," he snapped.

Ebony grinned. "Not going to happen."

"Get him *fucking* out!" He was shoving himself up—after moving Vex away carefully. Pandemonium broke loose. Ebony got to his feet, anticipating an attack, and Drake grabbed Rook before he could throw himself bodily at Ebony.

"ROOK!" Vex's shout was the only thing that drew him up.

He turned back to her, rage melting from his face.

She clambered toward him, trying to tug him back down on the couch. She cupped his face in her hands, her expression a storm of worry. "I want him in here," she whispered. "Please. Can we keep him?"

Rook's expression twisted, and he glanced toward Ebony, then back to Vex.

"If... if that's what you want."

Her smile, even lopsided, was enough to brighten the room.

Everything seemed momentarily diffused until Ebony opened his fat mouth, looking all too smug. "Good boy, Harrison. It's about what *she* wants." There was a split second of silence as he tensed. "And *she* wants *me*."

Rook was off the couch in a second, a growl in his chest as he threw himself at Ebony.

"Oh for fuck's sake!" I snapped, catching him just in time. Ebony's grin was broad as Rook fought with me and Drake to get to him.

"She didn't say she wanted you alive!" he snarled.

Ebony's bark of a laugh was almost enough for me to miss the sound she was making. Rook stopped fighting, spinning back around. Vex was still curled up where he'd left her, giggling as she watched us.

It was cute until tears started leaking down her face.

"You stopped..." She managed through teary-eyed hiccups. "You stopped cuddling me so you could punch him."

"No, no, no." Rook was curling back up beside her in a second. "It's not like that."

"It is," she said. "I saw it."

He drew her tight in his arms, eyes wide and desperate.

"Promise me you won't stop cuddling me again to punch Ebony in the face?" she asked.

"I..." Rook hesitated. "I promise I'll try really hard not to."

Vex pouted. "That's not great, Rook."

Drake shoved his fist in his mouth, squeezing his eyes shut as he shook with mirth.

"I just... I don't want to lie to you."

"Okay." Vex hugged him closer. "I can appreciate that."

There was a pause.

When she spoke, her voice was a loud whisper. "If you do stop cuddling me to punch him, can you make sure you don't take long?"

"I can do that, Baby Girl."

"Like... less than thirty seconds?"

"Less than twenty."

Vex's hiccuping purr came to life in response to that.

Ebony's eyes were narrowed as he stared between them. "You really don't have the right to be mad at me, Harrison," he said. I shot him a warning look. He *had* to stop provoking Rook. "She can't leave you alone, and she hasn't even *seen* your ass yet."

Uh... what?

"My... ass?" Rook straightened, staring between us.

Vex looked adorably bewildered. "What's his ass got to do with anything?"

Ebony shrugged. "He kept coming in and out with those drugs when he was in a rut. Had all these slurred requests for tattoos. I couldn't get them all done, but—" He cut off as Rook scrambled on his side.

"Uh... are we—?" But I cut off, too late.

Vex, just as curious, tugged down the sweatpants to reveal the muscular curve of Rook's rich brown ass cheek, and across it—

Well, *damn*.

My own grin was spreading across my face.

"Oh my god!" Vex squeaked.

"What did you do to my ass?" Rook demanded, blazing eyes fixed on Ebony.

Drake cracked; he was wheezing and tears flooded his cheeks as he spotted the tattoo. Rook tried to turn, but Vex—still high out of her mind—clutched him tighter and I swear her eyes might have glowed again as she stared at the words.

"You asked for it, mate," Ebony said.

"What the *hell* did you tattoo on my—*OW!*" Rook jumped as Vex delightedly sunk her tiny little omega fangs right into Rook's ass cheek—and right across the words: *'Ken to a gold pack doll'*.

THIRTY-ONE

Chia pet's 4th day of life. Hair length: 1cm
   Days until execution: 5 days

VEX

Yesterday I had been running on pure omega instincts. I'd felt like *myself* for the first time in a long time. Like I could make change. Rook needed *me*. As stupid and cheap as any of that might be, it wasn't any more stupid and cheap than the fact that my name was tattooed across Rook Harrison's chest—and the whole of New Oxford knew about it.

It was so fucking obnoxious, and my heart glowed every time I saw it.

And he'd promised me a date tonight.

So everything should have been perfect when I opened my eyes this morning.

It *should* have been.

Rook was in my bed, still holding me against his chest, the warmth of his body so right against mine. Drake was on my other side and our fingers were tangled together. He was so pretty, eyes peacefully closed in sleep with messy dark hair scattering across his porcelain skin. Beyond him, Love was on his back, sleeping on the far end of the bed.

Almost the whole pack.

But the dread I woke with, was for his beautiful slice of perfection.

I wasn't destined for perfection.

It was then that I realised I hadn't checked my phone.

Not in a long time.

And—Shit.

Shit.

I hadn't watered my chia pet.

I hadn't watered my chia pet, and I hadn't checked my phone and both of those things were *paramount.*

It took me a long time to slip from Rook's arms without waking him. I had to scent mark a pillow and stuff it into his arms to get away. I had a lingering headache from my injuries, but nothing severe enough to merit pain medications—I'd had more than enough yesterday.

I hurried to water the chia pet, phone clutched in my hand, even when I hadn't looked at it.

I would.

That conviction made the weight of my commands less urgent.

The chia pet, however, had sprouted green hair. I leaned closer, inhaling. For the first time that aroma didn't bring me a second of fear.

It wasn't chia sprouts that made up its green hair.

It was wheatgrass.

I palmed my phone in my hand. I'd now peeked at it to find two texts from Zeus, but I hadn't opened them.

I'd do *this* first.

I was nervous in a way I wasn't with the others. I didn't know why, but Ebony was just... different. I tried and failed to knock on his door four times before I mustered the courage.

Finally, I rapped quickly and took a few steps back.

Silence passed, and I hugged myself tighter.

I took another step.

It was okay.

I didn't need to do this, not really.

The door creaked as I began to turn, and I jumped. Ebony's brows were drawn as he rubbed his eyes, and twilight grass flooded the hallway.

"It's the ass crack of dawn, I texted you the update, there was—Oh."

He froze, gaze falling on me.

Mother above, he was beautiful. His hair was down, and messy—well, messy for Ebony, which meant a few hairs out of place as it tumbled about his shoulders. He was wearing nothing but a pair of baggy sweats, and I couldn't stop my eyes sweeping over his glorious torso: rigid muscle with that dusky tan skin and a perfect V leading down into his waistband.

Oh, fuck me.

He was too much.

I realised my lips were parted as I met his eyes, though he looked no less stunned. His gaze had slid down to my bare legs, before he met my eyes again. He was definitely less sure than usual.

"I wanted to see you," I said, when he looked as if he wasn't going to break the silence.

"Why?" He just sounded so confused it might have been comical.

I tried to formulate my words but nothing came out. I might have looked pale because he frowned, stepping closer.

"I..."

Shit.

Don't burst into tears.

That *really* hadn't been the plan.

I'd already done that too many times.

I managed not to, but I must have looked on the brink of it because he stepped toward me in a second, perfectly alarmed as he drew my chin up, eyes scanning mine.

"Are you hurt?" he asked.

But everything right down to his scent was like a breath of air I hadn't been able to draw until this moment.

I shook my head, fingers closing around his wrist. Then, before I could think about it, I'd flung myself into his arms.

He held me like that for a long moment, then drew me up and carried me to the couch in his room. Every step into the space calmed my nerves, the cool twilight grass sinking into my very lungs.

"What do you need?" he asked.

"I uh..." I swallowed. "I don't know. It's stupid. Just a bit of courage."

Still, those texts were unread.

It was so much worse now, such a freefall after finally finding some true harmony in this pack. Some happiness with all of them there—even if I had been high.

"And you came to me?" He kept tucking non-existent strands of hair behind my ear mechanically, as if he wasn't sure what else to do.

"Nightmares," I whispered. Well, not exactly. It hadn't started until I was awake. But sometimes it was hard to pretend this wasn't one big nightmare.

"I thought the others were in your room," he said.

"They are."

"Aren't they comforting you?"

"They would have," I said. "I left."

A part of me had been scared of coming here for this, expecting him to consider it all silly, but Ebony was fixated on me like a puzzle to solve.

When I was with him, there was nothing else in the world but us. It was already working, my nerves were already so much better.

"They can't fix this."

"And I can?" he asked.

I nodded.

"How?"

"I just wanted to be near you."

He nodded, and I relaxed in his arms, content to sit in the quiet stillness of his strangely tidy room. Engulfed in twilight grass I felt safer than I ever had, and that was hard to reckon with.

"I don't know why you're coming to me today," he said quietly after a long silence.

"What do you mean?"

He considered that. "It will be a few more days before I'm finished with my gifts."

I peered up into those curious storm-silver eyes, considering that. "I liked the swan," I said quietly.

"Is that why you're here?"

"It's not why. But I liked it."

He nodded. "Explain why I can help and Love can't."

I felt a half smile on my face at those words. "It's not really important."

He tilted my chin up toward him. "I need to know."

I considered him for a long time, chewing my lip. "When I woke up, I was in my room and everything was perfect. Rook, Drake, and Love. It's everything... But I can't shake the feeling that this is the dream. I'm going to wake up and I'll be back there, and all of this was just something my mind made up..."

Ebony considered that, deathly still for a long time. "So you want to be with me, instead?"

"I just thought if I was with you..." I trailed off, suddenly realising what I'd been about to say.

"What?" He leaned back just the slightest bit. "Do I complete the dream?"

"It's just a change of environment," I said, throat dry.

There was a pause. "You don't need to lie to me, Vex." His half smile was curious. "It matters that you are with me?"

"Yes."

"And it matters that I'm your mate?"

I opened my mouth, then closed it, nodding again.

"And that's safer than the others."

"Yes."

"Because..." He mused, though I thought his eyes were twinkling. "When you're worried this is just a dream, I'm a solution because I'm never what you would have dreamed of in a mate."

I winced.

He was right.

"I'm... *sorry.*"

"That I'm not an omega's prince charming?" he asked. "Why would that upset me?"

I breathed a laugh, wondering why I'd been worried about that at all, now he'd said it.

He leaned close, palm cupping my cheek, storm-cloud eyes so sure. "I'm the nightmare of your nightmares, Vex. I don't *want* you to ever forget that."

I stared at him, finding no words to respond.

Finally, when a long time had passed and I found my voice, I dared ask the question that kept me up sometimes. I felt safe around him, but was that enough? If I somehow got free of this dark bond, would he still be interested in me? "Do you think you can really... love me?"

He blinked, cocking his head.

I nodded, throat dry. "Or what... what love would be for you?" I added.

"What love would be for me?" he repeated, a little humour in his voice. "You've been talking to my brother."

EBONY

Love?

I took a breath, staring into shining, golden eyes: the place around which my whole universe had begun to orbit.

Thrill, passion, and need, but... Love?

I'd given it thought. Despite our conversation, despite my promise and her demand that I be myself no matter what that meant...

But obsession would be a better word than love.

Obsession, or a claim. It was the most I'd ever had to offer.

So having Vex dog my every thought wasn't a sweet fuzzy experience that made me want to bake cookies like it was in the movies. Instead, it was unfamiliar. She was in every waking moment. Something that should be mine, and wasn't.

She was perfect. Even right now with sleep in her eyes, and messy bedhead. Her cheeks were rosy, face free of makeup, summer freckles uninhibited. She wore one of her long sleeved shirts with the embroidered sleeves. Sitting on my lap as she was, I was all too aware she wore nothing else but lace and socks.

"You're mine, and that will never change," I told her, drawing her closer.

"Is that love, to you?" she asked.

"I think..." I considered that. "For me, love is claim. I don't think it can be any more."

She cocked her head.

"Then... would you let *me* claim *you*?" she asked.

I paused, brows furrowing. "What do you mean?"

The vision of her crouching over Rook's body, eyes feral, flashed in my mind again.

I'd wanted that since the moment I'd seen it. She couldn't do that for me, not in the way she had for Rook, but...

"I mean..." She leaned up and I felt her teeth graze my neck. Then she drew back, her eyes twinkling.

I reacted instantly, lacing my fingers through her hair and drawing her back to my neck. I felt the warmth against my skin as she breathed a little laugh.

Then her teeth sunk in.

An omega's bite.

The world shifted.

Briefly, it was like the bond I shared with Drake when he was struggling. When he gave me his pain. Except then... *she* flooded my mind. So much more than I'd ever felt.

It wasn't permanent like an alpha's claim, most often it was an act of healing or intimacy, but it created the echo of a bond. It didn't matter: an echo of Vex in my silent mind was like a flash of fire in a void. Vex flooded my soul in a way even my brothers never had.

I leaned back, taking her in. She might as well have glowed for the way she stole my breath. It wasn't just that, either. The discomfort I'd felt since the moment I'd first seen her, slammed in.

"*This.*" I shut my eyes, trying to manage it. "This is why I hated you."

She paused, brows drawn.

"I heard you... singing." I'd heard her singing a lullaby through the door, and this was what I'd been faced with. At the time, I had made her the enemy for how I'd felt. I'd held onto that ever since.

She frowned.

"The day you arrived," I said. "I heard you singing and it... it made me feel like this."

"And you didn't want that?" she asked.

I shook my head, unsure of why tears were stinging my eyes.

I *never* cried.

"I didn't know what it meant. Or why..." I paused, trying to navigate what it was. "Why it hurts." But... hurt wasn't the right word. "It... aches like something is crushing my chest and I can't breathe."

She considered me for a moment, and then that mischievous smile crept onto her lips. She pressed a kiss to my cheek and leaned back.

"What?" I asked.

"Have you ever heard anyone describe what it's like when they see their mate for the first time?"

I shrugged.

"It's not always the same. Sometimes it's awe, or attraction, sometimes it's nerves. And sometimes, they say..." She paused, leaning back more, taking me in fully and I could see the anxiety in her own eyes as if she wasn't sure she should carry on.

"Tell me?" I asked. I wasn't used to the desperation in my voice.

"Could you be describing...?" Again, she trailed off, but she didn't need to finish as I realised what she was saying.

Love at first sight.

I'd heard it before when discussing scent matched packs, and yet never had I ever thought it was possible for me. It flew in the face of everything I'd just said.

I'd never loved anyone—not even my own brother. A laugh slipped out, but my mouth was dry. I'd hurt in a way I couldn't describe since the moment I'd seen Vex. "Love is supposed to be good. If this was love, it wouldn't hurt."

Her light laugh caught me off guard, and she just looked at me like I was mad.

"What would you say if it was?" I asked.

Our agreement was sound. She didn't want *this* from me. I didn't think I was truly capable of love, but if I was I pitied the person on the other end of that.

Her brows bunched as she considered.

Lord she was beautiful. I wanted to drag her closer and press my lips to hers right now. I wanted all of her. Mind, body and soul.

I drew up at that thought, something so much more gentle in it than when I'd desired her before.

Because she *was* mine.

And I was hers, and now she was in my head.

Nothing else.

Yet I'd claimed a lot of things in my life. My job. Drake. Even Rook—though he'd never admit it.

None of *them* hurt to hold.

"If it was, I'd like that." Her words drew me up.

She'd already seen the monster I was. She'd fallen victim to it. Our agreement. That was something I could manage.

This though? This was pure destruction.

But *why* was I fighting this?

If I wanted her to be mine I should be drowning her with the possibility of love. Isn't that what omegas wanted? If I gave her that, she'd stay, and I could keep her forever.

Again, that ache grew, the piece of her that was lodged within me.

Convince her, or you could lose her...

Only... I wanted her happy, even if it meant she didn't want me.

That last thought slammed into me like an iron weight.

I couldn't breathe, and I sat up, clutching her tight, trying to unravel this stupid, complicated shit in my brain.

"Are you okay?" Vex asked, worry in her eyes.

I shook my head, holding her so tightly it must have hurt, but she didn't say anything. Instead, she took my chin in her hand and drew me to face her.

"I'm fine," I told her.

"I think you're scared."

I had no answer to that.

"I'd take your love," she whispered. "However it looks."

"I don't..."

Fuck.

She was right.

This was fear. Rare and goddamned suffocating.

Insecurities were drowning me, something I wasn't used to. "You won't want me." My voice was rough.

She was going to see me like this, and then, when the bite faded, when I was the monster she was bonded to...

Again, her lips curved up at the corners, and with it, the ache that had been weighing me down also lifted. "Kiss me. And don't tell me what I want, Ebony Starless."

I drew her close, fingers weaving through her hair, and drew her into a kiss. As her lips found mine, I found courage, just like she'd come to me for.

"Do it again, Vex," I breathed, asking for the very thing my fears had been telling me to flee. "Sing for me."

THIRTY-TWO

EBONY

The low sound of Vex's lullaby changed me. The bite wouldn't last, but the things I was feeling while we were connected, they would. It was the most incredible high I'd ever had.

We didn't do anything other than lay in each other's arms. It wasn't what I'd imagined would happen the first time I made a real connection with my mate, but it was enough.

Until it wasn't.

Until the very weakness I saw in others reared its head.

After what felt like forever, she got up, something anxious in her eyes. "I'll be back."

Then she vanished into the bathroom.

I frowned, not sure what to read into her nerves until the phone in my pocket buzzed. Not mine.

The proxy.

My blood chilled as I tugged it out.

I'd forwarded the texts her pack lead had sent last night. She hadn't, it seemed, checked them until now.

Until she saw you, a little voice whispered.

I scrolled up, reminding myself of the last text. It had been a lot less chilling when I'd last read it.

> Pack Lead: You think fame will save you from what's coming?

Vex had replied.

> Vex: I didn't do it on purpose. They're celebrities. You didn't say this couldn't be public.

I waited, but no more texts came from her.

With difficulty, I forced myself to forward it on. If he replied again, I could delay before sending it.

Only, his reply came in moments, and... shit.

It wasn't one I could withhold.

> Pack Lead: I've had enough. I want to see you.

I had to send it, but it had never been this hard before.

My pulse was unusually elevated as I stared at the phone. Mechanically, I forwarded the text, knowing she was in the next room, receiving it.

She would be afraid. I didn't want to give her that fear.

I felt it from her the moment she read it.

The bite.

The damned bite she'd given me... I couldn't let it sabotage this. I *needed* this proxy to continue.

> Vex: You said you wouldn't until my heat.

> Pack Lead: I told you I wouldn't interfere. Now you've insulted me and pushed that generosity.

> **Pack Lead:** Tell Drake he's going to drop you off for a meeting with us and that he better come alone or all bets are off.

There was a long, long pause.

> **Pack Lead:** I'm not going to let it go, you little rat.

When the silence continued, I crossed to the bathroom.

She was still in there, afraid.

Before I could act, I received another from her. One that made me freeze. That made it almost impossible to keep sending them.

> **Her:** I'll ask Ebony.

Me?

I stared at it, and my fingers shook in a way I wasn't used to as I pressed send..

> **Pack Lead:** You'll do what your fucking told.

> **Her:** It's Ebony, or I won't come.

She was so strong. I could hear her on the other side of the door. Her breathing was short and sharp. She was in pain, fighting his orders.

I could feel the echo of her through this connection; she was no longer a bright light, instead she was a void of fear. I squeezed my eyes shut, trying to shut this new connection down.

It was almost impossible.

My mate was in pain and I couldn't do anything about it.

> **Vex:** Let me.

I hated the next text that came in from her. I hated that she was begging him.

> Vex: Please
>
> Vex: I'm doing everything you wanted.
>
> Pack Lead: Fine. Your choice. Choose Drake, and I'll leave them out of it. Bring Ebony, you'll both be punished.

What did that mean?

I waited a while, not wanting to make her suspicious before I knocked on the door.

"Vex?"

I heard movement from within, and her voice was weak. "Y-yes. I'm fine."

"You've been in there too long, I'm coming in."

"N-no it's—" But I was already pushing the door open, relieved to find it wasn't locked. She was curled up in the corner, knees to her chest, and when I entered, she shoved her phone into her pocket desperately.

Her face was streaked with tears.

"I'm okay, I—" But she cut off as I strode across the room toward her, not willing to leave her alone a second longer.

"Come here," I murmured, drawing her up into my arms and carrying her from the room. I sat us on my couch, feeling my own rage simmering beneath the surface as she trembled in my arms.

From agony.

Agony she'd suffered fighting for Drake.

Why was she afraid of Drake coming? I knew she was protective over him, but was there something more to it?

And why had she chosen me, instead?

"Ebony..." Her voice was a raw whisper. "I need... I need you to do something for me. But the others can't know."

I tugged her closer, heart settling as she made her choice.

We were protecting Drake.

That, I could do.

VEX

I don't know why it had been Ebony.

It was just a truth that had become an anchor in my life since I'd returned to them. I knew in my bones that he would protect me.

He parked his ridiculously nice car in the location Zeus had sent. He'd told the others we were going out, and said nothing else. He would do this for me, even when I could tell it hurt him. Hurt, or... disturbed him. That was what I was getting through this connection—a big tangle of emotions that were hard to unpack.

"Are you okay?" he asked, jaw clenched.

"I'll be back before you know it," I said, though there was no lightness in my voice. "Promise."

He just stared at me, then his gaze slid across the street where a black limo was pulling in. I could see the calculation in his eyes.

"Please," I whispered. "Just let's get it over with."

Zeus knew he was coming. What if Ebony tried something and it didn't work?

It would make everything worse. Zeus could ruin the whole thing.

I hated this. I hated how fucking impossible it was, even when they were right there. When Ebony was metres from them.

But that, I realised, was the point.

It was why they'd asked for Drake.

To torture him some more.

I shut my eyes, calming my breathing. I felt something unusual on my wrist as I tugged at my embroidered sleeve. I tugged it up to find myself looking at a peach and green bracelet. There were two silver charms on it: a waffle and a falcon.

For a while I stared at it, lips parted. Could it be what I thought it was? Now that I'd pulled my sleeve away, I caught the faint scents from it. Rainfall and fire tangled with jasmine and myrrh. I'd been high out of my mind yesterday, but I remember Love mentioning visitors. I stared down at the glittering silver on the bracelet.

Havoc and Prey had come to visit me?

"They *remembered* me?" I whispered, looking up at Ebony.

He nodded, examining my expression. "The nurse said their scent settled you." I felt a little flash of green from him in the bond at that, and almost found it in me to smile, which was a gift in itself.

"You're glad they came?"

I nodded. I'd been hurt and they'd come, and they weren't my scent matches or anything. They'd just shown up like... like maybe I mattered...

I tugged the bracelet off.

"Keep it safe for me?" I asked, holding it out to him. I didn't want Zeus to read into the foreign scents. He was good at picking out what I cared about.

Ebony nodded.

"And don't... scent mark it."

He narrowed his eyes, a faint smile twitching on his lips. "No promises, Little Omega."

"Okay." I steeled myself. Zeus might be worse now, after my happiness with my mates, but I had a newfound courage. From Ebony and the bracelet in his fist. "I'll be in and out, and then we'll go back and it'll all be over."

And Rook was going to set up a date with me tonight...

It was going to be okay.

· · ·

"I gave you space, Vex," Zeus said. "I told them you could do what you've done all along. Cerus, on the other hand. He has doubts."

Today, he wasn't alone. For the first time, Cerus was at his side. His short black hair was gelled back, and his dark brown eyes looked like voids.

I hated how vulnerable I felt, with my fists balled in my lap, kneeling at their feet.

"I hope Ebony waits like a good dog," Zeus snorted. "If he breaks the rules, I won't give you back."

I clenched my jaw. Ebony knew that. He wouldn't. But I was regretting the bond between us now. I had to manage my fear more carefully.

Zeus glanced at Cerus as he went on. "He doesn't know if we're doing enough after you made that scene on TV. That you have enough rules to make sure you don't fuck this up. Most of all, he's worried." Zeus leaned back, a sneer on his face. "He's worried I'm going soft. That I've given you too much leash and now you're smashing all the china."

Cerus looked bitter, as his gaze slid from Zeus to me.

"He's worried, because he's used to more cruelty from me. But that's a mistake. I'm *not* cruel, I'm practical. There's a beautiful day waiting for me at the end of this. If we want this to work, they have to be obsessed, Vex. We're not going to get there by making your life miserable, by banning you from affection or tripping you up. You're pathetic enough without my commands making it worse."

None of it was a question. There was something wrong. Zeus wasn't like I was used to. Was he talking to me, or Cerus?

"Have you fucked them, yet?" Cerus asked.

I nodded, heart racing in my chest. "I... yes."

"All of them?"

I shook my head, shutting my eyes.

"She's fucking useless. Almost died for them, and they still don't want her?"

"What *was* that about?" Zeus asked. "Trying to get around my order? Off yourself before this all comes crashing down."

"It *wasn't* on purpose."

"Climbing into a cage with three rutting alphas? Could have fooled me." Zeus laughed.

"I was protecting my mate."

Zeus leaned forward slightly, voice ice cold. "I'm sure they went rabid over it, too."

Again, I didn't know what to make of him. There was a half smile on his face plastered on like a mask. He was silent through the bond.

"There was that incident, a few nights ago," Cerus said. "What was that?"

My mind raced, trying to place the timeframe. Shadows flickered in Zeus's eyes as I watched.

Fuck.

The night Love had bitten me. I tried to keep my breath steady, remembering his rage through the bond.

"It was nothing." My voice was dry.

"Nothing?" Zeus asked, suddenly stiff.

"I—" but I cut off as Zeus's aura burst into the small space, then he was closing his fist around my neck.

"Nothing?" He shoved me against the floor of the limo. Panic shot through my system, despite all my attempts to hide it.

Ebony would feel it.

He *couldn't* come.

But this was different than when Zeus had hurt me for the videos. There was no camera. No purpose. His eyes were blazing with madness.

I clutched at him. The world was spinning.

No no no.

I'd been here before. Seen this before.

I wasn't going back there.

It was too loud.

My own whispers were amplified through the palms I clutched to my ears as I squeezed my eyes shut. Still, it was too loud.

An aura shattered the lyrics of a song.

I tried again like she'd told me to. I tried and tried until there was nothing but me and the words I whispered to desperately drown out the violence outside.

"Zeus." That was Cerus's voice cutting through the panic. Just as black blossomed in my vision, the pressure was gone.

I gasped for breath, clutching my throat.

"Stay," Zeus growled as I tried to pick myself up. Then I felt something heavy on my throat.

His boot.

I clutched it, trying to free some of the pressure, half my mind on trying to fight the fear clogging my brain.

Ebony.

Ebony couldn't come.

"I swear, you little gold pack rat. You let anything like that happen again, and I'll make sure this meeting feels like a kindness. *Now, tell me what happened.*"

I tried to clear my mind. I'd seen this before, but I could survive this. I had something my mother never had. Something I had only claimed because of her.

"Love... Love bit me," I stammered.

"He *bit* you?"

"On... on your b-bite."

What flooded through the bond from Zeus was more unsettling than anything else. Rage, like I expected, but that wasn't all. With it I felt a vicious jealousy.

Claim.

And then with what must have been an almighty effort from him, the bond slammed shut. I was left with Cerus, a lingering sense of vile want and... I blinked, trying to find him in my vision.

I could feel his discomfort, and when I saw him, his gaze was on Zeus.

Zeus had a snarl on his face, clearly oblivious to his pack mate's dissatisfaction. "Let's solve both our problems in one. Ebony and Cerus."

Finally, the weight was gone, though the command wasn't. I couldn't pick myself up, not yet.

"They've all bitten you at least once?"

I nodded. He knew the others had. It was part of the information he'd pried from me while we were together after the Gala. When he'd been taunting me over not being good enough for them.

"Good." His voice and tone told me he thought it was anything but good. "Get on your knees, and beg Cerus for a bite right where Ebony gave you his."

No.

Tears flooded my vision as I steadied myself on my knees before Cerus. I was desperately hugging my arms to my chest.

No.

The only bite I needed to tether me to this pack was from Zeus, but that didn't stop the others from biting me, too. More points of connection for alphas I despised. Just like Havoc had never rid herself of the shadow of bites from her past, I would never be free of this one.

But that bite, the one Ebony had given me all that time ago on the roof beneath the sun. *It* was mine.

Love was my pack lead.

Ebony was my alpha.

I clung to that mantra.

Drake and Rook: they were mine.

Not Zeus, not Cerus. They'd had to force a dark bond to make that claim. A memory flashed in my vision. Ebony with burning silver eyes, taking my wrist and pressing his teeth to it.

"Show me where he bit you."

I lifted my wrist, thumb already tracing the place Ebony had bitten, strength waning as I fought the other half of his command.

"Beg him," Zeus commanded.

"I will... never..." I grit my teeth, so proud there were no tears this time. "I will *never* ask for that." It hurt, but not like when I fought other commands, as if by trying to command that, Zeus was violating the very nature of this bond.

They had taken. I hadn't given. And he couldn't make me ask for that.

Zeus grinned and I felt his fleeting moment of pleasure as my pain rushed through the bond between us.

"I was going to ask him to make it neat, but if you want a nasty scar..."

The frightening loudness was gone, followed instead by a ringing silence.

My mother was curled up at the edge of her bed. I'd snuck in to see her even when she'd told me not to. I didn't care. I hated when they left her alone like this. She was an omega. She needed touch. I knew she needed it even more after they hurt her.

And they knew it, too. A foul cycle of dependence designed to punish an omega who failed to give them what they wanted.

"No my little one," she whispered. "You have to go."

But I slipped my arms around her neck and held on tight.

307

"There's a bird in the storm, and nobody knows..." I began to sing, my voice almost free of fear, just like she managed for me.

If they wouldn't, I would hold her until she stopped shaking.

I clutched my knees to my chest in the passenger seat of Ebony's car.

I was back with my mate, and that was all I could focus on.

I'd survived.

Ebony hadn't come charging in, though there was a massive dent in his car's dashboard that hadn't been there when I'd left. He'd seen Cerus's bite and his face had gone ashen, silver eyes a furious storm. Then he'd looked away. I'd never seen him this close to it: the dark bond that stopped him from claiming me the way I knew he needed to.

Fragile and scared, barely able to breathe, I watched him as he stared from the window. Would this be more than he was capable of giving? I'd seen an alpha's pride wipe them clean of sanity. I'd seen it push them to rejection, even of the one they were supposed to love.

"He was mad about what Love did..." I swallowed. "He bit me on the neck, over... over his bite." My voice was weak.

Ebony turned to me, eyes narrowed. "Love?"

"This wasn't his fault. I... I wouldn't have it any other way. But please don't tell him."

He nodded slowly. "Give me your wrist."

I stared at him, unsure.

Still, I lifted my arm and revealed the bite again. I saw the way his eyes darkened and in this temporary connection, I felt his hatred of it.

"I can't do the same," he said. "I won't risk you getting hurt." His eyes slid to my neck, and I realised there must be a mark forming. I'd have to put makeup over it when we got back. I didn't want them seeing it.

There was a flicker of depravity in Ebony's gaze and I felt it in our bond. It was a void, something bottomless and vicious. In a blink, it was gone.

Then he reached into his pocket and drew out the bracelet from Havoc and Prey. Their faint scents rose in the air around us, but he didn't flinch.

Carefully, he slipped it onto my wrist and pulled the dangling strings so it fit perfectly just past the bite. Then, to my surprise, he leaned down.

Instead of pressing his teeth to the bruised and bleeding mark Cerus had left, he pressed his lips to it, instead.

THIRTY-THREE

VEX

We were back in my nest's bathroom.

Ebony was tense, pulling out a med kit and trying to be neutral as he examined the bite on my wrist.

There was a knock, and Ebony went to answer it.

"It's Drake," he said, returning to me. "Do you want to see him?"

I nodded, then paused, looking down at the angry wound across my wrist. It made my stomach turn every time I saw it, and I had to shove away the memory of the cruel look in Cerus's eyes as he'd done it. "It's okay." My voice was rough. "He can come in."

I heard Ebony say something under his breath, and then Drake stepped in, clearly trying to measure his expression as he crossed to me.

"I'm sorry," he whispered, voice tight.

I lifted my hand to him, but he was already tugging me into a hug.

I inhaled blackcurrant wine, my heart already settling.

Ebony finished cleaning the bite and wrapped it up

completely. Then he readjusted Prey and Havoc's friendship bracelet over top.

"Do you want to go on a walk or something?" Drake asked. "Get some space."

I nodded. "I'd like that." Space sounded good. I knew Love and Rook would be upset when they heard about what had happened—inevitable, since there was a bandage wrapped around my wrist now—but I wasn't ready yet.

Drake was always safe, though.

We walked down to the little creek in silence.

"Are you okay?"

"I think so." I squeezed his hand. "Holding on." I swallowed. "Rook's setting up the date tonight. He was so excited."

"You can wait, I know he'd understand—"

"No." I cut him off. "I want it."

No.

This part with Rook, I hadn't had it yet, not like I had with Drake. I wouldn't give Zeus that.

"Okay, well. Why don't I talk to him—tell him he's not allowed to say a thing about it? If that's what you want."

I leaned my head against his shoulder with a smile. "Rook *and* Love?"

"I can do that," he said.

I shut my eyes, letting him lead us down the path for a little while.

Leaves rustled, and I could hear the faint trickling of a stream in the distance. I inhaled the petrichor in the air from the sprinkle of rain overnight. It tangled with the earthy scent of trees and soil.

"You always hold on," he said into the quiet afternoon. "It's the strongest thing I've ever seen."

I swallowed, squeezing my eyes shut harder. "I don't have a choice."

"No. You... you *do*."

I opened my eyes, blinking up at him, processing the conviction he gave to those words.

"You do have a choice. You choose to keep fighting." He squeezed my hand tight. "I was... I was in this bad situation for a bit—a few years ago. I know how easy it is to give up."

He looked lost for a moment, a flash of panic in his eyes, and my pulse quickened.

Was he talking about...? "The... Lightning pack?" The words felt almost too dangerous on my tongue. But it wasn't a violation of my commands. *He* had said it. I was following the conversation.

He glanced up at the leaves above, more tense than I'd ever seen.

"Yeh. I thought I was being courted as a permanent addition. Made me..." He shrugged, a slight wrinkle in his nose. "Stupid."

I stared at him, knowing there was a frown on my face, but I waited, unsure if he was finished.

"There's no guarantees in this industry, right? It was a once in a lifetime shot. And I needed it more than most people. But they knew that, too."

"It was bad?" I asked quietly. "With them?"

He shook his head, then winced. "Yes. But like... not at the time—or I didn't *think* it was. I don't know. It's hard to explain." He cleared his throat. "You don't need me dumping on you, anyway—"

"I want to know you."

It was a truth that was separate from Zeus, from my situation. He was my mate.

He took a breath, eyes darting around the sun kissed leaves above. "I've never talked about it. I know that's stupid. Love put

313

me in a bunch of therapy, and I just..." He rubbed his face. "I couldn't."

"You don't have to tell me, if it's not right."

He nodded, still looking so lost in a way that broke my heart. "It was like... no matter how bad it got—it's just pack life. If you're struggling, it's your fault, not theirs. If things get worse... if they're moving too fast, it's because you can't keep up, not because *they* are doing anything wrong. You're gonna be pack, you can't say no or you're saying no to their way of life, and then the contract could vanish. So you just... survive, even when it's worse and worse, and all the time you think you're the crazy one."

He'd stopped walking, and my grip on his hand was like a vice. There was a lump in my throat.

I knew nightmares could fester, locked away by silence, and this one... I could see it had been locked away for so long.

"And then you find out they never cared..." He looked sick. "H-how much damage they did, because you were never going to be in the bond. And it's too late. You're so..." He swallowed. "You're so broken that no pack in their right mind would ever want you."

"But this pack—"

He let out an anxious burst of laughter. *"In their right mind."*

I couldn't smile, though. "How did you end up with them—this pack, I mean?"

"Ebony. He..." Drake breathed another laugh. "He poached me."

"Poached you?"

"Way I know it, he seduced Ronan Kit and got him to spill about the Valley Boy's cast. The Lightning pack had more name recognition and influence so they'd got in on it. Thing is, London Clearwater is known for his integrity. Won't hire a pack for a movie unless he thinks they're a good fit."

"And... the Lightning pack were?"

"Only one thing tipped the scales."

"What?"

"Well." Drake snorted. "He liked me."

"So Ebony poached you."

Drake met my eyes at last, a little more confidence in them. "He did more than poach me."

The question was right there and a desperate need shoved at me.

What did he mean?

What happened? The answer might give me the reason I was here. Zeus's commands, they wouldn't stop me—not if I was letting the conversation take the direction it should.

I might be able to get one step ahead of this.

I opened my mouth, about to ask, but the words got stuck.

He was vulnerable: fingers crushing mine, face so pale it looked like he might faint as he told me something he'd never told anyone. He was sharing his pain—pain the Lightning pack had given him. Pain he'd carried all these years.

This conversation was a gift, and I'd been about to bring his demons right to its doorstep. Zeus might as well be standing next to us, listening in.

I shut my eyes, steadying my breathing. "I'm sorry, Drake."

His fingers wound through my hair and he dragged me against his chest, holding me tight. I could feel him shaking.

"I love you," he whispered, voice thick. "And seeing how strong you are gives me strength. Because none of that was the worst part. It wasn't what they took, it was what I gave them. I tried so hard for so long. I gave them so much of me and they crushed it. Now I just act and go on walks and, I don't know, watch TV? There are all of these holes I carry everywhere and I can't get them back."

I drew back, staring up at him. "Was it like... the makeup?" I asked, remembering how he'd pushed after what Zeus had said.

How he'd told me not to let them steal it from me when I'd been afraid to even look at it.

"He tried to take it from you." His voice was rough. "Tried to make it into something... cheap or shallow so whenever you touch it, it's... w-wrong. But you took it back from them in... in days. And it's been years and I still haven't—"

"That's not fair." My voice shook as I cupped his cheeks and made him look at me. "I had you."

He shut his eyes, though I could see the smallest shimmering tear on his dark lashes.

"Tell me one thing?" I asked. "You don't have to do anything with it. Just... tell me one thing you lost."

He finally managed a half smile, hands settling on my waist. "You're going to make fun of me, Dreamgirl."

I laughed, and suddenly tears were hot on my cheeks. "I will *not*."

"God." He inhaled sharply. "You're going to make *me* cry."

"Good. Now tell me."

He snorted. "I um... *really* like to garden." He blew out a shaky breath, and he loosened, frame relaxing as I held him.

I felt the smile light up my face.

"Like, stuff to cook with. We had this little space in the back where I grew up, and I used to grow all these vegetables. Couldn't do anything like it at the academy, so then when I moved in with them..." He trailed off, jaw clenched. "I don't know. I haven't done it in a while." His smile was sad. "And I just... I think you're so impressive that no matter what, you walk away *you*, Vex."

I held him tight against me as my tears wet his shirt. It wasn't just grief for him, though. It was anger. "I want that for you, Drake," I whispered.

"Maybe... Now you're here."

"Well, now that I am, I'm never going to leave you alone." I felt the smile tugging at the corner of my lips. "So, you're not really going to have a choice."

I wanted the date tonight with Rook to be perfect. Not just the date, but also the rest of my time here.

The day was weighing me down, and I knew what I needed if I wanted to be free.

I found Ebony in the gym, beating up a training dummy. One was already cracked, its fluffy innards spilling across the floor. His aura died instantly when he saw me.

"I... need to ask you something," I said, crossing toward him.

He tugged his wraps off. "What is it?"

"It's about the negotiations with the pack... For me."

His eyes dropped down to where I was wringing my hands, and his brow furrowed.

"I need you to help me... if they don't go as planned..." I trailed off, wincing and half expecting him to interrupt, but he didn't. "I need you to promise me something."

"What's that?"

"I can't..." I took a breath, processing all of Zeus's commands, trying to make sure I wasn't breaking any. I could fight them, but Zeus would know, and his demand for silence was the one he valued most. It wasn't worth what waited for me if I did break it. My heart thundered in my ears. "If something goes wrong... I don't want to live like that." I swallowed. "I don't want to, but that's... that's what will happen." My voice shook. Zeus had told me what it would look like. They would hide me away somewhere my mates would never find me. Either that or... or there was a promise of worse, a threat so dark I'd drowned it from my mind...

Ebony's jaw clenched, his eyes narrowing as he analysed me. It was grounding, holding that silver gaze, knowing the objectiveness of what he offered was exactly what I'd come for. After a long moment, he spoke. "You can't kill yourself?"

I released a breath at those words, even as the weight of Zeus's command paralysed me from even a nod. He cocked his head, eyes more calculating than I'd ever seen them. It took him an age to speak, and when he did, his words were slow. "There's nothing on this planet I wouldn't give them for your bond, Vex. That *we* wouldn't give them."

"I know..." I whispered. "But... but what if... What if something goes wrong?"

Zeus had scared me today in a way he never had before.

Something was wrong. I could feel it.

There was a long silence, and I saw the resignation in Ebony's eyes as if this was something he'd already considered. "What are you asking?"

"You know... what I want," I whispered. "Please um..." God, I almost cracked then. "Please don't make me say more."

Still, he didn't move. He didn't draw me against him and comfort me, and for that, I was grateful.

I both needed and feared the answer already in his eyes. My mind went to Zeus, to Cerus, to Triton, a million terrors catching up to me, flashing in my expression for him to see.

"I promise you something no one else can, Vex," he said at last. "I *swear* there is no world that exists in which you walk away belonging to that pack."

My vision blurred with tears for the millionth time today, and my breath caught as he said what I needed to hear. That last, smothering weight, threatening to steal my happiness from the time I had left with them, it was gone. I drew him into my embrace, holding tight.

For the first time, I was sure.

"Thank you."

THIRTY-FOUR

ROOK

Vex was so perfect it was unbelievable. She was perfect, *and* she was giving me a chance.

She'd spent the afternoon with Ebony. I had a *bit* of a connection with her right now—since a stoned ass-cheek bite was apparently only enough for a half-bond—but she'd been rocky all afternoon. And then Drake had dragged me and Love into the theatre to tell us what had happened.

My blood chilled just thinking about it. About the fact she could just be taken on their whim, hurt while she should be in our care.

Still, when she turned up to the roof for our date, it was with a timid smile, and all of her anxiousness melted away. I averted my eyes from the bandage wrapped around her wrist, knowing she didn't want me to bring it up. Even when it almost got a growl from my chest.

But she wanted me to focus on tonight, so that's what I'd do. Going out might be a little crazy right now after how public we'd just been, so I'd grabbed wine and food and blankets and brought her up to the roof because the September stars were almost as beautiful as she was.

She lay on the daybed beside me, pointing up at different constellations as she tried to guess them. I had to pull an app up so we could keep track.

I already secretly ordered a dozen packs of glow in the dark stars with the intention of putting them all over her nest ceiling. I paid attention to her favourites. Orion was one, I determined. He was going right above her bed. Although... I narrowed my eyes at the belt.

It was a dude.

Could be an alpha.

Maybe I'd put it a little further away.

Every time I turned off the app, I'd leave my camera open and nudge it toward her hopefully. I knew I had a lot of work before I caught up to Drake. But still, I could use just one measly—

I cut off as Vex jumped to her feet and set down her glass of wine (second of the night). "This is my favourite!" she exclaimed.

She liked Heart's music, so I'd left it playing in the background.

Next thing I knew she was dragging me up to dance, and I wasn't going to say no—though I managed to snag my phone before she did. She wrapped her arms around my shoulders and let me hold her while she sang along.

Fuck she was mesmerizing.

I don't think I'd ever seen her this comfortable before. Was this what she was like with Drake?

I wanted to be safe for her. I wanted it so badly.

When the song ended, I wasn't ready for it to be over, but she was already singing along to the next one.

Her voice was a lyric mezzo soprano, and her lower notes were full and rich. The most impressive part was that sometimes she'd waver, or *'cheat with the tongue'* as my mother always put it, showing that she wasn't trained at all. Her voice was incredible without the training or money put behind mine.

She didn't mimic Heart, either, she sang her own harmony beside him, giving a different meaning to the words.

"Wait, wait," I cut her off, unable to stop myself. "That was good, the middle part, just hold that a little longer, you can slip into the next verse easily."

She nodded, a frown on her face.

"Sorry. If you don't want me—"

"No." Her smile was genuine, if still a little anxious. "It's okay."

"It was the..." I tapped an imaginary piano key before humming an E3, which made Vex smile. "That one. Try drawing it out right before you stop phonating, and try the three note riff like you did before."

She bit her lip, blinking up at me.

"Instead of the two note riff, I mean."

"So uh..." She was pink in the cheeks. "I mean... I mostly just watched internet videos and sang with my mom."

"Oh, like..." Shit. My mother was an opera singer, there was no musical stone left unturned when it had come to my education. "Right before you drop into the whisper, last time you..." Again, I tapped imaginary fingers on ivory, dusting off old skills I hadn't touched in a long time as I mimicked what she'd done, shifting through the three notes.

She grinned. "You don't think that's too much?"

"You can pull it off."

"I totally didn't realise you could sing."

I shrugged. "My voice is all paid for. No passion. Doesn't have soul to it like yours."

"Oh right. Your parents... Your mother! I totally forgot. Shit. I'm going to have to work hard to make them proud."

I felt my heart clench as I stared down into her twinkling eyes, bright and golden in the outdoor fairy lights around us. Eyes my family would never accept. Eyes that glowed in every video I'd seen of that moment in the arena, when she had turned on two alphas—a growl in her chest—to protect me.

I shook my head. "You don't have to do that."

"I mean, I'd like to, family is—"

"Here's the thing about my mother." I cut her off before she could be even sweeter to a family that didn't deserve it. "Firstly, she wouldn't have the capacity for pride unless you were Diana Ankudinova herself. Secondly, she'll never meet you, so it's a nonissue."

"You don't want me to meet your parents?" Her face fell.

Oh. "Shit, no it's not like that, Vex. I don't want *them* to meet *you*. They're vultures and you deserve better."

She frowned, and I could see the hurt in her eyes.

"They... would never." I winced, clearing my throat. "I saw them last week. They made it clear they'd never approve of a princess bond like this. Not in a million years."

"Oh. Right." Her voice was weak. "But, I mean, they're like world famous. I get it—"

"I'm *more* world famous than they are, and I say they can get fucked."

There was a nervous smile on her face.

"That's why I did what I did, Vex," I whispered. "It wasn't just about the cage. No one can come for you anymore, not without coming for me too."

I hadn't had a moment of regret. She'd shown me there was more to all of this than money and fame.

She could smile—even right now as she faced things I could never imagine. And tonight, beneath the stars as we sipped wine and danced, I knew none of it had been fake.

"You find happiness, Vex, no matter what," I said, voice rough. "My family...they find everything else, and call it enough. No one can get between us now. Not the news. Not anyone. I'm not willing to give them a chance to hurt you."

"O-okay," she whispered.

"I can't touch them." My heart clenched as I thought of the alphas who had left that vile bite on her wrist. "But I don't need to. I just need to make you believe that tonight could be forever."

She paused, jaw clenched as she held my gaze with an intensity I'd never felt. "What if I'm scared?"

I stared at her, feeling the faintest flash of panic in my chest. But she needed more from me now. I cupped her cheeks. "It's okay if you are, Vex. But you don't need anyone's permission to dream."

That was who she was. Someone who smiled, who wished and dreamed no matter what. I'd seen it myself. I'd seen who she was.

"Will you help me?" she asked, voice choked. "I... I n-need you to help me because I don't want to stop, but I'm... I'm so scared." She stared up at me, stunning golden eyes glittering brighter than the stars above us.

I nodded, running on instinct, terrified that I might be misunderstanding. I was the one who'd hurt her the most. The one who'd taken the longest... But something had changed between us. She wanted something to believe in, and I could give her that. "Yes."

Her lips quirked up in the faintest smile. "You'll catch me if I fall?"

"Every time."

"Okay," she whispered. "Then can you help me paint everything with dreams until I can't remember what's chasing me anymore."

I grinned. "Now that I can do Baby Girl. Any dream, you name it. I can take you anywhere you want to go. I'll build you a castle if you want. I'll funnel all the musical knowledge in the world into you just to spite my parents. You'll be unstoppable,

Vex. And you're going to make it big, and the *radio* will play you, and my mother might have a heart attack—if that's what you want."

"To give someone a heart attack?" she asked, eyes mockingly wide for a moment.

"The singing," I snorted.

She giggled, and my heart swelled in my chest. "Okay. Deal. I'll... I'll be famous just so you can spite your mother."

"Deal."

Then, to my delight, she finally plucked my phone from my pocket and turned on the camera app. She took a selfie of us together while she made a goofy face, and I pressed my lips to her forehead.

My cheeks were hot as I tucked the phone back away. I couldn't rid myself of my own, very real smile, because I had my first ever Vex selfie.

Ha.

I bet Ebony didn't even have one of those.

THIRTY-FIVE

Chia pet's 5th day of life. Hair length: 3cm
  Time until execution: 4 days.

DRAKE

"What's that?" Rook asked, leaning against my door frame as I worked on the poster board plans I had for Vex's nest.

"It's uh..." I fumbled to cover it, but Rook was already striding into my room and peering at it.

"Damn... This for her?"

"I thought... maybe. If she wanted it. She gets final say of course, but—"

"She's going to love it." He squinted at the floor plan, grin bright. "You going to show her? *Please* let me be there."

"I can't. I mean. Not yet." I tugged it back, turning it over. "After."

Rook was scowling at me. "I think you should—"

"What do you want?" I cut him off. "I'm busy."

He ran his fingers through the tangles of black tumbling to his eyebrows, clearly trying to find his voice. "I'm sorry, Drake. I owe you an apology."

I stared at him. "You... do?"

"I knew how you felt about her. I even saw you together, and I was..." He trailed off, shifting uncomfortably. "I was jealous, before I mean."

"You were jealous?" I asked.

Of *me*?

Rook had everything I had, just without the baggage. He was more popular, more amiable.

"She was into you, and I had to blackmail her to get time with her."

"If you were jealous, then why didn't you just... stop acting like a cunt, and—"

"Because I didn't know—"

Anger rose like a flash flood, and I was on my feet, a snarl on my face. "If you say you didn't know she was your mate *one* more fucking—"

"No!" Rook raised his hands defensively, staggering back a pace. "I didn't know I *liked* her!" He swallowed, expression twisting. "I've never wanted more with someone. I didn't know what I was feeling when I saw her with you, smiling and shit when she hated me." He'd opened the bond up, and I could feel his shame on full display. "I kicked off. It was just stupid and nasty, and there's no excuse and you didn't deserve it anymore than she did." He rubbed his face vigorously, but I didn't know what to say.

I still felt that twisting hatred in my gut when I thought of how she'd felt when she was here before the Gala.

"I just... I want us to be good, you know?" he asked. "Not just for her. I... I miss you."

I swallowed through clenched teeth as I felt that blow. It was the part we'd never said out loud. Another casualty of all of this.

Love was... well, Love. Kinda quiet and odd, and just did this own thing. And Ebony was like a cold, ridiculously protective older brother. But Rook? He was a little slice of normal in this pack. We could just be friends and hang out.

But I hadn't felt that since Vex had arrived.

I didn't regret that; her arrival had shown me a side of Rook I didn't like. But it would be a lie to say I didn't want to find a way to get it back.

"I want to make it up to you," Rook added into the silence. "And I'm sorry."

"Yeh. You said that."

He nodded, palming his fist in his hand. "Okay." He took a step back, clearly unsure.

I spoke before he could leave. "I'm pissed because I didn't see it."

Rook considered me for a long time. "I told her to hide it from you."

"Love and Ebony, too? All of you were making her feel like that, and I fucking missed it."

"Because she loved you." Rook's voice was hoarse.

I stared at him. "She loves you more than she'll ever love any of us—she did right from the start. You didn't know because she was trying to protect you from it—from... from us."

I stared at him, lump still caught in my throat.

"I've seen what she'd do to protect what's hers. It's why I have such a long way to go before I deserve that from her. But you... you've always deserved it."

I nodded, but still couldn't find anything else to say, so he stepped back toward my door. "You uh... you need to show her that," he said, glancing at the poster board.

"It's not..." I swallowed. "It would be wrong. I mean, we don't know what's going to happen."

Springing something like this on her would be cruel. Rook's

eyes narrowed, but he said nothing else as he shut my door and left.

ROOK

Okay. Vex's date was a success. Drake was done, now it was time for Love.

I found him outside at the barbecue in the covered patio despite the sprinkle of rain.

"What are you doing?"

"She mentioned she liked barbecue when she was high," he said, as if that was obvious.

"Ask Drake. He's good at it, right?"

"*I* can barbecue."

"Can you?" I asked, sitting down on one of the benches. I'd never seen him barbecue in his life. As if to prove me wrong, he lifted the lid and poked what was inside with some tongs before shutting it again. It didn't smell of anything though, and I thought there was supposed to be smoke.

"You told Jas to add Vex to the website?" he asked with a sideways glance to me.

"Yes." I had. There were no public statements about her yet— not official ones. We should be making them. Regardless of dark bonds, she was our scent match. That was indisputable.

"But—"

"It's not like people haven't guessed anyway, and we have offered her the princess bond."

"Yes, but—"

"Ebony said our job was to give her hope," I said, measuring his expression. "That's what he said you wanted."

"Yes, but this...? This is—"

"Is *what*?" I chuckled. "Childish and naive? Just like me?"

"Rook—"

"No. *This* is what she needs. This is *right*. You want to live believing that you'll have no tomorrow with her—that's how we lose it."

He looked stunned as he stared at me. I was expecting an argument, but instead he just slumped down at my side. For a long second we were surrounded only by the light pitter-patter of rain on the pool's surface.

"Shit. I don't... know what's fucking right anymore."

"Then let us help you. She's our scent match, right? Not just yours—?"

"I know. I *know*."

I didn't say anything else, feeling something discordant from him down the bond. I wasn't used to Love's unease. When he finally looked at me, I could almost see the words forming in his head before he said them.

"Rook." He swallowed. "This last week... I should have done better. I'm s—"

"Nope." I cut him off. "I don't want to hear it." He straightened, looking thrown, but I didn't give him a chance. "I'd be sick of my shit too if I'd had to deal with it as long as you had. It's been my and Ebony's crap for years. Tracks if you can't see the forest through the trees anymore."

"What can't I see?"

"You've done a good job, and you don't owe me an apology. I —*I* owe you a thank you."

"For what?"

I leaned my head back against the stone behind me with a sigh. "You know, Ebony said I like him around because he makes me feel better about myself—which is *kind* of true, but that's not it. Not really."

He watched me curiously.

"Do you know how likely it was that I'd end up in a toxic pack, with all that my parents wanted?"

"I wouldn't exactly say we're—"

"Right there—that's what I mean. You did a good job. We turned out better than we should have because we always had someone fighting for that."

He opened his mouth, but I cut him off.

"You could have left him, but you didn't. Why, if you didn't want to try and make something good out of this?" I asked. "You want what everyone wants. To build a happy life for yourself. Not exactly simple, with Ebony, and then you took me on, too. You didn't have to—"

"Don't be stupid," Love snorted. "I couldn't have left you anymore than I could have left him."

"Exactly. Except you never wanted the fame, you just wanted a quiet pack and a nice, completely sane omega. Do you know how easy it would have been if you'd got on that train with your mom?"

His eyes darkened slightly at those words.

"You're a good person, and you did your—"

"No." Love's jaw clenched as he shook his head. I could feel the anxiousness from him. "It's *not*... like that." His gaze drifted for a moment, as if bracing to say something. "Before Vex, that fucking train was all I could think about."

A strange silence fell between us as I processed that, my heart sinking.

He rubbed his face. "More and more the last few years."

Damn.

I'd failed him more than I'd realised.

When I found my voice, it was rough. "The reason I liked Ebony was because you two have always been a package deal, and seeing what you do for him—that was something I'd never been around."

He watched me cautiously, still unsure.

"But I've been a cunt," I said, needing to find some way to

lighten these words. My chest was tight. "Because I've just been *taking*. For years, I've been taking that from you, and not once have I tried to... *be* better for it. If I had, then I wouldn't have hurt her. You're not responsible for that."

He said nothing, but I felt his anxiety loosen through the bond just the slightest bit.

"And I don't blame you. Anyone would be tired of that. How long has it been that you're the only one fighting for something better for us? Drake's not exactly a saboteur, but he's still... getting by, you know? Never been much of a future guy."

"Not until her," Love murmured.

"It's going to be different now. We have a chance at something better. Something real." My throat was thick all of a sudden, and I inhaled aggressively. "I... I definitely wouldn't be someone with that kind of chance if you'd left me. Neither would he. So... thank you. And I'll say it for him too, since I doubt he'll ever say it— even if he knows it."

Love breathed a laugh, but didn't meet my eyes.

After a long pause with no more words, I glanced at the barbecue.

We had been here a while.

"Do you have to check it or something?" I asked.

"Actually... I uh... haven't figured out how to connect the gas," he muttered.

I snorted.

We sat in silence for another peaceful stretch, and the bundle of nerves on his end of the bond unravelled slowly with every second that passed.

"It's going to be better," I said at last. "You're not on your own anymore. Now that I've seen this future, I'm not letting go. Not if it kills me."

THIRTY-SIX

VEX

I needed this.

I just prayed that Love wouldn't think I was insane. Then again, if he did, he could add it to the list.

But I'd felt a connection to him since I'd arrived that I'd never felt before. It was new.

Every time I saw him, I just... I wanted him close. I felt it with all my mates, but it was different for all of them. For Love, it was a desire to be closer, to convince him to tell me everything would be alright, even when neither of us could make a promise like that. But he had a way of making me feel like maybe... just maybe, he could make that promise. That the world would change for him.

So I picked out the best lingerie I could find and hurried to his room, getting myself ready.

I waited for him in nothing but black lace and a silken dressing gown. When he walked into the room, I heard his footsteps halt. Vanilla winter shifted to something wanting, but I caught the edge of nerves to it.

He crossed toward where I knelt and sat on the bed beside me. "Vex." His voice was rough, as if there was something stuck in this throat.

"I want—need—to..." I trailed off, trying to find the words.

"I can't do this if you're here because I hurt you the first time..."

I shook my head.

It wasn't so simple. I'd been reminded yesterday what it was like to have this forced upon me by Zeus. When I'd come to Love like this before it had been a daring choice to give him the same, to give him a chance to change the narrative. But those hours of silence were hard to shake, claiming far too much space for how little had happened in them.

"I'm here because I trust you—I *want* to..." I trailed off, trying to find my strength. "I want to give you what I will never give him."

That was what I had always wanted.

Again, there was silence between us.

"I'm yours, alpha," I whispered. "Command me, and there is nothing I won't do for you."

Again, his scent shifted, his want deepening along with his sorrow.

I felt the brush of his touch as he nudged my chin up to face him. My nerves vanished, pulse quickening. Goosebumps lifted across my body as I looked up into stunning ocean blue eyes.

It was different now. It could be different forever. He could never erase the pain he'd given me, but he could begin writing over it. Create new connections to this room, to this dynamic, to the very thought of handing him power.

"I forgive you, Love," I told him. "I wouldn't be here if I didn't."

His lips parted just slightly, a look of reverence on his face as he stared down at me. "But now, I need you to fix it."

This was a weapon. Trusting him and overcoming the foul circumstances in which we'd met, it was crucial. I knew that. Zeus's anger, as frightening as it had been, was proof of that. I hadn't seen it that way before, not until I'd seen the way Cerus had looked at his pack lead. There were fractures in the Lightning pack. With every claim I staked for my mates, I was rejecting the alphas who'd bitten me, scoring those cracks deeper.

And Love was my pack lead. I needed my bond with him to be unbreakable. He'd taken the first steps, now I needed to take this one.

"I..." He swallowed. He sounded rough and unsure.

I slipped to my feet, meeting his eyes where he sat, following those instincts. Instincts I'd decided never to doubt after Rook's rut. "I think you've been pack lead for so long you don't know how to claim something for yourself."

"I... don't know. What if it's more than that?" he asked.

I tilted my head, waiting. He ran his fingers through the strands of raven hair that escaped his plait.

"I want to claim you." He shut his eyes. "I *want* to give you the world, Vex. But I want to give it to them, too. I'm afraid I don't know how to balance it. What if I can't take care of them and you—"

I cut him off, pressing my finger to his lips and slipping down onto his lap. He groaned, fingers closing around my waist.

"What if it isn't either or?" I asked. Then I leaned closer, my breath at his ear. "We can care for them together."

His grip tightened as he shifted me closer, and I could feel how solid his cock was beneath me. It was an effort not to shift over it, to tempt him further.

Finally his grip on my waist vanished. He drew back, tilting my chin up to look at him. His ocean blue eyes were blown with lust. "Will you be *this* before them?" he asked.

I blinked, considering that.

Heat rose up my neck, enough that it might have been reflected in my scent for the way the edge of his lips quirked up.

"I would be this before the world," I said. "Tell me what you want, and it's yours."

"I want you, Vex, more than I've ever wanted anyone."

He took my hand, tangling his fingers between mine. I felt a smile tug on my lips. Nerves fluttered in my stomach briefly as we stepped from his room, but then I squeezed his hand in mine.

I *did* trust him, I realised.

This time he wouldn't leave me unwanted. He wasn't going to hurt me.

So I gave myself over to it.

He led me out to the living room. Rook was on one of the couches, flicking through channels, and Ebony was pouring himself a drink in the kitchenette.

Love released my hand as he settled on the couch, arranging a few of the cushions and unfolding one of the blankets.

Just like I promised, I lowered myself to my knees as he got comfortable, eyes downcast, cheeks blazing.

I felt their gazes on me in an instant. I would have known, even without sensing the way the scents in the room shifted. The caramel brandy turned rich, and twilight grass became sharp as blades.

Finally, Love settled with legs propped up on the couch, and a decent stack of cushions at his back. To my surprise he had a book in his hand.

He reached out, tucking my hair behind my ear. "Alright, Princess, on my lap."

Comforting warmth slid through my veins at his command, and I rose to my feet.

This was easier than I thought. I could feel the gazes of Ebony and Rook on me, but it didn't matter. Nothing mattered but Love.

It was easy to do this without hesitating when I got lost in his beautiful blue eyes.

I slipped onto his lap, seated upright, legs straddling his hips.

His eyes roamed my body, and I could feel his reaction. I bit my lip to fight from grinding down into his cock that was rigid beneath me.

His free hand dropped to my hips.

"Do you want it?"

I nodded before I could catch myself. Blood rushed to my cheeks.

"Good, because you're going to keep me warm while I read," he told me. He lifted the blanket and draped it over me so he was the only one with a view of my skin in lace. "Take it out."

My lips parted, a thrill lightning my veins, slick pooling beneath the lace that very soon wouldn't be enough to stop it trailing down my thigh.

"They're going to see how good you are," he said. My cheeks blazed even hotter. The other alpha's scents in the room burned with lust—and perhaps envy.

I nodded, reaching down and carefully tugging his sweatpants down. I paused as I felt his cock in my palm, eyes meeting his. Soft, warm and... fucking thick.

He flashed his canines in a rare grin.

"Will you be able to manage?"

I nodded, tugging it free.

"Show me."

The blanket had tumbled to my hips, revealing the lace around my torso to the others, but Love was the only one who could see me tug the lace out of the way and line up his cock.

"You're soaked," he murmured, setting his book on his chest, grip biting down on my thigh as he held me in place as he lowered me just onto the tip. I let out a little moan at the sensation of him stretching me out. Slick pooled further, leaking down his length. "They can't take their eyes from you. You like that, don't you? Your alphas watching?" he asked. "Eyes on me." He gripped my chin, halting me as I made to turn.

My chest was heaving, my own scent likely enough to fill the living room and hallways by now.

Very slowly, with a vice-like grip, Love lowered me onto his length. His pupils were blown as he watched me slide down inch by inch. I caught myself by my palms on his chest, a breathy moan slipping out as he filled me.

"Good girl," he breathed, when I had taken him all. I could feel the base of his knot pressed against me. It was huge, and my eyelids fluttered as I shifted just slightly so I could feel it. "Don't move," he commanded. "I saw how well you squeezed Drake the other night. You don't need to fuck me to keep me hard, right, Princess?"

I nodded as he adjusted me so I could settle onto his chest, relaxing over him, my head tucked beneath his chin, even if I only reached his collarbones.

A purr rumbled to life in his chest, and—shit.

A low moan loosed from my chest, the vibration just enough to stimulate that deep spot his rock hard tip was trapped against.

He didn't react. Instead, with one hand tangled in my hair, he lifted his book, and began reading.

LOVE

Tonight might be the hottest thing I'd ever experienced.

Nothing in my dreams could come close to having her here, curled against me, sweet body tight over my length, gripping me like a vice as I stroked her hair.

It didn't take me long to realise that she wasn't *just* turned on. This position, my purr, was pushing her toward the edge. Occasionally, I dropped my hand, tugging on her nipple through the lace she wore. Each time I was rewarded by the sweetest little mewl, and her body squeezing me again.

I was turning the pages for the simple motion of needing something to keep me distracted, but I couldn't retain a single word. If I put the book down, it would be hard not to fuck her into the couch right now, and I wasn't ready for this to end. Not yet.

There was no way in hell my cock was going soft anytime soon, but I was enjoying her efforts. Sometimes she would shift just the slightest bit, core clenching over me.

Fuck.

It was so hard to keep my eyes on the page when she did that.

Rook was facing the TV, but neither he, nor Ebony were watching it. Ebony had settled down onto the nearest couch, clearly throwing any other evening plans out the window as his eyes traced the way Vex was curled up on my chest. She wasn't trying to hide what we were doing—or if she was, she was doing a poor job of it. Her delicate fingers were closed around my upper arm, biting down when I shifted. She was letting out the prettiest little moans.

Earlier, when she'd knelt for me, Ebony's side of the bond cracked open for just a second, pure shock slipping through. When I looked up, he'd frozen with his hand on his glass. His pupils were blown wide, and I had to fight my momentary fear at the lust in his gaze as he took her in.

He wanted this from her.

Would she give it to him?

She trusted him in ways I never had. It made me afraid, sometimes. But then, I knew I had to let go of that if this was going to work.

I'd tried to send her away—had fought to protect her from him, and it hadn't worked. I'd been too late. My mate was in far more danger than Ebony could ever pose, and that meant he was a part of this. He had to be, and nothing here could be done in halves.

She trusted Ebony, and I had to trust her.

Drake joined us sitting next to Rook, looking a little confused at first as he caught sight of me and Vex. Rook leaned over and muttered something to him, and then the black currant wine shifted to lust just like the other scents had.

Something content warmed my veins and my purr deepened, getting her to squirm against me. They were all here, in this room.

My pack.

My omega.

She was a Goddess, and one that couldn't sit still.

My fingers slipped beneath the lace of her bra and tugged at her nipple again. I was rewarded by a more desperate sound as she squeezed me harder this time.

Fuck.

It was almost too much.

The living room was a veritable swamp of hormones right now, and it only took the slightest glance to confirm it. "You look so perfect, using that hot little body of yours to keep me warm," I growled.

Her nails bit down on my chest, a quiet, breathy sound slipping from her.

"Love…" Her voice was a needy whisper. I lowered my book at last, meeting those captivating golden eyes, not prepared for how mesmerising they would be, pupils dilated and overtaken by need. Need for *me*.

"Yes, Princess?" I asked, measuring my voice.

"I'm…" She let out another little moan as I reached down and rolled her nipple casually between my fingers, as if it wasn't making her whole body tense. "I'm going to…" She bit her lip, cheeks bright pink.

"Say it."

Her eyes darted around the room, and fuck, I had thought she couldn't grip me harder, but she managed it when she looked around to see how enthralled the others were.

"Am I allowed to come?" she whispered.

"Say it so they can hear."

Heat flooded her cheeks, but she barely hesitated. "Please let me come," she whined, all dignity forgotten.

"Just from keeping me warm?" I asked, hand sliding down to her hips again so I could hold her perfectly still as I rocked my knot against her.

She let out a low whine, her nails almost drawing blood against my chest as she gasped. "Please, Alpha."

I set my book down, purr steady, and reached down, pressing my thumb beneath her panties.

"Come then, in front of all of them," I commanded, as I closed my other hand around her throat, lifting her up and putting pressure on her clit.

She seized, and I almost came with her as her body clenched around my length. Perfect whines rose in her chest as she tumbled over the cliff, the grip of those delicate fingers now piercing as she clutched my forearm.

"Good girl," I purred, as her last shudder faded, and I lay her down.

Slowly, with my firm hold on her waist, I shifted, drawing out of her just a little before settling back in. Her melodic, desperate moan filled the air as I pumped into her again. She was breathless and felt like heaven.

I fucked her like that for a while, the heat in my veins at a boiling point. Then I gripped her hair, lifting her enough that she had to plant trembling palms on my chest. Her eyes were dazed as she met my gaze, almost vacant with the orgasm that had just shaken her.

I'd dreamed about this since seeing her with Drake. I pressed my thumb to her lips. "I'm going to use that sweet little cunt of yours to finish."

She tried to nod through my grip, but failed. "Yes, Alpha—" She cut off as I pressed into her again, eyes almost crossing.

"Are you sure you can handle my cock splitting you open like this?" I asked.

"Use me however you want, Alpha."

I groaned, almost burying my knot in her right then at hearing those words.

Holding her over me, I drove into her at a steady pace, watching each time I did. I could finish right now, but I wouldn't.

Goosebumps lifted on her skin, low whines slipping out every time the edge of my knot teased her. Finally, when I thought she was on the edge again, I sped up, blood on fire at the sounds she was making, at the way each thrust made her more dizzy with lust.

"You're going to take my knot," I growled.

"Mmmmhm." Her breathing picked up. "Yes, Alpha, knot me please."

I drove up into her, this time stretching her down around my knot.

She gasped, and when she came the second time, she wasn't nearly as quiet. Unable to move by the way I was holding her, her eyes rolled back, moans lifting through the whole room.

Fuck.

I groaned as she gripped my knot, rocking my full length into her viciously and filling her with my pleasure. As we both came down, the movie was still playing on the TV, but not an eye in the room was on it.

"I love you, Vex," I breathed.

It was, perhaps, the only thing that could have given her the strength to lift her head and look up at me, locked together as we were. Her eyes were still dazed, but shining as she met mine.

I drew down and kissed her, rewarded with her passion as she drove her tongue into my mouth. There was a smile on her face as I drew back and she leaned close, nipping my ear. "I love you, too."

THIRTY-SEVEN

Chia pet's 6th day of life. Hair growth: 5cm
Time until execution: 3 days

DRAKE

Rook was a first rate prick.

He had pulled up a big white poster board in her nest today—just like *I'd* made in *my* room. Well, he hadn't copied me exactly—he was pinning on travel shit, not nest shit, but still. At least his drawings were primitive stick figures—rubbish compared to mine.

Also, he'd asked Vex if he could print out a selfie of them and put it in her nest, and she'd said yes. So now I kept finding the rooftop selfie of Rook kissing Vex *everywhere*. It was slipped into discarded piles of clothes, drawers, and scattered under her furniture—as if she would look under there. She was an omega, not a mole rat.

I'd found one under my pillow this morning—which I'd only noticed because of the scent of caramel brandy when I'd woken—which meant he'd scent marked all of them too.

Fucking bastard.

I had selfies.

I could have done the same *ages* ago.

Despite all of that, it *was* quite fascinating to watch Rook and Vex. She'd really let him in.

I knew he was doing his best, but it was hard to shove down the little flares of rage when I thought of his history.

But she was trying to forgive him so I could do the same.

I was worried though, I couldn't bear the thought of him hurting her again, and this posterboard stuff was a dangerous game to play with her right now.

And my fucking idea.

And she was *all* over it.

"There'll be more," Rook was saying. "Jas told me we had a bunch of counter offers after the Dragon Hunters' announcement."

"Did you?" she asked, clear relief in her eyes.

"Yup. From all over. We could stay here on the East Coast, or there was one in California, Vancouver—"

"Canada?" she asked.

"We haven't gone yet, but they're massive on filming out there. We could go see the sights. I've got a friend who moved to Whistler last year and his parties are always awesome."

"Like..." She swallowed. "With me?"

She glanced at me.

Rook frowned. "Well, I'm not going anywhere without you, so I'd hope so."

"I can't travel out of the country..." She trailed off, looking nervous.

"That all goes away with the princess bond."

"Right. Yeh. I mean... I know that. I just..." She nodded, pushing the frown from her face as she looked back up at him.

"You'll be able to go anywhere in the world," he said. "Plus, I looked it up. There's an action movie that will be filming across Europe and Asia next year. I checked and one of the places is Kathmandu, so I got Jas to put out some feelers—" He cut off as he caught her expression, her eyes wide as saucers.

"What?" Rook swallowed. "Are you...?"

"Yeh. I'm... I'm fine."

My blood had turned to ice, though.

What was he doing?

"You would really go there with me?" she asked, looking between us.

I nodded with a shrug, though the smile on my face was fragile.

"Well, we have some other things to check off the list first," Rook was saying. "Like the Pack Darling Part Two showing, and we've got to nail down your nest properly."

She was nodding, her eyes bright as she stared at him as if she was seeing a brand new person. I was feeling somewhat the same, actually.

"Do you think the others will want to go to Nepal?" Vex asked, looking between us.

Rook waved a hand. "Love'll be down the moment I tell him there's monkeys. Then Ebony will be outvoted anyway."

"Fuck yes," Vex hissed, adjusting one of the monkey cut outs they'd pinned to the board.

The moment we got a second alone, I grabbed him. "You *took* my idea," I hissed under my breath.

"Show her yours then," he told me.

"Is that a good plan?"

"What do you mean?"

"I mean... It's... She's not..." I swallowed. "You're giving her—"

"Hope?" Rook asked. "Isn't that what we're *supposed* to be doing?"

"Yeh, but this isn't... it's not fair—"

"She's done this more than I have. She'll tell me if it's too much."

"Done what?" I asked.

"I don't know... got through bad stuff. And anyway, manifest what you want, right?"

"Where did you get that? A self help site?"

Rook scowled, punching me in the arm. "My gran actually. And it's how I got through the academy." His grin was playful. "I get that you think I'm an idiot, but I'm still a world class actor. I didn't get that from nothing."

When she returned from the bathroom, I watched them more intently. Rook was cutting out pictures from a magazine while Vex found places to put each piece on the board.

They were building a future.

My heart twisted.

A future she might never have.

I shoved that thought away. Rook was right about one thing: If Vex wasn't letting that hold her back, I had no right to either.

Plus, Rook had found five different versions of himself from magazines and pinned them each onto the Nepalese sights along with the monkeys Vex was cutting out.

Rook wasn't just building her a future. He was building a future *without* me.

I ripped the magazine from his hand (the front page had a huge photo of a topless Rook with the title: 'Harrison Takes the Crown for his Princess') and began furiously sifting through it for photos of the rest of us.

"I did some research on omegas and travel," Rook was saying. "We can *'pocket size'* your nest and most of the time that's still comfortable, but we need to get the foundation down first if we're going to do that."

"Pocket nest?" Vex was grinning. "Let's make a collage for that too..." She trailed off, eyes darting around the board that was stuffed full. Well, it *wouldn't* be with a little less Rook.

"Ah..." Rook scratched his head—though I recognised the move as one of his acting quirks. I narrowed my eyes. "This one isn't big enough," he said. "Especially not with all of Drake's plans for your nest—"

"What?" Vex asked, spinning to me.

I stared at her, chewing on my lip. "I..." I swallowed, unable to take my eyes away from her at that moment. "I just... had some ideas."

"Can I hear them?" she asked, her golden eyes wide.

"I mean..." I palmed the back of my neck, refusing to look at Rook. "You could *see* them if you want?"

Her mouth dropped open in surprise. "You *drew* them?"

"Well, I made a poster board like this. They're nothing crazy. Just—"

"Drake's *nest* ideas?" She was getting to her feet, dragging me up with her. "I want them," she demanded, and fuck if her scent didn't just hit the room like a raspberry baking bomb.

Pretty golden eyes were fixed on me from amongst fluttering eyelashes and soft freckles on pink cheeks.

I opened my mouth, ready to tell her I'd get her whatever she wanted, only I'd forgotten exactly what it was.

"Shit," Rook snorted. "*I* didn't get this much excitement."

"Drake's special!" she said indignantly. That *didn't* help unscramble my brain, which felt like pudding right now. Of course, Rook had to ruin it.

"*That's* for sure—" he began, but grunted as Vex jolted slightly, still clutching my shirt. I think she might have kicked him.

"If you were first, you'd be special," she said, still not taking her eyes from me.

I grinned smugly, finally looking down at Rook.

"First *what*, exactly?" Rook folded his arms, glaring between us from where he lay on the floor.

Vex let me go at last as she began counting on her fingers. "First one to be nice. First one to say I love you—"

"She said it back," I added quickly, heat creeping up my neck, but Vex was still ticking fingers off on her hand.

"First date. First *ice-cream* date. First fuck. First knot. *Ever*. Like, *first knot ever*. And it was sooo—" She cut off with a squeak. Rook had leaped to his feet and clamped a hand over her mouth and crushing her against his chest from which a low growl was vibrating. "Right. I got it, Baby Girl. Loud and clear."

I was frozen all of a sudden, my gaze fixed on them. On the way Rook was drawing her against him. His gaze met mine with curiosity, then his touch landed on her hip and the hand clamped over her mouth dropped to her slender neck.

"Drake made you nest plans." Rook lingered on those words and her pupils blew as her gaze snapped back to me. He leaned down, lips close to her ear. "But he doesn't want to share."

He tilted her chin up, exposing her neck. She was still watching me, cheeks pink, pupils blown.

The words, the motion, it sent me over the edge. I slipped fingers through her hair, and had Rook by the neck, slamming him back a few paces to the wall before I crushed her lips to mine.

When I drew back, Rook tried to move, but a growl slipped from my chest this time, and he froze again.

"Drake," her voice was breathless as she tugged at my shirt. "I *want* the plans."

Right.

Yes.

"I'll get them."

I hurried from the room to grab my poster board.

I couldn't help but notice, as I laid it out on the floor for her to look at, the incredibly pleased smile on Rook's face.

VEX

It was the evening, and we were curled up in bed.

After filling both poster boards I was buzzing with excitement for all our plans. Rook and Drake had told me we were going to Nesting Needs tomorrow.

Rook was fixated on his phone, and when I peeked, I saw him scrolling @NestingGuru's videos with laser focus. Drake's phone kept pinging, and they'd shoot each other looks, all conspiratorial. I even saw Love and Ebony's names in the texts, which meant the conspiracy was pack wide.

My alphas were going to take me to Nesting Needs. Not even the bandage on my wrist covering the foul fresh bite could ruin my excitement.

Fighting my smile, I curled up in their arms, Drake on one side, Rook on the other.

Ebony and Love, they were the claiming kind. We'd be battling who had claimed the other until the day we died, I was sure.

But Rook and Drake?

I held on tighter, my smile wide as I tumbled into sleep.

These boys were mine.

THIRTY-EIGHT

Chia pet's 6th day of life. Hair growth 8cm.
Time until execution: 2 days

VEX

I'd heard a lot about Nesting Needs before, but I'd never actually been in one. It was, momentarily, enough to make me forget everything else in the whole world.

Where I came from, omegas were desired, sure, but that left them hunted. Topside, though? We were treated like queens, and it was something I was still getting used to.

I'd been on dates with rich betas, but it was hard to compare the occasional high-end date with the real world.

This was true value, built into the foundations of this warehouse-sized building dedicated exclusively to omegas.

And the shit inside was not cheap.

Their jingle: *'A maze of nests, you pick the best!'* was printed beneath the grand letters before the massive building.

The others—my alphas—weren't making an effort to hide themselves today, so we were getting stares. There was, however, a security detail of three alphas who were hovering behind us at all times.

We stepped up to the doors, and I read each of the posters outside.

'Check out the nest of the week—what makes Romeo Knight feel at home?', 'Half price on all beach themed nesting items', and *'Read our latest blog: What to do if your omega believes they want black lights in their nest, (Hint: they don't) and how to manage the fallout when they do sneak them in'.*

"Black lights?" I asked, brows furrowed. "But they don't sound so—oh." I cut off, heat rushing to my cheeks as Drake chuckled.

We stopped at the doors for a 'scent dampening spritz' which was mandatory if we wished to touch the rooms within. I tugged on Love's sleeve, and he let the employee mist us all down.

Inside, scent dampeners misted the air around us, though it wasn't enough to completely rid the rooms of other alphas and omegas. There were so many faint layers, though, that it all blurred into something a little less distracting.

Nesting Needs was, in essence, a village of nests. There were even fake cobblestone streets with lamps and a sky painted above. Each nest was different, some were wide, some two story, with every kind of decor imaginable.

"There's more to this than I thought," Drake muttered, stopping before the information board outside an earthy green 'hobbit's nest'. It listed the nest features, including colour themes, lighting types, fabric and texture combinations, sound and ambience, and even compatible fragrance and alternatives for different types of omega scents.

"This," I said delightedly. "Is going to be *amazing*."

DRAKE

Watching Vex in Nesting Needs was something else.

She'd sometimes flit from nest to nest quickly, but then she'd get stuck on one, and Ebony would have his notebook out, writing down the product number and interrogating her on all the variances.

It was cute, until a particularly aggressive line of questioning over the patterns of wallpaper that made Vex burst into tears. "I d-d-don't know," she sobbed. "I w-want the planets *and* the star sign design *and* the geo-geometric patterns."

"Okay." Ebony looked completely out of his depth as he sat down on the bed and tugged her into his arms. "It's okay Little Omega." He patted her head. "I'll get it custom done with all three, alright?"

She nodded, wiping her eyes.

"Do you know how insane it is, that you can make her cry *in* Nesting Needs?" Rook snorted.

"It's o-okay," Vex stammered. "It's v-very emotional in here. And it's worse because my heat's soon, so I'm a m-m-mess."

She was right. We passed at *least* two more teary-eyed omegas, one with three different types of potted plants clutched in his arms as he fled a nest and had to be chased down by staff.

Following that, what sounded like a pre-recorded announcement played on the intercom: *'All nesting omegas must be accompanied. Nesting Needs staff are not responsible for managing them in display rooms.'*

"How have you never been in one of these before?" Rook asked, as we stopped to grab a bite from the cafeteria.

"Have you?" Vex asked.

"No. But that's not the point. You're the omega—and didn't you say you dated rich guys?"

"Sure." She shrugged. "But I don't exactly trust a beta dude I'd met for two dates to manage nesting. That's a bit personal."

I frowned as I squeezed mustard on my hot dog and tried to come up with a followup question that wouldn't sound suspicious. "It uh... never got serious, then?"

"God no." She peered up at me from her fries. "All fun. I wanted a night where I could forget I was poor as shit and they wanted to bang an omega. Perfectly mutual, nothing serious."

Ebony, who had—unbeknownst to Vex—just arrived behind her with his tray, froze, his eyes narrowed. The paper cup in his hand crumpled, shooting pop everywhere.

I coughed loudly and changed the subject before he could get out his pen and pad and demand she write out names and addresses.

Love caught Ebony by the arm as we followed Vex from the cafeteria. I stepped past them, but not too late to miss him hissing, "If there's a list, they *cannot* go on it. *Do* you under—?"

I hurried out, knowing I might lose Vex otherwise, but I was stifling my grin.

When I next spotted Ebony, he looked sour.

"Oh my *God!*" Vex leaped onto the bed in the centre of the room. It had a big black skull and crossbones headboard. "This is the *BEST* room yet!"

Shit.

Again?

I sat next to her, tugging her into my arms. "Vex, if you don't tell us what about it *is* the best, Love will have the whole room delivered and set up before we can even make it home."

"I don't... know," she whined. The further we got into the city of nests, the more she seemed to be devolving into a primal fluff-obsessed omega. "It's everything. I want *all* of it."

"Okay. We'll get you all of it."

She sat up, staring at me, suddenly confused. "But not the lamps, right?"

"Um... Not if you don't want them."

"And the blankets aren't the best."

I nodded, fighting my grin and shooting a glance at Ebony and Love. Ebony was jotting things down on the notepad.

"Okay. Not the lamps. Not the blankets. Everything else."

"And the dressers and stuff. I liked the ones in the space room better."

I nodded.

"No dressers. Everything else."

The pout on her face, mixed with her glare, was the most precious thing in the whole world. "You're making fun of me."

"I'm certainly not." I drew her closer. "We're just trying to get it right. No wall colour, no blankets, no dresser. Everything else."

"Okay..." She swallowed, her voice fragile. "Maybe I just like the headboard."

I coughed to contain my laugh. "That's okay. We'll just get the headboard."

THIRTY-NINE

VEX

I loved today.

I loved the dreams that they were painting for me; the future that was starting to take shape.

We got home late, with a dozen boxes, more in the mail, and six custom orders that had been commissioned by Ebony, including the special wallpaper.

But when the Nesting Needs boxes were loaded up into the foyer, I didn't want them moved any further. "Do we have to put all this stuff in right now?"

"Nope. It's yours Princess," Love told me. "You can put it in the nest whenever you want."

My chest loosened slightly. "Okay. Maybe we'll wait a bit?"

It wasn't a lack of faith that made me want to stop here, it was just... "When I unpack them, everything needs to be perfect."

Love nodded, his gaze tracing to where I was palming the back of my neck. The darkness in his eyes was there and gone in an instant as I withdrew my hand. Faith or not, things couldn't be perfect while I still had this bite.

I wanted unpacking to be theirs, and *only* theirs. I didn't want the memories overshadowed by the darkness poisoning my neck.

"I was thinking, it's still nice out," Love said, changing the topic. "We've got a bit of summer left, maybe we could do takeout by the firepit?"

I grinned.

"Yes."

I was not ready for today to be over.

Rook tugged me in between him and Drake around the firepit.

Love was starting the fire, and Ebony set drinks and pizza down for us all to grab.

Their scents engulfed me. So, so beautiful and made of dreams. Ones I was too afraid to hold on to alone.

Sometimes when I closed my eyes, I was in free fall, as if the ground vanished beneath me and I was afraid this was a huge mistake. Last time Zeus had claimed me, it had been worse for the hope I'd had. And now the pain that awaited me on the other side, it was beyond what I could imagine.

But I'd seen it before: dreams without limit, claimed even in the darkest moments.

I wanted that.

I wanted my mother to be proud.

So, whenever that happened, whenever the ground gave out beneath me in that heart stopping second, I focused on them.

All of them.

My mates.

My anchors.

There was something entirely mesmerising about seeing them as a pack. The tension that had been there before was gone now.

I just listened to them talk for a while, sinking into Rook's arms.

Love and Ebony were arguing over past competitions, and who had come out ahead.

"I even won on the pack picks," Ebony said, sipping on his beer.

"What does that mean?" Rook asked, bewildered.

"I got the Drake pick—rightfully, I might add."

"Rightfully?" Love asked, mildly, regarding Ebony with a raised eyebrow.

"You picked Rook, I picked Drake. And Drake's better. Clearly."

"Ah yes, I forgot," Love said. "That's all the Crimson Fury pack really is: the Hightower brothers and their pets."

I giggled.

Rook nipped me on the ear. "Who said you don't count, too?"

I felt the smile creeping on my lips as I watched them jump into another debate—this one on acting skill, to which I had no contribution—other than to add that all my favourite scenes involved them with their tops *off*, and that was as far as I cared.

Stars peeked out from clouds above us, and—though the night air was warm—I was happy to accept Drake's hoodie to keep me warmer as they talked. Rook spotted him passing it to me and hurried inside to grab me a plaid blanket (just in case the hoodie wasn't enough).

I curled up in both, comforted by the smell of the crackling fire tangling with twilight grass, vanilla winter, black currant wine, and caramel brandy.

The trees across the garden rustled in the light breeze, and the shadow of the great maze loomed a little way away. The garden lights were on, and the pool glowed, its ethereal colours shifting across blues and purples.

This was the dream I'd asked Rook to help me paint.

I sank into it as they talked, the conversation becoming more and more erratic as the night went on.

"You are changing us, Vex." Love's voice was rough, dragging me from my trance after a while. "We're better for you being here. I know... I am."

"Oh, he's being vulnerable," Rook snorted, squeezing me against him. "You definitely changed him."

I snorted, but Love was smiling. "How do you think you're going to settle in? There's a lot of moving parts in a pack."

"This part isn't so new to me," I said before thinking about it. "I grew up in a pack."

I felt all their gazes on me in a moment.

"That's unusual," Love noted.

I nodded.

Omega-alpha pairings always had a chance at alpha kids, which meant pack experiences were often baked into them. Omegas, however, were born at random. The fact my mother had been one was pure luck. Or... well. She might not have seen it that way.

"I shouldn't talk about them. It'll kill the mood."

Rook swallowed, glancing sideways at me. "I hated, when you were gone, that I didn't know anything about you. I want to."

I shrugged, hugging a knee to my chest beneath the blanket. "Very traditional. Four alphas, one omega. Normal bond. Middle class. Average. And uh... they weren't..." I trailed off. "Good, you know?"

Their attention on me was suddenly... a lot. But they already knew so much. They'd seen my room. My posters and drugs. They'd already seen some of the most vulnerable parts of me, and they still wanted me.

That had been the heaviest burden, when I discovered I'd scent matched them: the fear of that rejection. The fear that there was nothing I could do to be good enough. And they'd managed to shatter that fear into a million pieces.

"Evan—pack lead—he was possessive in all the worst ways," I

said quietly. "Arrogant, always angry. There were constant pack lead fights when I was growing up."

"Did you have any siblings?" Ebony asked.

I shook my head.

"I think that's why they were so angry. After me, my mother didn't have any others. She told me later it wasn't until I was born, that she realised she couldn't. Couldn't bring any more kids into our family. When she took the injection, she never told them." The same shot I'd been given as a gold pack. The injection that stopped an omega from being able to have children for years at a time. "Like I said. My dads weren't good, and she was always afraid they'd hurt me. They threatened to sometimes."

There was a silence, broken only by the crackling of the waning fire.

Love broke it. "It sounds like she did the right thing."

I nodded. "It cost her. I don't know if they figured it out, but they blamed her. She became a burden. And they had a reputation by then, couldn't keep themselves in check long enough to court another omega—though they tried."

"Nothing came up about that when I searched you," Ebony noted, looking curious.

My smile wasn't warm exactly, but it was proud. "Like I said, they had a reputation. There was a murder—my dad was killed. It was mayhem. My mother saw it for the chance it was: she took me and ran. We moved cities, changed names and never looked back. But it was hard for her. She was bonded and in hiding. She had to be really careful. We weren't rich, but we were happy."

"What happened to her?" Ebony asked.

I chewed on my lip, eyes burning. "She got sick. Brain tumour. Happened fast. One day she was fine, and then... I was... alone." My throat was tight with words I'd never said out loud before. Drake's fingers squeezed mine, but I couldn't take my eyes from the fire as it popped and crackled. "'*Dare to dream, because a dream unfinished is just magic still waiting to steal you away,'* that's what she'd say. And she was dreaming until the day she was gone. Every night she would tell me all her plans for the next week, month... year..."

Lenny's Pizza Place for the four cheese with BBQ sauce instead of red.

Centennial Park's Autumn light display.

The Grand Canyon to see the sunrise.

My momma's dreams.

My voice shook, but I forced myself on. "I want dreams that strong. Dreams with enough power that only death can take them from me. Dreams that will live on even if I'm not here."

I let my gaze flick to Ebony for just the briefest moment.

He was absolutely still, eyes like liquid lava in the orange light of the dying fire, dancing shadows carving grooves across every inch of his frozen expression.

Then I focused on the fire again, jaw clenched.

I *could* do this with them. They were each little pieces of my soul, anchoring me; giving me strength I couldn't imagine without them.

"My mom would tell me her dreams every night, and then she'd sing me to sleep."

Drake reached up, thumb catching the single tear beneath my eyes before he cupped my cheek. I huddled against him, still holding my knee tight to my chest.

"I perfumed a week after she passed. Probably stress. Mom would have had a heart attack. She never wanted me to be an omega—well, she didn't say that, but only because we never expected it. It happened on the subway. I thought I was in trouble, but then this crazy dog found me, wouldn't leave me alone. Had my shirt in her teeth and wouldn't even let me go into my apartment without her."

I smiled at the memory. Of the great St. Bernard who'd followed me home and never left.

"It was one of my mom's dreams, getting me a dog so I'd be safe in the Gritch. But she wanted a Doberman, instead I got this goofy St. Bernard. But momma would have loved her anyway."

"She sounded amazing," Drake said, drawing me against him.

"She was." I smiled. She hadn't just kept me safe, she'd kept me sane.

I owed her everything, right down to this moment, to this pack, who were fighting for me, even when the world had turned its back.

FORTY

Chia pet's 7th day of life, hair growth 7cm.
   Time until execution: 1 day

VEX

I caught Ebony in my nest the next morning, arms folded, examining the chia pet. Love, Rook, and Drake were downstairs prepping to bring me breakfast in bed.

Ebony hadn't joined the others in the nest overnight yet, and I wondered what was holding him up.

"What are you doing?" I asked, stifling my yawn as I reached him.

"You're watering it every day?" he asked.

"Are you questioning my chia pet mothering skills?" I asked, narrowing my eyes.

"Not at all, Little Omega."

"Is there something wrong with it?"

"No. I just want to make sure it'll live until tomorrow."

"What happens tomorrow?" I asked.

He just gave me a sidelong look that sent a little prickle up my spine.

Damn.

What *was* going to happen tomorrow?

I opened my mouth to pry, but he tugged my bottle of scent suppressants from his pocket.

"What are you doing with that?"

"Checking it over," he said. "I was looking through your meds. You used this to suppress your scent?"

Uh… "Yes."

"Every day?" he asked.

"When I was with you, yes. But before that just some days."

"Where did you get them?"

"I know a guy."

"I looked it up," he said matter-of-factly. "Bad scent suppressants can be dangerous—"

"They're clean," I snapped, tugging them from his hands.

He narrowed his eyes. "A *guy*?"

"I'm serious. These are good. What is this? I know how to take care of myself."

He raised his eyebrows, and I glared.

"Why didn't you use the heat clinics?" he asked. "I help fund them."

"You think I didn't want to?"

He cocked his head, clearly unsure.

"There's two, Ebony. In the whole city of millions of people. There's *two* clinics. Even with a cab, if it wasn't rush hour, the closest one was half an hour away. Where I lived in the Gritch District, sometimes I had to wear scent blockers just to leave my house—even with Aisha. My hormones have been out of balance for years. If I'm lucky, I get ten minutes warning and I can take a pill to delay it by another hour—and it's agony. Sometimes omegas get caught because the amount of pain they're in is a walking beacon. So I have to get somewhere safe, I have to do it fast, and I have to pretend I'm not in pain the whole time. If I'm slow, then I start losing my mind—all the drugs and heat turn my brain to soup."

There were protections and programs, but not ones that gold packs qualified for. Another move in the incentive game the government played to dissuade omegas from avoiding the injection.

He considered that, cocking his head. "What about the pill you took the other week? Delay it by a day, a week, a month? Then you know—?"

"Do you know how expensive those are?" I asked. "And even then, it's just the same thing again. It comes on fast with no warning."

He blew out a breath. "But if you *can* get to a clinic—"

"Have you ever been to one?" I asked.

"I attended an opening."

"The neighbourhood outside those clinics have the highest rates of heat entrapment in the whole city. Predators wait for omegas nearing heat who can't get a spot—and there are *so* many who can't. But at home, I know I have the drugs. Would *you* toss that coin?"

He stared at me for an age, his jaw ticking as he processed what I'd said.

Finally, he nodded. "Okay. I understand. I failed. I should have pushed for more clinics so you were safer."

"You're... going to do that?" I asked, heart lifting.

"Why?" He frowned at me. "You're safe. I don't have any more mates."

My nostrils flared, and a growl rose in my chest before I could catch it.

He cocked his head, a smile playing on his lips. "That's very cute."

"You're going to set up more clinics," I said.

"Am I?" If it wasn't Ebony, I'd swear the smile on his lips was playful. "What do I get for that, Little Omega?" he asked. "I'll need a lot of convincing."

EBONY

I found her waiting in my room later.

That was odd, because I was sure by the way her eyes had darkened when I'd made the comment about the clinic that I'd screwed up. She'd stared at me for a long moment, then dropped the pout and dismissed me from her nest.

Now, I was frozen in my tracks, staring at a fucking siren in my bed.

I'm going to need a lot of convincing.

That's what I'd said.

Fucking lies.

I'd set up a thousand clinics across the city if it meant she would do this for me every night.

Once, when doing my own stunt at the edge of a cliff for a movie, I'd looked down and believed my harness wasn't attached. For one ice cold moment, my heart had felt like it tripped over itself, believing I was definitely about to die. I wouldn't go so far as to say I'd been afraid, but the thrill had been memorable.

Somehow, that was exactly what I felt right now, staring at Vex waiting in my room like a queen.

It tripped over itself a number of times, in fact, and when that mischievous smile spread across her face as she drank in my expression, it was like my heart clawed at my rib cage.

It was hotter because *no one* entered my room except her, and she certainly didn't do it without me. But she was reclined on the edge of my bed, tantalising black lace clinging to her skin.

I strode toward her, every goddamned instinct in my body screaming at me.

Bite her.

Claim her.

I drew up, chest heaving, right in front of my bed.

Something halted me. The same thing that had halted me every time. The bond I hated putting a name to, stopping me. It was a thing I *knew*, but couldn't feel. But even if I couldn't see it, or touch it, I knew it was there as surely as I knew Drake's stupid fucking 2005 minivan was down in the garage right now, rusting in the same air as my Lamborghini.

"You came in here without me," I said.

Her smile widened, and she tangled her ankles together, drawing her knees up playfully as she leaned back on her elbows.

Her claim—the bite on my neck—had faded in a day. But I wanted her again, however she'd let me have her.

"I have plans," she said.

"And those would be?"

"Do you want me, Ebony?" she asked.

"You know the answer to that."

"I want to hear you say it." She'd changed. She was more confident around me than she had been before. That made me feel good. A little burst of pride in my chest, because it was a claim of a sort, too.

I could feed that.

I wanted *more* of that. "I want you," I told her.

"And what would you do to make that happen?" she asked.

I cocked my head, examining her and unable to dispel a rush of hope.

Would she let me?

"What would you like me to do?" I asked. This wasn't coming for free, I could see that by the twinkling mischief in her eyes, but she didn't know how much I would be willing to give if it meant I could take her on my bed like this.

She was fucking mine.

It grated every day that I couldn't bite her. And even in this, the rules were different. I couldn't, like I did with most things in life, take what I wanted without asking. There would be nothing left of what we had. And it would hurt her.

I couldn't hurt her.

It was a new set of rules that were slowly—awkwardly—twisting into existence for me. It was of the same flavour as what I had with my pack, but so much more intense.

Vex slipped to the edge of the bed, so her legs were dangling on either side of mine. She looked up at me with those beautiful golden eyes, a half smile still curving plush lips that were now tantalisingly close to my crotch.

"I want to see you on your knees like I was for your brother."

VEX

I didn't *believe* it was going to work, but it felt... fun. And I wanted to see what would happen.

Ebony's jaw clenched as he gazed down at me.

He was a specimen, dusky skin and rippling muscle vanishing into white sweatpants. *Who could even pull off white sweatpants?*

Fuck me.

He was the type of man who just... gave off power no matter what he did, it had been that way since the first moment I'd met him.

And so my mouth went dry with shock as he sank to his knees before me. Perfect and statuesque, he placed his palms on his lap and dropped his gaze just like I had.

"Is that what you want from me, Little Omega?" The sultry

husk to his voice set my hairs on end as I picked my jaw up off that floor.

I narrowed my eyes, trying to hide my spiking arousal that I knew he'd catch in my scent. Instead, I got to my feet and did a repeat of what I'd done the first time I was in his room.

Ebony needed clear communication and boundaries. Give him that, and there was nothing for me to worry about. And creating a complete mess of his room—that was the first step of the message I was about to send.

When I was done, and his room was a tip, I sank back down onto the bed beside him. Then I lifted my phone and shot off a few texts to Rook.

> Me: Come and fuck me in Ebony's room.

There was a pause.

> Rook: Is this an assassination attempt?

> Me: You're not famous enough for it to be classified as more than a murder.

There was a longer pause.

Was he not going to come?

He wasn't really that afraid of Ebony, was he?

> Me: Where are you???

> Rook: Wait. You're serious?

> Me: Crystal.

> Rook: Crystal serious?

> Me: Do you want to bang me in his room or not?

> Me: You bang me or he does. Your choice.

Rook: Put it like that, death's a small price.

I dropped the phone down on Ebony's lap and shifted back on his bed. A low growl sounded from Ebony's chest as he read the texts, and his eyes flicked up to me where I was laying, leaning my cheek on my fist as I watched his every reaction.

"I didn't say you could look at me," I said.

A sneer curled his lip, but to my surprise, he dropped his gaze back down. "He's *not* coming in," he hissed.

Bolstered by what he was willing to do already, I smiled. "He certainly is."

"You think I'd allow that—*and* you don't even plan on letting me fuck you?" Something feral rose in his voice as he said it.

I shifted to the edge of the bed, and rolled on my back so my head was hanging off the side and I was gazing into Ebony's upside down thundercloud eyes. I couldn't help grinning.

He was hot and dangerous. And he was also ridiculous. This was just a room, but he was more mad about inviting someone in than he was that I'd wrecked it. "Well," I said, reaching out and brushing his cheek with my fingertips. "We're about to find out."

By the way he leaned into that touch ever so slightly, like a man dying of thirst, I had the sudden and shocking realisation that this was about to work.

He was going to let me do it.

"Rook's pack. His claim counts the same," I said.

Another growl rose in the air, and it sent heat spiking through my veins.

"Oh. *Shit.*" I glanced up to see Rook leaning against the door frame. "He's *in* the room?"

"*He* is right fucking here," Ebony snapped, about to turn, but I cupped his cheek more insistently.

"Shh," I whispered, tugging his chin up and pressing my fingers to his lips. He looked like a feral dog about to snap its leash. But he clenched his jaw, eyes burning as he re-fixed his gaze on his hands as if it physically hurt.

Holy. *Shit.*

I rolled over so I was upright, then leaned forward, pressing a kiss to his cheek. "Good boy," I said loud enough that Rook would hear.

Ebony's hand snapped up and he seized my hair, dragging my face an inch from his. His chest was heaving and his eyes burning as he fought the urge to... Well, I wasn't quite sure. Slowly, with a pained expression, he released my hair and lowered his hand back to his lap.

"And you *won't* touch yourself," I added.

I might be flying too close to the sun right now, but the thrill in my veins was enough that I didn't care.

"You can come in," I said, glancing back up at Rook.

Rook didn't hesitate, eyes sparkling with delight as he dragged his gaze from Ebony and looked around. "Don't know why, but I always thought it would be tidy in here."

FORTY-ONE

VEX

"Wreck me," I whispered in Rook's ear. He leaned back, chestnut eyes alight with lust, a smile on his lips.

"You know how recently I rutted, are you sure that's how you want it?" Rook asked me.

I nodded.

He grinned, tugging his top off. Fuck he was something to look at, rich skin rippling with muscles, I was entranced, completely.

"Safe word."

"What?" I asked.

"You want me feral, Baby Girl?"

"Yes."

"Then." He tugged me closer, breath tickling my ear, voice a low growl. "You're going to need a safe word."

My pulse skyrocketed with anticipation and Ebony breathed what could only be described as a hateful laugh.

"I..." My brain scrambled as I stared up at him.

"I'll give you one if you like," he said.

I nodded.

"If you need me to stop, say... how about... *cuck*?"

I giggled as I heard another growl from the end of the bed.

Fuck.

Fuck this was hot.

"You're a mess and I've barely touched you."

A whine slipped from my chest. He *still* wasn't touching me. Not as much as he *should* be. I reached down to his boxers—which were offensively *present*.

At the sound I made, he reacted in an instant. He flipped me, fist in my hair and grip on my thigh as he dragged me back against him.

"You claimed me, Baby Girl," he breathed. "That means I'm yours, body and soul. *I* fuck *you* and please *you*, not the other way around."

I felt him shifting behind me, and hoped that meant he'd rid himself of the boxers. I gasped as his fingers found my clit and my low moan echoed around the room as he lined up his cock with my soaked entrance and drove into me without warning.

My fists clenched on the sheets and I heard his groan above me.

He let out a breathy, "Fuuuckk..."

I whined as he drew out and then slammed back in.

Yes.

This was what I needed.

My first orgasm rushed in far too quick, with Rook's fingers at my clit and his cock stretching me out. I loved the sounds he was making, too: his low groans of ecstasy as our bodies connected for the first time.

EBONY

This absolutely shouldn't be working for me.

It shouldn't, and it absolutely was.

None of it made sense, least of all my rigid cock, hosting a hard-on the likes of which I'd never felt. The thought of her rejection of me *in my own room* after she'd destroyed it just sent more blood down south. And definitely not at all the heat in my veins as I watched Rook's chiselled form rail her like no tomorrow into my Egyptian cotton sheets.

She was fucking captivating and completely at his mercy. She threw her weight into trying to fuck him back a few times, but he cut it off instantly. The message was clear: he was fucking her tonight, not the other way around, not for a second. And I watched for those beautiful moments in which she tilted her head, golden eyes finding me as Rook sent her over the edge of another orgasm.

Rook.

Not me.

Even though I was responsible for the stupid etching across his ass that he was currently flashing me—which was probably the reason she was letting him do this to her in the first place.

And it was... fuck.

It was hot.

I was mesmerised by them. I loved, even more, how sometimes I couldn't tell her moans from whimpers. Sometimes she fought him so he had to seize her wrists in one hand, hair in the other as he pinned her to the sheets, railing her until her indistinguishable whines turned into moans and her eyes rolled back.

Once, it had looked like she was fighting him to get to me, her fists scrabbling on the bedsheets. He seized her by the hair, arching her neck so she was looking right at me as he fucked her into another climax.

"Good girl," he purred as she reached it, dragging her up against his chest by her neck. "Eyes on Ebony while I ruin you in his bed."

Her teeth caught her lip so hard I was surprised it didn't bleed. She let out a feral moan, shattering again over the same climax as his fingers found her clit.

I was in a trance, unable to look away from her lean frame dwarfed by him as he impaled her, her rosy nipples perky and dark beside her pale skin. Her blown pupils were fixed on me.

I was cracking, a low growl slipping from my throat. My cock throbbed like an iridium rod at melting point, but she'd been crystal clear.

Rook grinned at me. His eyes flashed with just the faintest trace of the wildness he'd had in the cage, the echo of a rut only just out of his system. He had stamina too, which was good—*bad*—because it meant this show went on for far longer than it had any right to.

He turned her on her back. His touch was always soft and tender when he readjusted her, and I'd lost track of how many ways he'd fucked her into oblivion.

I was good at sex. Like, I was: I'd put my work in—had to, to sleep my way around the industry. But... fuck me.

This would be less humiliating if he was a bumbling minute man.

But he damn well wasn't.

"Ankles over my shoulders, Baby Girl," he told her.

I almost groaned at that, my own body red hot, but there was no way in hell I was going to blow my load kneeling at the foot of my bed when Rook hadn't even busted a nut *in* her.

She was so tired she shook, and for a moment I wasn't sure she could keep up. Her expression was dazed as she tugged her knees to her chest. He had to raise her ankles the rest of the way.

His hand dug into her waist dragging her against him. When

he drove into her like that, she let out a breathy gasp, back arching, those cute nails with chipped black polish digging into the taut muscles of his back.

"Fuck." Rook's eyes squeezed shut as he groaned, free hand shaking to hold him up.

Fucking finally.

He finished in her like that, driving deep as her low moans filled the air.

She was spent enough that she was a trembling mess. He drew up, tucking her hair behind her ears. I could see the glitter of sweat across her skin.

"You were perfect," he whispered. "So fucking perfect Baby Girl."

She was almost cross-eyed as she stared up at him, chest heaving, exposing beautiful pale breasts to me.

He kissed her, long and deep and I saw the way she raked her nails across his back again as he did.

"You wait here," he told her, then shifted to the edge of the bed.

Right beside me.

"Like what you see?" he asked, and I knew there was a cocky grin on his face as he grabbed the edge of my under sheet to clean himself off.

I'd fucking burn it.

"I made you Harrison," I snarled under my breath. "Remember that."

He clapped me on the shoulder, unaware of how close the movement brought me to diving at him.

He laughed. "Thanks, mate."

I stifled another growl, knowing it would only vindicate him as he got to his feet. She lay on her back, chest heaving, eyes following where he'd vanished into my bathroom.

He returned with a cloth and took care of her, snagging her lace and helping her back into it. Then gave her a kiss and left.

Thank.

Fuck.

He was gone.

Vex slid to the foot of the bed beside me, and I was hard all over again for how aroused her scent was. Raspberry and lust.

Fuck, I wanted her.

I'd eat her out right now, Rook or not, if she'd let me. Instead, she pressed the crook of her finger to my chin and lifted it.

Her golden eyes were blazing as she looked at me. *"Never* use your power over a vulnerable population across this city as a leverage point for sex again. Is that clear?"

"Perfectly."

That's what this was for me, a learning experience.

I'd underestimated this—*hugely* underestimated it. And she was making sure I knew that.

I didn't resent that—though I maybe resented Rook a little for capitalising on it. But this was just another puzzle, and I'd figure it out like I'd figured out everything else.

Plus, when it came to this particular issue, I had a plan in motion already that would fix it.

"And you *won't* get off to what you saw tonight," she told me. "Or at all, until the first time I decide you can fuck me."

Shit.

Well... *shit.* I tried to unclench my jaw. "Careful, making a demand like that," I murmured. "Be *sure* you're ready for the monster you've created by the time I do catch up with you."

"I can handle you, Ebony Starless."

FORTY-TWO

Chia pet's 8th day of life. Hair growth: 9cm.
  A singular black tear has been scribbled down its cheek.
  Time until execution: 0 days

EBONY

"Wait—Wait!" Rook caught up to me as I reached the fence at the very back of the garden. "I want in!" he said, tugging a black jacket on as he did.

I turn on him, not hiding my irritation. "For fuck's sake," I muttered. "You're like a rash I can't get rid of."

"You're doing something for her, right? One of your psychopath revenge things? I want in."

Rook wanted in on tonight—after *yesterday*? I snorted. "Not a fucking chance."

"I'm coming," he insisted.

"This is *mine*."

"We're pack, she's *our* omega."

Oh, *now* she was ours. Ha. "She's mine, you're hers by the way it's looking," I told him.

He grinned, not even phased by that. "So I'm not a threat."

"You can't handle this, go back inside and cuddle her."

"I can handle it," he snapped. "Plus, I could blow this up in a moment. Sneaking out the back, wearing all that, you don't look like you want any attention tonight."

I bristled. "You'd ruin it, when it's for her?" Fury edged into my voice.

"I'm not losing the upper hand she gave me last night."

I glared. But shit... He was right. He could ruin it in moments. All that planning. All that time.

For nothing.

"If you come, you'll do *exactly* as I say."

"Yup."

"You won't get in the way."

"Done."

"And if it gets too much, you'll shut the fuck up and wait in the car."

"Too much?" Rook's grin was all too cocky. "Not gonna happen."

I sighed

You know what? Fine.

Fucking. *Fine.* All of his puppy-dog excitement was going to go poof the moment he found out what we were doing.

I was looking forward to it, actually. Double win. Vengeance for Vex, and breaking Rook's little brain.

He wasn't a total idiot, I supposed. He was wearing dark clothes with a hood, and he'd masked his scent. There was nothing identifying him as an alpha, or—with a mask—Rook Harrison. He was even wearing deep green contacts, which was a bit of an overkill, but whatever.

We walked a couple of blocks, clearing us of the neighbour-hood and landing us in a park. Then we got into a taxi that would take us to one of the beaten down warehouses I used to keep my other vehicles—it just kept everything cleaner. The Crimson Fury pack's address was known, but this way we were just two men taking a cab into town. Perhaps it was good Rook was here; two of us instead of one. Changed up my M.O.

"Once we get out, you're not Rook Harrison anymore, alright?"

Rook nodded, taking the cloth mask I handed to him. It was enough for now, but I had better ones.

"This is all very... organised," he prodded as we crossed toward an old car behind the metal warehouse fences. It was innocuous enough that it would look abandoned, though there was a worker here that made sure it was functional a few times a month.

"*Premeditated*," he added, playing with the word on his tongue as if just to be annoying.

I rolled my eyes. "Celebrity-hood is limiting." I handed him a pair of black gloves and slipped on mine.

"For *what*, exactly?"

I shrugged. "Anything I'm feeling. Sure you don't want to back out?"

"Not a fucking chance."

"Right. Great. Wait here."

It took me no more than ten minutes to slip to the storage facility next door and find my locker—kept under another alias, pre-paid for years, and completely untraceable. I scanned the different bags before grabbing one out. None held anything damning in them by themselves—worker equipment and other such things.

Rook was quiet as we drove, eyeing the bag I'd dumped on his lap curiously. He didn't open it, clearly trying to prove he could listen no matter what my plans were tonight.

We pulled up before the address I'd been given. It had taken some serious digging, and help from my mysterious contact that had helped with the whole production tonight, but he'd come through.

Luckily for me, what Vex wanted more than anything else in this world was noble enough that it wasn't hard to find characters who aligned with that. Now, I was on the brink of sending the go-ahead for those New Oxford fireworks I'd been building towards.

But not yet.

This part, I needed to do myself.

"What's inside?" Rook asked, following my gaze and peering at the house beyond.

It was a nice property. A small house on a plot of land in a nice neighbourhood. It was, unsurprisingly, the closest thing to an upstanding neighbourhood one could get from the Gritch District. I'm sure it would have been an inconvenience for him to travel too far for work.

Its singular occupant lived alone—though he had frequent visitors, women mostly—and none stayed long. That was barring the nights he was out until late, but I knew his job held demands far beyond normal work hours.

I'd had this place scouted extensively, and I was confident we wouldn't be interrupted. Still, I had eyes on the place, ready to alert me if anything out of the ordinary happened. And to clean up after I was done, since that part was dull. I was only here for this vile stain on alpha-kind.

There were, I had learned over the last week, many different kinds of vermin in his line of work. Some even with the full white picket fences, wives and children, or even packs who might have been none the wiser. They would be by the morning, though.

I started the engine again and then drove us down the back alley, where I found the spot perfectly shielded by bushes and trees, while still close to the house.

"So... What are we doing?" Rook asked at last, as I tugged

open my backpack—the one I'd brought from home—and withdrew my gun.

"Hunting."

He looked sceptical as I cracked the gun open to check the vials inside.

"Hunting?" he asked.

"Yup." I tugged out a cloth and carefully tipped just the smallest amount of the silver powder into the centre. Then I opened another vial and added the light sedative. All set, I wrapped it neatly and put it in my pocket.

"You really sure no one knows you have that?" Rook asked.

Agritox. A silver bullet, it was referred to sometimes. Alpha's poison. But I was sure. "It's safe."

I only had half a vial left, and I kept it for special occasions. I paused, a thought creeping in, one that I'd had before, but I hadn't had the opportunity to explore... With a smile, I added another small amount of Agritox to a vial of normal saline. I swirled it, watching curiously as it dissolved.

"This is starting to get a bit concerning, mate."

I ignored him, instead watching the last few swirls of silver disappear into the clear liquid.

"Tell me that's just for assurance..." Rook blinked as I pulled a second gun from my bag. A real one.

This was just for assurance, though I would need it—much later in the night, anyway.

Rook was right about how closely Agritox was tracked. The only reason I knew this vial was written off as a loss was because I stalked the tracking of this substance almost as closely as I stalked the drug rings amongst celebrity actors.

I tugged out my burner phone and shot off one text.

The go-ahead.

Drawing up the rest of the drugs I needed and capping the

needle, I turned back to him. "You are going to wait in here until I say you can come."

"*What?*"

"This part's delicate," I said. And mine.

He *could* come, and rather unexpectedly, the idea wasn't as appalling as I'd imagined. It wasn't because it was Rook, obviously, but one of my pack with me? The thought was strangely comforting.

I think... I'd even allow him to help if he had the stomach for it.

But I wouldn't give him this part.

I fitted a full mask over my face and fixed my hood so it covered any trace of my silver hair.

Blood began rushing through my veins, the first traces of excitement stirring.

Vex truly was the most incredible woman in the world. Not only did she give me a thrill I'd never had before, but her wants? They aligned with justifying *this*—the thing that would soon slip into second place for the best feeling in the world.

I knew what the first would be: Her trembling beneath me like she had beneath Rook last night coming apart from my touch.

After tonight, she would let me.

Fuck, I couldn't wait until her heat, when I could do it to her over and over and it would never be too much.

I checked my bag once more, making sure I had everything, and left Rook waiting in my car.

This alpha had security cameras all over this place. An abnormal amount, compared to his neighbours, but not at all surprising considering what he did to afford a house like this. Tonight, though, those cameras were having some serious technical difficulties, and last night's video would be replacing anything they might catch.

Tugging a key from my pocket, I slid it into the lock, turning it with perfect slowness so as not to make a sound.

Usually, at this time of night, he would be in the living room, watching TV. His evening routine consisted of a few trips to the kitchen to restock on drinks and food, but nothing else.

Tonight, however, he wouldn't be in the living room. Not after the text he'd just received.

The back door creaked only a little as I opened it and slipped in.

Sure enough, I heard a thump from upstairs. Something heavy hitting the floor. A suitcase, perhaps? Footsteps on floorboards above were hurried, and the shuffling was desperate.

Perfect.

I caught his scent in the air: confirmation that he was everything I was hunting. But right now, it was gross old wheatgrass with only the faintest hint of fear.

Not quite what I'd wanted.

Easily hearing each of his movements upstairs, I made myself at home.

I set my bag down in his living room. It was spacious, with an old-style arm chair—appropriately dramatic, I thought—and hardwood flooring. I tapped on it. Real, not laminate. Had to be careful with that.

I picked up the glass on the table, swirling the golden liquid within. Scotch, perhaps. It smelled smooth and expensive.

There was another thump upstairs, as if something had fallen over. He was doing my job zealously, covering the footprints that would lead to his own grave.

Still, I was impatient to begin. I shifted the mask from my face for a second, downing the remaining scotch—not nearly as good as I'd hoped.

I sat down in the armchair, tugging a marble from my pocket

and setting it down on the smooth surface of the coffee table, watching it carefully for a moment.

Satisfied, I repositioned it and dropped the glass upon the floor.

The shuffling from upstairs halted, and a smile found my lips.

I shifted into position, waiting pressed up against the wall around the corner from the staircase as I heard him descend one creak at a time.

"Who's there?" a low voice growled.

I took a deep breath, enjoying the stronger edge of fear to the wheatgrass in the air now.

Of course, the edge of a gun was the first thing to slide into my vision as he turned the corner. Just as primitive as could be expected from a man like him. Though his aura wasn't out, which was a testament to his familiarity with situations like this: guns and auras could be unreliable.

And he really was making my job easy. His gun was equipped with a silencer. I'm sure after the warning that had just sent him into a panic also made him uneasy about drawing gunshot attention to his house. But a gun wasn't enough to save him.

Nothing would be.

Right on cue, the marble hit the ground, making a resounding low *thunk, thunk, thunk* behind the armchair as it bounced on hardwood. His fear skyrocketed, and it was a sweet, sweet drug in my lungs.

"Who's there?" His demand was more aggressive this time.

He took one more step forward, damning himself with far too much ease.

I grabbed him, aura out, cloth in my fist as I pressed it over his mouth. His aura hit the air right after mine, but almost instantly it began to wane as the powder hit his lungs. I had his other arm in my grip so that when the gun went off, I could aim it into the back of the couch.

Not ideal, but I'd let my guy know, and he'd hide it.

Wheatgrass wailed, struggling against me as I crushed the cloth against his mouth with vicious strength.

He seized once, twice.

"Tonight," I breathed in his ear. "You're going to be more afraid of me than she ever was of you."

Again, his fear spiked.

Beautiful.

And then he went limp in my arms.

FORTY-THREE

ROOK

Holy.

Fucking.

Shit.

I walked into something from a true crime documentary.

Like... I'd had a faint inkling of what this was, but it was another thing to see the clear tarps across the floor and wall. To *see* the alpha on his knees in the middle of it. He was gagged and bound, face ruddy and eyes wide with panic as Ebony stood over him, silver eyes curious and fixed on me.

"Oh *dude*..."

Fuck.

Double fuck.

This was bad.

Really. Really bad.

"*What* are you doing?" I asked, voice a rasp.

"Field trip."

"No no no. *This* is too much. The second car... the sneaking around—fine. But... This? The... tarps?" My voice was weak.

"For the blood."

I swallowed. "Right. The blood."

"Well." I could almost hear the smile in his voice. "That part's up to you."

"Up to *me*?"

"I could go either way. There's less after they're dead, and I can make a man scream without spilling a drop, but I wanted to cover all my bases in case you had a preference."

Preference?

"I didn't think you were actually..." I ran my fingers through my hair, staring around again. *"Oh fuck!"*

We were screwed.

Completely screwed. And I was here.

I was an accomplice.

"I'm surprised. I thought you had me all pegged." There was something delighted twinkling in Ebony's gaze as he watched me melt down. He crouched down beside the struggling alpha, lifting a cloth beside him to reveal a neatly laid out line of... oh God.

Torture instruments?

"No." I lifted my finger, shoving down my nausea as I crossed toward him. "It's a *fucking* myth that most people like you do this. You're supposed to be running businesses, climbing politics, claiming positions of power"—my voice dropped to a hiss—"Not actually cutting people up and tossing them over bridges."

The wails of the alpha became more desperate.

Ebony looked rather pleased. "Despite the fact that you alluded to it the other week, you still missed the most important piece."

"What?" I asked.

He plucked out the thinnest knife in the case. I realised, as he'd spoken, his aura had edged into the space. One brief flicker at a time with more control than I ever felt. But his eyes were burning, the knife spinning in his grip.

He sighed, one long exhale as he considered the man before him.

I felt him through the bond in that moment, free falling into something thrilling, alive, and vicious.

Then, before he was consumed by it entirely, he moved lightning fast as he stabbed the blade into the man's forearm—right through his sleeve and flesh. I clamped a hand over my mouth as the man howled through his gag and I took a step back, as blood spilled onto the plastic below.

Oh *God*.

Ebony sang the words, low and vicious, and a chill ran up my spine. "What you missed mate, was the hormones."

He knelt on the alpha's back, knee pinning him to the ground as he dug his fingers into the wound. Then he was ripping back the sleeve of the man's shirt. I could see the skin beneath, tangled with the fuzzy black lines of a faded tattoo.

"Vex is waiting. We don't have all night, so if you don't want to..." He turned to the alpha beneath him. "Don't think you'll be needing that anymore." My stomach lurched as he slid the edge of the knife into the man's forearm, right down a faded black tattoo.

"What's... what is that?" I asked, voice weak. "Why?"

Okay.

There *had* to be a reason, right?

He was mad, but he wasn't like... this mad?

"The human trafficking ring in New Oxford... it's run by alphas, and yet they almost exclusively traffic omegas and alphas. It's a snake, eating its own tail. Rather appropriate for tonight, don't you think?"

"Trafficking ring?" I asked.

"Oh. Yeh." Ebony turned to me with bright eyes and said, as if it was an afterthought, "He's the one who sold Vex."

"*What?*"

Ebony cocked his head, looking down at the alpha still

shaking on the tarp. His eyes became dark. He lit in the bond, a tempest of fury for a split second. "*This* is Wheatgrass—as Vex has dubbed him. He works in the tunnels of the Gritch District. It was his people that ripped her from her home after they tracked her from that internet post." He returned his blade to the alpha's cheek, pressing hard enough to get a wail through the gag, but not enough to break the skin. "He kept her in a windowless room by herself for weeks before securing the best offer he could find. Then he forced her to wash in front of him, dress and look pretty so he could cash in, all while waving a gun around to make her comply."

My eyes fell to the alpha, blood still dripping onto the tarp from his forearm. A chill hit my veins, every hair on my body on end.

Everything changed in an instant.

I felt the rush of joy from Ebony through the bond as he watched my reaction. Then he stood and held the knife out to me. "You can have a turn. Let loose. I checked the vicinity; the property's big and there's no one here. If anyone comes, I'll know. You can use your aura if it feels good."

As if to show me, he gave the tied up man a kick in the ribs, getting an agonised grunt out of him. The movement jostled his gag free, and he was moaning in an instant. "P-please," he stammered. "I swear I'm not who you think. My name is Wrenly Hammond. I-I'm an outreach worker at the Gritch Districts East Community Foundation—"

"Shut up." Ebony kicked him again.

My voice was high. *"You got the wrong guy?"*

"Get a grip." Ebony rolled his eyes. "I don't get the wrong guy."

"He's—"

"His name *is* Wrenly Hammond—though I prefer Wheatgrass. But he isn't an outreach worker."

"P-please, I am." The man's desperate hazel eyes were fixed on me. "You have to believe me. I g-got the tattoo with friends when I was young. It doesn't mean anything." He struggled against the bonds that held him desperately, eyes wide and terrified.

It was chilling, seeing an alpha brought to his knees like this. I glanced at Ebony, but he was fixated on the man struggling, a glint in his eyes. He was focused on the same thing I was, but for a different reason.

"E—" I cut off before saying his name. "We should check, right? What if—?"

"Oh for fuck's sake. I don't get the wrong guy. Here."

Ebony grabbed the man by his hair and dragged him up to his knees. Then he crouched down. "A short while ago you got your hands on a *very* valuable gold pack omega. She must have been worth a thousand times as much as most of the poor souls you steal."

"I d-don't know what he's talking about—" Tears were flooding Wrenly's face as he looked at me. "I swear. L-look I have a sister. Niece and Nephew—"

"He's telling the truth." Ebony sounded pleased. "In fact, you took all of them across Europe last month. Tickets were booked last minute. It was a very expensive trip—especially the private tours in Pisa. I wonder what they would say if they found out how you paid for that—as an outreach worker in the Gritch."

"It was inheritance, I was—"

"Now," Ebony cut him off. "This omega, she would have been particularly valuable because she already had mates. In fact, that's why you targeted her. Because she posted online about the celebrity pack to whom she had scent matched."

"I swear I don't know... Please!" He was begging me now. "Please, I'm not who you think."

"M-mate, we should be sure—"

But I cut off as Ebony did something that turned my blood to ice. He tugged his hood down and removed his mask.

No.

I took a step toward him, but it was too late. There was a nasty smile on his face as Wrenly Hammond looked right into the face of Ebony Starless.

I watched as his eyes bulged. It was recognition, but not the way I was used to. Instead, his skin went a sickly shade. That was terror in his eyes, no doubt about it.

Not the reaction I had expected. Not the reaction anyone should have to seeing Ebony in person, unless—

"You took my mate," Ebony growled.

Shock seemed to have paralysed Wrenly Hammond entirely, and his eyes darted to me for a moment. It wasn't desperation like before, instead he was scanning my features as if he were trying to figure out who I was.

"Our mate," Ebony added.

"Who did you sell her to?" I asked.

He whimpered. "I, I d-don't know. We don't get that kind of information about clients."

A low growl rose in my chest as he confirmed the truth. "But you were the one who set it up?"

"I leave them at the door. I don't see names or faces. That can get us k-killed." Again, his eyes darted between me and Ebony in panic. "Please, I do have information you could use. If it's the Hounds you want, I could—"

"No need, Wheatgrass. We're here just for you."

"But... Ebony, what if he does know—?"

"He won't know anything special," Ebony said. "If he did, we can't trust him not to lie."

"N-no—I know things that c-can be of use—" He cut off as Ebony replaced the gag. "Don't worry, Harrison. We don't need him."

· · ·

So.

I got it.

Just a bit.

Love would never know, but there was a thrill to this, to carving out revenge for Vex across flesh and bone. To the sounds of his screaming. Even down to the warmth of his blood that soaked through my gloves.

Every time the alpha looked close to passing out, Ebony would jab him with another needle. His pupils would constrict and he'd scream for me a little longer.

"He's not so nice to the others, I hear," Ebony said as I worked, goading me on with delight. "If he can get away with more, he does—but Vex's value wasn't worth the risk. Funny, though, that it's not enough. He still has ladies over here so often."

Rage boiled up at those words as I looked into this man's eyes, red edging into my vision.

How many had he hurt?

How many like Vex?

My knife dug in—his thigh this time. His face was thoroughly fucked up.

"Which do you prefer?" Ebony asked him. "The women you pick up at the bars, or the omegas who can't fight back?"

He didn't reply, panting in agony.

I twisted the knife to elicit a howl. My stomach's flips of discomfort were gone. Instead I felt an echo of what Ebony did.

My instincts were on overdrive.

He'd hurt her.

Hurt others like her—omegas. A *violation* of what we were.

"Answer him," I twisted the knife again.

He just shook his head, sobbing. Tears curdled with blood on his cheeks from the cuts I'd made.

After a long time of carving flesh from bone, I felt satisfied, and I got to my feet, dropping the knife down on the tarp.

The pitiful groans were unending now. He was still awake.

Last night I'd been serenaded by Vex in Ebony's bed. Tonight, I got this.

Not bad at all.

"Almost done?" Ebony asked. I could feel his peaking excitement through the bond. He was on a rollercoaster of emotions that were usually so rare for him.

"Not yet."

He got up from the armchair (now with its own tarp) and took a breath, eyes scanning my work. I could feel a little appreciation from him through the bond.

"I didn't think you'd be so... into it." He crossed toward me. "Finally doing something of value."

"Get fucked." I turned on him as I ripped the knife out of Wheatgrass's thigh and jabbed it in his direction. "You need me. I'm valuable—not just to the pack, but to *you*, specifically."

"I don't *need* you," Ebony scoffed.

"You know what?" I asked. "People like Drake, because he's shy and all emo and shit. Love's a pillar—and he can be pretty funny in his roles. But I'm the flavour. You don't think people are going to get sick of the same old Ebony Starless villains, eventually? I'm the spice rack—I make your bland old chicken villain seem like something new every time."

His expression tightened. "I'm not chicken."

"You're good chicken, if that makes you feel better."

"I'm *not* chicken."

"You *need* me. Why do you think they always cast me in so many scenes with you?"

"Because Love likes to make me suffer."

I grinned, jamming the knife into Wheatgrass's stomach to a low groan. "Bet you the next solo spotlight, Love's never asked for that in his life."

"Watch where you're sticking that," Ebony snarled. "You'll kill him before I get a turn."

I left the knife buried in his gut and got to my feet.

"Fine. I think I'm done."

Once again, his eyes swept across the scene, taking it all in. Enjoying it. Then he crouched down, fisting the whimpering alphas hair and examining my work.

"You know what?" He said, turning his gaze on me as I sat down in the armchair. "Maybe you aren't as bad as I thought."

"I don't usually make a point of advertising it around you." I snorted. But I could see the strange... something in his gaze that continued to linger on me. I lifted my hands. "Oh no. Absolutely not. Shut that look off."

"What look?" He *almost* seemed startled.

"There's nothing between us."

"What?" he asked, a sneer curling his lips.

"You're getting all... claim-y. You claimed Drake. Love's yours. But not me, Ebony. There's no claim. No thank you. Not one damn thing—*nothing*—between us."

He sneered. "I'm not *claiming* you."

"Good," I said. "Then we're golden."

He paused, glancing back down at Wheatgrass for a long moment before flicking his eyes back to me. "I didn't realise you didn't want my claim that bad."

I narrowed my eyes. Oh no. No no no. "That *wasn't* a challenge."

"You fucked her in my bed," he murmured. "Only one way I let that slide."

I folded my arms, all my irritation draining away as he reminded me of that, and returned my attention to the alpha.

"You said you can make them scream without a single cut? Go on then."

He perked up, finally ripping his eyes from me. "I can." He

tugged out a pouch and withdrew a needle. "I've always been curious. What do you think would happen if you put Agritox right into an alpha's bloodstream?"

I stared over the metal railings at the peaceful flow of River Oxford below, stretching into the infinite darkness of the night.

"And you're *sure* about this?" I asked.

"After tonight," Ebony said. "No one will be looking for him in this city."

"Why?"

"He got a text before we arrived that sent him into a panic. His home is in a state of chaos—exactly what you might expect of a criminal who just learned he'd been discovered. Packed in a hurry and his suitcase is missing. He escaped just in time for the fireworks."

"The fireworks?"

Ebony grinned. "We have an omega to go home to. The night has only just begun."

FORTY-FOUR

Chia pet's 8th day of life. Hair length 9cm.
   Time until execution: 113 seconds

VEX

I jumped as the door to my nest banged open.

It was late—really late. But Ebony had promised me a date tonight and I was waiting up with Drake and Love.

Ebony stood in my doorway. He smelled of twilight grass and a fresh shower, and I'd never seen him glowing like he was right now.

"Ebony?" I asked, but he was crossing toward my window sill, eyes fixed on my line of gifts.

I tugged away from Love's arms and ran to him, heart taking flight in my chest as he picked up the chia pet.

"What are you—?" But he took my hand, chia pet in his other fist as he tugged me from the room. It was hard to keep my footing as he walked so quickly, but all of my omega hormones were on overdrive.

I didn't care that it was late.

I didn't care that he hadn't said a word—or that he was dragging me outside—or that I had no idea why. We were in the garden and Ebony shoved a planter off a pillar and slammed the horrifying chia pet in its place.

I froze as he picked up a gun that had been waiting on a nearby day bed.

"Ebony—" I began, but he was ignoring me.

He ripped a fistful of its wheatgrass hair out, tucked it in his pocket, then pressed the gun right up to its gaping mouth.

"Wait—!"

But without a moment's warning, he pulled the trigger.

I let out a squeak of shock as chia pet guts exploded everywhere.

FORTY-FIVE

ROOK

Vex couldn't stop bursting into fits of manic giggles.

Ebony had swept her into his arms and carried her into the nest where he'd shooed out everyone but me. Then he'd sat her down on the couch and told us to wait before vanishing.

"It's real?" She whispered to me, as she picked little pieces of soil from her hair.

"It's real," I said with a grin.

She narrowed her eyes at me like she was going to ask more, but then pursed her lips through a little smile.

Finally, Ebony was back, and in his fist he held a tall glass cup filled with a light green smoothie. In it was a straw and an umbrella.

He pressed it into her hand, sitting down on the couch and turning on the TV. From the drink, I caught the undeniable scent of wheatgrass.

"What uh...? What's going on?" she asked.

"The fireworks," he said, glancing between her and the TV. "For you."

I frowned as he found a news station, and we were instantly met by breaking news read out by frantic reporters out in the New Oxford night.

Along the bottom was the line: *"New Oxford in a state of chaos as police sirens are heard across the city."*

"There's been a leak," The reporter was saying. *"A major leak of information. This is big. Anonymous tips are one thing, but this isn't just some nut job on the phone. From what I know, there's evidence behind every claim, and there are* mountains *of it."*

Vex could not take her eyes from the screen. The smoothie clutched in her fist like it was a lifeline.

Then we were shown clips of police raids. People being dragged from houses and arrests being made on drug charges: possession, trafficking, importing and exporting goods. *Perhaps* not newsworthy, but for the fame of the people who were taken— and the sheer volume. It was, it seemed, never ending.

First, it was a bit repetitive as reporters across the city caught wind of celebrities being arrested in their homes.

Vex got to her feet, eyes wide as the Evening Star's logo appeared. Her eyes shone, and she took a little sip of the smoothie, unable to look away.

Ebony had the Evening Stars symbol he'd gifted her in his hand already. When Dean's name popped up on the screen, he dropped it into a wide basin and lit it on fire.

Vex looked over the moon as the edges of the picture curled with flames right as the TV showed a swearing Dean Trance in pyjamas being shoved into a police car.

When it had burned to cinders, Ebony funnelled the ashes into a tiny decorative glass jar and pressed a little cork cap on top before returning it to her window sill of doomed gifts.

He really had a thing for theatrics, I was starting to realise.

I supposed he *had* chosen acting for a career.

It didn't end at Dean Trance, though.

"It's not just police out there, I've never seen so many GPRE squad vans in one place in my life."

"What does that mean?"

"Gold Pack and Rogue Enforcement squads are no joke. They're set up to face more than just your run of the mill criminals. Whatever's going down in the Gritch tonight, it's massive. If you ask me, the arrests are just the beginning."

Vex frowned at the screen, clearly unsure what to expect.

Ebony was tense where he sat, and I could imagine, if he seriously was the mastermind behind this—which was complete insanity—that he might be anxious to see how it went down. But the slight edge of nerves to his scent, it didn't seem to be about what was on the screen at all. He could barely take his eyes from her.

"There's more tonight than celebrity arrests. We've finally got news about the disturbances in the Gritch District. It's been confirmed that the New Oxford GRPE and police force have raided an underground base host to a network of human trafficking."

I heard a little breath of shock, and then Vex crossed toward the TV, standing right in front of it, smoothie clutched in her hands as she watched from an inch away.

"Please be aware, some of the images you're about to see might be disturbing."

They weren't wrong. Next thing we knew there were frail looking omegas and alphas being ushered out of an old theatre building in the Gritch, escorted by police, and a sizable number of body bags.

"The theatre right there, 'Jamie Hill Arts Centre' appears to be one of the entrances. We've also had reports of no less than sixteen members of the GPRE and police that have also been taken into custody tonight."

"How could something that big be under their noses the whole time?" I asked.

"It's not so much that it was a secret," Ebony said mildly. "It's the power and money behind keeping it. Enough of that was destroyed tonight that it made a raid viable."

"It's...?" She swallowed. "Really... gone?" Vex asked, looking back at Ebony.

"Gone?" Ebony grimaced. "No. Can't make a promise like that, Little Omega. But we certainly put a dent in it."

Finally, when the news cycle began repeating, and the only fresh news was another rich idiot being shoved into the back of a cruiser, Ebony reached over and tried to tug the smoothie from Vex's grip.

"It's well finished."

"It's not." She glared at him, ripping it back and taking another teenie sip. There was a *little* left at the bottom.

Ebony's eyes narrowed.

"The smoothie was a bonus. Not the main act."

She bared her teeth. "I *like* the smoothie."

"Stop drinking him and let me take care of you."

I snorted, though he was right. I'd never seen someone make a smoothie last as long as Vex was making this one last.

Vex froze, eyes wide as Ebony finally managed to free the cup from her grip. Her face had drained of colour.

I straightened, alpha instincts on full alert as I tried to find the threat. I followed her gaze but it was still fixed on the smoothie that Ebony had set down on the table. Frowning, I looked back at her. Her expression was nothing short of panic as she finally turned back to Ebony.

"*W-what?*" Her voice was a rasp. Ebony was frowning, clearly as stumped as I was. "You... didn't...?"

Ebony cocked his head, clearly trying to understand. Then his eyebrows rose just slightly and he glanced at the smoothie, too.

"Ebony." She mounted him like an angry koala. "Ebony *tell me what was in that smoothie.*"

"I..." He trailed off, glancing at me like I could help him. "Well..." He scratched his chin, and I swear he looked uncomfortable. "I thought..."

"Wait...?" I said, feeling the blood drain from my face as I realised what he was saying. "You... you didn't."

We'd left Wheatgrass's apartment to be dealt with, but Ebony had wanted to dispose of the body. Was it possible...? Could he have...? I wasn't watching the *whole* time...

"I thought it was just wheatgrass." Vex murmured, nearly breathless.

"I mean... yes. It... *was*... wheatgrass," he said.

"What does that mean?" Her fists closed in his shirt as she shook him the best that her tiny frame could. Her voice was shrill. *"What was in the smoothie, Ebony?"*

There was a long silence as Ebony looked to me as if for help.

My mouth was open in shock.

How could he think—?

Then he burst into laughter. He bundled her into his arms and got to his feet, walking them both over to the bed.

"Ebony!" Her voice was a screech.

"I didn't put alpha in your smoothie, Little Omega." He patted her on the butt before tossing her onto the sheets.

"Oh, fuck no!" Vex hissed. "You can't—" she let out a little squeak as he caged her in.

Oh. Okay.

We were doing bed things now.

I followed them in time to see Vex's furious expression as she tried to wiggle out of Ebony's grip. "You're so fucking pretty when you're all angry," he told her, fist in her hair as he dragged his lips along her neck.

"We. Aren't. Doing. This. Now!" she snarled, but her cheeks

went bright pink as Ebony's touch slipped beneath her dress. "You can't make me think I ate people and then finger bang me!"

"I think, actually, I can."

She glared at him, but her pupils were blown with lust. I watched as he slipped his touch beneath her panties. She let out a sound somewhere between fury and lust, and then she'd grabbed him by the face and was kissing him.

My first instinct was to join in, not wanting to be left out, but then I paused.

Maybe I'd give him tonight.

He'd kind of earned it, really.

FORTY-SIX

VEX

Ebony had kept to every promise he'd made. Even when it should have been impossible.

Twilight grass saturated my nest as I deepened our kiss.

He was everything I could never have predicted. And perfect, all the same.

I groaned as his tongue explored my mouth, his grip on my waist holding our bodies together as I wove my fingers through his hair so he could never get away.

I loved him.

I knew what his love was, and it was enough for me.

It was who he was.

His grip dropped from my waist, fingers dipping into my core again. I moaned into his mouth, wanting more.

I broke away, brushing a loose strand of his silver hair from his eyes as I stared into them. "I want you."

"I have permission?" His voice was low, breath hot at my ear as he nipped it. "Loosen that leash, and I'll fuck you until you're full of my seed." His lips trailed my neck, thumb brushing my stomach. "And then I'm going to keep it all inside you with my knot so that pretty little body of yours can't escape while I make you come until you beg me to stop."

I shivered, lips parted as my words fled me. It was all I could do to nod.

I wanted all of that.

And then the truth rushed in. The dark reality that waited in the wings.

Zeus's promise.

Not a command, and somehow worse for it. The last thing he'd said to me before he sent me back to them. The one promise he'd made that sent fear rocketing through my veins whenever I thought of it.

Ebony drew back, eyes narrowed.

"Something's wrong," he said.

I swallowed, trying to shove it down, trying to return to the moment before, when I didn't remember. When it was just me and him.

I couldn't.

Sickness turned my stomach.

"I need..." I let out a breath, and he released me, shifting back on the bed. "I just need a moment."

I hated seeing the confusion in his eyes as I fled to the bathroom, knowing I was so close to losing it completely.

I hated that I was pushing him away for fear, when I'd promised them dreams that would live forever.

EBONY

Vex had been in the bathroom for a while.

Something had gone wrong.

Had it been me?

I thought I'd done everything right, followed the rules...

My phone buzzed, and I glanced down at it.

> Unknown: This blew sky high, man. Way more than even we planned for.

I glanced at the TV to see there was a fresh news cycle that hadn't been there before. It might well be the middle of the night, but there was no lack of new information.

"It's more than that, Jo. I've just heard reports that there are more people coming forward. This might go further than just the trafficking ring, I have word that there have been two arrests tonight —seemingly unconnected—but my sources tell me they might be citizens who were involved in the ring from the outside."

"What do you mean by that?"

"Buyers. It might be legal to dark bond a gold pack omega, but it certainly isn't legal to participate in the buying and selling of alphas and omegas—which is exactly what this organisation has done."

I stared at the screen, shock seizing my whole system.

I'd never considered that.

Was it possible... Could the police possibly find who had bought Vex? They hadn't helped because she was dark bonded, and we had no evidence she was purchased.

Even if they couldn't, if the pack who'd bitten her were watching this, they might be panicking.

I froze.

Her phone.

I didn't have it.

I'd been too distracted when I'd come in.

Shit.

Shit.

I dashed from the room and hurried down the stairs to the garage. The backpack I'd taken tonight was on the floor beside the door. I unzipped it and ripped the phone out. Even as I watched, it lit up.

Shit.

I paused, then into the driver seat of my car, shutting the door before tapping the screen on.

Sure enough, he'd made contact. Not just once, but... *fuck.*

There were dozens of texts, and a voicemail.

I read through the texts several times, piecing together broken words and sentences until they made sense. He was drunk... had to be. And panicked. I could tell.

> Pack Lead: Enjoy the night you little slut.
>
> Pack Lead: When they leave you behind you'll never have a good night again.
>
> Pack Lead: Or maybe better, maybe you've fucked him and I get even more entertainment.
>
> Pack Lead: The stupid dead bitch, trusting a man who'll never save her.

I stared at it trying to figure that out. He was completely off balance.

I forced myself to tap open the voicemail, every sense on high alert. Would he have hidden his voice in this? Not drunk as he was, surely?

I pressed play to hear angry, slurred words through the voicemail.

"Don't get confident you little rat. Like I don't know why you're happy tonight. You think we're like those others? That we're getting caught?" There was a pause, and then he was speaking again, more slurred than before. *"On second thought, go on. Trust what they're saying. Believe I'm going fucking soft, like I would ever want his seconds. Screw it all up like you've done since you started you dumb fucking bitch. Fuck Ebony fucking Starless so I can watch you*

get torn to pieces in a hunting arena." There was the sound of a crash, a low growl. *"Delete this fucking message. And call. Me. Fucking. Back!"*

That voice...

I recognised his voice. I couldn't place it—not exactly with the slurred speech and shitty voicemail quality. But I *knew* it. Not that I should be surprised, but still... *Hearing* the voice of the man who'd bonded my mate.

My heart was racing out of control. Unfortunately, not like earlier, when I was riding a high.

But none of that was the worst part.

The worst part was the realisation of what he'd said.

He'd singled me out.

He'd told her... I frowned, playing it again to confirm, to let the voice sink in a little deeper.

My blood froze in my veins.

He'd told her if she fucked me and we didn't save her, he would have her killed.

A hunting arena.

It wasn't something I was intimately familiar with, but I'd come across it on the dark web. Places where the trafficking ring was only the tip of the iceberg. You had to go deep into the underworld to find things like that. Where the rich played with the poor like toys. There were warehouses, pit fighting, and more. But hunting arenas: that was where omegas were killed by alphas for entertainment. And I knew there were packs who did it to rid themselves of dark bonded omegas they were tired of. It could damage the pack bond, but not always if the omega hadn't been bonded long, or if they'd been held at arms length within the bond.

I almost jumped as the phone buzzed again.

> Pack Lead: You want to know what really keeps me going, even knowing those pathetic alphas are banging my omega?

> Pack Lead: At the end of the day you're mine. I control it all. I decide if I keep you.

> Pack Lead: There's one video that keeps me going. I can't stop watching it. I even showed it to the others, and they've been begging me for it ever since.

Next thing, a video came through the texts.

> Pack Lead: Look how fucking pretty you look like that.

It was of Vex. She was in that familiar limo, and her eyes were a rich brown, the same as they'd been before the Gala when she'd worn contacts.

"Don't push me Vex. It can always get worse," the alpha murmured. "For example, I think the others would love to see this."

She squeezed her eyes shut.

"What do you think I should do about how much you made me want you?" he asked. He took her by the hair, twisting her neck toward him. "You can give me something to work with, and you can return to them untouched. Or you can fight me, and leave me to claim what I want another way."

Vex's eyes opened in shock as she stared up at him.

But he wasn't done. "Tell. Me." The command came again.

Tears streamed down her face, but I'd seen that look in her eyes. It was the look she got when she was sure about something. When she wouldn't give in no matter what.

"I w-won't."

She was shaking with the agony of fighting the bond.

"All of this pain, just to avoid telling me a little about him."

"It's not yours," she choked out. "None of it is—"

"You are mine." His voice was a low growl as he shook her. "Whatever you do with that pathetic mate of yours, it's mine, too. If I want to call you here after, you'll tell me what I want to know."

"Drake isn't yours. He never will be."

Drake?

My mind raced a million miles a minute trying to piece together what was happening. He wanted to know about Drake?

And they'd just been together, by the sounds of what he was saying.

Still, something wasn't quite right. Something tugged at the edges of my consciousness, just out of reach.

"If only you knew," the alpha laughed. "Don't you want to give me a little something? I'm getting a little antsy for the omega I've bonded. You're proving so much more interesting than I anticipated."

Vex shook her head again, and it seemed all she was able to do. Fighting the command was destroying her.

Still, she didn't give up.

"I won't..." she gasped, low whines slipping from her chest with every breath. "I won't."

I noticed how the camera panned closer, lingering on her tears and agony.

Finally, he let her go, and she collapsed to the floor of the limo. She curled up, clutching herself.

417

"I'll let you off the hook. There's enough here for me to make do with after all."

The camera cut off and my phone screen went blank. I was left with a dull ringing in my ears.

I knew.

I knew who he was.

From his voice, and from what he'd asked for.

Drake.

He wanted her to tell him about Drake.

The full truth settled onto me like a cold blanket, each piece of the puzzle falling into place, revealing a picture before my very eyes. There were so many packs it could have been, all with their own twisted vendetta, but somehow, this was the worst.

I knew who they were, but more than that...

Shit...

I was reacting in an instant.

I was on my phone, texting Leighton. She needed all of this information right now. We could get ahead of this. I fired off texts to others too, to anyone that could help until there were no more to send.

Until the truth came crashing in.

I sat back, head pressed against the seat as the phone dropped to my side.

Because I knew what Zeus Rogan would ask for.

It was over.

I don't know how long I sat like that, cycling through every possibility, always landing back where I started: to the impossible choice.

The one I could never make.

I needed more options. A part of me wanted to get on a plane and fly her a million miles away...

And then deal with the trigger commands, her agony and suffering...? Suffering like I'd just seen on that video.

It wasn't possible.

I might be able to survive in a world knowing I'd condemned anyone else to that. But not them. Not my pack.

Not my mate.

I returned to Vex's room first, whole body numb.

Love would have to be told that I'd discovered, and... *fuck*. I would have to tell Drake, but I couldn't let the Lightning pack find out we knew, so first I had to go to her. I had to find a way to forward what he'd sent without breaking her.

I froze at the doorway to find her waiting for me like a siren.

She sat on the bed, a silken nightgown hanging open to reveal her beautiful pale skin. She was wearing black lace panties, but her breasts were bare, just covered by the edges of the gown. I crossed toward her, looking down, into her eyes that shone in the pale light of the lamps.

She was waiting for *me* like this?

I stared at her, taken completely off guard.

"I... I want you," she whispered.

She *what?*

"Vex."

"I'm sorry. About before. I was nervous. But I know what I want." She was so sure, looking up at me, and there was a smile on her face.

I just stared at her.

I'd seen the promise Zeus Rogan had made to her.

That one that condemned her for choosing this. One that was a fool's choice, but for one thing: she trusted me.

I've got you, Vex. I will always keep you safe. Those words rocked me, the impossibility of what waited like a looming beast casting a shadow across everything.

Could I make that promise?

The future was impossible.

I knew what they'd ask for. There was no path that led to victory. My mind felt like it was stuck in a maze slamming into dead end after dead end with no way out.

"Ebony?" she asked again.

Anger rose in my chest.

Why *was* she trusting me like this? It was mad.

Foolish.

You make her feel safe. You built that foundation from the ground up. She is coming to you for everything you ever wanted her to come to you for.

And now...?

"I can't," I said.

I didn't know enough. I needed time to get ahead. Needed time to find a way around this—for an option beyond the two before me. If I did this now, without a plan, might I be condemning her?

It was then that I realised how far that this entanglement had gone, that the lines had blurred, that her safety and my victory... they were, perhaps, becoming the same thing. And that meant neither choice I would have before me would be a win.

But one would mean hers...

Was that enough?

Her expression broke and she shrunk, arms wrapping around herself. "You don't want me?"

"I..." I trailed off, trying to figure out what to say. "I'm not ready."

"Oh. Okay." She drew back, biting her lip. "That's okay." There was a silence, and I could see the insecurity in her eyes. "Did I... I didn't do anything wrong?"

"No." My voice was rough. "Never."

She nodded. "Okay."

She hunched her shoulders, taking a breath and forcing the smile back on her face.

Then she buckled, and raspberry treacle flooded the room like a drug, setting off every alpha instinct in me.

"No." My voice was gravel as I caught her.

No.

"E-Ebony." Her voice trembled with far too much fear for someone so brave.

No.

Not now.

Her heat.

Her heat had hit.

But that meant... They were going to take her back, and I—

"I'm scared." Her face crumpled, her breathing picking up.

I needed more time. There was something caught in my throat. I *needed* a third answer.

But there was no more time.

"E-Ebony." Her voice shook.

I hadn't moved. She was shaking in my arms, and I'd done nothing.

She was mine, and she wasn't. She... she never would be.

I couldn't win.

Not unless...

Those beautiful golden eyes glittered with tears, staring at me. Trusting me.

I blinked, and the third, and final door appeared before me: The last option.

The one I'd never had before her. I didn't know if it was victory, it didn't *feel* like that. But it wasn't loss, either.

It was something else.

Something new...

And maybe... maybe it would be enough.

The last gift to break. The black necklace: it would be no more.

"Bite me," I whispered.

"What?"

"I need your bite."

"I don't understand."

"I made you a promise," I told her, drawing her chin up and steadying her. She clutched my wrists, her breathing ragged.

Before now, promises had meant so little. I could lie with ease, could treat the world however I wished in order to get what I wanted. And yet now, in a game where there was no victory, everything else shifted onto a playing field I'd never seen.

When those words—that promise—it possibly, maybe could mean something... And if it did, perhaps I'd claim one small win after all.

I drew her close enough that I could feel the heat of her tears trickling onto my neck.

"Bite. Me."

She was still breathing heavily, terror in each of those sounds. It was hers, and then, like a blinding flash of light, it was mine, as her teeth sank into my flesh.

I sagged, wrapping my arms around her and holding her close.

"I'll always keep you safe."

This was it, I realised.

The beginning of the end.

ROOK

Something was wrong. I could feel it.

Or I was hyper attuned to the strange silence from Ebony after how bright he'd been earlier.

And that was when I saw her through my balcony window.

A slight figure in an oversized sweatshirt stepping down the driveway and into the darkness. The high of the night crashed into a stone wall as I realised what I was looking at.

My mate, walking away.

A limo waited on the street beyond. A pack here to take her back.

I was backing up, then sprinting down the stairs in seconds.

She hadn't texted, but I couldn't leave her to do this alone.

I caught up to her as she neared the gates, already in earshot of the low hum of the limo's engine. She spun as she heard my footsteps and her lips parted in surprise.

Her heat.

I caught it around the edges of her scent, present, though faint as if shoved off by drugs.

Fuck.

She drank me in, head cocked, a distant expression on her face. Then she reached up, tracing the lines of her name across the goosebumps of my chest.

It was hard not to glance at the limo. Hard not to let my aura slip out. "Are they...?" I cleared my throat. "Are they in there?"

"Yes."

I didn't realise I'd taken a step forward until I felt her hand on my arm. "Please don't," she whispered.

I paused, looking back at her with a pained expression. There was a long silence between us as I warred with every instinct in my body.

Didn't she know I would die for her, if it meant freeing her of this?

But it wasn't that simple.

It never had been.

I stepped back, jaw clenched, turning to her.

"I love you, Baby Girl," I whispered. "I love you more than I've ever loved anyone."

Her eyes became glassy, and then she leaned close. I cupped her cheeks, drawing her closer. But she put her hand on my chest.

"Kiss me when I'm back."

When they wouldn't see.

When this would all be over.

"Tomorrow," I told her.

"You promise?" she asked.

Her warm palm pressed against where my hands cupped her cheeks, and she closed her eyes. Her soft lips curved up at the corners, and she became, in that moment, complete. Every fragment of the puzzle I'd desperately scraped together over the last few weeks, coming together in one moment.

She was hope.

A lighthouse enduring in a void that should have swallowed it a thousand times. The impossible smile that defied every odd.

This omega, with breathtaking golden eyes, glittering with everything we had no right to have lost: she was our missing piece.

I searched for my own smile, needing to leave her with a gift. In that moment, I understood her strength for how painful it was when I found it: Soaring, agonising hope that tore open a void beneath me.

"I promise," I whispered. "We've still got dreams to chase."

FORTY-SEVEN

ZEUS

I stared down at the two objects before me on the oak desk. Either both would play a role tomorrow, or neither would.

I picked up the vial and tilted it, watching the disruption of the silver dust within. Enough to make an already vicious weapon deadly. Not enough to be traced in the body.

Yet, I'd believed in this plan since the day of its conception. Why would it change now, with one night to go?

The quietest voice whispered in my head. *Because of her.*

Upturning plans, wreaking destruction—in my mind, *my bond, my pack.*

Quivering with fury, I set the vial down carefully.

She'd ruined everything else, so could she have, possibly, changed the equation completely?

Why should I not leave this to her, then, too?

Her's would be the choice that damned him.

VEX

I clenched my fists around the sleeve of my shirt, around the inscription my mother had sewn.

It was the one line of lyrics I held most dear, the one line I hadn't had the courage to sing, even after all these years.

Back in the room they had trapped me in for months, the dread returned. Cruel whispers sowing doubt, telling me that I might have left my mate's home for the last time. The Lightning pack may ask for something I couldn't allow to be given.

I wasn't just running from the Lightning pack anymore. I *was* the Crimson Fury pack omega, and that meant I would protect them.

I could survive this: I had a piece of each of them with me.

An offer from Love.

A connection with Ebony.

A promise from Rook.

And Drake's secret, his missing piece that I knew he could take back.

I jumped as the door handle turned, but it wasn't Zeus who entered. Instead, Cerus stepped in and crossed toward me.

"Don't," he said as I made to get to my feet. He sat down on the bed at my side.

Cerus was calm, almost eerily so. He had short black hair and what seemed like a permanent scowl on his hollow face. His scent, unhidden, could perhaps have been nice to another: savoury and perhaps from a bakery shop. All I could smell was charred toast.

"I think Triton is obsessed with you."

Triton?

I stared up at him, unsure of what he wanted. I'd barely met Triton.

Cerus was stronger in the bond than the others for the bite on my wrist, but even with that he was quiet. He wasn't looking at me, gaze fixed on the floor before us.

"There's not a day that goes by without more omegas in his quarters. He's always been insatiable, but it's got out of hand."

I didn't say anything, though, heart flighty, all my nerves on edge.

His eyes trailed up to me slowly, something hateful in them. "That doesn't bother you? Knowing your alpha has been fucking omegas by the truckload?"

"He's not my alpha."

Cerus turned to me fully, gaze calculating as he drank in my expression. "Is that so?"

"*They're* my mates." All of this was to get them to trade for me, was it not?

"You're very invested in my pack for an omega who doesn't consider herself ours."

"Invested?" I asked, unable to hide the shock from my voice. "You bit me. I don't want to be here."

His lip curled. "Is that what you're going with?"

"It's the truth."

Cerus snorted, but his nose wrinkled as his expression twisted. "Zeus is calculated, quiet—he was the clear choice for pack lead. Though he was never quite as cruel as Zephyr even if he has the same dark streak."

"Why are you telling me this?" With every word, a chill was creeping through my blood.

Something was off about all of this.

"Because I want him back," Cerus said. "And *you* have taken him from me."

"*Taken* him?" I stared.

"All that time you've spent alone with him, what have you been doing?"

Me?

I got to my feet, heart pounding.

"I don't even recognise him anymore," Cerus said. "So tell me, what is it you want?"

"I want to be with them."

"I don't believe you," Cerus said, his voice chillingly calm. "I think you found a way to get around Zeus's commands. I think you told them who we are—or perhaps you convinced him to loosen that particular order."

"Convinced... *Zeus*?"

Cerus got to his feet, towering over me, dark eyes voids of ice cold anger. I took a small step back, but running wasn't an option. I couldn't get out of this room.

"He's the only one who sees you," Cerus spat. "When you came back to us, he didn't want us visiting. Then Triton came in, and you attacked him. Zeus did *nothing*."

He grabbed my wrist, dragging me back, his expression twisted in a snarl.

"He's been changing since you arrived, more and more with every visit. I couldn't quite put my finger on it until I really paid attention to you."

"What do you mean?"

He lifted my wrist. I tugged back, but his grip became painful. "I've been paying close attention since I gave you this, and you know what I found?"

I couldn't move, every instinct on high alert as I stared into his cold eyes, feeling his thumb running along the bite he'd left me.

"While our pack lead has been losing his mind..." He cocked his head. "*You*, our dark bonded omega—our *slave*—is with her mates, and..." His lip curled. "You're *happy*."

A chill ran down my spine at Cerus's words. My mouth was dry, lips parted but I couldn't speak. What he was suggesting was absurd, but my instincts were on high alert. Cerus looked dangerous right now. Too quiet.

Too calm.

"You poisoned him."

I shook my head.

"What have you got planned for tomorrow?"

"Planned?" My voice barely worked. "I want them. My mates. It's all I've ever wanted."

"You're lying to me—"

"I *can't* lie—"

He dragged me closer. "You can if you convinced him to remove truth commands."

"I haven't convinced him of anything!"

Cerus barely seemed to hear me. He looked mad. *"Now* he wants you? Thinks you're ours after all, when you were never more than a—"

"Cerus." Zeus's word cut through the space, and the alpha before me froze. "Let her *go."*

FORTY-EIGHT

VEX

Cerus's chest heaved, a snarl on his lips as he finally dragged his eyes to Zeus.

"*Now* you crack, Cerus? When tomorrow, we get everything."

"Me?" Cerus asked, nostrils flaring. "When all you want is to walk away with a pet? Don't you care about revenge anymore?"

Zeus sneered. "They're the same thing."

"Which do you care more about?" Cerus asked. "If it came to it, which would you choose?"

"It won't," he said, stepping into the room. "Walk away, Cerus, and *maybe* I'll let you join us for her heat."

I shivered as my blood turned to ice, but neither of them seemed to notice me.

"Her *what*—?" Cerus looked wild, stepping toward Zeus. His charred scent became enraged. "I want *vengeance*, Zeus. That's what this was. I won't let you take that from us for the sake of *obsession*."

Zeus closed the last few steps between them, his full height enough to dwarf Cerus. "We'll do it the way I want to do it."

Cerus's aura split the air. Zeus, as if expecting it, released his instantly.

I staggered back in shock, feeling the shift in the bond.

A pack lead fight.

As Cerus swung at Zeus, I made for the door. I reached it, ripping it open, terror scoring my veins, when I drew up.

Dammit.

Dammit.

Zeus had commanded me not to leave.

It was leave, and suffer, or... I jumped violently at the crash from behind me. My breathing was ragged, fist trembling as I clutched the doorknob, staring into the hallway beyond.

It didn't matter.

Triton had appeared down the hall, Achlys right after him.

I stepped back before they could see me, eyes darting around the room. The brawling alphas crashed into the armchair on the far end.

I did what I'd done a thousand times in my life—I hid. This time, I made for the bed, squeezing under it just in time for Triton and Achlys to come bursting into the room.

I covered my ears, squeezing my eyes shut, a whispered lullaby sounding just for me as I felt the pressure of their auras in the air.

Were they fighting each other, or hurting her?

I didn't know.

It hurt not to know. The temptation to lift my hands and stop singing was unending, but she was always firm when she told me what to do.

"Don't come out too soon. Wait. Wait until there are no more auras and then wait some more. And always whisper, don't let them know where you are."

Always whisper.
Always whisper.

It wasn't until the auras were gone that I shakily removed my hands from my ears. The crashes had stopped.

I blinked my eyes open, then flinched at the sight before me. Cerus was on the ground. Blood trickled from his mouth. The armchair Zeus had favoured on his visits was on its side behind him. He was still but for faint breaths, eyes shut.

I could see Zeus's black boots beside him, nudging him onto his back.

"Take him to his room." I saw him being dragged out. Triton's old beer and Achlys' foul scent of bitter onions faded back to just traces. Until it was just stale cigarettes lingering.

"Are you hiding, Vex?" Zeus murmured.

I clamped my hand over my mouth to cut off my reply, but there was no pull trying to force me to answer, as if he didn't care if I did or not. He paused for a long moment, then walked toward the bed, each step bringing him closer. When he reached it, he turned, and I heard the shift of a mattress as he sat down.

Then he shifted, boot tapping the foot of the bed. "Come out."

It wasn't a command, which was worse.

I shut my eyes, breathing shallow.

"He was obsessed with my brother," he murmured. "I think he's gone a little... mad." There was a pause. "They're gone though. They won't touch you tonight." Another long silence passed as I tried to gather my courage.

"Don't make me force you out."

Slowly, with blood roaring in my ears, I dragged myself from beneath the bed, more frightened of the idea of him dragging me out.

Zeus was far too relaxed for a pack lead who'd just fought to keep his title. There was blood trickling from his temple, but otherwise he looked unharmed. He beckoned me toward him. I braced, then stepped closer, eyes fixed on him now, trying to understand what I was looking at. There was something wrong with all of this.

I stopped before him, just a pace further than I knew he'd let me remain if he had to command it. His pupils were blown as he looked me over with a frown. He took my hand, head cocked, staring into my eyes with far too much interest. "Tell me, what did you decide?" he asked. "Did he have you, in the end?"

I stared at him, uncomprehending.

"Ebony?" Zeus clarified. "Did he have you?"

I shook my head, mind racing. *That's* what he wanted to know right now?

Only, my answer was wrong.

I'd *wanted* Ebony. I had just been too late.

"Good," he breathed, nodding almost to himself. "Good. You chose right, Vex. You know the truth."

The... truth?

What did that mean?

The little spark of me still blazing from Rook's goodbye, it pushed me to open my mouth and tell him that I had wanted Ebony, but Zeus's whole frame loosened and there was a faint smile on his face.

It drew me up. He reached up to my face, and I flinched. He paused, lips pressing into a line for a moment, but then he shook it away.

"You're scared," he said.

I had no response to that. I could barely manage my breathing.

"I was angry, but now there is nothing for me to be angry at anymore," he said. "Come here."

Shock hit my system at that command. He lifted his hand to me, beckoning me into his arms. He was right, though. I was afraid. Afraid enough to fight that command, afraid to know what it was he wanted of me tonight.

He sighed, grabbing me by the wrist and dragging me toward him, instead. "Do you have any idea how lucky you are, that it matters to me?"

A breath of fear escaped me as he dragged me onto his lap, still facing him. My nails dug into his arms, fight-or-flight kicking in as I tried to tug away.

"Good, good," he said again. He held me tighter, something content in his voice. "That's what I want. Learn to fight me the way I need and we can make this work."

I fought a low whimper, hating his closeness.

"You're afraid of me because you can feel it through the bond. You know how much I like it when you hurt. It's wired into me like it's wired into them, but that doesn't mean it has to be bad." His touch was gentle as he ran fingers through my hair. "I don't want to ruin you. I could, though. Remember that. Think of all the ways this dark bond could be used to cause your ruin."

He forced my chin up so I was looking at him.

"But I won't because you are..." He trailed off, expression wavering as if he'd said too much. Then he shook his head. "You put yourself between your mate and two alphas—the man who'd hurt and rejected you." His gaze was burning. "*That* was when I knew you were special. Even with those eyes. You're more special than I realised."

I couldn't move, though my eyes closed as his hand brushed my throat in a silent threat. "Don't let it get to your head."

I was shaking, eyes tight shut, needing this to be over. But he said nothing for a long time, holding me close.

"Do you want to know the truth about my pack?" he asked at last. "I didn't foresee how weak my brothers would be in the face of a bond like this."

The words, as strange as they were, gripped me, and I almost opened my eyes.

"They're more obsessed with you than I'm happy with," he went on. "It's not an accident that I visit alone, despite what Cerus might say."

I saw his eyes flick to the armchair that was tipped over.

"They wanted you before your heat, but I don't have faith that the experience won't blind them. I don't trust them not to sabotage this. When you go into heat with us, when we can claim you properly, then I'll loosen their leashes."

"*If.*" My word was a rasp, the first I'd had the courage to say.

His grip on my chin dug in and he let out a breath of amusement. "Vex, *you* had so little faith that they would save you, that you didn't lie with your mate. I think we can begin discussing our future together."

My heart sank, goosebumps rising on my skin. He had it wrong.

He was stroking my hair, the touch frighteningly gentle. "I'm going to hide you away so well, they will never find you. They'll spend the rest of their lives knowing you're out there, unable to find you. Unable to touch us for fear of what might happen if they do..."

I took a breath, shoving away his words. I had trusted Ebony.

I *did* trust him.

They would save me.

Yet, I couldn't open my mouth to say it, all my instincts screaming at me not to.

"I could reject that princess bond tonight," he said. "End it now."

I grit my teeth, forcing down my rapid breaths as ice slid through my veins.

"But look what you've made of me, Vex. Fighting my own..." He sighed.

I couldn't focus on anything but those words.

I could reject the princess bond tonight.

One errant moment, one choice from him, and this could all come crashing down. I couldn't move, didn't know how to speak.

"But see, look at you." He drew my chin to face him. "I'm no fool. I know you're appeasing me. Does it help you relax to know I won't do it?"

A low breath of relief escaped my chest at those words.

He laughed, drawing me closer. "They won't save you. I just need you to see it for yourself. To understand how lucky you are that I've decided I want you after all. I know you'll come around. You'll choose right. Even *you* know, deep down, they will leave you behind."

What was he saying?

"That after tomorrow, you'll only have me."

"I thought... you wanted them to trade for me." My voice trembled.

"The truth?" Zeus breathed. "He will not give what I ask. He was never supposed to."

I shook my head. "I d-don't understand."

"The trick was never you. It was him. He's going to leave you, and when he does, he'll break them."

Ebony. I knew he was talking about Ebony.

"But you wanted them to fall for me," I said.

"Them. Not him. And when he fails them, it will be a slow destruction of the pack. Torturous. Unending. I'm sure Love will cling to it, thinking he can hold it together. For years, perhaps. Until he realises there is nothing left to save."

I took a deep breath, calming myself.

"But *you* were the prize I didn't plan for. Their own mate they gave up on. As they break, they'll know that—know that I have you. You're going to make yourself beautiful tomorrow morning. The princess they'll never have."

I tried to block him out.

I needed to let him continue. He was fracturing, the bond was telling me that. Let him speak lies, and tomorrow Ebony *would* save me.

He would.

They all would.

"And then, with time," Zeus went on. "You'll come to love me just like you fell for them."

"I will *never* love you." I tensed, knowing it was a mistake, but Zeus only laughed.

"You fell for the men who tormented you—the mates who *rejected* you. I am no different. Better even, than that monster the universe paired you with."

No.

No.

"I wanted him." The words slipped out, desperate and damning. "Ebony. I... I wanted him." I almost shut my eyes again, pulse out of control.

"What?" His voice was low and dangerous.

"I..." Shit. I knew I should stop but I couldn't stand this. Couldn't stand him comparing himself to my mates. "I wanted him. *He* said no."

There was a long, harrowing silence.

My throat was completely dry as I watched the fury twisting his expression. "You think they're going to give what we ask of them tomorrow? That they care enough?"

Yes.

I... I did.

They'd promised. *He'd* promised.

Given me hope like I'd never had.

I believed in them all.

Zeus looked mad. "If, by some miracle, you're right, Vex, I will ensure you wish you hadn't been."

"W-what does that mean?"

He ignored me. "You won't be, though." He looked disgusted, shoving me from him with such aggression that I crashed to the floor. "And when you finally learn that, you'll be crawling back to me."

I crawled into the bed, curled up and shaking. I clung to my sleeve, to that last line I'd never found the courage to sing, and whispered my lullaby, holding them close, my voice cracking with each line.

Aisha.

"There's a bird in the storm, and nobody knows..."

My mother.

"And she sings for herself as the cold rains grow..."

Drake.

"No matter how deep digs the thorn of the rose..."

Love.

"Or that words become lost as the wild winds blow."

Rook.

"No matter the doubt, or how dark the shadow..."

Ebony.

I loved them.

I loved my mates, and they would save me.

FORTY-NINE

DRAKE

It was a twenty-five minute drive from our home.

Twenty-five minutes: That was all it took for me to be looking at a huge property that had been host to every nightmare I'd ever had.

The Lightning pack was inside, and this exchange—for my mate, for Vex—would be made on their terms.

The terms of a pack who had once tormented me.

We were in my van. It was almost three o'clock: the time they had set for the exchange.

The conversation around me was furious, though I could barely keep up. Leighton was on speakerphone and had been for the last half hour as we'd driven here.

"He's almost into the security systems, but we're running out of time, Love."

"We can't go in there without backup," Love replied.

Right.

That's what the text had said. No weapons. No phones. No backup.

Come alone, or you'll never see her again.

"You *will* have backup." Leighton's voice was cold through the phone.

There were kill orders on anyone taking a job at this location, that's what Leighton had said. They'd planned this for far longer than we had to react to it, and had the money and resources to spread the word far and wide.

"No one who makes money in this business will touch it," she went on. "I've called in every favour, Love, from your people and mine."

"I *need* guarantees we aren't all going to be shot the moment we step in there," Love said.

"They're afraid of the law," Ebony put in. "We know that much. They've been too careful."

"Until we're in their systems, we don't know how close we can get," Leighton said. "I can't risk tipping them off that we're here."

Dread slid through my veins, demanding we go. Vex was in there *right now*. With them.

My nightmares.

I took a breath.

The others were still talking. Leighton was replying to Love.

"This isn't how I would like to run this either, but we don't have time. They want a meeting now and heat could hit at any moment. Once we're into their security, we'll be on standby. The moment she's in your bond, or if things go south, we can get there in minutes."

If things go south?

"Are we almost there?" Rook asked.

"Their security is a fucking fortress." I heard the irritated male snarl through the phone. "They can't know I'm here and you only gave me *hours*."

"He's good," Ebony snapped at Rook.

"You said you've never worked with him before—"

"There was no one else, but he's good for it. You think I didn't do my fucking research?"

I balled my fists, measuring my breathing.

We would get her out. I didn't care what the cost was. The threat we'd been sent was too much, with the promise that we'd never see her again. It had even set Ebony on edge.

A memory flashed in my mind. Vex bundled up in my hoodie and a plaid blanket in our garden at night, golden eyes molten in the dancing firelight.

I shut my eyes.

I'd caught Ebony earlier and made him talk to me.

"We need to discuss what they're going to ask for."

"You aren't going back to them." That was all he said.

"She can't stay there," I said.

"She won't."

"If they ask for me—"

"You aren't. Going. Back." He'd grabbed me by the shirt. "Do you understand?"

But it wasn't that simple.

I knew it wasn't that simple.

Zeus was pack lead. He hadn't been as bad as Zephyr, but he'd been cruel. Cold. And he was calculated, always. It's why they'd done so well in this industry.

Until Ebony.

"You'll release Drake from his contract."

"Like fuck we will—"

"That's not all." Ebony's voice was cold. I remember how he'd

looked at me right then. Like I was his, and he'd burn the world down for me. Then his gaze drifted back to the pack who'd broken me. "I have enough here to end your career. But that last clip is more than enough to land Zephyr in jail—if I decided to release it."

There was silence in the room. An unending terrible silence that Ebony broke.

"I want more than just the contract."

"Drake." That was Rook's voice pulling me from the memory. "You ready?"

"Yes." I swallowed. "She needs us in there *now*. We need to get her out."

Love's hand was on my shoulder. "We've got to be—"

"You don't understand. *You don't—!*"

"I know, Drake." Love cut me off as I cracked. "I know I don't." His ocean blue eyes were calmer than they should be. "Take a breath. We need you solid."

I was shaking, but I nodded.

"Alright." That was Leighton's voice. "That's it. He's in. Go."

LOVE

Nothing could prepare me for what it would be like, stepping into the Lightning pack's house. We were unarmed, outnumbered, and out of time.

The others were vacant from the bond.

I got it. Panic could be infectious. But despite the urge to shut down my end, I remained in case they needed me, taking a breath and calming my nerves.

Any of them might need that calm at any moment.

We passed armed alphas at the doors, and my gaze slid to the guns at their belts. They were masked and clad in black as if ready for a fight.

They checked us for weapons and phones.

We'd brought none.

Get her out today. Those were Leighton's final words to me. *You get her out today or you might never see her again.*

This pack was ahead of us at every turn, and now we were walking in, completely open. They were safe from the law because we'd never proven they'd bought Vex. They'd fought to protect that.

They still had a lot to lose, and whatever it was they were going to ask for, we'd give them.

Revenge.

I knew that was their ultimate goal.

They'd already forced us to blow up the Dragon Hunters contract. I was prepared to give up more. If they wanted us to lose everything, to suffer, to see our humiliation, I would give them all of it.

I didn't care, not if it meant her safety. We *couldn't* lose everything, not anymore. She was pack, and she'd shown us we already had the world if we had each other.

The rest paled beside it.

Let Zeus Rogan give me his stupid list. Then we'd take her and this would all be over.

I clung to that as I stepped into a grand living room. It was a massive space, with sprawling rugs, modern, sleek couches and a tall ceiling.

The pack awaited us at the far end of the room, in front of a roaring fireplace. They were standing but for Zeus, who was reclined in an armchair.

And she was there, with him.

Seeing her on his lap was like missing a step. My heart slipped out of rhythm for just a moment.

She wore a silken gown of red. It was elegant, and not her at all. Her hair was tied up in a bun, and... I stilled for a moment as my eyes slid to the silver collar around her neck. A thin chain hung from it, and Zeus had it wrapped in his fist.

The shot of fury from Ebony through the bond was the only thing that calmed the rage boiling my veins. I took a breath as I walked in ahead of the others.

I'd never, before this moment, been more glad for my brother.

We would get her back and then he would find them. There was no leverage in the universe, not from me, nor anyone else, that would stop him.

Vex's eyes were downcast, though she must know we'd entered by the way her frame tensed. I noticed Zeus's touch drop to her waist possessively.

I fought the low growl in my chest, calming myself again. I *had* to stay calm for them. For her. So instead, as I approached, I forced myself to examine the pack.

Achlys's gaze was fixed on us, Cerus was at the back, jaw clenched and expression dark, and Triton was leaning against Zeus's chair, eyeing us all with a sneer.

There was... something wrong. I could sense it as Zeus lifted a hand, indicating that I'd come close enough. I was perhaps ten feet away.

Ten feet from her.

Her scent was in the air, raspberry and treacle.

She was afraid, but I could see she was fighting to hide it. Her fists balled in her lap, gaze still down.

"Love." Zeus's smile was broad, but I noticed that when his gaze passed over us all it lingered on Drake and skipped over Ebony.

"Welcome."

"Skip the introduction," I said evenly. I pulled the small black notebook from my pocket—the one he'd demanded we bring, and tossed it at his feet. "Tell us what you want."

"And if this is a part of it?" he asked. "I've already seen how pathetic you are. His eyes dropped to the book at his feet. "Desperate to make it up to your own mate after your arrogance destroyed her. Now I get to see all your pitiful faces as I claim what's yours."

He curled his fist around the chain, drawing her tighter against him.

It took everything in my power not to move.

Zeus leaned down, pressing his lips to her neck before baring his teeth, dragging them against her flesh.

I'd taken a step when her eyes snapped up to mine, stalling me. I noticed the tiniest shake of her head, her eyes were begging me not to react. I flooded our bond with forced calm, holding my hand up, jaw clenched.

It was as Zeus's grip dropped and closed around her thigh, that Drake's aura split the air. He stepped forward before any of us could move.

Triton reacted first.

"NO!" Vex's cry broke my heart and adrenaline burned my veins as Triton pulled out a gun, drawing Drake up mid stride.

"D-don't hurt him." Vex's voice broke.

Drake's aura was still heavy in the air, as Triton pointed a gun right into Drake's face, only a foot away.

"Get your dogs leashed, Love," Zeus laughed.

"Drop the gun," I ground out.

"Look at you, Magpie." Triton sneered. "Back after all this time, and we have your pet."

"Don't fucking touch her." Drake was shaking, eyes on Zeus.

"We can do this without her here," I said.

"But she wants to be here," Zeus said calmly. "Tell them you want to be here, Vex."

"Stop it!" Drake snarled.

Vex said nothing, but she was tense, teeth drawing blood from her lip, her knuckles white with how hard she was squeezing her fists closed.

"Don't hurt him." Her voice was rough, thick with tears unshed. "Please, don't hurt him."

"Then tell them."

She looked back to me, expression crumbling. "I need to... I *want* to be here."

"*Drake.*" It looked like it took everything in him to listen to me, but he stepped back at last.

"Zeus," I said. "*Tell me* what you want."

"This is about you and me, Love."

I stared at him.

Me?

Not Drake or Ebony?

Relief flooded my system. That was good.

"Your pack ruined us on your watch, Love," Zeus said. "Your brother *humiliated* us."

"Give me the damn list," I said. "Tell me what you want me to do. I'll do it."

"There's no list. Just one thing. The only payment that will suffice." The smile on Zeus's face sent a chill down my spine, something soul deep in me knowing that what was about to come, it would be bad. "An eye for an eye," Zeus said. "Seems only fair."

"What does that mean?"

"What did your pack do to us?" he asked.

"Tell me what you want me to do." With every second that passed, it was harder to keep my voice even.

"You misunderstand. This is about you, not because it's you who'll pay, but because it's you who will suffer."

What did that mean?

We'd taken Drake from them. I knew that. But Drake was

pack. I would move heaven and earth before allowing Drake near them. Zeus had to know that wasn't an option.

Except taking Drake wasn't all that had happened.

I *knew* it was worse than that. That truth was one I realised I'd been burying deep until now, my mind working overtime to avoid what it might mean.

I'd arrived when it was long over.

Drake—a young actor I'd never noticed before now—had found me, dragging me back to Ebony. We got there far too late to do anything.

I found my brother standing over the body of a trembling alpha. He was shattered, his aura flickering in and out.

His pack was gone.

"What have you done?" I grabbed Ebony, but all I got were those curious silver eyes.

In his hand was the cleaving iron. The one the alpha had just used to tear himself apart.

"We're safe," Ebony told me in perfect calm. "He won't tell."

I glanced down again at the seizing body of Zephyr Rogan.

Cleaved from his pack on his knees before my brother—that's what Drake had said.

"Why?"

"Honestly?" Ebony's smile was cold. "Was just curious if I really had it in me to push an alpha that far."

It was Cerus who stepped back, reaching into the fireplace and drawing out an iron rod.

My heart turned to stone.

I knew what it was.

And I knew, before Zeus spoke, that what he would ask for

was an impossible request.

"I want your brother on his knees before a mate he'll never have," Zeus said. "And I want to watch as he cleaves from your pack."

FIFTY

LOVE

"No." My voice was rough. Not that. "Ask for anything else."

"There is nothing else, Love." Zeus's eyes were bright with delight. "That's the price of her bond."

A harrowing silence passed, and my eyes slid to Ebony, finally trying to withdraw from the bond as my dread became infectious. I felt a flicker from Rook, as if he realised the truth like I did.

It was perfectly impossible. No one could force an alpha to cleave; it had to be by intent. The process was dangerous and unpredictable, sometimes leaving an alpha unable to ever form a pack bond again. He would never be able to rejoin our pack—and that was if it didn't kill him.

It felt like the world was crumbling around me. What he was asking for crashed in like a storm.

Ebony was absolutely still at my side, eyes fixed on Vex.

Was he running through the options just as I was?

Had he come to that same conclusion?

I knew, already, what the outcome would be.

For all I'd spoken to her about Ebony offering something

comparable to love, it fell to pieces before this request. My brother was a man of claim and victory. It was the only two things in the world from which he could comprehend value.

There was no beyond.

No sacrifice.

And it was in that distinction that lay the impossibility. It came down to one simple thing: If he cleaved, she would no longer be his.

He would never do it.

"No." Vex's desperate voice tore through thoughts made of tar. "It could kill him."

"He was willing to take that risk with my brother," Zeus said.

"If he cleaves," I said, scrambling for a way out. "The scent match could shatter. Then she won't be our mate, and you won't be able to complete your end of the deal."

That was it, right?

He *couldn't* ask for this.

"I would have suggested you offer her the princess bond for insurance. She'll join your pack the moment our bargain completes. But you were desperate enough to have done so already."

"Ask for something else."

"This is it, Love." Zeus was so sure. So absolute. He shoved her from his lap, fist clenched around the chain holding her steady as he got to his feet. He grinned, one arm spread as if he'd won. "Proof that your pack is more broken. Broken enough to leave your own mate in the arms of—"

He cut off as Ebony stepped forward, something vacant in his silver eyes.

"I'll do it."

Those words were followed by silence.

My heart was racing a million miles a minute. Drake and

Rook were both back in the bond. Rook was shocked, and Drake was a ball of turmoil and dread. Neither spoke.

"You're lying," Zeus sneered, and there was something strange in his eyes. It didn't make sense, but I could swear he was angry.

Ebony didn't reply, instead reaching down and picking up the iron that still glowed a dull red. Three times, he had to press the brand to his skin. With the third mark of that slender arrowhead upon his flesh, it would be done.

"NO!" Vex fought Zeus, trying to reach for him. "You *can't.*"

"On your knees, dog," Cerus snarled, ignoring her.

With absolute control, Ebony lowered himself to his knees before them.

"Wait, you can't! *Ebony—!*" Vex cut off as Zeus clamped his hand over her mouth.

I stepped forward, but Rook's hand was on my arm.

What would this mean, though?

I'd lose him.

But we couldn't leave her.

Zeus just stared down at Ebony, expression frozen. Cerus shifted forward, eyes narrowed as he watched. "Do it like you made him do it." Hatred laced each syllable.

I could barely breathe.

Was this right?

We needed to free her. We were at the mercy of their demands. Even if backup arrived right now, it wouldn't matter. If this pack got out alive, she would still be theirs.

That was if our backup was enough.

If we weren't all killed.

But if he cleaved...?

I'd lose him.

Half a decade of regrets, denial, of dreams that went beyond this life we'd built, they all crumbled in that second.

I didn't want to lose him.

He was my brother. My little brother; the one our mother had left behind. The one the world would leave behind, if I let it.

And if he left me now, I don't know if I would ever get him back.

I'd taken another step, and I didn't know why anymore. I knew we were out of options. Rook's grip tightened. "You *cannot* take this from him," he said quietly.

"The deal," Ebony said. His voice was rougher than I'd ever heard. He gripped the iron in his fist.

"An eye for an eye, Love?" Zeus said. "I will do to your pack what yours did to mine."

I felt the bargain settle upon us. The weight of a promise that, once fulfilled, would complete the bond.

That would hand Vex to us.

With those words, Ebony lifted the branding iron. With a deep, shuddering breath, he pressed it to his neck.

FIFTY-ONE

VEX

The commands didn't matter. The pain didn't matter.

I tried to lunge for Ebony as he lifted the iron to his own neck.

He might die.

It was all I could think.

But Zeus dragged me back against his chest, hand still clamped over my mouth.

Ebony's silver storm eyes found mine.

No—!

But the scent of burning flesh tangled with the alpha's scents in the room.

It was sickening.

Vile.

I gagged, eyes burning, fear scorching my system.

Again, I threw my full weight into Zeus's grip. He *couldn't* do this.

A loud *CLANG!* Jolted me from my thoughts.

Ebony had sagged, the cleaving iron slipping to the marble.

The connection between us—the one he'd asked of me last night—wavered.

Something was wrong.

Wrong beyond what was before me.

He was my mate, and I *knew*... My eyes found Love. His brows were furrowed. He had to know.

Something was wrong!

His eyes met mine, and I tried to convey it somehow, tried to make him understand.

He had to stop this.

Love took a step forward, but Cerus moved, grabbing the gun from Triton and pointing it at Love.

"Stay," he growled.

My teeth found Zeus's hand, and I bit down, making him flinch.

"NO!" I screamed. "You have to stop—!" With a vicious tug on the chain around my neck, Zeus crushed my mouth with his hand again.

"His choice," Zeus breathed in my ear. "He knew the risks. Now stay *still*."

Ebony was ashen and panting, his palm pressed to the marble floor. His aura was wavering. His fingers closed around the rod again and I tried to scream once more through Zeus's grip. When Ebony pressed the brand to his neck for the second time, it was with a low growl of agony.

The connection between us vanished.

Wild terror shook me but I couldn't move. Love was still facing the barrel of Cerus's gun.

Tears flooded my cheeks. They *had* to stop.

Love took half a step.

"I swear I'll watch you die before you get in the way of this," Cerus hissed.

No.

He needed me.

I could barely see through the tears.

He needed me, and I was failing him.

Ebony collapsed, his body hitting the floor. I screamed again, but Zeus's grip was tight.

"Look at that," Zeus breathed. "He *tried* to save you, but he's too *weak.*" He sounded pleased.

But Ebony was, through wretches, reaching for the iron, shaking fingers curling around it again.

No...

No!

Again, Ebony seized, a growl slipping out as he gasped for breath. His aura flickered in and out like a shuttering window in a storm.

"It's better this way," Zeus breathed to me. "That you get to see this part so close."

He dragged me down until he was on his knees with me, pinning Ebony on his back.

No!

Let it go.

Don't do this!

But I couldn't scream any of it, still silenced.

Even if this worked, if he cleaved and I was free... I sobbed, staring into silver eyes that were so determined. I couldn't do this without him. Didn't he know that?

He lifted his hand, but shuddered again, arm falling.

"Help. Him." Zeus's command of me was like nothing I'd ever felt.

Every other command he'd ever made fell away for that one order: something so weighted that my hands were moving before I could stop them. My fingers curled around the iron that Ebony held.

I trembled.

Zeus's grip on my mouth was still agony as he goaded me on.

"Go on," he hissed. "Help your mate save you."

Tears were streaking down my cheeks, splashing into silver hair beneath me. Storm cloud eyes held mine, agonised but somehow sure. It was the worst pain I'd ever felt, fighting that command, trying instead to hold the iron away from his neck.

I wouldn't do this.

"Here's the thing about your perfect mate," Zeus's voice was a low growl in my ear. No one would hear him but me. "He told Zephyr if he didn't cleave from the pack, he'd release all the dirt he had on us. Ruin us."

Still, I fought, and Zeus's hand dropped from my mouth, closing instead around my wrist, shoving me closer to Ebony.

It was inches away from its last stroke.

"And then do you know what he did a few months later? *After* he'd destroyed my brother?" Zeus hissed. "He released it anyway."

My blood turned to ice as I felt the victory from him down the bond.

"An eye for an eye, Love? I will do to your pack what he did to mine."

That had been the deal.

I knew, in that moment, the truth.

The truth of the deal, of his confidence last night: Zeus wouldn't give me up. He never would have. Even if Ebony cleaved, I wouldn't be theirs.

Only... Ebony wasn't just cleaving, he was dying. I knew it in my soul.

My mate was dying.

Tears blurred my vision.

I wouldn't let it happen.

I'd fought for this. Fought never to be here so she would be proud. I'd sworn I would never again helplessly watch as someone I loved was threatened.

. . .

"Hide, and never sing louder than a whisper, my sweet Lily."

So I sang, with my hands around my ears. "There's a bird in the storm and nobody knows..."

I whispered on, a vicious aura around me, a storm outside this time.

My fear was too much.

And that last line, the one I'd never spoken since I'd forgotten to whisper.

The closet door was ripped open and in spilled the light of the living room beyond. A flash of lightning through the window.

I could hear my mother pleading with him, telling me to run, but he told me not to leave.

I don't remember much.

I remember he was drunk.

I remember I was afraid.

And then my mother was there, a trembling fist clutching a knife to his neck.

Only... he'd laughed.

"You can't do it, Trinity." He stepped into the blade and she flinched back. "You can't, not even to protect her."

Like this, he wasn't someone I recognised.

I stumbled back.

But it wasn't me who'd been hit.

She was on the floor, expression twisted with desperation.

I'd never seen it—not in this way. She'd never let me.

My fists balled around the long sleeves of my favourite sweatshirt.

Today had been special. My pack dads had been gone for a few days, they did that sometimes. And the third Hunting Falcon's movie was out at midnight. She'd promised we could stay up and watch it. I'd picked out my outfit, so excited.

That seemed stupid now. We would have been asleep by the time he'd come home.

I stared, absolutely frozen, as a thunderclap boomed outside.

She was crying.

"You fool," he laughed.

I blinked, eyes flickering to the window for a second at another movement that shook me to my bones. Moonlight spilled through swaying sheer curtains, and wind slammed rain into the glass pane.

My mother whimpered from the blow.

I shook.

My fault.

I'd wanted stupid things and sung too loud. If I'd been quiet, she wouldn't have picked up the knife. And now I couldn't move as he kicked it from her hand.

It clattered across the hardwood, away from his attention.

"You can't stop me, you useless bitch." He'd grabbed her again. It felt like my heart was trying to burst from my chest it was beating so hard. Her eyes were wide as she looked at me.

They were a rich brown, not gold.

Desirable.

Beautiful.

Frightened.

I glanced again at the window. Out to the storm that usually made me more afraid than anything. "We're bound," he was snarling. "You have my bite."

He moved again and my breath caught.

I was frozen, clutching the sleeves of my stupid sweatshirt. Instead of looking at the storm this time, I dropped my eyes, finding the glinting silver of the knife that had come to a stop before my fluffy socks.

"You can never kill me."

Tears blurred my own fingers as I reached down.

And somehow, at that moment, I wasn't frozen anymore.

. . .

It was the last line of the song. The one embroidered on the cuff of the shirt I'd worn here.

It was the words I'd never sung since that day. The day I hadn't whispered.

A promise.

A dare.

I'd done what my mother never had. I'd claimed gold like she hadn't.

The beautiful brown eyes in the memory faded for silver, equally as ruined as hers.

My mate.

My love.

The one who would die if I had been her.

There's a bird in the storm and nobody knows,
  And she sings for herself as the cold rains grow.
  No matter how deep digs the thorn of the rose,
  Or that words become lost as the wild winds blow.
  In face of the doubt or the darkest shadow,
  Because free is the bird
  Where nobody goes.

FIFTY-TWO

EBONY

I'd never lost in my life. Not irrefutably.

And yet, this was it. Once I'd done this, there was no coming back.

She was above me, terrified eyes holding mine. Her grip was on the iron too, helping at his command.

Zeus Rogan's command. The vermin who'd dark bonded my mate.

But I only had to endure this once more. My body and aura screamed at me. I was in agony, my neck feeling as though it was on fire.

Was this how it was supposed to feel, when an alpha cleaved? I knew there was a chance I would die. It felt like I was dying. The world was fading in and out.

Just one more searing burn, and my pack would be gone.

She would be gone.

Three doors.

Door number one: denying Zeus's requests. Staying with my pack, and losing her. It wasn't an option, and never had been.

Even if it was, I'd seen what had happened the last time she was taken. We wouldn't survive it.

The second door: cleave and leave. And I'd lose her and lose them.

I had chosen the last door. The third door. The only door.

Cleave for her. Save her and save them—even if it meant I would lose her.

It was a chance at something I'd never in my life done... That was why I valued Drake, wasn't it? For those moments where he offered me something new—something I'd never felt.

I'd never lacked curiosity.

So I kept going, clutching the choice I'd made, finding, somehow, a relief in it. Something... new. Conviction. Commitment.

I'd been right. It *wasn't* a loss. Not completely. It *was* a win, of sorts.

Even if it hurt. Even if doubt was tearing me to shreds like it never had. I dragged the cleaving iron closer, relishing the shiver of fear that crawled up my spine.

Except, the burn never came.

I forced myself to focus in time to see Vex shatter before my very eyes. Tears cascaded down her cheeks as she shook, pinned by Zeus.

And then her scent hit the room like a storm and her eyes flashed a brilliant gold. For the briefest moment, I felt her with me in the bond—really, truly here.

And she was more than I could have ever imagined.

It had worked. She was safe.

Her scream of fury echoed above me.

The last thing I saw was her turn and lunge for Zeus's throat.

The world faded, and I felt my pack bonds fray as I tumbled from a cliff into darkness.

FIFTY-THREE

DRAKE

Vex lunged for Zeus, her scent in the room nothing short of wild.

She was feral.

It took me a moment to process what I was seeing: her teeth sinking into his neck. What followed was blood and chaos, as she shattered his commands and killed him, as she destroyed his pack.

I knew because she blazed to life in our bond, which wasn't possible. Not unless her pack was gone.

She blitzed into our bond, brilliant and jarring, at the same second Ebony's fear blinked out.

The void he left was almost enough to cripple me. What we felt, though, was nothing to what the other three alphas in the room had.

An errant gunshot went off as Cerus crashed to his knees with a strangled howl. Triton lunged for Vex, murder in his eyes.

I dived after him at the same time as Rook, but Achlys crashed into his way.

Vex.

Fuck.

Triton was—

"NO!" Aura out, I collided with Triton just as he reached her. His hands—about to seize her neck—instead closed around nothing as I bowled him over.

He snarled, green eyes wild as he looked at me, though there wasn't much left of the alpha I'd once known. Every ounce of nerves and terror I'd felt when I'd learned it was this pack who'd taken her burned through my system in an instant.

In seconds I had him by the neck. The power my aura leant me was overwhelming.

He tried to shove me back, but I'd always been stronger. *Then*, it hadn't mattered, but now he couldn't throw me off. Everything that he *was* came flooding in. Every twisted moment, every taunt, every nightmare.

I couldn't breathe.

He'd become her nightmare.

They'd all become her nightmare.

Because of me.

His face was ruddy, strange choking sounds coming from him. My hands were around his throat. I should... I should stop.

The thought came too late, fury blinding me.

But I had to—

A glint of silver flashed in my vision. A blade in his hand—

SNAP!

My whole body shook as he went limp, neck twisted at a foul angle in my grip.

ROOK

We had to survive until backup arrived.

I was faced with Achlys. The last I'd seen, Love had slammed the massive dining table against the door before wrestling a gun from the fist of an alpha who'd come through it. Drake had gone for Triton. Vex, covered in blood, hadn't stopped clutching Ebony.

Make sure she doesn't let go. It was the urgent whisper of my instincts. A need as paramount as protecting her. One I couldn't explain.

Triton's gun had been kicked beneath the couch, and Cerus, recovering from his initial collapse, made for Drake now that Triton was down.

He'd be fine. Drake's aura was impressive.

I threw Achlys back a pace, and his leg caught the rack of iron pokers beside the fireplace. He tripped. He was wild, eyes void of humanity as he fought like a wounded animal—one set on killing the omega who'd shattered his pack.

He wanted to kill Vex.

I grabbed an iron poker and jammed it against his neck, crushing him against the wall. He howled, eyes wide as he fought me.

Another gunshot sounded from behind me, chilling my blood and almost making me turn, but I didn't have time. Our bond remained intact. Love was safe.

Almost intact.

Ebony was gone. I couldn't feel him.

Just make sure she doesn't let go.

I threw my weight into the iron rod I held, watching as Achlys eyes rolled back and his body went limp. I turned just in time to see the table thrown from the doorway. Love had a gun in his hand and a man at his feet.

Cerus was down. Drake was with Vex and Ebony.

I staggered to Love's side as he raised the gun with an unsteady grip. Blood was soaking his cream shirt.

BANG!

I jumped as the first black clad man fell forward. Love started, unsure.

Another gunshot, then another and, with a burst of a relief, I saw an alpha I recognised through the door. It was the distinct white hair and red eye of the seer who'd visited with Havoc in the hospital. I grabbed Love by the arm, but he was already lowering the gun.

It was over in moments. More people were stepping through the doorway—alphas, I thought.

I didn't recognise them until I spotted Leighton grimacing as she stepped over a body. Dressed in a white pant-suit, she was the only one not holding a weapon as she fired off directions. "Bastion, take Denzel, check the rest of the property. I think we got them all, but can't be too sure."

This was the backup she'd managed to get together.

"You're with me." A pale dark-haired alpha with tattoos up to his chin was waving at the seer. He was shrugging a backpack off as he crossed toward Vex, Ebony, and Drake. I followed, unsure as he knelt beside them.

Now that the initial threat was gone, my thoughts were scattered.

His scent was roses and blood? That was unusual. But... no, actually I thought maybe there was just a lot of blood in the room.

"I'm Cass," he was saying to Drake and Vex as his eyes scanned Ebony. "I'm Havoc's. I'm going to check him over, alright?"

Vex looked up at him in a flash at Havoc's name, but her grip didn't loosen on Ebony's shirt.

"Medics are on the way," Cass was saying, "but the faster we can treat the poison the better his chances. I need you to calm her down so I can—"

"Poison?" Love asked.

"He gave me access to his tracking data the government has on Agritox." I thought that was Leighton. "Connected a stolen vial to the middleman they were using for all of this."

"You didn't mention that—?" Love's voice was furious.

"I only *just* found it," Kai snapped as he helped Cass unpack medical supplies from the bag.

"If he's poisoned *and* he's cleaved, we need to make sure—"

"He hasn't." Vex spoke for the first time.

"What?" Cass's voice was sharp.

"He only... he only did it twice. The cleaving needs three."

She was shaking, blood, disrupted only by tear tracks, smeared across her face and neck, matting her hair and trailing down the thin chain that hung from the collar Zeus had placed on her.

I tugged my jacket off and reached for her. She flinched at my touch, but her eyes found mine and she let me move closer and wipe away some of the blood. "It's okay," I whispered. "Let him help."

Her eyes were wide, but she didn't move.

"Let her stay. I can work around her."

I glanced down at where her fists were balled in his shirt. "I-If I let go, he'll..." Her expression broke, fresh tears spilling out.

She was a force in the bond. Absolute. And I could feel her conviction with those words, her will almost a power in itself. And I felt it at last, the thing my instincts had been trying to say.

He was still here.

I could feel him by a thread, one she was clinging to.

But Ebony was still in the bond.

FIFTY-FOUR

VEX

My mind was hazy as I blinked heavy eyes open, trying to adjust to bright lights. Around me machines were beeping.

I was in the hospital.

Again.

I groaned, sitting up, still trying to place the feeling of dread in my chest.

"You're safe." That was Love's voice, and I felt his touch on my hand.

What... happened?

I tried to ask, but my mouth was heavy.

"You're safe," Love told me again. His touch brushed my cheek, calming me. "You've been given drugs while your hormones balance out, but you're safe."

I was safe. I was here with them. My mates.

But something was different...

I choked on a sob.

My dark bond was gone. In its place, I had a princess bond with my mates.

Only... One piece... it was on the brink of fragmenting—it had been, I fumbled for the connections around me, terrified until—

He was here. His bond wasn't quite right, as if it had been broken and put back together, but he was here.

His scent was here with me.

Twilight grass. Close. Sometimes, in my more lucid moments I could feel him beside me in the bed.

Blackcurrant wine. Caramel and brandy. Vanilla winter. They were all there, too. And sometimes other scents, too. Firewood and jasmine.

The world faded in and out, time becoming meaningless, but I clung to him.

"...*Will he live?*"

That question tugged my consciousness to the surface.

Ebony...

They were talking about Ebony. The voices were echoes in my mind, faded and fuzzy. It was a struggle to grasp them.

"*Live? Yes. But his place in the bond, I can't be sure. It's touch and go.*"

"*Is there anything we can do?*" Drake... *that was Drake's voice. He was here.*

"*Just stay with them. As far as I can tell, she's the only one holding him here. It's impossible to know if his bond in the pack will heal, or if, when she lets go...*"

No.

I wouldn't. Not until I knew he was safe.

This pack... they were my new dream. I wouldn't let it go.

I *wouldn't* let him go.

Time blurred more, and I heard fragments of more conversations.

"*...None of that pack survived. If they had, it was going to be bleak. Media got a hold of everything... We're keeping them out. I'll send you the statements to look over.*"

"Thanks Jas."

"Don't mention it. Rest up. You've got a back-load of offers. The acting will be here when you're ready to come back."

"That will be up to her."

Up to me? Was Love talking about me? I tried to consider that, but I was fading again.

"She's gone through enough. I want to be sure when she wakes..."

"Her hormones are levelling out. It should be safe for her to take these. It's a pill a day. It will keep it at bay until she's ready."

"Are you sure her system can handle it?"

"Heats are a state of vulnerability. While they can be healing, a traumatic heat is more damaging than any pill."

I shifted, curling closer to the warmth beside me. To the twilight grass that still felt too faint.

Not until he was safe.

I didn't want heat, not if it was without him.

EBONY

I woke over and over, nightmares trapping me in a vice. Still, I couldn't feel them. Not Drake or Love or Rook.

Panic set in again as I blinked through a foul white light and tried to get my bearings.

Where were they?

Gone.

Gone. And my mind was a barren wasteland.

My thundering pulse in my ears was all I could hear. The world span, shapes appeared but didn't make sense.

They were gone.

I reached for my aura, then buckled in agony. There was a sound, something loud... A low, agonised growl that I realised too late was mine, and then—

I stilled as the first shapes finally formed into something that made sense.

Golden eyes.

Beautiful and bright and soothing.

Vex.

And...

And she was... mine. I could feel it.

Horrid, hot, wet *things* were tumbling down my cheeks as she cupped them, bright eyes so wide and fearful.

Mine.

She was still mine.

That was the anchor that finally ripped me back into the world.

"Ebony!" Her desperate voice finally beat down my ear drums, and I realised her fear was of me. Or... for me? I blinked again, looking around.

I was in a hospital, halfway out of a bed, and attached by cords she clutched as she tried to push me back.

...She was still mine...

I remembered then.

I'd been falling into oblivion. The threads of my bonds to this pack were snapping. And then she'd been there, catching me because I'd tumbled into the void.

I sunk back down and let her straighten everything out.

It wasn't over. I hadn't lost everything.

Because if Vex was still mine, they were, too.

VEX

Three days of bleary, semi-conscious panic but he'd finally stabilised.

Ebony was going to be okay.

One more assessment was all we needed to be officially

discharged. Love, Drake, and Rook waited just outside, close enough that I could see them, and their scents lingered. I refused to leave Ebony.

To my surprise, it was an omega who entered, I knew from the faint scent of ocean breeze. She wore scrubs, had wavy dark hair tied up in a bun, and sat down in a chair beside the bed with a clipboard, adjusting rose-gold glasses. She was, perhaps, in her thirties, and had tattoos down to her wrists. Most interesting were her golden eyes and the faintest trace of a dead dark bond on the back of her neck.

"Nice to meet you Vex," she said with a warm smile. "My name is Jackie. I'm a trauma specialist with experience in gold pack specific events. I'm on your healthcare team, and I'd love to talk to you if you'd be willing."

"Are you like... a shrink?" I asked.

She gave me a dimpled smile. "My role is flexible to fit the needs of the omegas I work with, but I can talk you through any questions or feelings you're having, if that is what you want. I've looked through your file extensively. You were in a complicated situation, and I wouldn't be surprised if you had some questions I may be able to provide answers to."

"I do..." I said, voice hoarse.

"I hope I may be able to help you navigate it. Please, ask away."

"I..." Images of those last moments before I'd killed Zeus flooded my mind. Ebony drew me closer, feeling my discomfort.

There had been blood everywhere.

"When I attacked him. Do you know what happened?"

I know the theory, but some of it hadn't happened the way I'd thought it should.

"You fought his command, you fought his bond, and you rejected his authority as your pack lead."

"I rejected it?"

"A dark bond is a bond taken, not agreed upon. It's a lot more difficult than people realise, to bite an omega and keep them at arm's length in a bond. A dark bond—most especially with a gold pack—is a true exchange. One with costs. The pack may well have shattered at the death of their lead, but there's another, much more likely explanation from what I've heard from your alphas."

"What?"

"You destroyed that pack, Little Omega," Ebony murmured to me.

"I... what?" I frowned, peering up into his silver eyes. He was tired, the dusky tan of his skin, ashen, but he looked sure.

"Dark bonds aren't natural," Jackie said. "And nature has a way of balancing the scales—especially when a gold pack is scorned."

I swallowed, looking back at her, all the insecurities I'd been shoving down before Ebony was better, surfacing. "What's going to happen to me?"

"To you?" Jackie's expression softened, and she stopped tapping her pen as she examined my expression.

"I killed him. I'm gold pack..." My voice was weak. He was an alpha—I'd killed my own pack lead.

"It's very clear that Zeus had every intention of killing your mate. Blood was drawn fast enough that traces of Agritox were found in Ebony's bloodstream. Even if there wasn't, there's also evidence he'd threatened..." Jackie paused, looking rather sickened. "Threatened your execution."

I shivered, memories of Zeus's threats of Hunting Arenas worming their way back into my mind. I'd tried to forget it with all of my might. But... "Evidence?" I asked. How could anyone know what Zeus had said to me?

Ebony tucked my hair behind my ear. "He slipped up."

"So... I'm not in trouble?"

"No."

Still, I stared at her, not processing it. It flew in the face of everything I'd been taught to expect.

Jackie leaned back in her chair, considering, and returned to tapping her pen. "Zeus Rogan dark bonded an omega, forced her into proximity with her mates then tried to issue a command that she kill one of them—a gold pack and a rogue, no less."

"What does that mean?" Ebony asked.

"Gold packs and rogues are closer to nature than any of us. Least bound by artificial laws such as dark bonds. Your scent matches, with whom you'd fallen in love, were under threat. I can't imagine a force on earth strong enough to have got in your way. Not laws, not alpha auras, not dark bonds. I rarely get to say this, but be grateful, Vex, that you let those eyes of yours turn gold. Had you not, that command would have bound you, and Ebony would very likely be dead."

Goosebumps rose on my skin, and I tugged Ebony closer.

"Add the poison to the cleaving, I think most alphas—at the least—would have had their bonds broken. Your eyes and your connection with your mate is something to be proud of."

For the first time since we'd woken, the twilight grass in the room became something more. Not weak, or faint, but possessive.

Still. That was wrong. "None..." I cleared my throat, eyes darting around the rest of the room. "B-but none of this would have happened if I wasn't a gold pack."

"Forgive me if it's an overstep—but it seemed that pack had it out for your mates, with or without you."

"So..." I swallowed. "That's it. No charges. I'm just... okay to go."

I was... free?

"While I'm sure your mates have an army of lawyers queued up on your behalf, I'll save you the worry. I've already seen the

477

summary of the report to the GPRE by the Arkologist on your case, Dr. Henreka Davis. *'Alpha recklessly makes dares of nature and finds himself dead'* isn't a strong start to a prosecution."

I nodded, still reeling. "Thank you."

Jackie smiled. "Do you have any other questions?"

I shook my head. "That's all."

"I'd like to put you in touch with one of my colleagues. While I specialise in this side of things, you've gone through a huge trauma. She specialises in healing after events like that."

"A *therapist*?"

"I think it would be beneficial," she said as she got to her feet.

There was a time in my life I might have laughed at that—as if my life could be fixed by something like that. But even in this conversation, threads had begun to untangle that I hadn't even known were present. I felt... strangely light.

It wasn't just that. I'd never been in a position to have been able to afford one.

"Wait!" I called as she reached the door. She turned back to me. "Is this... what the others are getting?"

"The others?" Jackie asked.

"All the omegas and alphas who were rescued from the trafficking ring last week?"

Jackie's smile was sad. "Unfortunately roles like mine are new, and they aren't supported in the public system."

Something tightened in my chest. "No... no, you don't understand. What I went through was nothing." Not compared to what I knew went on. My mates made me valuable to them. "They need the help more than me—"

I hadn't realised how tightly my fingers had curled around Ebony's shirt until I felt his touch brush the back of my hand.

"We'll cover it." Ebony said to her.

Jackie fixed her golden eyes on him in surprise. "Efforts like this won't come cheap."

"Get my pack lead in touch with someone who can organise it."

FIFTY-FIVE

DRAKE

It was finally over. Vex was safe. Ebony was stable, and we could bring them home.

And somehow, stepping back through the doors to our home left me with a cold sense of dread.

I'd tried to go to her nest with her and the others, but I just couldn't do it.

Ebony found me in the theatre and took a seat beside me.

I shut my eyes.

I could feel him through the bond, faint—though growing stronger every day. I'd almost lost him... We'd almost lost him.

This pack, who'd taken me in, had paid the price for my demons.

After a long silence between us, I spoke, voice rough. "She told me I was enough. Even when you were all pushing her away, I was there for her."

"You were."

I shook my head. "But this whole time, it's been because of me. It's all because of me."

His calculating gaze found me. He took a while before he replied. "That's not how this works."

Bitterness twisted my expression. He was wrong. "They were my past. If you hadn't got involved, she would never have suffered."

He was going to try and make me feel better, I knew it was why he was here.

Well, he couldn't.

"I didn't," he said at last.

"Didn't what?"

"Save you," he said. "That's not what happened."

I turned to him, trying to figure out his angle.

"You were a trophy that I took from a pack I wanted to destroy. I didn't save you. I claimed you."

I breathed a bitter laugh, resting my head on the back of the couch.

Right.

"The day you got here," Ebony went on. "I didn't just make you an offer to join the pack."

I stared at him, jaw clenched as I tried to work out his angle.

"You told me," he went on, "that you weren't sure. You didn't believe my pack wanted your baggage—"

"And I was right. She might have matched you without me—"

Ebony snorted. "And then what? She posts online, gets taken, and a different set of pricks who take her to get to us?"

I was on my feet in a moment, rage flaring. "It would have been better than this. Anything would be better. You almost died—"

He got to his feet, matching me, and I was surprised at the flash of anger in his eyes. He was still faint in the bond, but he felt... different. "I don't make claims I don't defend," he hissed.

"I'm not worth that."

"That's not your decision," he snarled. "It was my choice. That is what I have to offer, and now you don't want it—?"

"No." My voice broke. "It's not like that. I just... it doesn't matter. None of it matters." I felt like I was in free fall. I didn't care about where he thought we should lay the blame.

My chest was tight. We were home, they were safe, and there was nothing else stopping me facing the truth. "They..." My voice cracked. "They took her."

My nightmares.

I was shaking.

Vex, my omega, who'd fought a thousand battles and survived. And I'd given her my monsters.

It didn't matter why or how.

All that matters was that I had.

Ebony's chest was heaving and he looked off-balanced. For a brief second, I thought he was going to punch me.

And then I felt a faint tremor in the bond. It was him, and his connection with us strengthened enough in that moment, that I finally understood what he was feeling.

He was... afraid.

It wasn't just this conversation, either.

He'd been like this since... well, since he'd woken, but his connection had been too weak for me to realise what it was.

"She's safe," he said. "And I didn't die."

Knowing he was off-balanced over everything threw me, unseating my own anxiety. Ebony was scared?

I frowned.

Of... what, exactly?

Only, I thought knew, and that realisation was shockingly comforting. I cleared my throat. "And... you're still in the bond."

"Yeah." His voice was rough.

I don't know why, knowing his fear, grounded me so much, but I finally found my footing. "You're... different," I said.

His jaw ticked and he took a step back. "I don't know if her bite is lasting longer this time or if she bit me again in the hospital."

"Bit you?"

"Yeh it... fucks me up in the head." He said, but caught my expression. "Don't fucking tell Love."

I smiled despite myself but he scowled.

"Don't get used to it."

I nodded. Still unable to keep from prodding him again in the bond.

He folded his arms, squaring me with a challenging look. "I heard you killed Triton."

"Uh... yeah." I palmed the back of my neck, mood lifting another degree as he flashed me a grin that was much more the Ebony I recognised.

I felt pride from him through the bond.

"Actually..." I shrugged, fixing my expression. "Cerus too. If we're counting."

Cerus had gone mad, and he'd lunged for Leighton after our backup had arrived. Ending him hadn't off-balanced me like it had with Triton. Triton was arrogant and selfish, but Cerus... he and Zephyr had been cruel. In that moment, as the light in his eyes had died, I'd silenced a thousand nightmares of my past, and a thousand more for the people he'd never hurt again.

"Good." Ebony grunted, clapping me on the shoulder before leaving. "They were your kills."

As he left, I let my hand drop from my neck and the silver scar upon it. The bite he'd offered me the day he'd joined the pack.

His promise of a new start.

VEX

I had time.

Not forever, these daily pills would fail eventually and my heat would come. But I had time to leave the hospital and heal.

So, I did, vanishing into the perfect little bubble that was to be my forever nest.

My *home.*

Before, even when they'd brought half my apartment into this nest, it hadn't felt like home. Not like it did now.

So, we got to decorating.

On the second day, while I helped Love and Drake put the gigantic skull and crossbones headboard together outside, Rook had dragged Ebony away to help with a 'super secret' project.

Later, when I'd returned to the nest, sweaty and exhausted from reading instructions wrong for three hours, he tugged me into the middle of the room and told me to close my eyes.

I hadn't opened them until he was back, hands brushing my waist.

My breath caught as I looked up. The lights were out, but the entire ceiling was covered in glow-in-the dark galaxies.

"Oh..." I'd been breathless, staring up at them, spotting the constellations that we'd pointed out on our date together.

Then he'd taken my face in his hands and drawn me close.

"I love you, Vex," he whispered. I stood on my tiptoes, dragging him into the kiss he'd promised me all those nights ago. A kiss for when I was free.

After three days of non-stop decorating, my nest was *beautiful.*

Literally, perfect in every way.

The colour scheme was switched to neutral darks. The enormous skull and crossbones headboard was set up (properly now) behind the pack bed. There was a massive stereo system set up beside the fireplace, with neon lights shaped like musical notes flickering on the walls around it. Warm Edison lights were strung above my bed, and a lava lamp bubbled on my side table.

A circle rattan chair draped with blankets and extra pillows sat beside the tall window, just right for curling up, and at its side was a decorative old fashioned lamp post standing in as a reading light.

Along the wall beside my bed, Drake had nailed up a massive magnetic dream board covered in a dark wood texture. It wasn't full enough, though, not yet—but it would be.

My favourite lyrics were written across the dark wallpaper in bright paint—that had been fun, though I thought Ebony might have cracked a tooth as I spray-painted words across his custom wallpaper.

Ebony was, day by day, returning to himself. The burns on his neck, already healed enough that they didn't need bandages—alpha healing. But he was returning in the bond, too.

On the third day, when the nest was almost complete, he took the black choker from my window sill and handed it to me.

"You get to burn it, Little Omega," he told me. "You freed yourself."

He took me out beneath the stars to where the others were seated around the roaring flames of the fire pit.

I stepped up to the flames, holding the necklace out, frozen for a long moment.

I felt Zeus's bite on my neck, the other on my wrist.

Scars that would never go away, not completely.

The necklace slipped from my fingers and tumbled into the flames below. I watched, listening to the flames pop as the fabric turned to dust. After a long, long time, all that remained was the scorched husk of the lock among the ashes.

I'd been standing here for a long, long time, Ebony at my side.

I shut my eyes, a tear leaking down my cheek as I felt them all here with me. Present, alive, so full of energy and love, even after all we'd been through.

The princess bond had opened, the connection present, accepted by Love, Drake, Rook, and Ebony. They'd all claimed me, all accepted me, all bitten me—and yet never with this dark bond gone.

"I'm ready," I whispered at last.

No more pills.

No more dark bonds or commands or fear.

Just me and my pack.

LOVE

"Dammit!" Vex had groaned this afternoon, flopping back on her bed as we cut out pictures for her dream board. "It shows up whenever I *don't* want it. Now I have four alphas in a princess bond and I wanted to be fucked and *where is it?* Nowhere!"

It was, admittedly, a little ironic. And it was driving her a bit bonkers.

I'd paused at my bedroom door earlier, hearing an argument in the living room beyond. Peering out I saw Vex hovering at Ebony's side on the couch.

"I'm not doing it," he was saying.

"You have to. Rook got you one. And you told me—"

"That was *only* because of your bite. You'll *never* repeat that, Little Omega."

She shook him by the collar of his shirt, eyes pleading. "You *have* to write it down. Come on. Please!"

"Fine." Ebony scowled. "But get me a different card."

"No."

"But—"

"Please! Please please please."

Wrinkling his nose with disgust, he plucked the pen from her grip. "Fine."

Later, I found an envelope tucked under my door.

I opened it to see a card inside. On the front was a cartoon bumble bee amongst the text, *'Thank you for bee-lieving in me.'* Inside, he'd written the words: *'You might have done a little more than I realised. Caring hurts like a bitch (glad I can shut it off.)'* Beneath it, in a poor imitation of Ebony's handwriting—*I'd* forged his handwriting enough times in my life to know—was an added, *'Thank you'.*

When I flipped it upside down, I saw, in miniscule letters at the bottom: *'she's withholding sex'.*

Snorting, I'd propped it on my bedside table.

But Ebony wasn't alone.

Since halting the heat suppressants, she'd decided to practise abstinence from all of us.

Which—fine. That was *totally* fine, and completely her choice, only this evening as she joined us at the firepit, (something that was becoming a pack habit) she'd selected a black lingerie set.

She was wearing only that and a silken nightgown that did a poor job of covering it.

"Wait, what?" Rook demanded, eyes bugging out of his skull as she sat down at Drake's side. "That means you want us to bang you, *right?"*

I couldn't look away from her either, knowing my scent was shifting just as obviously as Rook and Drake's. She looked like a queen, pale skin clad in lace, waves of silver-brown hair tumbling to her waist, the cute peach streak bright in the firelight.

"I'm turning up the hormones," she said. "But you aren't blowing your energy before it starts, they said I'm going to be *impossible."* She looked smug.

"Ebony's going to pop a vein," Drake chuckled. I grinned at the thought. At least the rest of us had been with her.

Sure enough, when Ebony arrived, he drew up as he caught sight of Vex. After a long moment he dropped onto the bench at her other side and pulled her onto his lap. "Give me one reason not to drag you over my cock right now?" he asked, drawing her chin up. "Or are you trying to send me into a rut?"

Her scent shifted in an instant, raspberry treacle dripping with lust. Her lips parted as she stared up at him. From the want I felt down the bond, I thought she might just be tossing her no sex rule out the window. Only, she folded her arms. "If you did that," she said. "You'd be missing out."

"Would I?" Ebony asked.

"I want to play a game."

He raised his eyebrow, and her gaze flickered to the maze entrance. "You've got a trophy to win back," she said.

A *trophy*?

His pupils blew, canines flashing as she got to her feet.

Okay.

So... No more no sex rule?

It was hard to tell.

"And when I catch you?" Ebony asked.

"*If* you catch me, then you can do whatever you want." She leaned close and I only just caught what she said. "Do you want me to fight?"

The low rumble of a growl sounded in his chest.

"There's only one thing that's going to be different," she told him.

"What's that?"

"You're competing against Rook."

FIFTY-SIX

ROOK

I would catch Vex first.

She'd given herself a minute head start, but Ebony—after shooting me a filthy glare—had vanished into the house, muttering about needing to grab something.

He was tapped in his head from the whole... cleaving shit.

I didn't care.

If it meant catching Vex first, he could watch *again* while I ruined her...

Fuck yes.

She was too beautiful tonight to pass up that chance.

Night had fallen, the stars and moon above were the only lights. I caught traces of her scent sometimes, telling me she'd passed by. Even from the traces, I caught her lust, as if she wanted us to catch her. I could feel it through the bond.

I caught twilight grass, too, which meant Ebony had finally decided to join us.

I heard a rustle in the bushes and spun.

The ground was cool against my bare feet as I took a step, peering down the tall corridor of hedges.

I tensed as I saw movement in my periphery and snapped my gaze down the other way.

Movement.

Was it her?

I stepped toward it and caught the faintest glint of something in the grass, reflecting the moonlight unnaturally.

I leaned down and picked it up, rolling it in between my fingers.

A... *marble?*

What the—?

I turned, much too late, twilight grass suddenly far more than a trace.

A hand—no, cloth—clamped over my mouth. I struggled against powerful arms and my aura flared—but so did his.

SHIT!

My eyes were getting heavy, the world spinning.

"You fucked her in my bed, Harrison." Ebony's voice growled in my ear. "Only one way I let that slide."

I tried to fight him, but the world spun. I felt the soft ground against my arm and back. The last thing I saw was Ebony's tanned face, white teeth flashing in a broad grin.

Shit...

Nothing in the world that made Ebony Starless smile like that wasn't completely fucked.

Nothing.

And right now, that was me.

EBONY

With Rook dealt with—*more* than dealt with —Vex was next.

I retraced my footsteps, all the way until—*There.*

Raspberry treacle tangled with the scent of cool soil.

And fuck if I wouldn't ruin her when I caught her at last. I could take my time. It would be a while before Rook woke.

I was glad she'd let him play. Now I had revenge and the *perfect* offering.

I froze as I heard movement. The faintest rustle of movement —just a bit louder than the gentle wind disrupting the surrounding leaves.

I took one step back so I was pressed against the hedge and went absolutely still, instincts on high alert.

My heart rate lifted, and I tilted my head, letting that sink in.

Both? The thrill of the hunt, *and* the thrill she offered?

Vex *was* everything.

Again, I let that moment replay in my head. Crimson blood spilling as she sank her teeth into Zeus's throat.

For me.

My perfect mate.

I tilted my head just the smallest amount as I saw movement. The pale skin of her foot crushing the plush grass came into view around a corner.

One more step and I saw the moonlight across her smooth legs. The flash of a silken black gown hanging open to reveal dark lace clinging to creamy skin.

She leaned forward, peering around the corner—looking the wrong way.

Silver-brown locks tumbled free, moonlight sliding across each like a reflection on water. She shifted enough for the silken gown to sway, revealing gentle curves over a slender frame. The bralette she'd chosen wasn't enough to hide the peaks of her nipples.

She went still, and I knew my scent had given me away.

She turned, and I saw the flash of pretty golden eyes, wide as she took me in. I launched toward her.

She let out a breath of shock and threw herself backward.

This time she wouldn't get away.

She'd managed to turn and get her feet beneath her, but I had her by the hair, dragging her against me. She wailed in shock and the sound, paired with the lust I felt from her through the bond, was like a pulse of heat straight to my cock.

When she'd asked if I wanted her to fight, I hadn't imagined this performance. Her claws were out, her eyes fierce as she fought me.

I loved seeing her like this.

I slammed her down against the grass, a growl in my chest as her nails caught my cheek.

She fought like a lioness.

Fuck.

This was a release like no other.

She struggled against me, a snarl breaking from her lips, but I had her pinned in seconds, wrists in one hand over her head as held her against the ground by her chest.

The lace was an easy obstacle to rid myself of, snapping in my grip with ease. I liked how she stilled when I did that, as if I'd convinced her, at last, that she was mine.

She was the only woman in the world who'd ever truly caught my attention, the only woman I'd ever killed for.

And she had killed for me.

I would fuck her until she couldn't remember her own name.

I used my free hand to adjust her hips and lined my cock against her entrance. She tilted her head, meeting my eyes as a breathy gasp escaped her.

I paused. We remained frozen for a long moment as I held her pale slender body against the rich green grass.

She had nowhere to go.

A whine rose in her chest, pupils so wide I could barely see gold anymore, and she shifted against me, fighting my grip to get closer.

Fuck.

I drove into her, getting the most beautiful moan from her chest. Pressing my weight against her as she continued to fight, I fucked her without mercy.

Mine.

She was fucking mine.

I kept my pace, pleasure building as her body tightened around me as if on the edge of her own orgasm.

Not fucking yet.

Not when she'd run from me.

I sunk into her, holding her hips firmly against me as I released her wrists at last. Then I pressed my fingers against her back entrance as I rocked against her, my knot stretching her open just enough to tease as I slipped my thumb into her backdoor.

She whined, pleasure soaring through the bond even when she scrambled to get away from me. Her struggles were to no avail.

I pressed my length again into her impossibly tight pussy and she let out another moan. She trembled beneath me, her fists ripping up grass as she gasped for air.

I reached out, gripping her neck and dragging her against me as I fucked her harder still, finally nearing my own release.

Fuck.

The orgasm that surged through me was like nothing I'd ever felt. I wanted more, but her whines were a siren's call, so I didn't knot her. I crushed her to my chest by her neck, feeling every moment as she climaxed, her whole body shaking. And I followed her over that cliff in the most intense orgasm of my life.

In that moment, I knew the truth.

Vex was my salvation.

The thing I'd been waiting for that would bridge me with the rest of the world.

"Bite me." Her plea was like another shot of adrenaline. "Bite me, Ebony."

Fisting her hair away from the back of her neck, I did, sinking my teeth over the darkness Zeus Rogan had left.

Over the mark of a man she'd killed to save me.

And with that bond we forged, my aura was complete again, full and stronger than it had ever been.

Hormones, lust, and ecstasy flooded my veins, leaving me a mess the likes of which I wasn't used to. Orgasms never ended like this. Not with the whole universe spinning out of control.

When I focused once more, she was limp and panting in my grip.

Mine.

I'd claimed her. She was full of my seed, utterly claimed in a way that no one outside of my pack would ever have.

Then I drew her into my arms and carried her to the centre of the maze, so very far from done.

VEX

Heat was sweeping away my inhibitions.

Never before had I been able to give into it. But I was in Ebony's arms, the warmth of his chest against my skin, enough to draw a purr from me.

For the first time, I let go, a wave of warm lust crashing in.

He would take care of me—give me everything I needed.

They all would.

"My perfect little omega," he breathed. "I have a gift."

Another gift?

He'd got me so many. Next thing I knew, he set me down and I felt the cool ground beneath my bare feet again. Twilight grass was everywhere. He'd marked me. Marked me and bitten me.

I was his. He was mine.

I hummed contentedly as I stared up into swirling silver eyes, another wave of heat cresting into my body. A whine slipped from my chest.

I needed him again.

Now.

"Vex?" That was Rook's voice.

Rook was here? My heart lifted.

Good.

I needed him.

"Ebony!" But Rook's snarl cut off as my gaze found him. I blinked, hazy mind clearing for just a moment as I processed what I was seeing.

He knelt on concrete up the steps of the gazebo in the centre of the maze.

Only... Oh.

Around his neck was a golden collar, and his wrists were cuffed behind him, the chains attached to the Alpha's Hook fixed into the ground. He wore his sweatpants, but he was topless, rich dark skin over rippling muscles, that tattoo marking him mine, clear across his chest.

"My gift," Ebony said.

"You *bit* me?" Rook sounded wild, eyes darting to Ebony. My gaze slid to his neck.

Just above the collar, beneath his jaw, was a bite.

That was hot.

Everything about the situation was sending lava through my veins.

I stepped toward him in a moment, transfixed.

He seemed to fully take me in, gaze soaking in my body. "Fuck

Vex..." He looked, for a moment, like he'd forgotten everything else.

I rushed up the steps, and as I approached he fought the chains, eyes desperate.

My alpha.

My mate.

Then he let out a hiss of rage as Ebony dragged me to a halt right before him, his grip in my hair. I turned to him, eyes wide.

"Ebony!" My voice was a whine.

A growl rose in Rook's throat. "You didn't think this might be fucking *insensitive*?"

Ebony smiled. It was quite mesmerising, and for a moment I didn't know who I wanted to look at more.

"Insensitive?" Ebony asked. "She's spent enough time chained by alphas. I thought she might want one in return." Ebony's gaze slid to me. "What do you think, Little Omega?"

"I want him," I whined again.

Ebony grinned. "Good girl," he purred. "He belongs to you." Ebony's fist closed around the chain at Rook's neck, dragging it back and forcing him upright. Another growl from Rook and I felt like I was on fire.

Again, I tried to step toward him.

"But *you* are mine," Ebony said. "Show him that. On your knees for me first, and I'll let you have him."

"Ebony—" Rook snarled, but I barely hesitated, dropping to my knees and reaching for his cock.

He groaned as my lips found him and took the tip into my mouth. Caramel brandy was desperate in the air and it was enough to make slick pool between my thighs.

"Fuck..." Ebony groaned, grip tangling in my hair as he dragged me over his length, fist still gripping the chain at Rook's neck.

ROOK

She was tumbling into heat before my very eyes. It was as beautiful as it was infuriating.

"Ebony," she whined when he let her surface for air. Her eyes darted to me. *"Please."*

"You'll have him when you earn it."

He dragged her over his length again until she couldn't breathe, but fuck if it wasn't captivating. Raspberry was thick in the air.

I groaned, fighting again to get to her, but Ebony yanked me back, fist still around the chain. His eyes were dancing when I found them.

Again, he drove right into her throat, and her nails bit down on his thighs. I felt her lust through the bond.

I was rock hard, every instinct dialled up to fifteen.

She was my omega. She was going into heat.

I fucking *needed* her.

He held out way too long, and she was desperate by the time he finished.

"Good girl," he growled as he choked her, blowing his load right down her throat, fist tight in her silver-brown waves. Her eyes didn't leave him the whole time, not until he let her go. She sagged, catching her breath, already turning to me.

"Now I want to watch while you use him."

Despite the insanity of all of this—that he'd drugged me and bitten me and then chained me to an Alpha's Hook—I didn't care. Because then her warm skin was on mine as she wove one arm around my neck, the other reached down and freeing my cock.

"Fuck Vex," I breathed as she straddled me.

I groaned, her delicate grip on my cock as she lowered herself over my tip.

Again, Ebony was in the way, drawing her back by her hair again. "Wait."

Vex paused, lip caught in her teeth, as she glanced up at him desperately.

"Beg, Harrison. Then she can fuck you."

I didn't care. Not when I felt her slick against my tip. Not when her scent was like a drug. I didn't even care that Ebony was still fisting the chains around my neck, holding my back at an arch.

"Fuck," I moaned. "Please. Use me."

Her eyes flashed with delight and she sank over my length, a petite growl of pleasure in her chest as she claimed me. Those eyes of molten gold not leaving mine for a moment.

She fucked me like a lynx.

Ebony kept the chain at my neck stiff, making it impossible for me to move, but it didn't matter. She was mesmerising, arms draped over my shoulders, finding a good position to rock over my length, eyelids fluttering every time she took me to my swelling knot. And the sounds she made were beautiful.

I groaned again, fighting an orgasm. I had never been this close to finishing this fast, but this was the hottest thing that had ever happened to me.

Finally, when I'd felt like I'd been close to bursting for forever —absolutely determined not to finish before she did—she let out a pretty little whine, her eyes lifting to Ebony.

"Don't come yet," he told her, fist still in her hair.

She whined again and by the satisfaction in his gaze as he glanced at me, I wondered if he knew how close I was.

"Fuck him harder."

I grit my teeth, blood on fire as she drove her tight little body over me harder, shuddering every time she took my full length.

Pretty sounds rose in her chest every time she sank all the way down.

Ebony tightened his grip on her hair, arching her neck. "Good girl. Keep going."

She moaned, eyes squeezing shut. She was *so* tight, her sweet cunt squeezing me with every movement.

She let out another whine, and I could feel her desperation through the bond.

"Look at me while you finish," he commanded her, not letting go of her hair, the chain from my neck still tight in his fist.

Fuck.

She came, and that was it. All I needed.

I groaned as her golden eyes snapped open to look at Ebony, a gasp of pleasure escaping her lips as she sank down, now fucking me with slow strokes as—with each one—she trembled with the first orgasm of her heat.

FIFTY-SEVEN

DRAKE

"Drake?" Her voice was low and melodic. "Where are we going?"

"Just getting you to the nest, Dreamgirl."

She was so perfect, purring in my arms as I carried her up the stairs. I could swear her scent was stronger now than when I'd first scooped her into my arms. Love was right behind me—though he'd told Ebony he wasn't coming in until Rook was unchained from the Alpha's Hook.

I set her down on the bed.

"Drake... Love?" she whispered.

"We're here," I told her.

She was dazed, pupils dilated as she glanced between us. Her scent alone was enough to make me rock hard. It was one thing to know that her heat was coming, another to be feeling it.

Okay.

So this was heat. Real, actual heat with the most important omega in the world.

We had this, right?

Even if we hadn't done it before.

"I really need you to fuck me." Her eyes were wide.

Right.

Yes, *that*.

Love dropped down on the bed beside her. "You have *four* alphas to consolidate a princess bond," he said. "You are going to be thoroughly fucked."

She didn't even give him a chance to remove his clothes before she was climbing him, palms at his cheeks as she drew him into a kiss.

I tugged off my shirt as Love tried to balance kissing her back with removing his pants. "I want you both." She finally let go of him to help him with his shirt. "And I want *bites*."

"And you're going to get them, Dreamgirl," I told her, sinking onto the bed beside them, examining

I'd seen them together before in the living room, but there had been a whole lot less to *see* there.

Love flipped them so he was pinning her to the bed with only his boxers remaining. "We're going to ruin you and claim you," he told her.

She giggled. "Doctor said *I'm* going to ruin *you*."

I didn't doubt that. My brain was already working slowly, my blood was scorching hot as I watched them, transfixed.

Love growled, caging her in, and... damn.

He'd never looked so much bigger than her than as he pinned her to the sheets, lining up his tip to her entrance. She arched against him, panting. Her hair was still host to shreds of grass and soil smudged her pink cheeks. *That* sent imaginings through my sluggish brain, wiping away the moment of worry.

Ebony had taken her in the maze.

Fuck, they would have to do that again when I could watch.

That was a surprisingly warm thought. Safe—truly, now I was in the room with her heat hormones in the air, watching as Love kissed her. When he broke the kiss, he glanced up to me. I felt him in the bond, fully present, every feeling laid bare for me.

An offering.

He'd sat at my side before the fire last night before the others had arrived. "If you need anything for her heat—or if you want to have time with her privately, I can—"

"No." I'd cut him off, hating even the thought of it. "I want to try."

I was determined. This was one of the things they'd taken I'd never even realised. Vex wasn't the only one who'd dreamed of a pack. I wanted to be a part of it—a part of her heat.

He nodded.

"I think... Maybe... if the bonds are open. That will... help."

When they bonds were open, they weren't... other. I could see them fully, there was nothing hidden, nothing to be afraid of.

I dropped down on the bed beside her, tucking an errant strand of silver-brown hair behind her ear. "I want to see how hot you look taking him, Dreamgirl," I told her. I made sure my end of the bond was open too, so they would both know how true that was.

Her smile sent my heart tripping over itself.

It was more true than I'd even realised. I was spellbound as Love readjusted his grip on her hips and slid into her with perfect control. His blue eyes were fixed on the way her lips parted as he stretched her out.

Damn. That was really hot.

I would never be *with* any of my pack aside Vex, but I was, for the first time in a long time, able to appreciate the beauty of this. Love's pale, muscular form driving her into the sheets. Her breasts were pert and nipples peaked as she gasped with pleasure, arching against him, nails digging into his skin as she begged him for more.

Her eyelids fluttered as he picked up his pace. I palmed my

own cock through my pants, but then she was reaching out to me, eyes glittering with need.

Her pheromones were like a thick blanket in the air and, just like the openness of Love in the bond, this security she felt couldn't be faked. She wanted our pack for her heat. This incredible and fierce omega, who'd fought harder for her happiness than anyone ever should, felt safe with us. With Love, Ebony, and Rook.

That meant more that I could quite explain.

I knelt beside her, and she tugged my pants down, taking my shaft in her fist, pumping it a few times before letting out another little moan, fist tightening. I repositioned so I could comfortably press my tip to her lips. She shifted forward, wide eyes holding mine.

I pressed in, slowly at first, enjoying the view of her lips around my length as little mewls rose in her chest. Love continued to fuck her, nudging her against me slightly with each thrust.

Her hand returned to the base of my shaft, gripping it tight again. I readjusted once more, fingers weaving through her hair to help, then slid my length down her throat.

It was fucking heaven.

"You're taking us so well," Love told her.

A stuttering purr rose in her throat as she was fucked at our mercy.

She finished before either of us, with my length down her tight throat. Love picked up his pace, driving into her harder as he began playing with her clit. Each time he rocked, he inched those pretty lips further over my cock, letting her squeeze me so tight.

Finally, Love dragged her off my cock. She let out a furious sound of derision that was quickly stifled as Love pressed his knot against her teasingly. "You got him nice and ready," he breathed, dragging her against his chest and repositioning so he was propped up against the pillows and headboard. "Now you're going to take my knot *and* him, right Princess?"

"Yes!" She nodded, and I could see her fighting to sink down over his knot.

Instead, Love lifted her hips giving me a perfect view of his thick cock impaling her. She whined again, nails digging into his chest.

"Knot me," she demanded, something bratty in her voice.

Love laughed. "You're going to take me so well while he watches, aren't you?" he asked as he lowered her down again to the edge of his knot.

She growled, fighting once more to take it, but he held her hips with an iron grip.

"Look at him," he commanded.

Her golden eyes snapped to me as I knelt beside them both, drawing her close and kissing her. I wanted to see how she looked when she took him all. She groaned, releasing a breath at my lips. I drew back.

Her eyes rolled back as Love dragged her down over him completely.

"You feel so good," he praised. I saw the smile curve her lips, contentment in her eyes as he rocked into her. It didn't last long.

"More," she pleaded, even more urgent now she'd been knotted, shivering with need. "I want you."

I moved behind her, pressing a finger to her entrance, feeling her slick.

Fuck that was such a turn on, but she whined again, spinning on me with blazing eyes. "Now!"

Love chuckled, and she tensed over him.

I pressed into her, just an inch at first, but there was a siren's moan in her chest. "Look at you, Princess," Love breathed, stroking her hair.

She lowered herself against his chest, curling up so her stunning eyes found mine.

I would never forget that moment. It was the most captivating image I'd ever seen. She bit her lip, making little mewls of pleasure with every inch I pressed in.

Fuck she was tight, her body gripping me like we were made for each other.

I slid the rest of the way in.

We *were* made for each other.

She was my Dreamgirl.

"Mmmmhm..." she tried to shift back, feeling my knot against her, but her brows knotted. She was still trapped over Love.

"You feel so good, Dreamgirl," I told her.

A purr rose in her chest at the nickname. I pumped in a few times, knowing I was rocking her against Love's knot.

Then I picked up the pace, fucking her harder. Her nails biting down on Love's chest as she kept her eyes on me.

Her whines grew louder with each thrust, and Love leaned back, jaw clenched.

Finally, her eyes rolled back with another wave of pleasure.

Shit.

She tensed, and I pressed my palm to the sheets, bowing over her and hearing Love's groan as he finished too.

LOVE

"What do you mean, you've *lost* the key?" I snarled.

Ebony was scratching his head. "I left it on the side table. It's gone."

"You left it on the side table *in* her nest?"

"That's where we were before this."

"Love!" That was Vex calling for me.

It was only Drake in there at the moment and her scent was distressed.

I poked my head around the door. "We'll be right in, Princess." Then I turned back to Rook and Ebony with a glare. "What the fuck are we going to do?"

Ebony was a fucking idiot. He'd been able to undo the cuffs at least, thank God. This heat was supposed to be wild, and we couldn't do it with an alpha down. "The Alpha Hook stunt was one thing. But this—?"

"Love?" At her voice, I spun in the doorway, heart dropping.

She was there in a silken dressing gown and nothing else, arms folded, a pout on her face. "It's my *heat*, where—?"

Rook took a step back, but too late. Vex's eyes widened as she saw him.

Ah.

Shit.

Rook went ashen, standing there looking like some kind of Aztec porn star, topless with a golden collar and chain around his neck. It held a painful similarity to the nightmare from which she'd just escaped.

But to my surprise, Vex's eyes lit up. She all but staggered toward him, stretching on her tiptoes and pressing a kiss to his cheek. Colour flooded his face. Then she wrapped the chain in her hand and was tugging him back into her nest.

Ebony's mouth dropped open. *"Wait—!"*

I put a hand on his chest as he tried to follow them. "Oh no," I snorted. "You did this. You live with it."

When I stepped back in, Drake was returning from the bathroom, two glasses of water in his hands. He froze, staring. Vex had shoved a *very* smug looking Rook onto the bed and mounted him, chain still clutched in her grip.

She looked back around at us, seeming, only then, to notice the tension. She paused, a frown on her face.

"What?"

I palmed the back of my neck. Even Ebony looked a little thrown.

"Nothing, Princess." My voice was a little weak. It was kind of impossible to shove away the flashes of memory of Zeus holding such a similar chain and collar.

She chewed on her lip, clearly not liking the tension in the room. Then she said, as if it were the most obvious thing in the world, "I killed him."

There was a long silence.

Of course Ebony broke it, crossing the room and dropping down beside them both. "You did." He wrapped his arms around her, running his lips along her neck, hands roaming her body and making her squirm. "You ripped out his jugular, Little Omega. It was the hottest thing I've ever seen."

The room was instantly *re*-flooded with delighted raspberry and treacle heat hormones.

I opened my mouth, then shut it.

The universe had matched her with us.

With Ebony.

I really, *really* needed to start remembering that.

FIFTY-EIGHT

ROOK

Insatiable was an understatement, but I was not going to crack on day one of her heat. We would, as her alphas, hold out until she was in dreamland. That meant Love was grabbing a snack while Rook and Ebony downed electrolytes.

I was taking care of our princess.

I didn't know how many hours it had been, but I'd never felt better.

Particularly not with a goddess straddling my face, golden chain clutched in her fist as I drew her down over my mouth.

She let out a sweet little mewl as I found the right spot with my tongue. Still gripping her hip with one hand, I pressed two fingers into her centre. She was soaked with slick, and she tasted so sweet.

How the fuck had I got this lucky—*and a view like this?*

I knew when I got a good spot because I would feel the urgent tug on the collar at my neck, dragging me against her. She was so bratty and demanding, holding that chain, and I didn't think it was possible for me not to be hard, seeing her with it. My down time was record low. I'd do anything she asked like this.

I needed to piss off Ebony more often.

I drove my fingers in faster, adjusting so I could slip my thumb into her back door.

"Fuuuckkk," she moaned.

That's it Baby Girl.

I needed her to cum, I wanted another taste.

I felt her tense as I sped up, and she was shuddering that way she did when she was riiigghhht on the edge. The chain was pulled so tight I was under threat of suffocating and ending up alpha heaven.

Take me now.

It was time. She'd asked, but I'd been waiting for the right moment, and with her riding me like this, body about to give out —it was perfect. Still pumping into her, I adjusted my chin and sank my teeth right into the soft spot of her inner thigh.

She gasped, chain going taut and dragging my teeth along her flesh just a little. The princess bond lit like a firework and she climaxed with a moan, spilling right into my mouth and down my chin and neck.

Yup.

This *was* heaven.

Raspberry treacle heaven.

"Rook," she mumbled as I drew her down against my chest. She was, it seemed, *maybe* getting tired.

"Yes?" I asked, brushing her peach streak out of the way of dazed golden eyes.

She yawned. "I love you so much."

"I love you too, Baby Girl."

She might be tired, but her scent told me she was still horny.

Well, I could work with that. I tugged her lower, guiding her hot core over my length and letting her relax on my chest.

Holding her hips, I rocked into her, enjoying her cute little purr as I did all the work so she could rest up as I gave her all the orgasms she could ever need.

LOVE

Vex was a storm of hormones that scrambled my brain, making me forget that there was a world at all, outside of this nest.

It was heaven.

Just our pack. No one else.

And our omega.

My omega.

It felt like it should be a dream. But then I'd hear the serenade of her low moans, and I knew I could never come up with a dream as incredible as this.

I leaned against the door to the bathroom, a warm cloth in my fist, watching as she took Rook and Ebony from either side.

Drake was absently refilling the bowl on the bedside table with protein bars from the drawer, eyes fixed on them. His hand missed the drawer three times as Ebony, who was rutting her from behind, fisted her hair and pressed her mouth deep over Rook's cock as she shuddered with an orgasm.

The chain was still coiled around her fist, even with Rook's cock so far down her throat her lips brushed his knot.

She was insatiable, though. Completely and utterly insatiable. Seconds after Rook had finished, and Ebony had dragged her back onto his lap, she searched the room for more. Her hair was wild, spilling around her cheeks. Not enough to obscure the way her eyes locked with mine as Ebony twisted her nipple.

She whined.

It didn't matter how spent I was. Every time she looked at me like that, my cock was rock hard, my need for her absolute.

I crossed toward her and knelt, drawing the—now cool—cloth

over her skin, which was glistening with sweat. She let out a little gasp as Ebony tugged on her nipple again, his other hand circling her clit and sending her into another shuddering orgasm.

"Love," she whispered, when she'd recovered, and I'd tucked her hair behind her ear.

"Yes?"

"I want all of you at once. You keep... relay racing me."

Rook choked on the water he'd been sipping.

"Well," I said, unable to help the grin on my own face. "Clearly, we're slackers." I tugged her from Ebony and onto my lap, adjusting her just right.

She sank down on to my length while Rook pressed into her from behind. Watching that expression of bliss as she was overwhelmed never got old.

"You're not going to come until you've finished us," Ebony told her. She nodded as Rook hooked her arms behind her, holding her suspended as she sank down to my knot.

Fuck, that was a sight: watching her get impaled over my length as Rook rocked into her from behind. "There you go," Ebony breathed, his one free hand dragging her by her hair to Drake's cock. "Show him your tongue."

Vex depressed her tongue, eyes fixed up at Drake who groaned at the sight before pressing his tip into her mouth. Her other hand reached out, fisting Ebony's shaft as Drake began fucking her throat deep.

Every thrust of Rook's sent her onto my shaft, and I was nearing my own orgasm in no time, pressing up against her to make sure I was going deep. One of my hands was on her hips, the other free to roam from her clit to her nipples.

Her lust soared through the bond, stronger than before as Rook found a rhythm, Ebony occasionally dragging her lips from Drake's cock and onto his. She was shaking, nearing her own climax.

"Don't come," Ebony growled as he pressed his knot right up to her lips. She shuddered, eyes almost crossing as she was held at the edge.

Finally, I dragged her down, watching as she stretched over my knot. I spilled into her with each thrust from Rook. She groaned, trembling harder as I circled her clit, and Rook picked up his pace. With each thrust she let out a whine. Lust was like a vicious creature in the bond, demanding reprieve as Ebony edged her.

Fuck that was something.

"You won't come until he knots you," Ebony told her.

Her whine was deep and low with Rook's next thrust, her chest heaving. Ebony held her deep over Drake's length as he pumped into her, and I could feel Drake nearing his own climax. In the last second, Ebony switched, dragging her lips to his tip and letting her fumble for Drake's shaft.

Rook groaned, and her whole body seized as he pressed his knot into her from behind.

He let out a breathy "Fuuckk" as Ebony dragged her back to Drake, letting her catch one more deep breath of air before Rook and Drake finished in her at the same time.

Tears were tracking down her cheeks as Ebony dragged her lips over his cock one last time, and I renewed the speed of my thumb on her clit.

"Good girl," Ebony breathed. "Come, Little Omega."

Her sounds were desperate as she came, lips still trapped over Ebony's cock, and the feeling of Rook's knot rocking into her sent me over another cliff.

When Ebony released her, she was still shaking from the orgasm.

This felt right, with the whole pack as she'd wanted.

"I'm going to bite you, Princess," I told her.

Her delight was a shot through the bond, and I arched her

neck and leaned down, pressing my teeth to the front of her neck, wanting every person who ever met her to see it.

She shuddered in Rook's grip, her connection with us in the bond momentarily like a firework, her scent became that storm of possession again as I claimed her fully and completely.

With every orgasm, Vex tumbled further into the throes of heat.

I thought heat started with the craziest part, but day two was when she was feverish with need.

This was madness. I hadn't, before now, been able to conceive of a single person being able to have that many orgasms.

With each one, she became more feral.

Ebony was like oil on the fire, sometimes spending an hour with her knotted against him, making her cum over and over. Once it got so bad she could barely catch her breath as she trembled, each lungful of air ragged.

When I finally ripped him from her, telling him in no uncertain terms that he wasn't supposed to orgasm his omega into an asthma attack, she almost burst into tears.

He grinned at me, sank back into the sheets, then grabbed her by the hips and dragged her over his face. She then managed a truly impressive feat, as she spent her next orgasm with arms folded, actively levelling me with a death glare.

I'd had to give her an inhaler.

I supposed it was telling, at least, that there was one in the heat medical kit we had in the cupboard.

Fucking idiots.

FIFTY-NINE

VEX

The full fury of my heat had broken at last and it was everything I could have ever dreamed of. A blur of passion and love and lust. I'd never, in all my life, felt as safe as I did in this nest with my mates.

I don't know what day we were on. Three... maybe four? We'd ordered take out half a dozen times at least by the amount of paper bags accumulating at the door.

It would be another day or two before it was over completely, but I was back to myself. I could take heat breaks, go outside or downstairs to the kitchen to help cook breakfast (even if it was to discover it was five o'clock in the evening).

Drake was the last to bite me.

"You want to know the truth, Dreamgirl?" he asked, when I'd finally brought it up. "I just can't decide how to make it perfect."

"Perfect is you and me," I whispered.

"Then I just want to hold you," he murmured, drawing my back against his chest. "I would hold you forever if I could."

I smiled, wriggling against him and biting my lip with pleasure when he slipped into me from behind. His lips brushed my neck.

"Where would you like my bite, Dreamgirl?" he asked.

Warmth was spreading through my body with each rock of his hips. I smiled, thinking about it.

It wasn't until I felt him press his knot against me, a low hum of contentment in my chest as I wriggled against him, that I thought I knew. He chuckled, turning us both so he was on top of me and I could see his beautiful violet eyes. Then he stretched me out with his knot, his groan of pleasure a twin to mine.

I cupped his face, drawing him into a kiss. Then I lifted my wrist to him, the one with the dark bite Cerus had left.

"You want me to cover it?" he asked.

"No." That didn't feel right. I didn't want his bite touching Cerus's at all. "Above it." When I looked at my hand, I wanted to see his claim first.

"I can do that, Dreamgirl."

He drew my wrist to his mouth and pressed his teeth to the base of my palm.

I let out a breath as I felt the connection bloom. He flooded my mind, love and passion and... I thought that might be peace.

"You saved us," he told me as he drew his teeth away.

"We are going to heal together," I whispered.

"We already are." His smile was breathtaking.

I curled up in his arms, content.

This was bliss.

I was, somehow, on the other end of hope. There was no dark bond chaining me anymore.

And my heat, the thing I'd spent so much of my life afraid of, had become something full of light and joy and happiness.

The last of the darkness torn away.

EBONY

I woke up to hear omega-light creeping footsteps on the rug beside me.

Sunlight filtered through the windows, though it could just as easily be mid-afternoon as early morning. Time hadn't had meaning in a while, and my whole body was sore.

I saw a flash of brownish-silver waves.

What was she doing?

I squinted, not moving an inch.

I saw her creep around the bed and slide something that sounded small and made of metal on the bedside table. When she clambered back into bed, curling up at my back, I lifted my head to see what it was.

A grin spread on my lips, and I turned to her, drawing her tight enough into my arms that she let out a tiny little squeak.

"What are you doing, Little Omega?" I asked her.

She pressed something cold against my chest. "You won it back," she whispered.

I looked down to see the cleaving iron she'd stolen from me all those weeks ago. A purr rose in my chest, and she snuggled closer, a pretty smile curving her lips as she closed her eyes.

She was my world. A woman who wanted me as I was.

As she tumbled back into sleep, content as I purred, I peeked back around to where she'd crept.

Behind me on the side table was the gold key to Rook's collar.

EPILOGUE ONE

DRAKE

Vex's heat was over, and we were settling into a new normal.

One where we weren't singularly focused on the next acting gig, and our pack had a sense of cohesiveness. The pack really was starting to feel like a pack. It was a strange thing, as what we had now wasn't something I'd noticed we were missing. But my brothers were truly starting to feel like a family—bickering and all.

Yesterday I'd caught Love lecturing Ebony on how it was *never* acceptable to steal from his omega's nest and replace her things. As the argument got heated, I couldn't help peering around the corner. Ebony had bundles of fabric in his arms and his jaw was clenched in rage.

"Put them back," Love demanded.

"Mine are *better*," Ebony snapped.

"I don't care how many Crimson Fury pack pillow cases you bought. She wants—"

"My omega is *not* sleeping on a Prey Nightingale—"

"She certainly *is*"—Love jabbed Ebony in the chest—"and you are going to *deal with it!*"

I had to clamp a hand over my mouth to stifle my laugh.

"Now!" Love snarled. "Put. Them. *Back.*"

I'd never clocked Ebony as a tantrum kind of alpha, but there was no other word for it as I watched him dump the entire bundle of Hunting Falcons pillow cases over Love's head before stalking off.

I was working on my plans for Vex, converting one of the offices on the first floor to a recording studio. Rook had hooked me up with some industry contacts who knew how to get it done well.

The contractors were in the house today, hard at work, as we were taking advantage of Rook's decision to take her for a full day of shopping.

He'd sworn they'd take all day and had a lot to do. All I knew was that they were going to find the perfect charms to give to Havoc and Prey for friendship bracelets. And find housewarming gifts for Gambit's family—Rook had managed to find a family and omega friendly apartment building that had openings. There was, however, also a mystery gift for Vex that he had conspired with Love about, and the two of them were buzzing with excitement over it, and completely tight lipped.

What would take the whole day, though?

Plus, Rook had sworn to Vex he would get her a gift that would trump every gift Ebony had ever given.

That wasn't a competition I would ever willingly enter.

While we had contractors in, Love was also discussing renovations in the garden. He wanted to convert the little cove of seating on the covered patio into a new firepit. We were enjoying the evenings with pack time, and he wanted to be able to continue into the winter months.

Meanwhile, I was in Vex's nest, examining her dream board. It now spanned half the wall and was starting to populate.

She'd open four more sections, one for each of us to fill.

It had been less than twenty-four hours, but Rook's section was almost full.

He'd received a document in the mail this morning. Within the hour, he'd mounted it in a golden frame and hung it right in the middle of his section. It was a very official letter stating he had been wiped from the Harrison Pack will.

Around it were dozens of selfies of Vex and him—though we were, at least, featured in most of them now.

In Ebony's space there was one photo, one I was sure Rook had left. It was Vex beside the rooftop pool, a snarl on her face as Ebony wrestled two inflatable arm bands on her as he insisted on teaching her to swim. Beside it—also a Rook addition—was the card he'd bought for Ebony at the hospital. It was an out of season Grinch Christmas card, and inside were the words, *'his amygdala grew three sizes that day'.*

I smiled, eyes lingering on my empty space. The one I was here to fill.

"What's that?" I'd asked this morning, peering at plans that had replaced the ones I'd made for her nest (we'd taken those down now they were all implemented).

"My plans," she said. "For you... But only if you want them."

I tugged them from the magnet, examining them. A smile spread on my face as I realised what I was looking at.

"A greenhouse?"

She looked unusually flustered. "I thought maybe you could show me... I mean..." She went bright pink. "Only if you—?"

I drew her into a kiss. "I'd love to show you, Dreamgirl."

. . .

Still, it wasn't as simple as just pinning them up like it had been for Rook. I'd spent all day gathering the courage, keeping them folded in my back pocket. But I didn't know when she'd be home, and I wanted them there when she got back.

It was easier now, looking at every dream on here—the ones she'd had the courage to hold onto. If she could do it, then so could I.

So I lifted them and pinned them to my open space upon the dream board.

EPILOGUE TWO

EBONY

Rook thought he was getting a *better* gift than I'd given her?

Never going to happen. Rook didn't have the brain cells to come up with the kind of gifts that—

I froze as I pulled a protein bar from the mini fridge, hearing a desperate scrabbling of nails on hardwood and a squeak. I spun to see Vex crashing into the living room, launching herself after the black *creature* that was careening across the marble, a pink collar —larger than its whole body—in its teeth. It tripped face first, skidding the last few feet into my foot before it was on its hind legs, scrabbling at my jeans.

It dropped the collar and let out a delighted bark.

Oh no.

"Rook got me a *puppy*!" Vex squealed.

A *dog*?

That was his gift?

That cheating *bastard*.

Gifts were supposed to be expensive perfumes, nest designs, or the slow torture of unsavoury alphas—gifts were *not* puppies. Didn't they put that on Christmas posters or something?

My grimace faded at the look on Vex's face as she caught up to the uncoordinated creature still struggling to scale my leg.

She was beaming.

Damn.

Well. *Damn.*

A gold pack in a princess bond was basically a monarch. If she said this little... I squinted.

Doberman?

I wrinkled my nose.

If she said this little doberman was pack then...

Fuck.

"Aren't you supposed to... not like animals or something?" Vex asked, peering down at the playpen I was putting together.

I snorted. *What a primitive take.*

Even if it was accurate.

Frankly, every dog on the planet could catch fire and burn to little puppy cinders and I wouldn't give a fuck. But *Princess Jasmine* was pack now, so her weaknesses were, *unfortunately,* mine to protect.

I could appreciate Aisha, she'd proven herself and protected Vex, but how did we know we could trust this one?

She was a glossy black with rich mahogany patches, far too active, and *painfully* incompetent when it came to survival instincts. Still, she seemed to respond well to the stash of treats I kept in my pockets, so she *could* be bribed... That made her more reliable than most humans, I supposed.

I didn't know it was possible to find a being worse than Vex when it came to self preservation—Love had let slip the *hitch-hiking* attempt—but Princess Jasmine was staking a claim for champion.

How the fuck was I supposed to take care of a creature I wasn't in a bond with?

EPILOGUE THREE

VEX

I woke, surrounded by my pack.

Princess Jasmine was stumbling across every alpha on the bed, growling every time any of them moved until she reached me. I caught her earthy scent, reminding me of Aisha. I cuddled her close, huffing it, a purr rising in my chest.

Love reached out to me, hand brushing my cheek, and Princess Jasmine opened an eye, tensing. With a smile he drew us both into his arms.

"I love you," he breathed, and my purr deepened. "You are more than anything I could have ever dreamed of." He held me tighter, and yet I could feel a tremor run through him.

I turned, peering up, still clutching Princess Jasmine in my arms.

"Are you okay?" I asked.

He smiled, but his jaw was clenched. "I need you to hear me when I say this, Vex," he breathed. "You chose those golden eyes and because you did, the world has made you pay. But if you hadn't..." He trailed off, his breath catching. "If you hadn't, Vex..." He couldn't seem to finish, but he didn't have to.

And his words were a salve on that age old burn.

"I'm sorry," he whispered. "For every moment you were alone. That we weren't there."

And I couldn't speak as I hunched in his arms, drowning in his scent of vanilla winter.

"You are incredible, and I will never tell you those golden eyes are less than the most beautiful thing in the world. Without them, this pack would not have survived."

For a moment, it was like my throat closed up as I shook in his arms, his words washing over me. And they were a shocking relief.

A weight lifted I hadn't even known I was carrying.

I felt one tear trickle down my face.

Princess Jasmine stiffened for a moment, then licked me right across the cheek. For a moment, she wasn't Princess Jasmine at all. Her tongue was huge and slobbering and demanding, backed by the weight of a dog large enough to ground me. There was a smile on my face as I curled up, safe, with Love's arms around me.

My nest was complete.

I had my pack, my puppy, and, in the centre of my dream board, I'd mounted the embroidered sweatshirt that Ebony had extracted from the Lightning pack mansion. Beside it, hung the pink glittery collar that had started all of this.

I remembered that day at the signing, standing in line with her collar. It had felt like an ending; I hadn't known what was going to come next, or what I would do without her.

But she had led me to them. To a fight for a happily ever after that was worth every moment.

Now four signatures were scrawled upon it: My pack, with a thousand dreams of untapped magic waiting to steal us away.

The End.

Thanks so much for reading! This is my first ever full grovel book.

Let me know what you think! Did you like the guys by the end? Who was your favourite?

Drop me a review here!

What's next?!?

I would love love love to do some bonus content for Sweetheart, however!!! This duet became a giant! 235,000 words later, and I'm going to let the crew rest a little. I do have some plans for some HEA episodes, but I don't want to make timeline commitments right now!

Are you going to do a story for Prey?

I sure hope so, there is some plans in the works, but I have a few other projects first <3

Visit Mariemackay.com for more books by me.

THE POISONVERSE

*

NEED AN ENEMIES TO LOVERS TO TIDE YOU OVER BEFORE BOOK TWO'S RELEASE?

Read Havoc now!

"I'm the omega who killed my alpha. Now the rest of his pack decides my fate..."

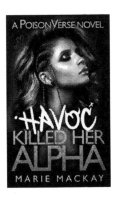

*

WANT MORE POISONVERSE?

Havoc Killed Her Alpha - *Marie Mackay*

Forget Me Knot - *Marie Mackay*

Pack of Lies - *Olivia Lewin*

Ruined Alphas - *Amy Nova*

Lonely Alpha - *Olivia Lewin*

And more to come...

Go to PoisonVerseBooks.com for more.

What if I read Havoc, but I don't know why is she friends with Prey?

Find out how in the the waffle battle novella on my Website, Mariemackay.com

Printed in Poland
by Amazon Fulfillment
Poland Sp. z o.o., Wrocław

28321829R00305